Valor

The Arinthian Line: Book Three

SEVER BRONNY

This book is a work of fiction. Names, characters, places and incidents either are the product of the author's imagination or are used fictitiously, and any similarity to actual persons, living or deceased, establishments of any kind, events, or locales is entirely coincidental.

Library and Archives Canada Cataloguing in Publication

Bronny, Sever, 1979-, author
    Valor / Sever Bronny.

(The Arinthian line ; bk. 3)

Issued in print and electronic formats.

ISBN 978-0-9937676-4-7 (paperback).—
ISBN 978-0-9937676-5-4 (ebook)

       I.   Title.

PS8603.R652V35 2015   C813'.6

C2015-904466-9
C2015-904467-7

Version 1.0

Copyright ©2015 Sever Bronny Ltd. All Rights reserved. Map and cover by author using creative commons and commercial licensing. "Valor" cover font by Steve Deffeyes, deffeyes.com. For information about permission to reproduce certain portions of this work, please contact the author at severbronny@gmail.com or via
www.severbronny.com

Northeast Solia, Northern Sithesia

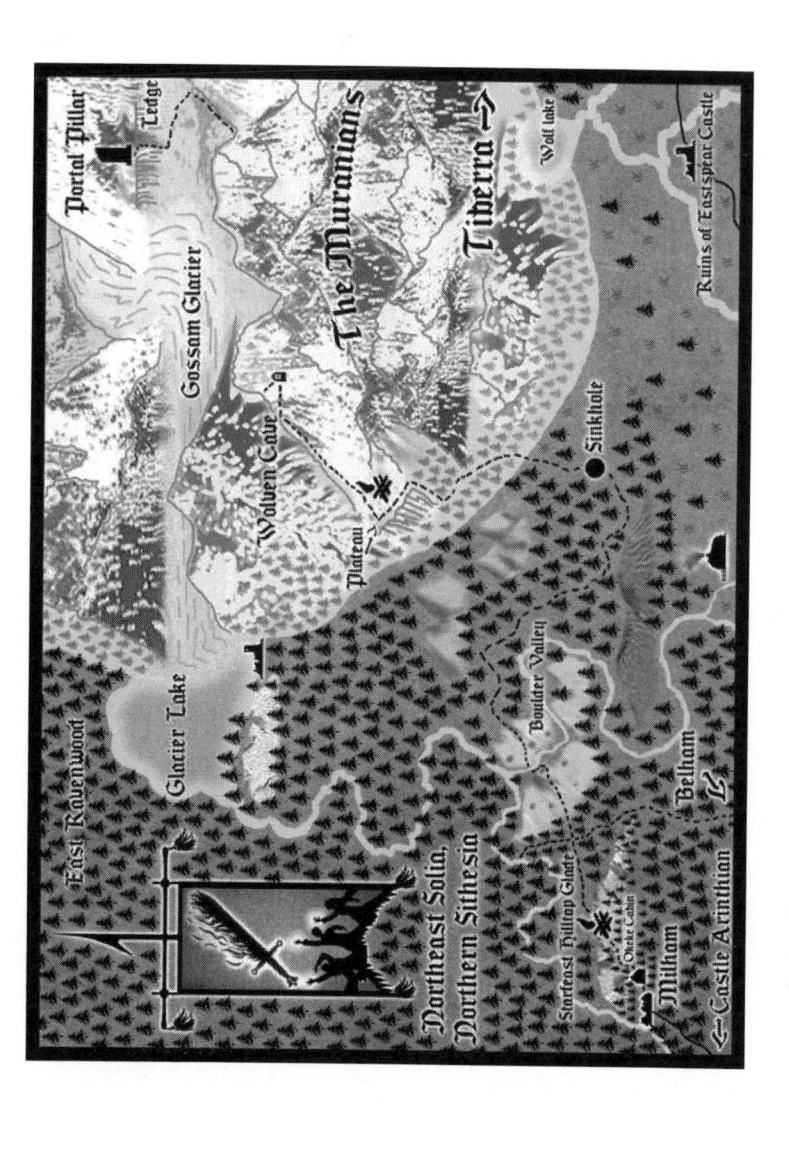

- First Ravenwood
- Portal Pillar
- Ledge
- Gossam Glacier
- The Muranians
- Glacier Lake
- Wolven Cave
- Plateau
- Tiberun →
- Wolf Lake
- Sinkhole
- Ruins of Ensispear Castle
- Boulder Valley
- Startcast Hilltop Glade
- Oozte Cabin
- Milham
- Belham
- ← Castle Arinthian

THE TALLOWS

Augum Stone tightened his grip on the reins, urging the black warhorse onward. The sun clung overhead in a cloudless azure sky, its rays reflecting off glimmering waist-high snow, forcing him to squint. Three days had passed since they left the remains of Sparrow's Perch. Three long, drab days of nothing but the Tallows, its tall yellow grass peaking through the endless snowy expanse. Well, almost nothing—the trio had managed to practice arcanery now and then.

Raven-haired Leera Jones clung sleepily to Augum's waist, head bouncing on his back to the rhythm of the horse. She startled awake and blankly stared about.

"We there yet?"

"No."

"We close at least?"

He did not reply.

She gave an exasperated sigh, squeezed his midriff tighter, and nuzzled closer like a cat seeking warmth. Usually her touch would have sent a thrill through his heart, but he felt dull and empty ever since Mya Liaxh had died in his arms.

That reminded him—it was long past time to check the Orb of Orion, he was sure of it. It remained where they had left it, in the ruins of the Legion camp at Hangman's Rock. Luckily, they possessed an engraved pearl that allowed them to see and communicate through it. The girls took turns. They knew it would be painful for him to look and thus spared him the burden. He was grateful, but it needed to be checked. He didn't want the Legion claiming Mya's body and ... and raising her from the dead.

He cleared his throat. "When's the last time you looked through the orb?"

Leera removed her hands from his waist, yawned and stretched. "This morning. Still nothing."

"Can you look again?" He tried not to imagine Mya's long jet hair lying in the snow, partially buried; her once brilliant almond eyes, now vacant.

There was a pause. "Guess so." Leera dug the pearl out of her robe and concentrated. "Nothing."

He wanted to ask if she was sure. No, what he really wanted to ask was whether or not Mya's body was still there.

"Want to practice arcanery?" Leera asked.

"Not really." They were supposed to be studying for their 2nd degree but he hadn't been in the mood to practice today. Actually, he'd been forcing it the last few days—the loss of Mya had tainted those pleasures too.

Leera's hands returned to his waist. "You're thinking about her."

He shrugged. Of *course* he was thinking about her, what did she expect? Always the same memories too. The time he used oxy to save her life. Their dance together in the ancient underground Leyan city. The last look she gave him as she died, his hand on hers, pressing the wound on her throat.

VALOR

Robin Scarson had murdered her. He regretted not tearing Robin's arms off when he had the chance—he could have used the Banyan beast back when Robin was sitting in the snow, defenseless. Instead, he chose to let him go. Now he knew the consequences of that decision.

"I miss her too," Leera whispered. "I miss her too ..."

He didn't reply. He wished she wouldn't talk about Mya. She didn't understand how he *felt* about her.

Unlike after the massacre at Sparrow's Perch, there hadn't been an arcane memorial ceremony to dull the pain of loss. Nana had not recovered enough to perform the powerful spell. Bridget and Leera had been as supportive as possible, but the pain was beyond the reach of even their friendship.

For the umpteenth time, he thought of turning the horse around and galloping back. He imagined picking Mya's body up and stealing her away, calling on the Unnameables—on any power that would listen—to help. He thought of ways to bring her back to life. Crazy ways, ways he dared not speak of.

The snow whooshed as the horse plowed it aside like waves in a frozen ocean.

Augum glanced ahead to the other two horses. Albert Goss and his son, Leland, led the group. They sat on a similar warhorse whose packs bulged like the chins of a well-fed man. Mr. Goss was middle-aged with spectacles and a balding head, while nine-year-old Leland was blind and mute, a result of lightning burns inflicted by Augum's father. Every time Augum laid eyes on the boy, there was a guilty pang in his stomach. *His* father had done that, one of countless atrocities.

Bridget Burns and his great-grandmother, Anna Atticus Stone, rode next on a languid chestnut mare. If Augum could have a choice of any girl to be his sister, he would choose Bridget. Compassionate, smart and loyal, with long cinnamon hair and a pert nose, she had been particularly supportive since Mya's death.

His brow creased with concern as he worried about Nana, wheezing in Bridget's arms, sick with a potent fever. It had taken hold of her after the recent battle with his father at Hangman's Rock, and worsened daily. She was too old to be sick.

The scion, embedded at the top of her sleek staff, caught the sun, blinding him momentarily. Fifteen hundred years ago the Leyans presented it to Augum's ancestor to help fight a legendary necromancer by the name of Occulus. It was more than just a powerful artifact though—it was a piece of family history, the only scion passed down within the original receiving family, generation after generation, for the entirety of that fifteen hundred years.

This was his inheritance, this ... burden. He didn't want it as it was keeping his great-grandmother alive. Sometimes he thought she was speeding their training along to prepare him for inheriting it.

He looked away from the scion, still seeing a ghostly afterglow in his vision. So much to worry about, yet it should be a happy time. After all, it was the fourth day of Endyear, the celebration marking ten days until New Year's Day, or "Founding Day" as warlocks called it, referring to the day arcanery had been formalized into elements 3340 years ago.

Every breakfast, Mr. Goss marked the occasion by lighting a candle on a bed of holly. Normally, the candle was kept lit day and night until Founding Day. Except no one was about to hold a candle in this weather for the sake of tradition, especially not while on horseback.

Augum almost smiled. He loved all the Endyear traditions, but Merrygive the most. Merrygive called for the young to go to the doors of the old and volunteer to help around the house or farm in exchange for butter cookies. Butter cookies always tasted better during Endyear.

VALOR

There were games, singing, dancing, music, and traditional tournaments of sword and bow. There was the communal hunt, the top prize awarding three bushels of hay, candy apples, two loaves of bread, and a barrel of sweet mead. Sir Westwood, his guardian at the time, won two years in a row, downing a plains elk one year and a buffalo the next.

Then there was the winter Star Feast held in the dead of night under a blanket of stars. It was what everyone else looked forward to the most. Typically, boys asked girls to attend, though the reverse wasn't unheard of. It was the only time parents did not, by tradition, step in the way of such requests, mostly because it was quite a public affair. Not that Augum had either back then—parents or friends. He had longed for friends, mostly someone to relate to, share dreams, fears, failures and triumphs with—but the other children hated him. He hadn't dressed like them or talked like them. He was either too learned or too quiet. Above all, he was *gutterborn scum* in their eyes.

And parents? He had known the Pendersons, with their foul breath and vile children. He had been a slave to them, working on their farm like Meli the mule. He had also known Sir Westwood, a stern guardian and capable mentor. But he had not had *parents*.

Augum sighed. Butter cookies, games, the Star Feast ... that was all back when things were simple, back when he strove for nothing more than knighthood. Willowbrook was a pile of ashes now, Sir Westwood dead and gone, murdered by the Legion.

He spotted something ahead. "What do you think that black dot is in the distance?" he forced himself to ask.

"The Waxman farm," Leera replied groggily. "At least it better be, else I'm going to go mad and eat my turnshoes or something."

The Waxmans were friends of Mr. Goss' and might provide food and shelter until Mrs. Stone got well. After, the group would make its way to the Muranian Mountains to find Occulus' castle and retrieve an ancient recipe for making a portal to Ley before his father got his hands on it.

Her hands adjusted at his waist. "Think Mr. Goss is lost?"

He shrugged, in no mood for banter.

She sighed, her head returning to his shoulder. "Let me know when you want to switch."

Clouds slowly gathered on the horizon as the day snailed along. The wind was calm, a welcome relief from the usually gusty Tallows. The cold still bit at Augum's ears though.

The speck in the distance grew closer, soon splitting into two, then three, then four distinct structures. As the sun kissed the western edge of Solia, Mr. Goss stopped his horse, waiting for everyone to catch up.

"I think we can get there before nightfall if we ride through supper. Is everyone all right with that?"

"Sure, Mr. Goss," Bridget said, holding a sleeping Mrs. Stone in her arms.

Augum and Leera gave lackadaisical nods.

"Good." Mr. Goss drew the blanket tighter around his son, who sat silent in front, and resumed the pace.

Leera dug inside her robes, withdrawing the pearl.

"See anything?" Augum asked.

"Give me a moment." She concentrated. "Hmm."

"What is it?"

"Thought I saw movement, but I think it was just a rabbit or something."

Augum had the urge to see for himself, but the memory of Mya's smiling face promptly changed his mind.

"Hold on, I see a Legion soldier …"

"What do you mean? Where?" He pictured the typical soldier—shining black armor marked with a burning sword emblem, matching pot helm, and sword.

"There's another one." Her voice dropped to a whisper. "And another. Looks like … looks like a column of them, filing out of the woods. Fifty at least."

He turned. "Any warlocks?"

"Yes ... and his robe's got black and red stripes—"

His knuckles whitened on the reins. That could only mean one thing—a necrophyte, an apprentice necromancer.

"There are other people with them ... villagers, I think," Leera continued. "They're fanning out. The necrophyte is telling them to pick up the bodies. Oh—"

"What? What is it—?"

"Haylee's one of them."

Haylee Tennyson was one of Bridget and Leera's former academy schoolmates. She was their age and studied the ice element. She had joined the Legion along with Robin as a necrophyte but revolted to save the trio's lives. Unfortunately, she disappeared trying to stop Robin's wraith during the Battle at Hangman's Rock.

"She's in chains," Leera reported.

"Is she all right?"

"She's a mess ..."

He didn't want to think about what kind of revenge Robin would exact for her betrayal. What pained him most was that until Mrs. Stone got better, there was nothing they could do for her.

"She's making her way over to the orb," Leera said.

"Think she'll recognize it?"

"She's seen it plenty enough. At least I think she has ..."

But Augum couldn't recall ever explaining to Haylee how the orb worked. "Maybe we could teleport her out somehow. Suck her through the orb or something."

Leera made a sound with her lips suggesting he was crazy.

"I don't know," he said, "I'm just saying maybe Nana could figure it out," but the more he thought about it, the dumber the idea became. Nana couldn't even stand, let alone perform arcanery.

Bridget looked back and raised an eyebrow. "What's going on?"

"Leera's listening through the orb. There're soldiers."

Bridget slowed her horse, drifting close.

"It's *him*—" Leera said through gritted teeth.

Augum stiffened. He didn't need to ask who. He only wished there was a way to arcanely throttle Robin through the orb.

"He's harassing Haylee," Leera reported, "making her remove weapons off the dead."

"Maybe he'll find the orb," Bridget said.

"He's coming closer. We have to be quiet now."

Augum and Bridget stopped their horses, allowing Mr. Goss to canter ahead obliviously. They had once overheard conversation within the orb via the control pearl, back in Evergray Tower. Erika hadn't even been aware of them listening in. If they weren't careful, someone could do the same to them.

Leera eventually opened her eyes and pressed a finger to her lips. She removed a cloth from her pocket, wrapped the pearl in it, and stuffed it in her robes. "Think they'll be able to hear through that?"

"Doubt it," Augum said. "So what happened?"

"Robin found the orb. He made Haylee stick it in his horse's pack. Can't see or hear anymore."

It was exactly what they had hoped for. Now, if they were careful, they might glean some useful information through it.

The sky turned to fiery dusk as they caught up to Mr. Goss.

THE WAXMAN FARM

"This is it," Mr. Goss said, dismounting at the edge of a rustic wooden fence, portions of it collapsed. "It is unfortunate we lack a horn to announce our presence."

Augum, Bridget and Leera dismounted while Mrs. Stone wearily sat up in the saddle, coughing.

Mr. Goss stepped over the fence and urged the horse to do the same. Leland, who stayed on his father's horse, moaned.

"It is all right, son. We are almost there."

Leland moaned again impatiently.

"I know that is what I said earlier, but we really are almost there."

Augum noticed the dark windows and broken shutters, the pileup of snow on the sills. The Waxmans were supposed to be a large family, yet the place looked deserted.

They slowly approached a barn, its planks grayed from the sun.

"Hello? Is anyone there?" Mr. Goss called out.

No reply.

"Most unusual."

Suddenly a lone figure dressed in furs peaked out from behind the barn before disappearing.

Mr. Goss waved excitedly. "Hello there, is that a Waxman I see!" He turned to the trio. "Must be one of the younger children."

They made their way around the barn, coming across a set of footprints that led to an earthen home, its windows shuttered.

"Let us put the horses in the barn and make ourselves presentable," Mr. Goss said. But after stepping inside, his face darkened. The barn was empty, stripped of its animals, its farm implements, even its hay.

"I fear for the fate of my friends," he said quietly, tying up his horse. "Let us see who this person is."

They walked over to the earthen house. Mr. Goss opened the plank door. It squeaked on rusty hinges.

"Hello?"

Nobody replied.

"It is all right, we mean you no harm. We are mere travelers in need of rest."

Augum stepped into the dark abode after Mr. Goss, noting a dirt floor covered with straw, a dusty trestle table and benches, a hole for a fire, and a broken ladder-back chair on its side. There was an open doorway off to the right to the only other room. The place held the lingering scent of cooked meat, herbs and smoke.

"I know you are here, please do not be afraid," Mr. Goss said.

Augum raised his palm. "Shyneo." Lightning spidered along his wrist and fingers, flooding the room in a bluish glow.

"Leave me alone, I not do nothing," said a thickly-accented and quivering voice from the doorway of the other room.

VALOR

Augum pointed his palm in that direction in time to see a small fur-clad figure scurry into a corner like a trapped rat. When the boy looked up, Augum's first thought was that his face was painted white, before realizing that was his actual skin color. Multi colored jeweled rings pierced his nose and lips. His eyes were as black as coal.

Mr. Goss took a tentative step forward. "But ... you are not a Waxman."

The boy looked around as if searching for an escape route. His fur hood fell away from his head, revealing straight milk-white hair that dangled just past his ears.

Mr. Goss dropped to one knee, voice soft. "What happened to the Waxmans?"

The boy's eyes darted about, fixing onto Augum's shining palm. "You not *them*, no?"

Mr. Goss kept his hands open before him. "Them? Them who? Do you mean the Legion?"

The boy only stared at Augum's palm, breathing rapidly. Augum extinguished it, plunging the room into dim darkness. The boy eased his breathing.

"Are you talking about the men in black armor?" Mr. Goss asked gently. "Is that who—"

"Burners. Burn animals. Burn people." The boy made a wavy gesture mimicking fire and looked at Leland. "Burners."

Mr. Goss glanced back at his disfigured son. "Yes, Burners. The Legion." He turned back to the boy. "And where are your parents? Are you all alone here?"

"Papa come soon. Papa strong. He hurt you if you hurts me."

"We will not hurt you, I promise." Mr. Goss withdrew a chunk of biscuit beef and held it out. "Have a bite." The boy only stared. Mr. Goss made a biting gesture. "See? This is good. Mmm, good."

The boy slowly reached out, eyes shooting between the dried beef and Mr. Goss' face. He snatched it and quickly withdrew, eating as fast as a squirrel, never taking his eyes off Mr. Goss.

"What is your name?"

"Ettan."

"Ettan. That is a nice name. My name is Albert Goss. This is my son, Leland, and that is Augum, Bridget, Leera and Mrs. Stone."

Ettan glanced at the frail old woman. "She old. Old maniye."

A chortle escaped Mrs. Stone's lips that quickly regressed to a coughing fit.

"Please, Mrs. Stone, have a seat," Bridget said, taking her by the hand and leading her to a bench by the table. Mrs. Stone wheezed her way over, eyes closed.

Ettan wiped his runny nose on the back of his sleeve. "Old maniye dying?"

"She'll be fine," Augum said. "She's just tired. What does maniye mean?"

Ettan tapped his skin. "Sapinchay." He pointed to Augum's skin then to Mr. Goss'. "Maniye."

"Oh, you mean our skin?" Mr. Goss asked. "Maniye means darker skin?"

Ettan nodded. "Iya." He pointed at Mr. Goss' face. "What that?"

"You mean these? These are called spectacles." Mr. Goss took them off and offered them to the boy. "They help me see better."

Ettan stared at the wiry frame. He reached out, snatched them, and tentatively put them on. His eyes magnified. He tore them off his face and retreated. "Andava, andava—!"

Mr. Goss picked them up off the floor and gave them a wipe. "Sometimes I want to do the same thing, but unfortunately for me, I can barely see without them."

"Papa say bald die quicker under sword."

Mr. Goss surrendered a nervous laugh. "Yes, well, uh, I will be sure not to get into any sword fights anytime soon."

He stood up, dusting his knee. "May I ask why you are all alone, Ettan?"

"Waiting for Papa. He gathering. He come soon."

"Gathering? Oh, you mean food."

Ettan shrugged and stuck out his hand.

"Hungry little fellow." Mr. Goss handed the boy more biscuit beef. "Is this your place now?"

Ettan shook his head.

"And you know nothing of what happened to my friends, the Waxmans?"

"Burners take away."

Mr. Goss's head dropped. "Are you sure?" he asked quietly.

Ettan shrugged while he chewed, eyes solemnly watching Mr. Goss.

Mr. Goss nodded slowly. "Can we stay here and wait for your papa with you?"

Ettan shrugged again.

"I'm sorry, Mr. Goss," Bridget said quietly.

"Thank you, Bridget."

Augum gave Mr. Goss a pained look. "I'll get the supplies."

Leera sat Leland down beside Bridget and Mrs. Stone. "I'll help."

The pair left the earthen home, only to hear distant galloping. They quickly ducked back inside the doorway.

"Someone's coming!" Augum said.

Ettan rushed to the doorway. "Papa here!"

They watched as three horsemen jumped the fence, their armor catching the fiery hues of dusk. They had colorfully painted faces and rode gray mares.

"Ho!" called the lead rider, drawing a curved blade. "Who with my son! Come!"

Augum was about to step outside when Mr. Goss held him back with a hand while striding past. "We are just some weary travelers looking to quietly bed down for a few days. We mean you no harm."

The lead rider boomed a laugh revealing black teeth. A single golden tooth stood out like a beacon fire. He was a very muscular man with the same snowy white skin as Ettan. His milky hair was so long it touched the saddle. A series of jeweled rings pierced both his eyebrows, and blue lines streaked across his face, curling around his sharp brows and pointed nose. Strips of bloody cloth dangled from his well-worn iron plate.

The man pointed his curved blade at Mr. Goss's head. "He been under knife!" and laughed anew, this time joined by the other riders, both also as white as snow. One wore bloody chainmail under a great red bearskin. Rabbit and squirrel skins hung from his horse along with an assortment of pots, silver cutlery, and clothes. The other wore battered plate mail under a buffalo hide. Strapped to the back of his horse was a deer carcass.

The lead rider raised his chin. "You have younglings."

Mr. Goss glanced backward nervously. "Yes, yes we do. One of them is my son."

Ettan shouldered past Augum. "Papa, maniye have sick old woman and boy put to Burner fire."

"Ettan speak good maniye tongue, yes?"

Mr. Goss cleared his throat rather quickly. "Oh yes indeed, he is marvelous. My name is Albert Goss—"

"Goss. Weak name." The rider turned to his comrades. "Like swamp juice." The other two laughed.

The rider smacked his sword against his muscled chest. "Rogan the Conqueror." He then pointed it at the chain-mailed man. "Hushu." He swung his sword the other way. "Chikota."

The man wearing plate mail and buffalo hide scowled.

Rogan gave a nod. "We are Henawa."

"Henawa—of course! I have heard tales, but I have never—oh, this is such an honor! This is my first experience with your people." Mr. Goss turned to Augum, smiling. "The Henawa are from northern Ohm. They sometimes travel south with the snow in winter, retreating in the summer." He glanced back to Rogan. "Well it is a pleasure to meet you, Rogan the, uh, Conqueror."

"You maniye. You not travel. You hide in walls, stone, earth. You burn Henawa."

"No, no, that is not us, I assure you. That is the Legion, and they are very bad." Mr. Goss shook his head gravely, frowning. "Legion very bad."

Rogan grunted. He sheathed his blade and dismounted, stroking his horse on the neck before handing the reins to his boy. He strode past Mr. Goss into the home.

Mrs. Stone coughed, keeping her eyes closed.

"She dying."

"No, she's only tired," Augum said, standing between Rogan and Mrs. Stone.

"She dying. Leave her. We go."

"We're not going anywhere with you!" Leera said.

Rogan's eyes narrowed. "Maniye females no talk to Rogan like he small." He raised his hand to smack her.

"Shyneo!"

Three palms immediately lit up, one glowing ivy, one water, one lightning.

Rogan took a step back. "Nuliwi …"

"That's right," Leera said. "So don't try anything."

Rogan hooked his thumbs into his belt and cocked his head. "Nuliwi bring many furs in trade."

"You're not trading us like slaves, you're going to leave us alone, or, or—"

Rogan gave an amused chortle. "Or what maniye nuliwi do?"

"Or Mrs. Stone will turn you into a turnip!"

Everyone glanced at Mrs. Stone. She groaned and rested her head onto the table.

Rogan scoffed. "She sick. We leave her. Dying nuliwi no good."

"NO!" Augum took a step forward, palm outstretched. "We're *not* leaving her. We're *not* going with you." He'd be damned if they were going to be taken captive *again*.

Rogan the Conqueror studied their glowing palms with coal eyes. "Hmm. She sick. Shaman help." He nodded. "Bring old woman. We make trade and heal." He sniffed loudly and walked out the door. Mr. Goss, who had been kept from entering by Hushu's curved blade, scampered out of his way.

Rogan swung onto his horse. He reached down and plucked up his son like a sack of potatoes, dumping him behind.

"Maniye hurry or Papa mad," Ettan said.

Augum glanced to Mr. Goss, who seemed frozen in place, eyes as large as an owl's.

"Maybe the shaman can help Mrs. Stone," Bridget said.

"Either that or we fight," Leera said under her breath.

Augum took a moment to think. Nana was too sick to perform arcanery, the warriors looked quick and strong, and Centarro, the most powerful spell they had in their arsenal, *might* help overcome them. Or not. But what if Nana got worse? What if there was no food for leagues, and they passed up this opportunity to have her healed? Rogan gestured for them to move along to their horses. "Henawa have roof, fire, meat. Maniye come."

"I think it's worth the risk," Augum said. The others nodded.

Mr. Goss lifted a moaning Leland up onto his shoulders. "Shh, son, it is all right."

"Burners," Rogan said as Mr. Goss walked past, eyeing Leland.

Hushu and Chikota nodded. "Burners."

The trio followed next, helping Mrs. Stone walk. She took tentative steps, skin hotter than fire.

"Where do you think they're taking us?" Augum asked quietly, glancing over his shoulder.

"Don't know," Bridget replied.

They helped Mrs. Stone onto her horse first. When they were ready, Rogan took the lead. Ettan stared at them like a snowy owl watching a field mouse.

The column rode south into a cold moonless night, the sky sprinkled with glimmering stars and a smattering of clouds.

THE PAST TO LIFE

The scars on Augum's back tingled when he spied a particular pitched-roof house and barn. "I know this place …"

Leera squeezed his waist lightly. "Aug?"

He spotted a familiar oak and recalled a pack of kids chasing him up its trunk, stones being thrown, his body smashing to the ground. Mr. Penderson had whipped him right over there for being too tired to finish his chores. It had been pointless to explain that Garth, the oldest Penderson brat, had forced him to sleep in the barn that night. The man didn't appreciate "trying to pass the load", as he liked to put it.

"This is … The Farm," he said, a sick feeling in his stomach.

"You mean the place you ran away from as a child?"

He could only surrender a tense nod as they passed a well. He remembered dangling upside down from its rope, laughter echoing.

VALOR

Leera's voice became increasingly disbelieving. "The place your mother dropped you off at to be taken care of? *That's* where we are?"

"Yes ..." Everywhere he looked, memory stabbed at him like Garth's finger when making a point. He had scratched his knees up good fixing the thatched roof of the barn; spent quiet rainy days within, Meli alongside, her ears flopping this way and that. He recalled burying himself in the prickly hay, the brats stabbing pitchforks into it in search of him; remembered feeling Meli's tired last breaths as Mr. Penderson's whip rained down on the old mule in the field where crabby corn had once grown.

They heard singing as they rounded the corner of the earthen home. Hushu let loose a piercing cry, taken up by Chikota and Rogan and quickly echoed by a slew of voices. Soon they were in view of a large timber fire surrounded by about twenty figures. The barn stood behind, randomly stripped of planks like a beggar missing teeth. A dozen large horses milled within, grazing on straw.

"Ho!" Rogan called.

"Ho!" voices shouted back.

A flock of snow-skinned and snow-haired children immediately ran over to inspect the new arrivals, especially Mrs. Stone. They shouted out in the Henawa tongue, pawing her saddlebags and yanking at her robe.

"Hey, don't touch that!" Bridget said, smacking at the hand of a young girl trying to tug the staff. One of Mrs. Stone's brows arched slightly, but other than that, she seemed untroubled.

Rogan, Hushu and Chikota dismounted, ignoring the children. A few fur-clad women came to help unlash the deer carcasses and the rabbit and squirrel hides. They eyed Augum and the others with distrust.

A very fat man with a tremendous amount of piercings waddled over. A great bearskin was draped over his back, the head resting on the man's scalp. Food clung to his long milky beard. He clutched a waterskin in one hand and the remains of a roasted bird in the other. A long hide shirt decorated with beads and bones hung down to his knees.

"Chunchuha!" the man said, raising his waterskin and showing black teeth in what Augum thought might be a smile.

"Chief say hello," Rogan said, picking up his son and tossing him to the ground. The boy landed on his feet like a cat.

The chief reached over to Augum's robe, feeling the coarse woolen cloth between his fingers. He turned his great head to Rogan. "Maniye nuliwi."

Rogan gave a small nod. The pair then exchanged rapid shots in their language.

The chief glanced over at Mrs. Stone and scowled. Rogan made dismissive gestures, pointing at the trio. The pair argued for a moment before Rogan spit on the ground and walked away, arm around a husky woman.

"What's going on?" Leera asked.

"Don't know," Augum replied.

The chief barked at the people around the fire. Half a dozen fur-clad young men rushed over.

"Hey—!" Bridget yelped as one of the youths yanked her off her horse. Two others did the same to Mrs. Stone, who gave no resistance. Hands pawed at Augum and Leera, stripping them off the horse. Only Mr. Goss had the wherewithal to dismount quickly, holding a moaning Leland close.

One of the youths snatched the rucksack from Bridget and tossed it to the children, who immediately began pawing through it.

"That's ours, you brats!" Leera called, but no one paid her any attention, except Ettan, who chewed on a finger, staring at her. She began struggling with her captor. "Let go! Where are you taking us?"

VALOR

"Taro, taro! Onusha!" the youth said, twisting her arm and shoving her forward. The other men prodded Augum, Bridget and Mr. Goss with sticks. "Taro!"

Two youths dragged Mrs. Stone along. When one of them tried taking the staff from her, he jumped like a bitten dog, complaining loudly to his friends. They only laughed, saying, "Nuliwi, nuliwi!"

Augum witnessed a dirty child wearing deerskin run away clutching their ornate blue book on Arcaneology, eyes wide in delight. The rucksack contents quickly dispersed among the crowd. Some of the adults joined in, rifling through the satchels hanging off the horses.

"Great, there goes our stuff," Leera muttered.

"If I recall correctly, I think we have to gain their respect to get it back," Mr. Goss said.

"How do you know that, Mr. Goss?"

"My father left me an old tome I read as a child, written by a renowned adventurer by the name of Codus Trazinius. It was called *A Solian's Recounting of Distant Lands*. If we ever make it back to Sparrow's Perch, I will be sure to—"

One of the youths pushed Mr. Goss along. "Taro, taro! Onusha!"

"Shyneo," Augum said just as one of the boys stepped near, only to spring away. Augum locked eyes with the chief. "Where is the shaman? We made a deal with Rogan—"

The chief eyed Augum's palm before gesturing impatiently. He spoke a few terse words.

"Chief say we talk tomorrow," Ettan said.

Augum extinguished his palm. His eyes narrowed at the chief. "Tomorrow then."

They were marched into the house. Augum was only too familiar with the crudely vaulted ceiling the Pendersons threatened to hang him from; the squeaky timber flooring that gave him away when he tried to go unnoticed; the primitive stone hearths the brats had shoved him into.

He did not notice his fists curl. The place made him angry. Angry that he had suffered so. Angry that the brats got away with so much.

There was a pantry kitchen, a room for the servants, and a large bedroom, each abundant with ghosts of his torments. The long trestle table and benches—which he was never allowed to sit at—remained, but most of the other furniture seemed to be missing.

Winter was a hard time, especially for farmers. Now that war had come, famine was right behind, and it didn't surprise him too much to see the place in disrepair like this. He wondered what had happened to the Pendersons.

"Taro!" A youth herded them into the bedroom, shutting the door behind them. Augum heard the youths settle around the table in the kitchen, snickering.

"Who's there?" asked a timid female voice from the darkness.

Leera held up her palm. "Shyneo." It flared to life, shining watery blue light on a large bed against the near wall, under a shuttered window. The dresser, chairs and blanket box that had once been here were missing, but what caught Augum's attention were two dirty figures huddled in the far corner, precisely in the same spot he used to sleep. The Pendersons forbade him room on the large bed, forcing him to sleep on the floor, mostly to keep an eye on him. Sometimes he was allowed to sleep in the servant room, the barn, or outside.

"What be that devil light?" the boy asked.

Augum knew that voice. His blood immediately began boiling.

"We mean you no harm," Mr. Goss said, placing Leland on the bed while Bridget and Leera helped Mrs. Stone lie down.

"Who you be!" the boy demanded. He had ruddy cheeks, long auburn hair tied back, and a muscular physique. Muddy and torn trousers flopped over turned-down boots. A ragged fur coat hung around a splattered linen shirt. He seemed to be protecting a girl of about Augum's age. She, too, had long auburn hair in a ponytail, face as muddy as her dress.

"Who we be ..." Augum said. He took a step forward, ready to flay the boy alive, to slam him through the wall with his bare fists.

But he was held back by Bridget's firm grip. "Aug?" she whispered, searching his face. "What's the matter?"

"We are just some weary travelers," Mr. Goss said, unaware of Augum's reaction.

"And that devil light there?"

"It's a spell," Leera replied. "I can do it too. Means we don't need candles."

The girl whimpered. "Thems is witches! Don't eat us, we ain'ts no good."

Leera scoffed, taking a seat on the bed. "We're warlocks, not bears."

"Let me go," Augum hissed. There was a beating to attend to.

Bridget only gripped him harder. "Stop it, what's gotten into you?"

"*Some* of us are warlocks," Mr. Goss added. "My son and I are as ordinary as country pie."

Leland moaned.

"What's wrong with him, why he all melted?" the boy asked.

"The Legion burned him with lightning."

"Oh. So he a freak now—"

"—he isn't a freak'!" Leera replied, scowling.

"Well he don't look right."

"Where is your family?" Mr. Goss asked.

"They took Pops and my brother for them war. Wanted to get me but I hid with my sister. Mum's around too. Hold on now. You there—shine that devil light on your face!"

"Shyneo." Augum raised his crackling palm.

"Well I'll be. I knows you! You're that stupid gutterborn—"

Augum surged forward, dragging Bridget right along. Something about the look on his face, perhaps combined with his lightning palm, made the boy's face turn ashen.

"Unnameables help me!" he squealed, almost climbing the wall to get away, his sister shrieking.

"Aug, what are you—" Leera grabbed him too, but even with both girls holding him, there was an unquenchable inner fire that raged, giving him strength. It took Mr. Goss' quick intervention to stay him.

"My word, Augum, what in Sithesia is the matter, my dear boy?" Mr. Goss turned to the boy and girl. "I assure you, he is not like this usually."

Augum allowed himself to be withdrawn.

"You know them, don't you?" Bridget asked, holding one of his arms with both hands.

"Buck Penderson and his sister Wyza," Augum spat. Buck was the younger of the two Penderson brothers, but just as brutal.

Buck relaxed and grinned. "So it *is* you. Got you some gutterborn courage since I last sees you."

"Please don't use that kind of language," Bridget said.

Leera guffawed. "So you're the demented loons!"

"Now, Leera, let us not be rude," Mr. Goss said, tentatively letting go of Augum, but remaining close by. "We must be cordial in the predicament we find ourselves in."

"But Mr. Goss, these are the kids who bullied Augum when he was a boy!" She took a step forward. "Let's turn them into raccoons, or smear them into manure like what's-his-face."

Wyza shrieked, struggling in her brother's arms. Mr. Goss held up his hands. "I assure you they jest—"

VALOR

"You stay back, keep that there devil light away," Buck said to Leera. "Or I'll smash my fist into your face and break them pretty teeth."

"Not before I shove you through that there wall without a face," Augum quickly replied, not even realizing his voice had taken on the commoner twang Sir Westwood had take so much care in expunging.

Mr. Goss cleared his throat. "Let us be civil. Settle down, everyone, settle down. May I ask how long you have been in this room?"

"Must be twenty days and some now," Buck replied after a tense silence, keeping his eyes on Augum. "Them savages done setup camp right here. Legion took most of our flock first, barbarians ate the rest. Mum's been feeding us, workin' for them savages in the mean. She don't let us leave the house or talk to them."

Even the sound of Buck's voice strained Augum's nerves. He associated that vile twang with lies, curses, and more lies.

"It's you, you be the reason for this," Wyza said, pointing a filthy finger at Augum. "You done been a curse to us since the first day your hag mother dumped you here."

Augum's light flared. "You *dare*—" but he was stopped once again by the girls and Mr. Goss.

One of the Henawa youths kicked the outside of the door, barking a shout.

"We should be quiet," Mr. Goss said, adjusting his spectacles. "Please, I implore civility. Augum, I am sure Buck and Wyza here have long grown out of their habits. And Buck, Wyza—I can personally testify what kind of boy Augum has become. You will hardly recognize him, I assure you."

Buck scoffed. "Fancy pants wordsies coming from a bunch of uglies." His beady eyes returned to Augum. "So now you is even more wicked, a witch—"

"Warlock," Augum corrected. "And you're just as stupid, I see."

"You grew some nerve, gutterborn. I sees I is going to have to fix that. Whatever you is, you done no good then and you done no good now. To me, you is as flea-bitten as the day you come."

Bridget squeezed Augum's arm. "Now is not the time. Let me take over Shine, you rest your energy."

Still glaring at Buck, he nodded reluctantly, sat down beside Mrs. Stone, and extinguished his palm.

"Shyneo," Bridget said. The room filled with a soft green light as vine entwined around her hand. Wyza and Buck watched with stony faces. Bridget gave them a warm smile, but Buck only spit on the floor, his sister mimicking.

Leera gave them a disgusted look before sitting beside Augum. "What do we do for food?"

"I regret asking everyone to skip supper," Mr. Goss said. "I am a hasty fool."

"It's all right, Mr. Goss," Bridget said. "How were you to know?"

Augum took Mrs. Stone's withered hand in his own. It was hot to the touch. Nonetheless, it calmed him. "How are you feeling, Nana?"

Usually she'd open her eyes or squeeze his hand, but this time there was nothing.

"I fear she is gravely ill," Mr. Goss said. "We need a healer."

A sullen mood fell upon the group as they made themselves as comfortable as they could in the cold room ... and waited for the morrow.

THE HENAWA

Augum shivered awake at the crow of a rooster, a sound he had not heard since living in Willowbrook with Sir Westwood. He blearily opened his eyes, finding himself on the dirty plank floor of a dusty room. Horizontal rays of sun pierced a shuttered window, daggering into the near wall. Mr. Goss slept beside him, his steady breathing sending up plumes of fog.

Augum sat up, rubbing his elbows, sore from the planks. He spied Mrs. Stone asleep on the large bed, Bridget, Leera and Leland curled up beside her. Buck and Wyza lay on the far side of the room. Both looked terribly uncomfortable.

Might be a good time to take a look around. He quietly got up and placed his ear to the door, hearing snoring. He turned the handle. It squeaked and the door popped open. The sound brought back memories of Mr. and Mrs. Penderson storming out of the room, throwing an insult or kick his way, before ordering him to get to work.

Two of the Henawa youths lay asleep on the floor, covered in thick furs. Augum gathered his charred robes close and tiptoed around them, pushing through the front door.

Outside, he squinted against a sharp sun floating in a spotless sky. The fire pit smoldered, the snow around it muddy and well trodden. Tall hide tents stood between the pit and the old mill. Skins hung on racks, drying. The air was still, the only sound the distant trickle of the Gander, the river he had followed to Willowbrook years ago.

He spotted movement on the barn roof—it was the rooster, watching him. He wondered how it had survived everyone's hunger.

A heavy man pushed aside a tent flap, stepping out into the cold, milky chest bare. He burped and stretched. It was the chief, minus his bearskin. A moment later, a woman exited the tent. She had long auburn hair and wore a pale linen dress.

Augum's skin crawled. Mrs. Penderson ...

She picked up a handful of snow, washed her face, slipped on a pair of old turnshoes, and reached into the tent, removing a covered basket. She smacked the chief on the arm and said something sharp. The man groaned and disappeared inside the tent, emerging a moment later with all three of the trio's Dramask wool blankets. Mrs. Penderson, who in the meantime had fixed up her hair, wordlessly yanked the blankets from him and proceeded to walk Augum's way.

He stood there, watching her approach, wondering what he would say to her, feeling oddly calm. She came right up to him as if expecting him to be there after all this time. The sun had creased her face over the years, but her blue eyes sparkled as coldly as ever.

"You."

Augum nodded at the blankets. "Those are ours."

She reared back, ready to deliver a vicious slap, the kind he was all too familiar with. But for the first time ever, he caught her arm and held it firm.

"Never again," he said, flexing his jaw.

"You gutterborn wretch, this be all your fault," she hissed, yanking her arm free. She glanced past him. "What you looking at, you little maggot?"

"You old," Ettan said, chewing on his finger.

Mrs. Penderson spat on the ground before the boy. "I'd smack you too if your pappy wouldn't go on and scalp me for it." Then she marched inside the house.

Augum watched her go.

"She no like you."

"Feeling's mutual."

"You has dirty face." Ettan skipped off.

"Wait, do you have any food?"

Ettan stopped. "You gather."

"You mean I can hunt here?"

The boy shrugged before skipping off again.

"Can I at least borrow a bow or something—?" but Ettan was gone.

Suddenly there were shouts from within the house. He ran back inside, jumping over the two Henawa youths, who were slow to get up, and raced into the bedroom, where he found Mrs. Penderson screaming at Mr. Goss and the girls.

"—you done get out of my house, you filthy gutterborn—"

She dropped her basket and started swinging wildly at Mr. Goss, who wore the startled expression of a man who had suddenly stepped on a wasp's nest.

Wyza ran over, feebly trying to stop her mother. "Ma! Ma don't, they is witches, Ma—they is witches!"

Mrs. Penderson recoiled as if stung. She grabbed Wyza by the arm and yanked her back. As thin as she looked, there was ferocity there stronger than mere muscle. She jabbed a finger in their direction. "You stay back or I'll call them savages and have y'all scalped!" She snatched her basket, the Dramask blankets, and quickly withdrew into the corner.

Mr. Goss drew on his spectacles. "Ah, you must be Mrs. Penderson, it is a real pleasure—"

"You shut that gob and stay back, you hear? You ain't got nothin' to scalp but that don't mean you don't bleed like a stuck pig."

"Now Mrs. Penderson, I hardly think—"

She whistled sharply and the two Henawa youths appeared.

Mr. Goss held up his hands. "All right, all right, we are backing away, but we really mean no harm."

"You hang yonder and keep them mitts where I can see them."

"Really now, Mrs. Penderson, this is hardly necessary."

She watched him out of the corner of her eye while her children dug into the basket like a pack of hungry wolves.

"That's our food!" Leera said, watching them scarf down biscuit beef and dried apple slices.

Bridget turned away. "Ignore it."

"Hell I will." Leera raised her arm and beckoned. A dried apple flew out of the basket, much to the astonishment of the Pendersons.

"Told you they is witches," Wyza said as the three of them took ridiculous measures to hold the basket.

"Next time it'll be your eyeballs," Leera said, handing the apple over to Bridget to give to Mrs. Stone.

Mrs. Penderson held her children a little closer after that.

The snow-skinned youths began conversing in Henawa, sometimes gesturing at the trio while using the words maniye and nuliwi numerous times.

"Excuse me, but do you have something to eat?" Augum asked them. They gave him a blank look. He repeated his query while making the gesture to eat.

"Spudi maniye," one of the youths said to the other, who chuckled.

The front door squeaked open and heavy boots thudded across the planks. Rogan the Conqueror sauntered in, sporting a great many scars across his bare chest. His long milky hair flowed down his back. A large necklace of bones and animal teeth hung around his neck. His son Ettan peaked out from behind his massive legs.

The youths immediately stopped talking as Rogan looked around the room, sniffing the air like a bull.

"Excuse me, sir," Augum said, "but, do you have any food?"

"You nuliwi. You make food with magic."

"That's not how it works—" but Rogan was already talking sharply to the youths. They nodded before moving to stand in the hall.

Mr. Goss gently cleared his throat. "Mr. Rogan, sir, we really do need to eat. My boy is hungry, and we have not eaten since yesterday afternoon."

Rogan glanced over at Leland sitting quietly on the edge of the bed, his scalp melted, eyes sightless. The man grunted before strolling over to Mrs. Penderson and yanking the basket out of her hands. She grabbed Buck and Wyza and wilted into the corner, baring her teeth at him but saying nothing. Rogan stared her before casually reaching into the basket and withdrawing smoked fish and a small jar of honey. He shoved the basket back at her before walking over to Leland, gently placing the fish and honey into the boy's hands.

Leland moaned.

"It is all right, son," Mr. Goss said. "The man is only giving you some food. Now what do we say when someone does us a kindness?"

Leland moaned twice in succession. He then proceeded to share the honey and fish with their group.

Rogan cocked his head slightly before turning to Mr. Goss, making a gesture to his own head. "First boy born slow. We leave him forest."

"We'd never do that," Bridget said, placing Leland on her lap. "Ever."

Rogan grunted before aiming a steely-eyed gaze at Augum. "Go. Magic food."

Leera leaned close to Augum. "I think he means for you to go hunting."

Mr. Goss came between Rogan and Augum. "Good sir, I will hunt—"

Rogan pushed Mr. Goss aside, pointing sternly at Augum. "No. Him. He prove he man. Hunt magic."

"Will you send us that shaman soon?" Augum asked.

Rogan grunted. "Hunt first," and turned to leave.

"I'm coming too then," Leera said. "I'm also a warlock."

Rogan stared at her a moment before giving a brief nod. He departed without another word.

Augum wondered how they were going to accomplish this. He'd never hunted before using only arcanery.

"I come," Ettan said, still standing in the doorway.

Augum shook his head. "I don't think that's a good idea."

"I come or call Papa."

"Let him, maybe he can help," Leera whispered.

"Fine, but you have to promise to be careful."

Ettan shrugged.

"Do you need me to come?" Bridget asked.

"Probably best one of us warlocks stays behind," Augum replied, flashing the Pendersons a distrustful look.

ARCANE TRICKS

When Augum and Leera stepped outside, a good many of the Henawa were out of their tents, their children already running about making noise. The men sharpened and repaired weapons, probably readying to go hunting, while the youths tended to the horses or sparred.

Soon they were snatching glances of them. Mutterings of "nuliwi" and "maniye" abounded.

"I don't think it's a good idea for us to linger," Augum said under his breath.

Leera nodded.

They walked north, Ettan trailing, his little legs unable to propel him quicker over the waist-high snow.

"I'm so hungry I can't think straight," Leera muttered.

Augum's own stomach felt canyon hollow, but he already associated the farm with starvation, so it was a familiar state to be in. "Let's try the river."

They strode east, arriving at the partially frozen river, one of his few sources of joy as a child. He remembered drifting down its lazy current in the summer, gazing at the sky, dreaming of a better life.

SEVER BRONNY

Ettan watched a little ways back like a curious raccoon.

Augum smiled at the boy, seeing himself crouching by the banks in the same way. "I used to play in this river all the time," he said to Leera. "Learned to swim in it. Never thought I'd come back."

Leera thumbed at the house. "Bet you never thought you'd see them again either, or have to deal with a tribe of Henawa."

He snorted a laugh for the first time in what felt like months. "That's true. I guess we've been in worse spots, haven't we?"

"Uh, *yeah*."

They stared at the river together for a while, listening to its ceaseless gurgling, until an idea occurred to him.

"Ettan, do the Henawa fish here?"

The boy looked at him like he was stupid.

"Never mind." He turned back to the river. "Lee, you remember how we saved Bridget at the tower, right?"

Leera gaped at him until recognition dawned on her freckled face. She smiled. "Are you thinking—"

"—yes, exactly. The question is, alone or together?"

"Let's try alone first."

He took a tentative step out onto the ice at the edge of the river. He certainly couldn't afford to fall into freezing water right now. The ice seemed to hold his first steps, so he ventured forth. The gap in the center was just over a foot wide. He straddled it. The ice here was thin but held.

"Good luck," Leera said.

He looked down at the rushing water, conscious of Ettan watching nearby.

Concentrate, he told himself. You can do this. He placed his palm over the water and waited. A few small fish zoomed past. At last, a larger one trawled along. He concentrated on Telekinesis, visualizing the fish in his hand. It panicked and slipped away from his arcane grip.

VALOR

"Never even heard of this before," Leera said. "Arcane fishing ... who would have thought."

Another large fish swam past but he missed again. "They're too quick."

"Be quicker."

"You sound like Nana."

"I'm filling in for her."

A fish swam by and he yanked arcanely. It shot out of the water. He missed catching it with his hand but had the wherewithal to slap it aside on its descent. The fish tumbled to Leera, flipping this way and that. She shrieked and jumped out of the way. Ettan, on the other hand, started shouting in his native tongue before running off. The pair hardly took notice.

"Ugh, guess I got to do my part." Leera picked up a rock and brought it down, just missing the fish.

Augum winced. "Best to hold it."

She snatched the tail and slammed the rock down on the fish's head, breathing a sigh of relief when it stopped moving. She glanced up with a wry grin. "Bridget never would have done that."

"That's why I title thee, 'Fish Vanquisher'."

She smiled. "Shut up."

"I think that's a trout. Now we just have to do it a couple more times and we should be fine."

"Can't believe Telekinesis even worked. Let me try now."

Augum made an *after you* gesture and stepped off to the side of the bank as Leera took his place. She hardly started concentrating when there came a great commotion from the camp. Ettan soon reappeared with what looked like every male in the tribe, pointing and shouting at Augum and the fish, all clamoring to get a better look.

Rogan the Conqueror pushed through the crowd, shooing some of them back to the camp. They wandered off a little ways before creeping back on the periphery like snow foxes.

Rogan fixed a cold stare on Augum. He pointed at the fish. "You magic?"

Augum exchanged a look with Leera. "Yes, I, uh, I magicked the fish." Bridget would have been mad at him for using that word. Warlocks say "arcane" or "arcanery". "Magic" was for tricksters and fakes and parlor magicians.

Rogan explained to the crowd in their tongue. They hung on every word before returning their gaze to Augum.

"No, now it's her turn," Augum said, gesturing at Leera.

It wasn't long until a fish flew through the air. Leera made it look even better by actually catching it by the tail and throwing it aside for Augum, who promptly smacked its head with a well-aimed blow of the rock.

"Salmon," he said triumphantly.

The crowd erupted in cheers and equal shouts of alarm. "Nuliwi!" some called. "Andava!" others cried.

The cacophony was so great Augum feared they were going to get scalped then and there. Rogan issued commands. Runners dispatched to the tents. A gaggle of women and children quickly appeared, tongues clucking. Rogan sharply pointed at the stream, at the fish, and at Augum and Leera, all the while vociferously explaining in Henawa. He then turned back to Augum."Now you show why no need women no more." He explained the joke again in his tongue. The males all laughed while the women flashed sour looks.

Augum and Leera repeated the feat, this time even faster, and the entire tribe went wild—the women shouted at the men, the men pointed skyward and at the fish, and the children ran around screaming in a frenzy.

"Another trout," Augum said, trying to ignore the calamity going on behind him. They grabbed their fish and pushed past the throng, strolling back to the camp wearing slight grins. Before they even got to the door of the house, every single child in the tribe (and even some of the youths and one or two of the adults when they thought no one was looking) was pointing at objects and barking commands, trying to make them move.

"Ho!" Rogan called just as Augum pried the door open with his turnshoe. The big warrior pointed to the center. "We make fire. Maniye nuliwi cook here." He bared his golden tooth in a wide smile.

"Sure," Augum said, relieved.

"I'll tell the others, be back in a moment," Leera said, disappearing inside.

Augum strode to the fire pit where a youthful Henawa man and woman were finishing making a pyramid of planks and twigs. The barn continued to lose timber, even though there were trees around.

"Chunchuha!" said a burly voice.

Augum turned to find a grinning chief. The grin was identical to that of the bear's head sitting on his scalp. The large man began pointing at the fire and at the trout, speaking in Henawa.

"Chief want fish cook magic," Ettan said, joining the little gathering.

"Nuliwi," the chief said, nodding and smiling.

"Oh, uh, no, I don't know how to do that," Augum said, making an exaggerated shake of his head. "But some warlocks can cook their food arcanely, yes." He was thinking of Erika Scarson in particular.

Ettan explained to the chief, the translation far longer than what Augum had said.

Leera soon returned with Leland and the other fish. Bridget followed along with Mr. Goss, who helped a coughing Mrs. Stone. She jabbed at the ground with her staff, each step a trial. The bustle of the camp slowed as the Henawa watched the procession.

"Now really, Mrs. Stone, I hardly think you are in any shape to be outside," but she only waved Mr. Goss off impatiently. "She insists on some fresh air," he said to them, as they sat on a log near the unlit fire.

"Leera told me everything," Bridget whispered, joining him, along with Leera. "Didn't know it was possible."

"Neither did I," Augum replied.

"They look friendlier now."

He glanced around. It was true, the faces no longer showed open hostility, but curiosity, even amusement.

The chief strutted around the fire pit, long beard bobbing, as the throng slowly gathered near, some holding freshly caught fish, others deer or rabbit. He made a small speech in his tongue before gesturing grandly to the trio. Heads swiveled their way and watched.

Augum blinked. "Uh, what are we supposed to do now?"

Ettan pointed at the timber. "Make fire."

"But I told you we don't know how."

Ettan shrugged.

Murmurs began as the Henawa started to get restless.

Suddenly the timber erupted in flames. The crowd gasped, retreating a few steps. Augum turned to see Mrs. Stone lifting her staff away from the fire, eyes closed, breath labored.

The chief nodded and chatted with Rogan, the two agreeing on something, while the crowd talked animatedly. Rogan finally sauntered over, his muscular chest still bare as if the cold didn't affect him.

The crowd quieted.

"We not see this magic before. We see cup magic."

Augum's brows rose. "Cup magic?"

Rogan picked up a couple stones and made a show of swapping them around.

"Oh, you mean *cuppers*," referring to the gambling game he had seen some of the older men play back in Willowbrook. "That's more of a game really. What we do is called arcanery."

Rogan puckered his lips. "Arganeri." He turned to the group and pointed at the fire and at the fish. "Arganeri!"

"Argreenerie," the crowd mumbled uncertainly.

VALOR

Augum shared a smile with the girls. "Close enough," before returning his gaze to Rogan. He had a serious question to ask. "How will you honor our agreement to trade for a healer—or shaman or whatever—when all our stuff is gone?"

Rogan frowned while the crowd muttered. He spoke with the chief. It degenerated into an argument, with the chief pointing at Mrs. Stone and then pointing at the woods. Rogan finally spat on the ground and turned to face Augum.

"You teach son arganeri then you teach chief. We find shaman. Make old woman not sick."

"But I thought the shaman was here with you—"

Rogan gave him a blank look.

Ettan pointed north. "Shaman far away. Long ride."

The trio exchanged glances, asking the same silent questions—what if the boy didn't have the aptitude to learn Telekinesis, and how would they get around the language barrier?

Augum glanced Mrs. Stone's way. She sat with bowed head, clutching her staff as if her life depended on it—and in a way, it indeed did. She'd be able to discern in a heartbeat if the boy could learn arcanery.

Augum looked to Bridget and Leera. They gave reluctant nods. "All right, deal," he said, wondering how in Sithesia they were going to teach a Henawa boy Telekinesis.

Rogan gave a nod. "Good."

Chikota then showed Mr. Goss how to cut a fish properly and cook it over a thin cedar plank. One of the women even offered dried rosemary. Soon the scent overcame Augum's worries and his mouth began to water. By the time the first fish was ready, he thought his stomach would jump out of him and eat the fish itself—yet he let the first one go to Bridget, who slowly fed morsels to Mrs. Stone.

Chikota then showed them the same procedure with the other fish. Midway through cooking, the door to the house opened and out spilled Mrs. Penderson, Buck and Wyza.

Everyone turned to stare.

"We wants more food, you savages!" Mrs. Penderson called. "You don't have no right to stay here on my land without no payment. You don't have no right! You is going to feed my children or you is going to go!"

"Ma, please ..." Wyza said.

"Hush up, child, Ma is talkin'." She dragged Buck and Wyza all the way to the fire. She faced Rogan the Conqueror, eyes wild. "You hear me, you filthy savage? You pay or you go. We have a thing called rent in civilized society."

"Mrs. Penderson," Mr. Goss broke in, "perhaps now would not be the time—"

"Didn't I tell you to shut that gob, you spectacled freak? If my husband were here, he'd send you all to hell. You know he's part of them Legion now, don't you?" She turned to Rogan, who observed her curiously. "My husband's a Burner!" She gesticulated at the assembled crowd. "Burner!"

"Burner," some of them mumbled.

She fixed her gaze on Augum, her brows knitting together like crossed swords. "This be all your fault! You best get them savages out of here right quick—"

"Or what?" Augum asked, feeling his face grow hot. "What are you going to do to me that you haven't done already?"

Mrs. Penderson took a step back, gaping. Her knuckles whitened as she held onto Buck and Wyza.

"Ma, you is hurtin' me," Wyza said, squirming.

"Want me to smack him for you, Ma?" Buck asked.

Augum flexed his jaw. "Please try. Give me an excuse." He was tired of people trying to take advantage of him or his friends.

Buck glared but didn't move.

"You done have some nerve, boy. Should've beaten it out of you, I should've." Mrs. Penderson glanced around at the Henawa. Every single one of them watched her. Her gaze fell back on Augum. "You'll regret this, you wretch," and charged back to the house, dragging her son and daughter like piglets.

Rogan shook his head. "She demon eyes."

Bridget squeezed Augum's shoulder, whispering, "I'm sorry you had to grow up around that."

Leera suddenly yanked the trout from the fire. "Shoot, the fish burnt …"

MRS. PENDERSON

After a most delicious breakfast, the trio began the training. They started by practicing fundamental arcanery, as a focused warlock should on a daily basis. Mrs. Stone lay on the log while Mr. Goss sat beside her, watching. Leland stood with the trio, imitating their actions as described by Bridget.

"Think they'll give us our stuff back if this works?" Leera asked under her breath while they dimmed and brightened the Shine spell before a throng of Henawa, who *ooh*ed and *aah*ed with each wave of her hand.

"Don't know," Bridget replied. "Hope so. We need those spell books back."

Augum extinguished his palm. "Let's move on to Telekinesis."

They practiced raising and lowering burning sticks from the fire, much to the entertainment of the crowd. To push themselves, they pooled their efforts and arcanely lifted one of the bench logs. One of the youths jumped on it and it collapsed, eliciting a round of laughter.

Next, Leera asked to borrow something from the chief. Ettan translated and the chief departed to his tent, returning with an abalone-inlaid wooden bowl.

"Uh, you sure about this, Lee?" Augum asked.

"Trust me."

The chief handed the precious object over. Leera promptly smashed it against a rock. The crowd gasped and hissed. A few even drew weapons.

Leera calmly raised a hand. "Watch." She bent over the broken bowl and concentrated while splaying out her palms. The crowd howled as the pieces reformed. Some pointed skyward, some downward. Yet after the shock of it passed, many began bringing them things to repair, as well as things to break and put back together again. Children brought wooden toys; men pipes, blades and buckles; women bottles, paddles and ornaments. The trio did it all—it was good practice.

"I don't think we should do anymore," Bridget finally said. "Think of how they'd react to some of our other spells."

Augum imagined the Henawa hurling spears or axes at them just to see the Shield spell work, or even reflexively shooting them with an arrow after Slam.

"Agreed," he said, making an exaggerated panting sound while pointing at his hurting head. "We have to rest, Chief, sorry."

The chief frowned.

"Now you teach," Ettan said, stepping before the trio just as they took a seat. "Teach magic fish."

The trio glanced at each other before laboriously taking turns explaining how to perform the Telekinesis spell. Ettan and the chief merely stared. Needless to say, after many hours of trying, neither the chief nor Ettan managed to move a rock. The rest of the villagers—at least the ones that weren't hunting or working—attempted Telekinesis as well. Occasionally one of them would summon up the courage to point at a rock. When it didn't move, they'd study their finger quizzically.

Augum wasn't surprised it wasn't working—not everyone had the capacity to perform arcanery. Regardless, it was far harder than it appeared and required extensive and focused practice. He recalled his own bumbling attempts under Mrs. Stone's patient eye. He had failed countless times before getting anywhere, and he was learning from a legendary mentor.

"We're terrible teachers," Leera said, glancing longingly at Mrs. Stone.

Augum would have laughed at the absurdity of the situation if it wasn't so serious. Nana needed a healer. They had to come through somehow. "We *are* terrible teachers," he mumbled as the chief picked up a stone and angrily hurled it at the barn. It thunked off the roof near the rooster, which crowed in alarm.

Bridget curled loose strands of cinnamon hair around her ear. "Could certainly use Mrs. Stone's help."

That gave him an idea. "Sir, uh, Rogan—" Augum said, catching the attention of the big snow-skinned warrior. "Sir, I don't know if we're exactly capable of teaching you, but I know someone who is." His gaze fell upon Mrs. Stone.

"She dying. No good."

"She taught us though. She's—"

"—she's a legend," Leera cut in, making a grand gesture. "The best and most powerful warlock that ever lived. She can teach you how to fly even."

Bridget gave her a questioning look that she ignored.

"If you make her well, she'll teach you," she continued, nodding and elbowing Augum.

"Yeah, uh, she's the best," he added. "But you have to make her not sick now, not later."

Rogan studied them for a time. Ettan imitated his father, giving them the same appraising look. At last, Rogan turned to the chief and explained the situation. The chief looked

VALOR

annoyed and the pair spoke harshly for a bit. Chikota and Hushu joined in on the fray. Soon the entire tribe was arguing.

"What's going on?" Augum asked Ettan.

"Chief agree."

"What? But there's a lot of arguing going on."

Ettan only shrugged.

Rogan finally whistled and barked some commands. The camp turned into a hive of activity. Youths began preparing horses while men strapped on mismatching armor and weapons.

"Now what's going on?"

"They help old maniye woman."

"I don't understand."

Ettan shrugged.

Soon most of the men and some of the older youth galloped northward, sending up eagle-like war cries and kicking up plumes of snow.

"Hope nothing bad happens," Bridget said, holding Leland's hand.

They waited by the fire, occasionally helping feed it, while the snow-haired women tended to their children, mostly ignoring the maniye. Ettan actually showed Leland how to make a fire by rubbing two sticks together over wood shavings. He didn't say much, guiding Leland's hands to show him the movements. Mr. Goss watched with misty eyes.

Meanwhile, Augum, Bridget and Leera spent a lot of time trying to haggle for their spell books, something difficult to do when they had nothing to barter with. They failed miserably, though Bridget did succeed in showing one of the youths how to operate the spyglass.

"What was the point of that?" Leera asked, watching the youth trip over a log while staring through the spyglass.

"Guess I thought he'd like to see something he'd never seen before."

"Ugh. Now he'll never give it back."

They looked on as the youth explained this most miraculous of inventions to his cohorts. Soon the whole lot of them were on top of the barn, sweeping the horizon.

"Make sure to tell them not to look at the sun," Mr. Goss said to Ettan.

Ettan shouted at the youths. A moment later one of them tumbled off the roof with a shriek, sending up a cloud of snow.

Bridget wagged her finger. "That wasn't very nice, Ettan."

Ettan couldn't stop giggling, along with Leera. Augum had to avert his face lest Bridget see him cracking up too.

The day moved along almost entirely around the ever-fed fire. A wide curtain of cloud trawled overhead, bringing with it fat flakes of snow. They continued trying to teach Ettan and the chief arcanery, but nothing seemed to sink in. The chief eventually grew so frustrated he kicked the fire, nearly setting himself ablaze. As Henawa women and youths laughed, he cursed at them and limped off to his tent.

Supper consisted of deer, quail egg, skookum grass, durden root, and fish, which of course had to be retrieved arcanely, an occasion that demanded the entire tribe's attention, just in case their eyes had fooled them the first time.

"Hey, when did we last check on the orb?" Augum whispered after throwing a deer bone into the fire. He had traded a fish for its weight in venison. It was a worthwhile and tasty exchange.

"Oh, I completely forgot about that," Leera said, digging in her robe.

"Wait, not here," Bridget whispered. "Let's finish eating then go round back."

As a murky sunset graced the horizon and everyone relaxed around the fire, talking in low voices and nursing their full stomachs, the trio, one by one, disappeared behind the house.

"I think we're clear," Leera said, peeking around the corner.

"Wait, let me just check the window here." Augum peeked in through the gray shutters. The interior of the kitchen was quiet and dark. "All right."

Leera raised a finger to her lips and dug out the engraved pearl, their only possession besides the clothes on their backs. She closed her eyes and concentrated. "Nothing," she reported eventually.

"Here, let me see."

Leera handed the pearl over to Bridget.

"They must be mid-journey or something. What do you think?" She passed it on to Augum, who closed his eyes and saw darkness, but heard muted sounds. By the rhythms, he guessed the orb was in a horse's pack.

"What's that there magic you got goin' on?" asked a voice from the shutters.

The trio jumped. The pearl skipped out of Augum's hand and dropped to the snow.

"Mind your business, Buck," Augum said, trying to discretely figure out where the pearl had gone.

The shutter opened wide. "My pappy would still be here if it weren't for you, you hell-worshipping gutterborn."

"How so? I haven't been here in years."

"You done bring a curse on us. Now that you a witch, now we know it was your fault they took him."

"I'm a warlock, not a witch."

"You is a witch."

"And you're a gnat," Leera said.

Bridget rolled her eyes. "Leera, don't antagonize."

Wyza's head soon popped out the shutter. "What them witches be up to, Buck?"

"They is up to no good. They know it and I knows it. I see them looks of guilt leagues away." He turned to his sister. "Remember how we used to chase him up the tree and throw crab apples at him?"

Wyza cackled. "Yeah, he done right pooped himself, didn't he?"

Augum used Telekinesis to slam the shutter closed. "Oops, sorry about that!"

Leera laughed.

Bridget shook her head. "Really, you two, that was unnecessary."

"Couldn't help it," he said.

"Neither could I," Leera added. "Oh, come on, Bridge, it was funny—he did it without a gesture too. It was good training."

"Watch out!" Bridget pushed Augum out of the way just in time as a frying pan smacked the side of the house.

"HOW DARE YOU TOUCH MY CHILDREN—" Mrs. Penderson screamed, picking up the frying pan and aiming for Augum's head. He instinctively raised his arm and the pan bounced off a shield made of hard lightning. The shield disappeared as fast as it had zipped into existence.

"Mrs. Penderson, stop—!" Bridget shouted, but the pan smacked her on the forehead. She keeled over, clutching her face.

The shutters opened and out spilled the Penderson brats, grasping at Leera and Augum. Next thing they knew, Mr. Goss had whipped around the corner of the house.

"Now Mrs. Penderson, this is no way to—" he stopped to duck the frying pan. "Be reasonable, Mrs. Penderson—"

Wyza wrestled with Leera while Buck tussled with Augum. The boy was stronger but not as dexterous. Augum managed to get behind him and put him in a chokehold, before something hard clanged against his head.

He blacked out instantly.

MISSING ARTIFACT

"Never in all my years have I seen such a display," Mr. Goss was saying quietly, applying a damp cloth to Augum's head.

"Ugh, what happened?" Augum asked, trying to sit up, head throbbing.

"Just lay still. You took a hard knock."

He lay back down, staring at the ceiling. "Where's Leera and Bridge?"

"We're right here," Leera answered, tending to Bridget's forehead beside the bed.

Bridget only moaned.

He bolted upright. "The pearl—"

Leera's face went ashen. "Wait, you don't have it—?"

"No, don't you—?"

The girls exchanged a horrified look.

Mr. Goss' brows rose. "I do not understand—"

"We've got to go, Mr. Goss—" Leera said, scampering out the door, Bridget and Augum in hot pursuit. They bolted around the corner of the house, ignoring the looks on the faces of the Henawa, and ran to the scene of the altercation, where they immediately began digging through the snow.

"I don't understand it, I saw it fall right around here," Augum said, pawing like a frenzied dog.

"This is so bad, this is so bad—" Leera kept saying.

They dug up every foot of that area, shoveling the snow aside, freezing themselves to the bone in the process.

Augum, knees soaked, suddenly stopped, out of breath. "Buck must have it ..."

The girls stared at him gravely.

"Well we just have to get it back, that's all," Leera said.

Bridget got up, forehead still bleeding. "Let's go find them."

The trio marched back around the house, eyeing the camp. Sitting at the fire were Buck, Wyza and Mrs. Penderson, minding a plank of salmon.

Augum marched up to them. "Where is it?"

Buck's face scrunched as if something foul was in the air. "Where's what?"

"You know what I'm talking about. You took it."

Mrs. Penderson stood up to her full height, jabbing a finger into Augum's face. "You *dare* come accusing us of thievin' after what you done to my children?" Her voice was an angry hiss, a viper about to strike.

He had to resist the urge to back away from her reach. "We need it back. It's extremely important we get it—"

"—I don't give a cow's hoof what you want, you degenerate. It only serves you right to lose something of yours. *You* be the reason for all this here misery. Now I suggest you go on and leave us be right now lest there be a scene. And I don't care if all these savages witness it, for woe be the ire of a mother wronged." She glared at the trio.

"Come on, Aug," Bridget said quietly. "This is pointless."

"You're darn right it is, you little hussy. Now scoot!"

Bridget reddened but yanked on Augum and Leera's sleeve. "How rude," she muttered when they had walked a distance away.

"We're not sleeping in the same room with her," Leera said. "I might wake up with my hands around her throat."

Bridget dabbed a cloth to her forehead. "I think we have more important things to worry about."

Leera grimaced. "So what do we do now?"

They stood pondering a moment.

"I got it—Unconceal." Augum didn't know why he hadn't thought of the spell earlier.

"Might work," Bridget said. "We'll have to be careful, do it in such a way so it doesn't raise too much suspicion."

Augum rubbed his aching head. "Let's just hope that when we do find it, it won't already be too late." The Legion could be on their way right now. He pushed the thought aside, trying to assure himself that whoever had it probably had no idea what it was or how to use it.

The trio split up, Bridget to the fire, Leera out back.

Augum took the house. He splayed out his hand and tried to calm his thundering heart. "Un vun deo." He focused on that very subtle emanation in the arcane ether, a force pulling him in the direction of something purposefully hidden. But after a solid hour of looking, having drained his arcane energies, he came up with nothing other than a small carved horse hidden by one of the brats who knew when. Bridget and Leera came up empty-handed, trouncing into the house, hair askew, eyes puffy.

They moved to the pantry and spoke in whispers.

"I don't understand why it didn't work," Leera said, searching her robes for the umpteenth time.

Augum unconsciously did the same even though he had pawed through his pockets more times than was good for his sanity. "Me neither …"

Bridget, who had been staring at her shoes, suddenly looked up. "I know why it didn't work … it must have been hidden arcanely!"

He groaned. She had to be right. Only the 11th degree spell, Reveal, could find arcanely hidden objects.

"Wait, that makes no sense," he blurted. "No one here knows arcanery."

They exchanged looks. The mystery had deepened.

Leera crinkled her nose. "What if they hid it somewhere further?"

"Then it could be anywhere," he replied. "The fences—"

"—the river," Bridget threw in.

"The barn ..." Leera said with a sigh. "Ugh, we're in trouble."

Bridget peeked out the door, making sure no one was listening in. "We need to tell Mrs. Stone."

"What good would that do?" he asked. "It'd only make her worry and she's already very weak."

"Does Mrs. Stone even worry about anything?" Leera asked.

He gave her a look.

"Sorry," she mumbled.

"Let's just find the pearl," Augum said. "I'll walk the fences, see if I can find tracks or something."

"I'll take the river," Bridget said.

Leera gave an assertive nod. "Guess I got the barn. Good luck everyone."

They split up for a second round of searching. The sun had set by then, though snow continued to fall. Lazy snowflakes swirled in a gentle breeze, dimming the already hazy light of dusk. The children had gone to bed but the youths stuck around, watching from a distance. Augum's search at the old wooden fence was fruitless. Bridget and Leera's efforts also turned up nothing. Tired, cold and out of ideas, the trio decided to head in.

"Should we tell Mr. Goss at least?" Augum asked as they strolled over the well-worn ground near the fire, kept alight by a woman and man team who would routinely journey to the barn, stripping it of its planks one by one like carrion birds feasting on a carcass.

"Might as well," Bridget said. "He'll find out eventually anyway."

Mr. Goss was in the servant's room with Mrs. Stone and Leland rather than in the bedroom with the Pendersons. The trio exchanged relieved looks.

The room was dark and cold, the air stale. Three cots lined the walls. Mrs. Stone occupied one, staff at her side. Mr. Goss fed her fish soup, one spoonful at a time. Leland sat in the corner, back against the wall, humming a gurgling melody to himself.

Augum checked the Pendersons were nowhere near before clearing his throat. "Um, Mr. Goss, we have something to—"

"—I am afraid she is not doing so well," Mr. Goss said, putting aside the soup.

"What do you mean?"

Mr. Goss shook his head. "I wish I knew."

"Mrs. Stone's lips are moving!" Bridget said. "I think she's trying to say something." She placed her ear close to Mrs. Stone's mouth. "She's saying, 'Arcane Fever'."

Mr. Goss frowned. "I am afraid that is unfamiliar to me."

The trio exchanged worried looks. It was evident now, more than ever, they needed an arcane healer.

Mr. Goss adjusted his spectacles. "What were you saying, Augum?"

"Oh, uh ... nothing." He couldn't bring himself to compound the problem. "Excuse me." He left the room and pondered what to do in the corridor.

"Found it yet?" Buck asked in a sneering voice. He was leaning against the far wall, arms crossed.

Augum walked over. "Where is it? You don't understand, we need it back."

Buck glared down at him. "Oh, I'm too dumb to understand, that it? Well I don't even know what you be talkin' about, and I don't rightly care either. I hope you never find it, and I hope you get in all sorts of trouble for losing it."

Augum wanted to say something spiteful, but it'd only make things worse. Wyza schlepped out of the bedroom, wiping her nose with the sleeve of her muddy dress. She stopped upon spying Augum. "Ma, that gutterborn hell child is here again causin' trouble!"

The old instincts took over. "I wasn't causin'—" he began, but Mrs. Penderson was already in the hall, glaring. "You is lucky Mr. Penderson ain't here to give you the whippin' you deserve, boy." She brought Wyza close to her chest with one hand and waved him off with the other. "I reckon I prefer any beast to come a visitin' at Endyear other than you. Go on now, scoot! Don't you be talking to my children no more. They ain't got nothing to say to you anyhow."

The scars on Augum's back tingled as he bit his tongue and turned away, only to spot Leera standing in the hallway with a hard look on her face. He gave her a gentle tug on the elbow.

"Come on …"

She let herself be guided back to the servant room.

"I used to sleep here when they'd let me," he said, sliding to the floor against the far wall, absently picking at his fingers. "Wasn't allowed to use the cots though."

"You slept on the floor even though there were empty cots in the room?" Leera asked.

He nodded. It was hard talking about his past. Really hard, actually. But part of him was also tired of holding it in for so long, of carrying that weight around all his life. Maybe it was time he let go of some of it.

He avoided their gaze as he continued. "He used to whip me in this room. Actually, in every room. And the barn … the field. Come to think of it, she had a go at me almost just as much."

Leera squeezed his hand. "That Penderson witch? That's ... ugh, I'm going back out there—"

"No—" Bridget said. "Don't even think about starting more trouble."

Leera exhaled deeply before sitting down beside him, resting her head on his shoulder. "You don't usually talk about yourself, Aug. I'm sorry you went through all that. You know we're here for you."

"Let me see now, what was it Mr. Penderson used to say?" He switched to his best twang. " 'Keep your dog close so you don't have to go far to kick him'."

Bridget got up off the cot and sat on his other side, drawing her knees close and placing her chin on them. "You turned out very well though. Better than most people I knew with privileged upbringings."

He didn't know how to reply to that.

Mr. Goss looked over and gave a pained smile. "You are lucky to have each other. I am proud of you all."

Augum forced a smile, unable to meet Mr. Goss' eyes. What would he say when he found out Augum had lost the control pearl to the mythic Orb of Orion?

Ettan trounced into the room. "Can Leland play?"

"I am afraid it is a bit late, my dear boy," Mr. Goss replied. Leland moaned angrily.

"It is past your bedtime, son."

Ettan gave a pouty look. He dug into his pocket and retrieved a candle, holding it out to Mr. Goss.

"Is this for us? Why thank you, that is very kind of you."

Ettan left without another word.

Leera snorted. "We don't even have our flint and steel to light it with."

"That is quite all right. I can light it at the fire." Mr. Goss stood up, dusting off his worn tunic. "What a nice gesture," he said to himself as he left.

Leland sat down beside Mrs. Stone, groping for her wrinkled hand. He took it in his own and moaned quietly.

Then he began slowly rocking back and forth while humming *A Boy and his Cat*, a familiar children's melody.

The trio sat there letting the fragile song wash over them, Leera's head on Augum's shoulder, Bridget's on her knees. Augum, meanwhile, ruminated on their growing list of problems.

Mr. Goss soon returned cupping the lit candle. He placed it on the floor and put Leland to bed, the trio readying as well. Augum and Mr. Goss slept on the floor, Bridget and Leland on one cot, Leera the other.

Augum watched his breath fog in the cold air, wondering how he was going to go to sleep with all these turbulent thoughts running through his head.

"Good night, everyone," Mr. Goss whispered, blowing out the candle.

Yet as tired as Augum was, he simply couldn't sleep. The others all stirred too, probably from the bitter cold. Mrs. Stone's breath rasped even above the wind that whistled through the shutters.

He listened, unable to quiet his tortured conscience. Where was the pearl? Was Buck talking to the Legion in that moment, huddled in one of the trio's blankets? Were they going to wake up to an entire company of black-armored soldiers waiting outside? The thought was almost enough to make him sneak out and investigate.

As the night cooled more, his shivers worsened. He curled up in a tight ball. It barely helped.

"Aug, you awake?" Leera whispered, teeth chattering.

"Yeah ..."

"I can't sleep, too cold."

"Me neither."

"We need to find blankets."

He was more than ready. "Let's go."

The pair of snuck out of the room.

"Shyneo," he said, keeping his hand lit at a very dim level.

VALOR

They opened the door that led outside, the hinges shrieking ghoulishly.

Augum winced, listening for the Pendersons while freezing wind and snow blasted his face.

"We're all right," Leera whispered. "Go."

He could barely see past a few paces. They had to be extremely careful—it'd be all too easy to get lost in this, Shine or no Shine.

The gusts slammed into them the moment they stepped away from the shelter of the house. Both drew their hoods, but he had to keep his lit hand bare.

"I think a blizzard's coming!" he shouted over the wind. It meant the cold would get worse, much worse. It was imperative they find blankets.

Leera grabbed him by the arm. "This way!"

She led past the abandoned fire that had long blown out. A tent loomed ahead and she scrambled to find the entrance.

"Hello! Anyone in there?" she called. After a few more tries, a woman's milky face stuck out from a small door flap in the bottom.

"Please, we need blankets, can you help us?" Leera asked.

The women took one look at Augum's lit hand, scowled, and disappeared back inside.

"Let's try another one!" he said, moving on to the next tent. He was rapidly losing feeling in his hands and feet.

A tanning rack materialized in the driving snow. Leera immediately started yanking the flapping animal skins. He helped, hoping the Henawa wouldn't scalp them for thievery. They managed to snag five heavy furs and began dragging them back to the house.

Suddenly his palm extinguished, plunging them into suffocating darkness. "Shyneo!" but he couldn't feel his hand. "It won't light, you try!"

"Shyneo!" Her palm fluttered to life.

61

The pair dragged the furs, battling increasing winds. Augum hoped they were headed in the right direction. A plank, probably from the barn, almost speared Leera as it whistled past.

The pair exchanged a brief look before continuing. At last, they hit upon the wall of the house, right beside the shutters to the room the Pendersons slept in.

"This way—!" Leera dragged her shoulder along the wall.

The wind suddenly switched direction and their hoods blew off their heads. He felt his face and ears numb immediately. One of the furs caught the wind like a sail and was torn from his grasp, flying off into the night.

"Lost one!" he shouted, hoping his limp grip could last the final few paces.

"What!"

"Nothing, just go!"

They got to the door, the wind shrieking fiercely now. Leera turned the handle and pushed, but it wouldn't budge.

"What in the—" she reared back and plowed into it, but it held firm. She gave him a look that quickened his breath.

"Let me help!" He slid in beside her and the pair slammed against the door together. It still didn't budge.

"Telekinesis," he said, taking a step back. He felt weak, but they had to try.

They raised their arms. He didn't know if it was even working, his hand was that numb. The door pushed back a sliver before slamming shut. They fell against the door, panting.

"Buck, is that you behind there?" he yelled. "Let us in or we'll die out here!"

There was no response.

"If you're holding this door then damn you to hell!" Leera screamed, smacking the wood before shrinking against it, sobbing.

VALOR

He noticed her grip on the furs loosen and jumped on top of them.

"We have to go around!" he yelled just as her hand extinguished.

"I'm so cold," he heard her say, "I'm so cold …"

He threw an arm around her. She was shivering violently.

"Can't feel … my hands …"

"I know, Lee, I know." He repositioned himself, wrapping her in one of the furs, himself in another, feeling stupid for not having thought of it earlier. They were very heavy and thick, acting as great windscreens. "Shyneo," he said, but his hand did not light.

He hunkered down before her, further blocking the wind. They had four hides between them, and had to get them back to the others. His own teeth were chattering so much he could barely talk. He felt a light pressure, but he couldn't tell if she had a hold on him.

"You got me?"

"Don't know …"

He risked letting go of the fur in his other hand to check. She was holding him but he couldn't feel it at all.

Good enough.

He scrambled for the loose fur. As soon as he thought he had a grip on it, he began leading the way around the house, fighting the wind, hugging the wall, concentrating on his grip on Leera.

The pair struggled for some time, turning the corner before finally hearing the violent vibrations of a pair of shutters about to rip loose. He held the fur between his knees and used his free hand to bang on them. He did this repeatedly, but no one came. He screamed, but his voice was barely a whisper above the roaring blizzard. His eyes stung and he was too frozen to replace the hood back over his head.

"Why … won't … they … come …"

"Pantry …" Leera gasped.

He cursed himself and got a grip on the fur again. There was still another corner to go. The pair continued to hug the wall, moving at a snail's pace, the wind constantly battling them. When they turned the corner, they hit a whirlpool of air, threatening to suck them out into the black void.

He drew Leera close. She stopped shivering, and went limp in his arms. He pried the fur from her claw-like grip. "I got you," he said, picking her up and carrying her, the effort quickly sapping his remaining reserves of energy.

Soon he heard another vibrating set of shutters. He held on to Leera as best he could as he banged on them, hand feeling like a lead brick.

Please oh please let them hear him. This was their last hope. The cold had seeped into his bones and he was sleepy, so very sleepy. He reached up to bang again but instead felt a tug. Someone was yelling. He looked up but couldn't see a thing. Then he felt himself being pulled upward.

"No! Take her first, take her!" he shouted.

The grip loosened and he fell. One of the shutters was open and slamming itself against the side of the house. It sounded like a giant's hammer eager to smash his head in. He groaned as he used the last of his strength to heave Leera upward, feeling her body slip by, pulled over the ledge.

Someone yelled, but he couldn't hear what they were saying above the roar. The fur draped over his back threatened to blow away at any moment. He didn't have the strength to save it.

Someone jumped down beside him, snatching him in a great bear hug. He felt himself rise. A hand grabbed his neck, then his arm. He tumbled over the ledge, fur and all, coming to a stop on one of the cots. A moment later, he felt the weight of another fur, then another. Someone closed the shutters and the roar subsided.

"Shyneo," Bridget said, her voice shaking. The room lit up in a green glow amidst a flurry of activity. Mr. Goss was using one of the furs they had toiled over to wrap Bridget and Leland, Leera between them.

"Mr. Goss, your spectacles—" Bridget said.

"The blizzard has them now."

"Is … Leera … all … right …?" Augum asked through chattering teeth.

"I got her," Bridget said, "I got her …"

Leland moaned fearfully.

"It will be fine, son," Mr. Goss said, looking peculiar without his spectacles, like a painting without a frame. He took one of the furs and covered Mrs. Stone in it. "Everything is fine now," and wrapped himself in the remaining fur. "That was a very brave thing you two did, a very brave thing."

FAMILY REUNION

Augum woke stiff and sore, but warm. He peeled back the hide to see ribbons of pale sun paint the far wall. Dust lazily revolved within the rays like tiny flecks of gold, catching the light now and then.

Bridget sat quietly beside a red-eyed Leera, the latter tightly wrapped in hide. Mr. Goss and Leland were absent while Mrs. Stone snoozed away under a blanket of fur.

"Morning, Sleepyhead," Bridget whispered, smiling.

He sat up. "How is she?"

"She's fantastic," Leera croaked, "and can talk." A strand of raven hair fell across her freckled face. Bridget brushed it aside for her.

"Thanks, Mum."

Bridget only gave her a hug and a kiss on the head. "You two are hero—"

"—don't say it," he interrupted, rubbing his eyes. "Just ... don't." The last thing he cared about was the whole hero thing right now. "Where's Mr. Goss?"

"He's gone to boil water over the fire for more soup. Leland's playing with Ettan. You should see it out there, it's unbelievable. You can barely get around."

"We have to find it," he whispered, glancing over at Mrs. Stone to make sure she was still sleeping. Her breathing was even and slow. "We have to find the pearl. It's the only means we have of keeping tabs on the Legion."

Bridget's smile faded. "I know."

"Someone held that door last night," Leera mumbled.

"Maybe it locked itself behind us."

Bridget gave him a grave look. "There is no lock on it, I checked."

He recalled using Telekinesis to open it a crack, before it quickly shut again in their dire moment on need. Someone had to have been holding it, but who?

"I'll help Mr. Goss," he said, pushing aside the fur, hoping the river wasn't frozen over.

Bridget stood. "I'm coming with you."

"What about Leera?"

Leera scowled. "Ugh, I'm not a baby. Go already. I'll be up soon anyway."

Augum and Bridget exited into the hall, exchanging a look when passing the closed door of the Penderson bedroom. When he opened the front door, (there indeed was no lock on it), he stopped—the snow was chest high!

"Warned you," Bridget said, seeing the look on his face.

Henawa children and youths played in it, their milk-white skins sometimes making it appear like clothes were flying about on their own. A rough path snaked to the fire pit, the flames coughing a column of gray smoke into a clear blue sky.

"Certainly something, isn't it?" Bridget said as they approached the fire, tended to by a youthful woman who avoided their eyes. The bear-skinned chief squatted before it holding a skewered squirrel on the end of a stick. He slowly turned it above the flames, watching it sizzle.

"Chunchuha!" he said without looking up.

Augum gave a friendly wave. "Chunchuha."

They sat on the log to the chief's left, breath steaming. The man then started talking to them in his tongue.

Bridget shook her head and spread her palms. "I'm sorry but we don't understand."

The chief groaned. "Ettan. Ettan—!" The boy soon appeared holding Leland's hand. The pair had round snow splat marks all over. The chief started saying something to him. Ettan only nodded now and then. When the chief finished, Ettan turned to Augum and Bridget.

"Chief say crazy woman say you steal furs."

Bridget's brows crossed in indignation. "But we had to take them, we—"

The chief held up a hand, saying something to Ettan.

"Chief say he understand. Chief say you keep furs. Chief say you teach him more magic in trade. Better magic. Not boring."

The chief drew an invisible bow and let loose an invisible arrow, making a grand gesture of it.

"That is kind of you," Bridget replied, "but we do not yet know any offensive spells like that.

The chief grinned, appearing not to understand.

Bridget gave a resigned sigh but smiled.

The chief nodded and waved them off. Ettan snagged Leland's hand and shot away, while Augum and Bridget walked to the river.

"At least we'll be warm now at night," he said.

Bridget blew a lock of hair from her eyes. "Wish I could understand their language." She stopped to glance back at the tents. "I could see myself living like this."

"What, as a nomad?"

"As part of a community. I'd be a mother presiding over a gaggle of children, with a dashing hunter of a husband and a flock of dogs and chickens in tow."

"You'd be a fussy mother."

Bridget smiled. "Probably."

Augum gave her a playful elbow. "Nag them kids to death."

"Oh hush, you."

"And the husband," he mumbled.

She elbowed him back. "Double hush!"

After snickering, he added, "I'd come visit you."

"You'd better. But where would you live?"

He watched Henawa children run about in the snow. He hadn't thought of what kind of future he wanted at all. He'd been so caught up with just … surviving.

"Don't think anyone's ever asked me that. Always thought I was going to become a knight. I suppose I'd live in a small village, but one filled to the brim with friends."

"And what would you do for a living?"

"Warlock, for sure. Is adventurer-on-the-side a profession? I don't know. You?"

"Also warlock. I think I'd be a mentor."

"A teacher? At an academy?"

"Maybe I'd open my own. One for farm boys—"

"—like me?"

She smiled. "Like you. Common folk need to be educated about arcanery."

"Tell me about it."

Her face darkened. "Maybe I'd rebuild Sparrow's Perch. School and all. Then, after living a long life full of joy and laughter, I can be put to rest beside my parents."

Hearing her say that made his heart constrict. "Sounds like a good life."

She wiped her eyes. "Sorry."

He smiled warmly. "Don't be," and the two of them embraced.

"One day this will all end," he said, thoughts drifting to his father and the man's dark ambitions.

"Hope so," she said into his robe. "Hope so …"

"Hello, Chief!" Mr. Goss said, walking from the river, holding a slopping wooden bucket.

"It's us, Mr. Goss," Augum said, gently letting go of Bridget. He was still trying to adjust to seeing Mr. Goss without his spectacles.

"Ah, good morning, Augum and Leera. Feeling better?"

"That's Bridget."

"Oh my, of course it is." He reached up to adjust his spectacles but ended up poking his nose. "What a beautiful day, is it not? And look at all this snow! Brings the child right out of me, it does."

"I'm really sorry about your spectacles," Augum said.

"No need to be silly, I am incredibly grateful for your efforts, Augum, really. We would certainly not have made it to the morning without those hides."

"I'll go look for them."

"Please do not bother. I felt the wind take them. You would not find them in this snow if you had a year to search. Not to worry, I shall commission a new pair as soon as we get to a city. Now excuse me, I have some Henawa soup to make!"

"Can we help?"

"I am not a child, my dears." He strode past them, making to ruffle Augum's hair but accidentally hitting him in the face instead. He didn't even notice, whistling as he walked off.

"How well do you think he can see?" Bridget asked.

Augum watched as Mr. Goss repeatedly stumbled on the path. The pair of them exchanged a look before continuing to walk.

They arrived at the river only to discover it completely frozen over. A Henawa woman had just finished collecting water from a round hole in the ice. She gave them a wide berth as she strode past.

"You haven't fished with us yet," Augum said. "Want to give it a try?"

"Definitely."

He taught her how he did it and the pair took turns until they captured four fish, by which time Leera had joined them.

"I missed the action, I see." Her hair was askew, nose and ears red.

"No frostbite?" Bridget asked.

"Got lucky this time. If it weren't for those furs—"

"—if it weren't for those furs we'd all be dead," Bridget said. "You two are heroes. What, it's true, Aug."

It was Augum's turn to roll his eyes for a change. "We were just talking about what kind of lives we'd be living after all this is over, Lee. What would you—"

"—I'd be a famous warlock," Leera immediately said, using her hand to paint the sky with her story. "Known in every kingdom of Sithesia."

Bridget chortled, hand over her mouth. "You mean *infamous*. And where would you live? What would you do?"

"I'd live in a magnificent castle. I'd be an ... adventurer, yeah! That's a profession, right? Anyway, the castle would be a fixer-upper, there'd be a gazillion cats, and a dashing—" her eyes locked with Augum's for the briefest moment. His heart skipped a beat. Suddenly he envisioned himself adventuring with her, repairing Castle Arinthian together ... but he promptly looked away, confused by the hammering in his chest, the butterflies in his stomach. He had no idea how to react or what to do. Besides, anything like that was a lifetime away. He wasn't even a man yet, and there was still so much to learn, and so much to face—

"—prince or something," she finished, a note of disappointment in her voice. "But not the kind that you'd want to smear with manure."

"And I'd come visit you in your castle," Bridget said, giving Augum a particularly pointed look, "just to see familiar face—"

"We should go and make breakfast," he blurted, hurriedly grabbing the fish by the tails. "Let's get these on the fire then figure out a way to find the pearl."

"Right, cause there's always stuff to do," Bridget muttered, still watching Augum.

The girls sighed and followed along.

"What if Mrs. Penderson secretly *is* a warlock?" Leera asked as they made their way back to the fire. "And she's hiding the pearl arcanely and that's why we can't find it—"

He shook his head. "Impossible." There was no doubt in his mind that he would have known if she was a warlock, that she would have used her powers against him or to benefit her family at some point in the past.

He wondered how his mother felt showing up on the Penderson's doorstep with a baby in hand, canceling the Penderson debt to the Titan clan in exchange for his safe harbor. Had she judged his fate with that horrible family a better one than a life with his father? Had she even had a choice?

He frowned. "I wonder what debt the Pendersons owed my mother's family."

Leera chuckled. "Maybe money for cases of Titan wine?"

Augum recalled Mr. Penderson's chronic strong breath. "Well, he was a foul drunk ... Doesn't matter anyway. I wish she hadn't left me here, but it happened. Let's eat."

The trio joined Mr. Goss at the fire. They cooked the fish, talking about the blizzard, but avoiding the topic of the door and the pearl. Mr. Goss stared blankly around, evidently not able to distinguish much beyond blurred shapes, for when Leland came near he mistook him for one of the Henawa children. When the boy pawed at his father's face and discovered the absence of his spectacles, he surrendered a slow moan.

"Not to worry, Leland, not to worry." Mr. Goss fed him some soup before taking him by the hand. "Come, my boy, let us see to poor Mrs. Stone."

VALOR

"It's to your right there, Mr. Goss," Bridget said when he started down the path that led to the barn.

"Ah, indeed." He switched direction, one hand holding Leland, the other pawing the air before him.

The trio silently looked on.

Bridget sighed. "I fear for their safety."

Augum refrained from saying he feared for all their safety. After last night, he worried about the Pendersons the most right now—they were unpredictable. Even when he was young, he learned to sense their volatile moods, making himself as invisible as possible and spending as little time in their company as he could get away with. Yet it had hardly helped. The more time he spent here, in fact, the more those memories surfaced, memories he had long forced into some dark recess of his mind.

The door to the house opened and out strode Buck, adjusting his ragged ponytail. "What are you looking at?" he said on his way to the river.

Augum's eyes narrowed while Leera made a gagging sound.

Mrs. Penderson, Wyza in hand, exited the house soon after. The trio turned away.

"She's our age and she still holds her mother's hand," Leera whispered.

Bridget put a finger to her lips. "Shh!"

"If any of you disgusting vermin were any good you'd work that there mill," Mrs. Penderson said as she strolled by. Wyza stuck out her tongue as they walked to the river to join Buck.

"She reminds me of someone," Augum said, tapping his forehead. "Can't possibly think of who."

Leera chortled. "Erika was crazier."

"And being a warlock, more dangerous too," Bridget added.

He smiled to himself.

73

Leera pushed her deboned fish onto a plank. "What's so funny?"

"Nothing, just ... this, all of this, it's ... funny."

The trio looked at each other, at the fire, and at these strange snow-skinned people. Augum noticed the rooster perched on the roof of the barn, only steps from a Henawa youth glued to the eyepiece of their spyglass. As if on cue, the rooster crowed, as if it did not approve of the interloper in its presence.

Augum was the first to start laughing, quickly followed by the girls. It was the kind of unrepentant laugh from deep within, healing wounds, bringing light to darkness. When he at last recovered, he found the chief standing nearby, staring at them.

"Maniye nuliwi," the big bear-skinned man said, shaking his head and waddling off. "Maniye nuliwi ..."

Neither the nasty comments nor the dirty looks from the Pendersons as they made their way back from the river had much effect on the smiling trio. Their breakfast was slow and sumptuous, one they shared with Mr. Goss, Leland and Mrs. Stone. For that brief time, they forgot about her condition, about the lost spell books they needed to advance their degree, about the missing pearl, about Mr. Goss' lost spectacles, about the ancient castle they had to find, and about everyone that had died. For the span of a meal, they simply enjoyed each other's company, and eating fish they'd caught with their own hands.

Suddenly a distant cry pierced the stillness, immediately answered by more within the camp.

The trio shot to their feet.

"Rogan ..." Augum said.

Sure enough, a column of riders plowed through the chest-high snow, their milky faces proud and stern. The camp gathered—the women sent up shrill cries; the children shouted and hooted; the Pendersons spilled out of the house.

The riders circled, raising axes, swords and spears into the air, shouting triumphant cries. Rogan and his warriors were covered in blood. His face was a mask of ferocity and victory. He nodded at everyone who looked his way, raising his arm and squawking a sharp "HO!"

The final three horsemen that made it into camp dragged three bloody figures on a rope. One of them wore a tattered black robe, the other two the shining black armor of the Legion.

"Oh no," Bridget said, unconsciously squeezing Augum's elbow with both hands. "No, no, no …"

"The entire army is going to come down on us," Augum said.

"Please, sir, did they have a commander?" Leera shouted to him.

Augum immediately understood what she was getting at. The Legion commanders possessed orbs of seeing, allowing them to communicate with each other and the Lord of the Legion. If this column had a commander, he was sure to pass news of the attack on.

Rogan was too busy to reply. He swam through the adulating crowd with the ease of a fish in water. He kicked the captured men over one by one, until their bloody faces were visible.

Wyza suddenly cried out as if pierced by an arrow. She sprinted over to one of the men, sobbing the whole way, squeezing past Rogan the Conqueror.

"Father—!"

SUALA CHI

Augum, heart pounding like a Henawa drum, instantly recognized that bloody face, a face he forever associated with the stench of strong wine, a face permanently twisted with maniacal hatred.

In no time at all Mrs. Penderson was sheltering her husband's limp form, wailing and shouting, "He's dying! You done killed him! You done murdered my good husband!" Buck came rushing over, face aflame. The three Pendersons covered the man as if afraid of further attack.

Rogan the Conqueror watched with mild interest before yanking the robed one to his feet. He was an older man, maybe around sixty years of age. His back was bent, face lined with wrinkles and splattered with blood. A tuft of silver hair stuck to his wispy scalp. He wore black studded leather armor underneath a simple black robe emblazoned with the burning sword of the Legion. A woven rope snaked firmly around his chest, digging into the leather.

"Burners," muttered some in the crowd. "Burners!" The Henawa spat at the three figures. The Pendersons swatted at the ones that ventured too close.

VALOR

Meanwhile, Rogan dragged the warlock over. "Shaman." He cut the rope, handing it to Augum.

Augum looked up at the old man stupidly, not knowing what to say.

"What've you savages done!" Wyza cried next to her mother. "What've you done!" Her shoulders heaved with sobs. "Pappa's hurt ... Pappa's hurt real bad."

Rogan smacked the warlock as if he was nothing more than livestock for trade. "Trade. He make old woman well. You teach magic."

"Are you a healer, sir?" Augum finally managed to ask.

The man only nodded. His eyes told Augum they had seen far too much. They were full of pain and ... remorse.

"What's your name, sir?" Leera asked.

"Sam Ordrid, young lady," the old man gurgled, coughing blood. He wiped his mouth with his sleeve.

"I ... I was forced into the Legion ... I never—"

"It's all right," Augum said, handing over the end of the rope to the old man. Mr. Ordrid stared at the frayed end dazedly.

Some of the nearby Henawa started talking in low voices. Augum ignored them. He looked over at the Pendersons. Wyza was wild with fear. Buck and his mother swatted and spat at the Henawa like rabid wolves. And Mr. Penderson stared straight at Augum.

He recalled a particular moment back in Willowbrook when he had come home to Sir Westwood, clothes torn from a fight with Dap, swearing to the old knight that he hated that boy and everyone in that stupid village.

"Hate is like stones in your heart," Sir Westwood had replied. "They only slow you down and clutter your spirit. When the opportunity comes, leave them behind, for the road of life is long and hard enough already."

Maybe this was an opportunity for him to leave a stone behind.

"Please help us with my great-grandmother, Mr. Ordrid. But before you do so ..." He nodded at Mr. Penderson. "Can you heal that man first?"

Leera grabbed his arm. "Aug, you sure—?"

Bridget placed a gentle hand on Leera's shoulder, her eyes on Augum. There was a hint of a smile on her lips. "He is."

Leera hesitated but eventually let go.

Suddenly Rogan the Conqueror yanked the third man, a hapless young soldier, to his feet. He started chanting to the crowd in Henawa, the crowd throwing up shouts of either anger or victory when he paused for breath.

"Ettan, what's he saying?" Bridget asked, snagging the boy as he shouted along with the crowd.

"He say, 'This for Burner slaughter. For loved ones' spirits. For glory of Henawa'."

She blanched and looked to Mr. Ordrid.

"An entire company hit the Henawa further north. It was, it was—"

"—a slaughter," Augum said quietly.

Rogan suddenly threw the young soldier into the crowd. They hoisted him over their shoulders like a coffin. His limbs flailed as they carried him to the fire.

"Stop it!" Bridget called, glancing around feverishly. "Stop it—! Somebody do something!"

Augum wanted to shout for them to stop, to tell them it wouldn't bring back their loved ones, but all his mind saw was the fires that consumed Willowbrook and Sparrow's Perch, and the fire that consumed Mya.

Leera, who stood right beside him, seemed mesmerized. Was she seeing her family's feet dangling midair? The sky orange from the flames?

"I can't watch this horror," Bridget said, hand over her mouth. She ran back to the house, sobbing.

"Look away, young ones," Mr. Ordrid said. "Please, for the love of the Unnameables, look away now. Only I deserve to watch what is about to happen."

Augum and Leera turned away, the pair breathing in unison. Time slowed to a crawl. He was barely conscious of his hand finding hers and squeezing.

They watched as shadows played on the snow, shadows of hands rising in jubilation and revenge. They felt the heat on their backs and heard the celebratory cries, the lone scream, and the agonized weeping of the Pendersons.

When the celebration reached its peak, Augum retched. Leera was right beside him, heaving onto the snow. He had never been that sick, never. It took almost all the fight out of him, as if he'd been kicked in the stomach.

The tumult died down and Rogan made a new speech. The moment he finished, there was movement and the Pendersons began shrieking hysterically. The crowd roared as Rogan the Conqueror stabbed at the air with a curved blade while yanking Mr. Penderson to his feet, while his family struggled in the arms of Henawa warriors.

Mr. Penderson somehow found Augum in the crowd. His eyes lit up with that familiar malignant hatred. For a moment, Augum thought he smelled rank wine.

Stones in your heart, Augum. Stones in your heart ...

He knew what he had to do. He summoned every ounce of courage and strength and made a fierce whipping gesture, a gesture infused with old frustration, tired suffering, and faint hope.

"GRAU!"

The sound of crashing thunder tore the air, startling men and horses, children and women alike. It was the loudest thing he had ever heard, shaking the earth, forcing almost everyone to duck and cover their ears.

There was a ringing silence as Augum scrambled to his feet, trying to hold his stomach in check. "NO!" he shouted in the clearest voice he could, marching up to Rogan the

Conqueror, placing himself between the warrior and Mr. Penderson. "It won't bring them back! It won't bring your loved ones back!"

Rogan stared down at Augum as if he was a fly to be smushed. "Child know nothing of suffering."

There was no hesitation. Augum practically tore the robe from his upper torso along with his linen undershirt, revealing a naked back ridged with scars. He slowly turned in a circle for all to see. "But I do, I do know!"

Stones were dropping by the moment. He could feel himself growing lighter.

He pointed at Mr. Penderson. "This man did this to me. This man here! And I do not wish him dead." There had been enough death, enough sorrow, enough stones. "The Burners razed two villages before my eyes." He envisioned a woman running through a field, child in her arms. "They murdered my mother ..." Sir Westwood, straw dangling from his mouth. "My old mentor ... and ... and my friends." A tear, Mya in saltwater form, trickled down his cheek. "Revenge won't bring them back ..."

Rogan had been translating in a calm voice. When he finished, the crowd stared in total silence.

"Suala Chi," someone finally said.

"Suala Chi," repeated another. Soon everyone in the crowd was saying "Suala Chi," and nodding, before dispersing.

"Suala Chi," Rogan the Conqueror echoed quietly.

Augum dressed. "Suala Chi ...?"

"It is your name. It means *Brave Soul*," and handed him the rope tied to Mr. Penderson.

VORTEX

"I don't know what just happened," Leera said when Augum returned to her side, "but I don't think I'll ever see something like that again." She looked at him as if seeing him for the first time. "Why do you have to be so damn brave?"

Before he could reply, she drew him into a tight embrace, her hand gently stroking his back. "I ... I didn't know," she mumbled. "I'm so sorry."

"It's all right. Those stones are gone now." His spirit had never felt so ... light.

She let go. "Stones?"

He smiled. "Never mind." The pair looked on as Mr. Ordrid healed Mr. Penderson, his family huddled around.

Augum glanced skyward. Lumpy gray clouds filled the sky. A light wind had sprung up.

"I feel older," Leera blurted.

He snorted a laugh. "Me too ..."

The two friends exchanged smiles.

He scrunched his face in concentration and reached for her raven hair. "Come to think of it, is that gray hair—"

She swatted his hand away, flashing a scandalized look. "That's *frost*, Augum Stone."

He gave her a wry grin and shrugged. "I know."

Bridget finally came out of the house, face red. "What happened? Why are you two smiling?"

"I can't even ... I'll explain later." Leera nodded at the healer attending to Mr. Penderson. "But look."

Mr. Penderson's family brought him to his feet and a round of hugs ensued. Mr. Ordrid left them to it and returned to Augum. "Son, if you ever raise an army, you let me know. I would be proud to take up your banner."

"I'm only fourteen—"

"For now, but history is riddled with stories of boys like you. Boys that grew to become fine men. Fine men who became great leaders. Great leaders who became legends."

Leera punched him on the shoulder. "Look at that, a legend in the making. Besides, you're almost fifteen, and I'd follow you too." There was a softness in her eyes that made his ears burn. She stabbed at his chest with a finger. "Just don't let it go to your head."

"Now where is this great-grandmother I am to help?"

"Right. This way, Mr. Ordrid, this way." Augum led them into the house.

"What's going on?" Bridget sputtered, standing with a befuddled look on her face. "How did ..." before hurrying to catch up.

"Sir," Leera began as they walked, "why didn't you just teleport away when they captured you?"

"The Henawa are masters at surprise. My arcane energies were spent trying to save the fallen. Truth be known, part of me felt I deserved to be captured and hauled away like nothing more than a log. I have seen too much, and I did nothing to stop it. They would be right to burn me in the fire."

"Then you'd be no help to anyone. At least you can save lives still, make up for it." Augum said it casually, but the man stopped. His lip quivered as if he wanted to speak but could not.

Augum gestured to the servant room. "In here, sir."

Mr. Ordrid nodded, patted Augum on the shoulder, and entered.

Mr. Goss hurriedly stood.

"It's all right, Mr. Goss," Leera said. "He's here to help."

Mr. Ordrid made his way over to Mrs. Stone's side and gasped. "It cannot be, it simply cannot be ..." He kneeled by the bed. "This is ... no, but my eyes deceive me ... this is Anna Atticus Stone."

"Yes," Augum replied.

"Headmistress ..."

The trio exchanged looks.

Mr. Ordrid put a hand to his wispy scalp. "But that means ..." he glanced Augum's way. "That means you're *his* son."

Augum nodded slowly.

"You're the one they're looking for." Mr. Ordrid glanced at them all anew. "All of you. Mighty Unnameables, you are in great danger—" He stood up, eyes frantic. "You must leave here at once. The commander has already informed the rest of the company. The Henawa only came across a small detachment. They have no idea what kind of force they are up against."

Bridget paled. "The speaking orbs ..."

"Precisely."

"Then we must move quickly," Augum said, gaze falling onto Mrs. Stone. "Please, can you help her? She said something about 'arcane fever'."

"Yes, I know about arcane fever—it happens when one seriously overdraws one's arcane talents. It means she pushed herself to the very edge of arcane knowledge. Warlocks die from going over that cliff, but some feel out the edge, walk that line and come back. The fever of seeing the abyss is ..." He swallowed. "No, she is Anna Atticus Stone, she *must* survive."

Everyone glanced at Mrs. Stone, ancient lined face pale, breath slow and labored.

"She fought my father," Augum said. "That's what made her sick."

"The Battle at Hangman's Rock," Mr. Ordrid said quietly. "I have heard." He turned to them. "She is the greatest warlock alive. A living legend. I will do everything in my power to save her. I just hope it is enough. Now let us get to work, we have very little time. The process of curing arcane fever requires a mix of traditional and arcane healing. This is what I'm going to need from you ..."

He proceeded to give the trio a very specific set of instructions: they needed to gather stinkroot, oxy, fish oil, a flake of iron, a flake of silver, a flake of gold, a flake of steel, three candles, and a mortar and pestle. They were to do it as soon as possible because the Legion was probably on its way that very moment.

The trio split up the task—Bridget would gather the three candles, iron, flint and steel; Leera the fish oil and flakes of silver and gold; Augum the stinkroot, oxy, and mortar and pestle.

They raced off in different directions, each warning anyone who'd listen that the Legion was coming and that they had to pack up the camp and go.

At first, Rogan the Conqueror and the chief thought Augum had lost his mind, but after confronting Mr. Ordrid, they became convinced, and began shouting orders immediately, compounding the difficulty of the ingredient gathering.

The day had turned gloomy and windy. The Henawa youth with the spyglass scampered back onto the barn roof, ready to shout a warning should the Legion appear on the horizon. The women and men set to striking down the tents, a task that looked well rehearsed. Horses were readied and packed; waterskins filled to the brim; planks torn off the barn and strapped to steeds. Even young children had a hand in the process, gathering clothes and packing rucksacks.

Augum ran from tent to tent, begging for ingredients in a language none of the Henawa understood. They were far too busy packing to pay him heed anyway.

"Suala Chi!" Rogan called while Augum flew by. "Come." The warrior shoved the trio's old rucksack at him.

Augum could only gape stupidly.

Rogan gestured at the barn. "You take back horses," and strode off, shouting commands.

"Thank you," Augum muttered, barely able to believe it. Everything was there! Everything except their spyglass, which the Henawa needed; and blankets, which the Pendersons stole, but he didn't care. He quickly tracked down Bridget and Leera.

"Look, we have something to barter with!" he said. "Oh, and we have the horses too!"

"There's the flint and steel we need," Bridget said, taking them out. "Now I just need something to barter for the candles."

"Here, take the hourglass, I don't think we need it that bad."

Bridget took it from him and raced off.

"And I'll trade the saddles if I have to," Leera said, running to the barn.

Augum pawed through the rucksack. They couldn't afford to trade anything that was left, except maybe the sheepskin map. He thought about it—they could always use the stars, or at least Mrs. Stone could. This was all or nothing, after all. Besides, it had to be worth a lot. He yanked it out, heaved the rucksack onto his shoulders, and shot off, finding Ettan helping a gang of kids his age stuff supplies into sacks.

"Ettan—I need your help," Augum said, skidding to a halt before him, huffing. "I need to trade this map for stinkroot, oxy, and a mortar and pestle."

Ettan stared at him, bone white face as blank as morning snow.

Augum repeated himself, even making the stirring motions for the mortar and pestle. "Please, Ettan, you have to help!"

The boy casually glanced down at the map, before turning to one of the other boys. They began a somewhat heated exchange before Ettan suddenly walked off.

"Ettan, wait—" Augum had no choice but to follow. He searched the horizon, scanning for the telltale plume of kicked-up snow indicating a galloping army. Nothing yet, but it was only a matter of time.

Ettan yanked at the hide skirt of the husky woman Rogan was seen with. She barked at him, waving him off, but he pointed at the map, calmly explaining in Henawa. She scowled and snatched the map from Augum's hand. She asked Ettan a question while making to rub her behind with it.

"No, no—it's a map," Augum said. "A map." How does one explain a map?

Ettan shook his head and pointed at the horizon, then back at the map.

Augum nodded along. "Uh, right, I need mortar and pestle in trade." He made the stirring motion then squeezed his nose. "And Stinkroot. Oh and—" but she had already disappeared inside the tent, taking his map with her. He anxiously shifted his weight from foot to foot. At least he heard the sound of unpacking.

"She talk to me funny. I no like her," Ettan said, standing as if nothing troubled him in the world.

Augum flashed a sympathetic smile before scanning the horizon for the umpteenth time. The camp was in a tremendous bustle now. The biggest Henawa men ran from tent to tent, striking each one down. This one was the next to go. Why wouldn't this woman hurry!

At last, just as the men surrounded her tent, the woman came out holding two sacks, one of which she dumped to the ground, the other one she pawed through, ignoring the commotion behind her. The woman withdrew a small leather bag, tossing it to Augum. Inside was stinkroot, the familiar lumpy brown root with red welts all over. Never had something that stank so foul looked so good.

Rogan shouted commands, the sinews on his milky muscles bulging as he held a rope attached to the top of the tent. The woman then withdrew another object—a stone mortar and pestle, and Augum thought he was going to jump with joy. She handed it to him and immediately returned to packing while the tent collapsed behind her.

"Thank you," Augum kept saying over and over, but neither she nor Ettan seemed to notice or care. "Now I just need oxy. Do you know where I could find some, Ettan?"

The boy shrugged and walked away.

"All right, well thanks for these anyway!" Augum raced back to the house.

Mr. Ordrid couldn't believe how fast the ingredients were coming in. Bridget had already brought three candles, a rusted iron spoon and the flint and steel, while Leera had managed to trade a horse saddle for flakes of gold and silver, and fish oil.

"It's going to be uncomfortable riding that beast, but I didn't have a choice," she explained.

"Now all we need is oxy," Augum said.

"Try the mill," said a voice from the corridor. It was Wyza Penderson. Buck stood beside her, holding three Dramask blankets.

"Pappy hates you for what you done," Buck said. "Far as I sees it though, I—" he swallowed, unable to finish.

Augum smiled at Buck for the first time in his life. "It's all right. Thanks for these," and retrieved the blankets.

Buck quickly strode off, leaving Wyza standing there.

"I swears to you we never took that there thing you lost," she said. "And I know momma don't have it either." She stared at him a moment. "You should go on with them savages. We won't stop you none." Then she turned on her heel to pursue her brother.

"Well that was strange," Leera muttered.

"You should get the oxy, Aug," Bridget said.

"Right." He left the blankets with Leera before running off through the busy camp and careening into the old mill, practically swimming through the snowdrift at its entrance.

Inside he found remnants of two broken chairs, and empty shelves. Was Wyza playing a trick on him? He turned to the doorway, half expecting the brats to trap him.

No, that was a long time ago ...

He recalled sneaking into this place often with a borrowed book in hand—not that the Pendersons had many, mostly books they had received in trade for crops. They'd later either trade those books in town or use the pages as kindling.

He splayed his palm, concentrating on the arcane ether. He wasn't great at Unconceal, but he'd had some success with it. It was an effort to calm his breathing and shut out all the thoughts zipping through his mind.

"Un vun deo." His hand wavered before him. He soon felt the subtlest pull, following it to a spot in the wall. There he found a loose brick, which he promptly pulled away. Inside the small cavity, he found a series of leather pouches, each labeled with poor writing. The biggest one was labeled "Gold". It had to be the Penderson's secret savings. If he were younger, he would have stolen it instantly in petty revenge. Instead, he pushed it aside, scrambling between the pouches, until at last finding one with the word 'Oxy'.

He pumped his fist, before realizing Wyza must have known about the gold. Did she intend on him having that too? Perhaps as some kind of ... apology or thank you?

VALOR

He raced back to the house, leaving it behind.

"I got it!" he shouted, flying around the corner into the room and handing the oxy over to Mr. Ordrid.

"Everyone please stand in the hallway," Mr. Ordrid said.

They vacated the room. Mr. Ordrid then lit three candles in a triangular pattern on the floor. The trio exchanged looks—they knew all too well that was the sign of the witch.

"This arcanery is old," Mr. Ordrid said while crushing ingredients in the mortar and pestle. "It uses all the arcane elements. Do not be frightened, but feel free to look away. Above all, do not step into the room."

A piercing call like that of a hawk suddenly rose outside.

"We don't have much time," Mr. Ordrid said, never taking his eyes off the mortar and pestle. "They will be here soon." Then he began speaking an unfamiliar language that sounded ancient and difficult to pronounce.

The hustle outside increased—men, women and children ran about as commands were barked.

"They're leaving us—" Leera said.

Augum kept switching his focus between the wide-open front door down the hall and Mr. Ordrid, who began chanting.

The house darkened as if a black cloud had settled directly overhead. The wind increased, whistling through the shutters.

A large horse appeared at the door, rearing up. A snow-skinned boy was lowered to the ground by a muscled arm. He ran to Augum.

"I not like her," Ettan said.

"What?" Augum didn't have a clue what the boy was on about.

Ettan dug into his pocket. "She mean." He held up the engraved pearl.

Augum received it with both hands. "I don't believe it," he mumbled. He closed his eyes and looked through it. There, on the other side, the image curved from the Orb of

Orion, was a face with too much makeup and oversized earrings. He immediately closed his hand over the pearl and shoved it into his pocket.

"What is it?" Bridget asked quietly.

He put a finger to his lips and scrounged in his pockets. "A cloth," he mouthed. "Quickly." Everyone rifled through their pockets. Mr. Goss found one he had used for his spectacles.

Augum wrapped the pearl. "I don't know how much she knows," he said.

"Who?" Leera asked.

"Erika Scarson."

The girls blanched.

"Ettan! Taro!" Rogan the Conqueror called from the door, horse bucking wildly as the sky around the house blackened further.

Ettan glanced back to the door. "Chief say he no want you teach magic. He no like dark cloud. Bad spirits."

"We wish him well," Augum replied. "All of you, we wish you well." Bridget and Leera nodded along.

Ettan ran back to his father, stopping half way. "Bye, Suala Chi."

"Good bye, Ettan."

They watched as Ettan's father scooped him up, then bolted after his tribe, the last of the Henawa to go.

Augum turned back to Mr. Ordrid and Mrs. Stone. It was now so dark he could barely see the mortar resting on her stomach, rising with her rapid breathing. Sweat beaded her wrinkled face.

"Shyneo." His palm lit.

"Shyneo," Bridget and Leera echoed.

Mr. Ordrid's chanting strengthened along with the wind. The house shook. Suddenly, a great purple and black vortex opened up above Mrs. Stone. The space around the maelstrom wobbled and shifted. Within the vortex, a giant scaly hand appeared, pulsing as if its veins were aflame. A second hand soon appeared along with a giant, horned lizard-like head. It reached for Mr. Ordrid, yet at that moment, he bent down to light the contents of the mortar with the flint and steel.

The mortar exploded in a jet of fire and light, shooting up, beating back the demon. The thing screamed and lashed out. A battle waged before their eyes—the demon versus the light. It went back and forth, back and forth, until the light started fading and the demon began winning. It had half of its body out of the vortex, flexing great muscles.

Bridget screamed as Mr. Ordrid slowly turned to the group with a look of pure horror. Behind him, the demon reached for Mrs. Stone.

"Mr. Ordrid—!" Augum called, pointing.

The man snapped back around. When he saw what was happening, he lunged at the demon. There was a furious struggle as Mr. Ordrid lifted off the ground.

Augum saw his chance. He shoved at the air before him, aiming for the demon. "BAKA!"

The beast withstood his blow, but not Bridget and Leera's, who cast the spell immediately after. It dropped Mr. Ordrid and disappeared back into the vortex, which collapsed with a sucking sound.

All was quiet as the house began to lighten. Everyone rushed to Mrs. Stone's side, arriving just in time to see her open her eyes.

"Mercy, what are you all gawking at?" she asked, her withered face turning into her classic scowl.

The trio loosed celebratory cries of victory, and hugged, only to be cut short by a distant trumpet blast.

"They're here," Mr. Ordrid said, pale and out of breath. I'll buy you some time and distract them." He gave a final nod. "Good luck to you all," and ran off before they could reply.

"Mrs. Stone," Leera started in a rapid burst, "there's no time to explain now but that's the Legion. You have to teleport us out—"

For a moment, Mrs. Stone stared at her in confusion. Then she sat up, head swiveling to the wall in the direction of the charging Legion, as if she could see through it. Her chin rose a little. "Hold hands."

Everybody immediately attached themselves to the person next to them. Bridget stuffed the Dramask blankets into the rucksack and slipped it on. Augum considered doing the same with the hides, but they were far too large and there was just not enough time.

Mr. Goss helped Mrs. Stone stand. She glanced over at her staff. It jumped to a standing position, vibrating, then floated between them all, a silent lightning storm flashing within the scion.

"Be ready now," she said. The group tensed. She inhaled, pausing to look at Augum—and winked.

MILHAM

Augum, tumbling end over end while being pulled in all directions by what felt like a team of horses, had forgotten just how nauseating teleportation could be.

An implosive crunch signified their arrival as the group spilled onto the snowy ground like so many beans cascading from a jar.

Augum's recovery was slow. His stomach refused to allow him to stand. The others weren't doing much better, coughing and gasping. Mrs. Stone was the only one on her feet examining the area, panting frozen breaths, clutching her sleek staff.

They were in a small sunlit glade of towering pines, spruces and firs, the waist-high snow untouched. A creek trickled nearby, the only sound to be heard other than the occasional tweet of a bird. Clouds trawled in the distant east, overlooking the hazy tips of a string of enormous snowy mountains. The air was crisp and cold, their breath freezing before them.

"Where are we, Nana?"

"East Ravenwood."

"So we're near Castle Arinthian?"

"The castle is many leagues westward. This is the closest I have come to the Muranians. Hence we find ourselves here."

That's right, a warlock could only teleport to places he or she had visited.

"We will need supplies for the journey ahead," Mrs. Stone continued. "There is a village nearby. I deemed it best to walk in, lest it be occupied by the Legion."

Bridget dug out the three Dramask blankets, distributing them to Leland, Augum and Leera.

"Keep it for yourself," Augum said.

Bridget nodded and draped herself with it.

"Nana—the boy, Ettan, he had the pearl for a while there, and ... and Erika Scarson was on the other side. He talked to her."

"Did she see your face? Or hear you?"

"I don't know."

"Then we must assume she did. We must further assume they can deduce the general direction of our travels." She pursed her lips. "Please use greater caution when handling the pearl in the future."

"Yes, Nana." He subconsciously felt his pocket, wondering if Erika Scarson was listening in right then, and if she could hear them through Mr. Goss' cloth. He reached in and closed his hand over it, just in case. "Um, it is good to see you well, Nana."

"And I am glad to be well again. Arcane fever, sometimes referred to as *overdraw*, is a terrible sickness. It had only happened to me once before, after I fought Narsus. This time was worse, however. I am indebted to the healer and his arts."

"Where did the vortex go?"

"The arcane spell that you witnessed is called Abbagarro, and it predates the Founding. As to the vortex, one can only guess where it leads. Some say it is a portal to hell."

VALOR

The trio exchanged looks before walking the trail Mrs. Stone plowed for them. She strode erect, pawing lightly at the ground with her staff, braided ponytail bouncing. Mr. Goss was close behind, particularly careful of his steps, Leland in his arms. The trio took up the rear.

Leera took the time to quietly explain to Bridget what had happened back in the village. When she got to the part about Augum's back and how scarred it was, he felt his chest tighten. When she fawned on about how brave he was, he found himself trailing further and further behind, until he couldn't hear them. At the end of the story, the girls stopped to wait for him.

Bridget had a hand on her chest. "Why didn't you tell us?"

He shrugged, unable to meet her gaze. What was he supposed to do, show them off as if they were battle scars? A vicious drunk had whipped him.

"I should have stayed outside," Bridget said. "I'm sorry. I should have been there to support you."

Augum managed to crack a smile. "What would you have done, cheered me on?"

Bridget gave him a *don't be silly* look. Then she smiled. "I'm proud of you," and drew him into a hug.

"Thanks," he said, before they caught up to the others.

"What brought you this far east, Mrs. Stone?" Mr. Goss asked as they began following a near-frozen stream snaking through a wooded valley.

"I have travelled much further east than this, Albert, well past the Muranians, although I daresay teleporting to those places would hardly help us find Occulus' castle. Nonetheless, I once travelled here with my old companions in search of Castle Arinthian. The villagers were kind enough to point us in the right direction. Milham is a mining town that brings a diverse kind of folk. You can say its isolation has a certain appeal."

The stream eventually crossed a path. "Yes, this way," Mrs. Stone said under her breath. She stepped onto the trail, its pristine surface marred by recent footprints. Soon they came upon a snow-covered sign. She raised her hand and the snow arcanely slipped off, revealing the words *Village of Milham*. In the distance, they could hear the sound of children playing.

The path led past a log cabin with a steeply pitched roof, and behind it stood a small village surrounding a well. Some adults looked on and clapped as children with various skin tones threw snowballs at a wooden charger. An Endyear game, Augum realized.

A man dressed in heavy furs chopped wood beside the log cabin. He looked up, revealing an ebony face, short curly black hair, and a long beard, both flecked with gray. His eyes were shiny and bloodshot, as if they had seen too much sun.

The man's great black brows crossed as he gave them an appraising look. After a moment of contemplation, he raised an arm. "Happy Endyear. No harm?" He spoke with a slight foreign accent.

"No harm," Mrs. Stone replied, "and happy Endyear. We come seeking shelter, supplies, and the comforts of a warm fire. Does the Miner's Mule still stand?"

The man rested his hands on the top of his axe. "It does, my dear lady, though Huan has been fighting an uphill battle keeping the place upright."

"Would Huan be the innkeeper?"

"He would." The man looked past Mrs. Stone to the trio. "Would some in your party, including yourself, be warlocks?"

"They would."

"Then take heed—a Legion herald came through here recently with proclamations. He said all warlocks had to report to Eastspear—"

"—for the war effort, yes," Mrs. Stone said. "I am sure he also said that scrolls and spell books were banned."

"That he did—"

"—and would I be correct in assuming there was also a proclamation all able-bodied men were to present themselves at the nearest Legion office, in this case, also Eastspear?"

The man studied Mrs. Stone a moment. "You are indeed correct."

"Then I shall expect no complaint." She resumed the trek into the village.

"That is not all the herald proclaimed—"

Mrs. Stone stopped.

"They search for a group consisting of an old woman and three children, one of whom would be the son of the Lord of the Legion himself." The man's shiny eyes fell upon Augum.

"Perhaps it would be wise for our stay to be a short one then."

"Perhaps that would be wise indeed." The man buried his axe in a log. "Let us make a bargain. Some here mistrust arcanery, but that some does not include me. Healers are very hard to come by in this day, if not impossible. My son broke his arm in the mine. The bone has not set right. He cannot work. If you can heal it, I promise you safety in my own home, away from prying eyes."

Mrs. Stone stared at the man a moment as if contemplating his character.

"It would mean a great deal to me, and a great deal more to my son."

Mrs. Stone at last surrendered a nod. "Let us call it a bargain then."

The ebony-skinned man smiled and reached out a hand. Mrs. Stone took it. He pulled her hand to his lips and bowed slightly. "It is an honor, my lady. Kwabe Okeke at your service. My home is this way."

He took his axe and led them through the forest to another log cabin set between the trees. It also had a high snow-covered pitched roof. Saws, iron-strapped barrels and rope were stored against the log walls. Soft gray smoke rose from a stone chimney, dissipating into the towering evergreens, where the Muranians loomed in hazy outline.

"Please come in," Mr. Okeke said, opening the plank door.

The group filed in, immediately hit by the aroma of smoked meat. The place was roomy and warm, decorated with strange colorful furs, the mounted heads of unfamiliar animals, and ebony carvings of what looked like malformed figures in agony. The windows had real leaded glass, as well as outer shutters pushed open to let in the light. Two doors led to other rooms, in between which sat a great hearth. A fat Endyear candle decorated with holly sat on a ledge above.

Mr. Okeke eyed their torn and charred robes. He gestured at a thick trestle table made of yellow pine. "You must be weary from your travels. Please, have a seat."

"Thank you," Mrs. Stone said. "But first allow me to present Albert Goss and his son, Leland Goss—"

Mr. Okeke nodded while Mr. Goss said, "Greetings."

"And this is Bridget Burns and Leera Jones—"

The girls curtsied politely.

"It is a pleasure, young ladies," Mr. Okeke said.

"And this is my great-grandson, Augum Stone."

"Augum Stone. Most unfortunate for you, young one, to be the son of the man that murders many."

Augum tilted his head respectfully but said nothing.

"And I am Anna Atticus Stone."

"Yes of course. I am honored to share my home with you." Mr. Okeke gestured for them to sit at the table before taking off his heavy fur coat, revealing loose trousers and a belted chestnut smock covered in soot and oil. His arms and neck bulged with veins yet he was remarkably thin.

VALOR

"And when will we have the pleasure of your son's company, Mr. Okeke?" Mrs. Stone asked, taking a seat.

"I sent him to purchase potatoes. He should arrive soon, that is if some dramatic catastrophe does not befall him along the way."

"I am certain he will be quite all right in his own village—"

"The boy is over two barrels tall yet believes the tiniest cut will lead to his death. When he broke his arm, he made it sound like the world was ending along with his life." Mr. Okeke sighed. "I fear I have been too protective of the boy since ..." His eyes fell upon the ebony carvings.

"Those are most interesting," Mrs. Stone said.

"They are nightmare carvings. We Sierrans carve them when a bad dream clings to our nights. It is supposed to make them stop." He picked one up, slowly revolving it in his hands. "My dream is always the same," he said to himself. "You have been to Sierra before?"

"I have indeed."

He returned the figure. "Few in the north travel so far south. I myself came here with my wife when my son was but a boy."

"And what brought you, Mr. Okeke?" Mr. Goss asked.

"A search for a new life." The man glanced up at an expertly painted portrait of a comely ebony-skinned woman with bushy hair. "Alas, my beloved died years ago to a northern sickness. A most painful disease."

"I am so sorry to hear that," Mr. Goss replied quietly. "It seems suffering is a mark of these times. My own wife was murdered by the Legion, as were the friends, mothers and fathers of the girls here. My son still bears the scars."

Mr. Okeke glanced at Leland, who moaned quietly, before sweeping them with his gaze. "Troubled times indeed. They search for you now. They search for the boy and the scion."

Mrs. Stone rested the staff against the wall. "They do."

"They say if the Lord of the Legion attains all of these artifacts, he will bestow eternal life to his followers."

"A lie told by a liar. His heart is as twisted as …" Her gaze fell upon the carvings.

Mr. Okeke nodded and paced to the kitchen area, where he began preparing strips of salted meat, bread and butter. As his veined hands tore the bread, Augum's stomach rumbled, Leera licked her lips,, while Bridget stared hypnotized.

"And what brings you to Milham, Mrs. Stone?" Mr. Okeke asked, sprinkling spices onto the meat.

"We are in search of a castle lost to history."

"I am afraid I know very little of castles around these parts. My son probably knows more than I, for he has an arcane yearning which, all things considering, I simply cannot support."

"Has your son studied at an academy?" Leera asked.

"He very much wants to attend the one in Blackhaven, but he does not seem to understand it is under the control of the Legion. His only option there would be to become a necromancer. This, of course, I forbid him. Besides, I fear the moment he sets eyes on a real necromancer—"

The door opened and in walked a very tall and gangly ebony-skinned boy of about the trio's age, wearing a fur coat much too small for his size.

"Ah, this is my son, Jengo."

The boy froze upon seeing the group at the table, .

"Jengo—"

"Father, it's *them*!" His eyes darted about. "They'll execute us for sure—"

Mr. Okeke took a deep breath. "No such thing will happen. They are here by my invitation. Please welcome them as guests."

Jengo dumped the basket to the ground. A couple potatoes fell out and rolled under a chair. He was much taller than anyone Augum had ever seen. His face was oval

VALOR

with a large scar on his chin and he seemed to favor his right arm. Like his father, he possessed short, curly black hair.

"That's the Lord of the Legion's son right there. They'll burn the place down with us inside—"

"Enough, Jengo!"

There was a marked silence. "Hello, uh, I'm Jengo. I mean, obviously, yeah. But, uh, Happy Endyear ... I guess."

"Happy Endyear," the group replied.

Mr. Okeke wiped his hands. "This is Mr. Goss and his son, Leland. Over here we have Bridget, Leera and Augum. And this is Anna Atticus Stone—"

Jengo inhaled sharply. "Impossible, Anna Stone died—"

"—battling Narsus the necromancer," Mrs. Stone finished. "Let me assure you, young man, this is not a walking corpse you see before you."

Jengo gaped.

"Manners, Jengo. Please boil the potatoes for our guests—and mind you recover the ones under the chair."

"Yes, Father," Jengo replied in persecuted tones. He withdrew a cloth from his pocket, reached under the chair and gripped the potatoes with it, holding them as if diseased. He then retrieved the basket and hurriedly walked to the kitchen, head bowed.

"Your coat, Jengo."

"Oh, right." Jengo rushed to take off his coat and hang it by the door, but in doing so, he snagged it on a chair and tripped, nearly skewering himself on a figurine. He swallowed, mumbling something about death at every turn, while the trio quietly snickered.

Mrs. Stone cleared her throat, silencing them immediately. "May I remind my young companions that I expect them to observe the highest courtesies as Endyear guests."

"Yes, Mrs. Stone," they mumbled. As much as Augum had grown since meeting Mrs. Stone, she still managed to make him feel young and immature.

Jengo's cheeks reddened as he hurried to scrub the potatoes in a washbasin by the fire. When he thought his father wasn't looking, he readied to throw the wrapped potatoes into the hearth.

"Those ones too, Jengo."

"But they fell on the floor—"

"They have skin. You will wash them and then they will be boiled—"

"*All right*, Father, I get it," Jengo said, blushing while giving the trio a furtive look. He carefully unwrapped the two potatoes and threw them in the water. His face twisted in disgust as he resumed scrubbing.

Mrs. Stone leaned toward the trio. "Perhaps the three of you would deign to find the time to help our new young friend?"

Augum, Bridget and Leera scrambled to join Jengo around the washbasin, leaving Leland and the adults at the table. "Your hands don't look clean," he whispered. "If you don't mind, could you just *pretend* you're washing? I mean, don't actually put your hands in the water."

The trio exchanged looks.

"Guess so," Leera finally said. "So, uh, your father speaks formally, like he's—"

"Highborn? He was brought up in the royal court of Sandorra."

"Is that the Sierran capital?" Bridget asked.

"It is. Even though it annoys him, I prefer to speak in a more ... common fashion."

"How did you get that scar?" Augum asked.

Jengo gave his chin a dainty touch. "This grievous injury I sustained in an epic fight in the mines, one that almost brought down the place. It was I against the largest beast of a boy you'll ever see. He said things about my mother I wouldn't repeat to my worst enemy. He doesn't much like people that are different, which is weird because he's very different himself."

"So he's even taller than you?" Leera asked.

Jengo checked to see his father was busy in conversation before throwing a particularly scabbed potato into the fire. "Not taller, but certainly bigger. And meaner. And stupider."

"Augum's mother is from Sierra," Leera replied.

"Oh?"

"Her name is Terra Titan," Augum said.

Jengo stopped what he was doing to stare at Augum. "So your father is the Lord of the Legion, and your mother is a Titan?"

"Yes."

"You don't look Sierran."

"I'm not. Born in the Black Castle."

"Your father is the Lord of the Legion, your mother is a Titan, and you were born in the Black Castle."

Put that way, it sounded ridiculously improbable to Augum too. "Uh huh."

"But he's a farm boy first," Leera said with a smirk.

"Was," Augum corrected. And never will be again.

Jengo tossed another potato into the fire. "I heard the Titans feed their children wine to make them stronger."

"That's ridiculous," Bridget said. "And please stop wasting potatoes."

"But they're ... I'm sorry, I'm being insensitive and crass and tactless again."

Leera's brows rose. "Those are words Bridget would use."

Bridget and Jengo reddened.

"So we hear you want to become a warlock," Leera went on.

"Father told you, huh? You three are apprentices, right? I recognize the robes from a book. What elements?"

"My element is earth, Leera's is water and Augum's is lightning," Bridget said. "What's yours?"

"Oh, uh, I ... I don't actually know." He dropped his voice to a whisper again. "But I know a couple things about arcanery. I ... I even know a *spell*."

"You mean you learned one wild? Which one?"

Jengo checked over his shoulder before shoving the bowl aside—slopping some water onto a bear hide rug—and holding his palm out. His face strained as his hand flickered to life with a white light before fading out.

"That might be healing—" Bridget said.

"Really?"

"For someone with no formal training, it's very impressive. The healing element is three times rarer than the other elements. I think our class only had one healer."

Jengo smiled proudly. "I've been practicing. One day, I'm going to join the academy, but I have to convince my father to let me go first. Maybe you can help me—"

"You don't want to go to the academy right now," Augum said. "Not while the Legion runs it. Trust us on that."

Jengo's face fell. "I thought that's just something Father told me to scare me into not going."

"We had to flee the academy when the Legion came to power," Bridget said. "I'm sorry, but your father was telling the truth."

All the joy faded from his eyes. He dragged the bowl back before him, took up the brush, and resumed scrubbing. "Great, how am I to become a warlock now?"

"Well, we're on our way to learning our 2nd degree," Leera said, "and we're not even attending an academy."

"How is that possible?"

She glanced back at Mrs. Stone, talking in hushed voices with Mr. Okeke and Mr. Goss. "We're lucky to have a good mentor."

"Good? Try legendary." Jengo's eyes lit up again. "Do you think ... you know ..."

"You'd have to ask her," Augum said, "but you just have to make sure your father is all right with it, because I doubt Mrs. Stone will mentor you without his approval."

"Not to mention we're in the midst of travel," Leera added.

Jengo shot to his feet, almost knocking the basin over. "Father! Are you all right with me training with our guests in the arcane way?"

The table fell silent. Mr. Okeke slowly stood up, face grave. "That is a very presumptuous thing to ask, son. I am ashamed of such a question and I apologize to present company."

Mrs. Stone used her staff for support to stand. The trio politely stood as well. "We have precious little time for training, I am afraid."

Jengo's head fell.

"However—"

His chin rose.

"—if Mr. Okeke sincerely desires his son to follow the arcane path and permits us to stay a few extra days—"

Jengo could barely stand still.

"—then I shall endeavor to impart what lessons time permits."

Jengo brought his hands together. "Father, please ..."

Mr. Okeke studied him carefully. "On one condition."

"Anything, Father ..."

"Swear you will not attend the academy until it is free of the Legion."

"I swear."

"Then so be it."

Jengo was so excited he ran to hug his father, dwarfing the man in his clutches. He then bowed deeply before Mrs. Stone. "I am so eternally, blessedly, ever thankfully—"

Mrs. Stone took a patient breath while he rambled on, and paced around the table to stand before the boy. "Your father has informed me your arm was not set correctly.

Unfortunately, it will require re-breaking before I can heal it. Oh, do not look so frightened, child, I shall put you to sleep."

That didn't seem to calm Jengo, who breathed as rapidly as a squirrel. "Is there ... is there a chance of spell failure?"

"I assure you, my dear boy, you will be fine."

"May I offer assistance, Mrs. Stone?" Mr. Okeke asked.

"That would be welcome. Perhaps the use of a room—"

"Yes of course. Please, this way."

Mr. Okeke, Jengo, and Mrs. Stone filed into another room. After some highly dramatized moaning, there was a silence, but Augum and Bridget placed their hands over their ears, neither wanting to hear the bone being broken. Only Leera listened, and her face said she regretted doing so.

They returned not long after, Jengo tenderly rubbing his arm.

"Mrs. Stone, I ... I am so very grateful," he said, bowing deeply. "So eternally, respectfully—"

"That's quite enough, son," Mr. Okeke said, also bowing. "And I, too, am grateful, Mrs. Stone."

Mrs. Stone gave a courteous nod.

Mr. Okeke gestured at the basin. "I am happy for you, my son, but those potatoes will not boil themselves."

THE MINER'S MULE INN

The light steadily darkened as Jengo tended a pot of boiling water and potatoes. He peppered the trio with questions about arcanery, particularly how safe it was. They responded by telling him which spells they knew and which ones they were studying to learn next. He listened with rapt attention, remarking on how dangerous each one sounded.

Mr. Okeke decorated the table with candles and holly. "It is Endyear and we invite our guests to partake in the festivities. Perhaps we can all have a jolly game of Piggy Run after supper."

Jengo fished the potatoes out with a ladle into a large bowl. "Really, Father, that's a game for children."

"Ah, perhaps a game of cards or Cuppers for us old folk then—if Mrs. Stone and Mr. Goss do not object, that is."

"I have never gambled before," Mr. Goss said. "Annie disapproved of the practice." He gave a nervous chortle. "And you will have to bear with my sight. But seeing as it *is* Endyear …"

"I do not consider myself much of a gambler," Mrs. Stone said, frowning. "However, I see no harm in playing a hand or two—for entertainment's sake of course."

"Of course." Mr. Okeke scuttled to a cabinet and withdrew a dark stoppered bottle. "Nodian Heartfire wine. Only Titan wine is stronger *and* tastier."

"Augum's mother is from the Titan clan, Father," Jengo said.

"Is that so?" Mr. Okeke immediately began a lengthy diatribe on the many subtleties of Titan wine, the enormous grape it comes from, and the mystery of its making—all while preparing food. Mrs. Stone's lips thinned as he went on while Mr. Goss nodded politely. Leland finally moaned so loudly that Mr. Okeke stopped himself. By then the table was crowded with buttered and herbed potatoes sprinkled with bacon bits, roasted chicken, steamed peas and peppered leek soup. For dessert, Mr. Okeke served dried cranberries in sugar sauce and waffles covered in caramel. After supper, he served pine tea.

"That was a very fine feast," Mr. Goss said, cheeks colored from the wine. "Thank you kindly, Mr. Okeke."

"Ah, but feasts always taste that much better to those that are hungry. You have undertaken great trials."

Augum, eyelids drooping with the haze of stuffing himself, realized Mr. Goss and Mrs. Stone must have told Mr. Okeke some of the things they had all gone through.

The conversation continued in spirit as Mr. Goss, Mrs. Stone and Mr. Okeke moved to the living area, composed of a lush carpet of black and white striped fur on top of which sat two pine armchairs and a settee decorated with plush red and blue cushions. Everyone else remained at the table, where the trio brought out their blue tome and the burned yellow book on elements.

Jengo picked up the tome. " 'On Arcaneology: A Pupil's Encyclopedia of the Arcane Arts'." He looked up at them, eyes wide. "I've dreamt of such a book, I've dreamt of it, and here it is in my hands!"

Leera snorted. "Did you dream how thick it was too?"

"I'd read every word a thousand times."

Leera quickly gave Augum a *goody-goody* look.

Leland moaned twice.

"Don't worry, we promise to read it aloud for you," Bridget said, giving him a pat on the hand.

"We should check on the orb," Leera said.

Jengo looked up. "The orb? Is it … is it dangerous?"

Bridget patiently explained all about the Orb of Orion and how they were using it to spy on the Legion. "Problem is," she concluded, "it's possible Erika knows we have the pearl. She could hear through the orb by putting her ear to it. She just can't see us—"

"—we can see *her* though," Leera added while Jengo's eyes kept enlarging, "and hear her too."

"And we can also lock the orb in place," Augum threw in. "Anyway, we're supposed to look in on it regularly to see what the Legion are up to. With any luck, they still think someone else has the pearl."

Jengo looked between them, mouth open. "You mean to say they could be listening to us *right now*?"

Augum shrugged. "Maybe, but—"

"So they could be on their way *this very instance*—"

"Not very likely, but—"

Jengo placed his head in his hands. "We're all going to die. So these are the final moments of my life …"

Leera's arched brows sharpened. "Don't you think you're being a touch … oh, I don't know … *melodramatic*?"

"There's no point discussing anything. We should just wait here and accept our fate. It's in the hands of the gods now."

Leera could barely keep a straight face. "What are you talking about? Nothing's happening to us—"

"The whole village is gone already, we just don't know it yet. It's over. I'm sorry it ended this way, but there you have it."

" 'There you have it'? Ugh. Aug, just show him how it works."

Augum placed a finger to his lips before withdrawing a tightly wrapped bundle of cloth from his pocket. He carefully unwrapped it, closing his hand over the pearl immediately, hopefully muting the low voices coming from the living area.

Jengo only wrung his hands throughout.

Augum closed his eyes and concentrated on looking through the Orb of Orion. A dark room materialized before him. Chains hung from the walls and sharp objects glinted in the light of a single candle. The dim light highlighted long blonde hair, eyes half open, arms manacled above her head, and a stained linen dress.

"Haylee—" he said without meaning to.

Her face shot up, twisted with fear. Quick footsteps echoed and in strode Erika Scarson, leering at the Orb.

"Well Happy Endyear to me," she sang. "This could only be one of my favorite three kiddos. How glad I am you retrieved the pearl from that savage little brat. What a bore he was."

She got up close, face magnified by the curvature of the orb. Her icy blue eyes looked like oblong saucers, cheeks overly painted, nose toad-like. She wore an exquisitely embroidered rose-colored dress. Large earrings jingled alongside her wobbly head. The sound brought a shiver to his spine.

"Like my new earrings? I don't—they're not nearly as nice as the pair you *stole* from me." She gnashed her teeth a moment before her lips widened into a falsely sweet smile. "So now, who would it be looking through my precious orb? Could it be Squirrel, that upstart of a young lady, with that pretentious nose of hers? Or would it perhaps be that

VALOR

disgustingly filthy Freckles ... or maybe even the grand prize, that little hustler himself, who almost fooled me into believing he was my own nephew ..."

Augum didn't reply.

Erika stepped back, smiling. Her hand slowly went to Haylee's head. She got a good grip on her hair and yanked it up. Haylee whimpered but Erika didn't bat an oversized eyelash.

"This is my chance to redeem myself. I'm assuming you're clever enough to understand where I'm going with this." She pulled Haylee's hair harder, forcing her to scramble to her feet to catch up, tears freely running down her cheeks. Erika then ceremoniously drew a little knife and held it to her neck. Haylee yelped and stood on her tiptoes, breathing rapidly.

"You tell that old crone we want the scion and the pearl," Erika said, ignoring Haylee's struggles. "She can come to the academy. She has one day. If she doesn't come by sundown tomorrow, this little traitor gets it." She jerked Haylee's head away and walked off. Haylee collapsed, caught sharply by the manacles. She started sobbing.

"Haylee, it's Augum, we won't let them do anything to you—"

"They killed them ... they killed my parents ... my grandfather ..." she blubbered, hands dangling above her.

Augum's chest tightened. "Haylee, I'm ... I'm so sorry." Mere words.

"Augum ... help me ... please ..." Then her eyes rolled into the back of her head and she fell forward, limp.

"Haylee—!" but there was only silence and that single candle, standing crooked like some kind of cruel Endyear jape.

"They have her hostage," he said, letting the pearl roll out of his hand, barely noticing Mr. Goss, Mrs. Stone and Mr. Okeke standing nearby.

Leera immediately smothered the pearl tightly, wrapping it in cloth.

"And they killed ... they murdered her parents and grandfather ..."

There was a shocked silence.

"Poor, poor Haylee," Bridget said quietly. "Tell us what happened."

He relayed everything he had seen and heard.

"It's obviously a trap," Leera said when he finished. "Mrs. Stone, you can't go—they'll just take the scion and kill you—"

Mrs. Stone paced to the fire. "I was afraid of this very thing ..."

"Are we going to die?" Jengo asked in a weak voice that hardly matched his towering frame.

"Everyone dies in the end, son," Mr. Okeke said.

That didn't seem to help Jengo, who swallowed hard, forehead beading with sweat. He leaned towards Augum. "Are they on their way here right now?"

"I don't think so."

"But there's still a chance of it happening, right?"

They ignored him, instead watching Mrs. Stone as she stood staring into the hearth, hands behind her back. At last, she turned around.

"In the academy, you say?"

Augum nodded. "By sundown tomorrow."

"Then we have very little time. I must go immediately—"

"But Nana, it's a trap—"

"Mercy, child, that is plain as day. You do not think I plan on teleporting in there like some jester's apprentice, do you? No, what is required here is the finishing of something that I started a long time ago."

"What do you mean, Mrs. Stone?" Leera asked.

"Years ago, I began my studies of the Orb of Orion oblivious to the existence of a control pearl. Many things did not make sense then. Now that we are in possession of the pearl, perhaps I will be able to discover something to our advantage. The time has come to finish those studies. I must go to Antioc at once."

"Why Antioc?" Jengo asked in a wavering voice.

"The ancient library," Bridget replied. "But won't it be guarded?"

"Most certainly." The scion on top of her staff began humming. Clouds formed within, flashing rapid bursts of silent lightning.

Jengo focused his gaze upon it. "Is ... is that thing *dangerous*?"

Mrs. Stone glanced to the trio.

"I trust you to comport yourselves appropriately in my absence. Keep watch on Haylee."

"Yes, Mrs. Stone," they replied in unison.

She took a deep breath before focusing on the scion. Suddenly there was a tremendous implosive sucking sound and she was gone.

Jengo jumped, knocking the tome to the floor.

"It is all right, Jengo," Mr. Goss said, pawing the floor until he found the book. "That was merely Teleport."

"So ... so she didn't just ... disintegrate?"

Mr. Goss chortled as he handed the tome over. "Hardly. When you spend enough time around warlocks, you will grow accustomed to these things." His hand drifted up to his face to adjust spectacles that were not there. "Everything will work out. Mrs. Stone is a most competent warlock. Let us not underestimate her."

"Can I offer you more tea, Albert?" Mr. Okeke asked.

"That would be wonderful, Kwabe, thank you."

Mr. Okeke helped Mr. Goss back to the living area, leaving the youths sitting silently around the table for a time. Augum worried about Mrs. Stone. What if she sprung the trap and the Legion killed her? The thought was unbearable, but as much as he tried pushing it out of his mind, it remained like a stubborn splinter.

"So ... is there anything I can do to help?" Jengo asked.

"Aside from checking in on Haylee, I can't think of anything to do," Augum replied when the girls did not.

Leland moaned while pointing to the dark window.

"I think Leland wants us to ask around about the castle," Leera said.

Jengo perked up a little. "Castle—?"

"We're looking for Occulus' castle. It's supposed to be lost to time."

Jengo's voice dropped to a frantic whisper. "Why in all of Sithesia would you want to find *that* place?"

"There's something there we have to get," Leera replied." Anyway, it'll be exciting. It's a big adventure."

" 'Exciting'? 'Big adventure'? Do all warlocks crave death like this?"

"Leera's excited about anything involving death and adventure," Bridget said. "Anyway, Jengo, it's supposed to reside up in the Muranians in some hidden location."

"Occulus was the most powerful necromancer ever," Jengo mumbled, absently rubbing the scar on his chin. "Even I know that. I don't like talking about him. It'll definitely bring bad luck." He glanced at their eager faces. "I don't know where the castle is, but I guess you *could* ask Huan, the innkeeper of the Miner's Mule Inn. He's probably heard more stories than everyone in town combined."

"Is it too late to see him?" Leera asked.

"The inn's loud until dawn, especially during Endyear."

"I don't know, Lee," Bridget said. "Mrs. Stone preferred us to stay here. The Legion—"

"—is looking for an old lady with three children. We should be fine if only Jengo, Augum, and I go."

"You're taking an unnecessary risk, if you ask me."

"We'll be fine, *Mrs. Stone*."

"Ugh ..." Bridget raised her nose. "I suppose I'll just have to stay here and teach Leland about arcanery then."

Leland moaned in delight.

"You're too young to cast spells, but we can begin outlining the basics."

"Here, you might as well take this." Leera withdrew the wrapped pearl and placed it on the table before Bridget, whose lips tightened much like Mrs. Stone's.

Jengo looked to the window. "It's dark though, and there could be any manner of Legion monster out there—"

"Don't even think about changing your mind." Leera stood. "Come on."

Jengo swallowed but moved to his fur coat, Augum and Leera right behind.

Mr. Okeke stopped conversing with Mr. Goss and put down his tea. "Son, it is getting late. May I ask where you are going?"

"To the Miner's Mule, Father. We won't be long, promise."

"Just remember to play the good host, Jengo—no sneaking mead."

"Father, please, I'm almost a man grown—"

"This is not a game, Jengo, and put on a coat—"

"And I'm not a child!"

"Well you certainly act like one sometimes. Please do not embarrass me."

"Yes, *Father*." Jengo slapped on his coat and left with Augum and Leera.

"I'm almost fifteen and he still treats me like I'm eight," Jengo said as they trekked on a path through the towering snow-covered evergreens. Torches lined the route, pushing back the night.

"I felt the same way once," Leera mumbled.

"Hmm?"

"Nothing."

Augum suspected he knew what she meant—the last conversation between her and her mother was one she probably regretted.

Distant singing soon reached their ears.

"Sounds festive," Leera said.

"Just wait until the Star Feast tomorrow night."

Her face lit up. "That's *tomorrow*?"

"Yes. Shame you missed the sword and archery tournaments a few days ago."

"And Merrygive too," Augum said. Going door-to-door to help one's elders was traditionally done on the first day.

Leera scoffed. "Merrygive. You just miss the butter cookies."

"Oh, and you don't, with your famous sweet tooth?"

"Of course I do!" She glanced skyward. "I love Endyear …" she said wistfully.

A lonely feeling speared Augum's heart. Endyear was a time for family and friends. His father robbed her and Bridget of that, not to mention so many others in Solia. His best Endyears were with Sir Westwood, but now he too was gone.

"You'll still be here tomorrow, right?" Jengo asked Leera.

"Probably."

"So are you going to take someone to the Star Feast then?"

"The only boys I know around here are you and Augum, and look how ugly *he* is." She thumbed in Augum's direction.

For a horrifying moment, Augum thought she was being serious, until he saw the playful smile. He felt a light flutter. He'd never been asked to a Star Feast before, should he dare ask her to go with him? What about Bridget, who would she go with? If she didn't have anyone, she'd just sit all by her lonesome.

Then he thought of Haylee, hanging in that dreaded dungeon, and realized there were more important things to worry about than some silly late night supper.

"Who are *you* going with, Jengo?" Leera asked, blushing.

"Oh, I have someone in mind …"

VALOR

Augum felt that flutter dive. If he was going to ask her, maybe he should do it sooner than later ...

The singing grew louder as they walked past more homes with high-pitched roofs. The air was crisp and fresh, the snow sparkling from the light of the torches, each decorated with holly and vine. Soon they were in a plaza near the stone well marking the center of town. Four older women with mismatching skin tones and fur coats gossiped on a bench near a fire. Four men sang arm in arm behind them holding tankards. They were big and burly, coats smeared with mud.

"Miners," Jengo said. "Some come a long way. Money's good during war."

The men raised their tankards as the trio passed. "Happy Endyear!"

"Happy Endyear!" Jengo replied, Augum and Leera joining in half-heartedly, keeping their faces slightly averted.

"Don't worry, nobody will recognize you—the herald didn't bring a sketch of your faces."

They walked past a closed merchant shop named *Good Medicine* and on to the *Miner's Mule Inn*, a two-story log house with a balcony, on which people sat. Glasses clinked as the strangers bellowed with laughter.

Outside the inn, a man with a scraggly beard puffed on a long pipe, a wolf skin draped around his shoulders. He watched them as they walked by.

"You is that walking Sierran tree," the man said, slurring his speech.

"Well I am Sierran," Jengo replied with a smile and nod, towering over the man.

The man blew a cloud of blue smoke up into Jengo's face.

Jengo coughed. "What a dreadful thing, I'll be sick for a tenday ..."

"I don't much like your kind, you is too dark. Can disappear at night I say, sneak up on a man. It ain't right.

Damned by the sun you is. You go on back to where you come from."

"But Sierrans come in every color under the sun—"

"My mother's a Sierran," Augum said.

"Then you mammy is a no good—"

"Try not to strain that drunken brain, you oaf," Leera said.

Augum and Jengo stared at her.

The man's wandering eyes focused in on Leera. "What you just say, you darn squeaker?"

"I said, did you lose your cane?"

The man looked down. "I don't have no cane—" but they had already strolled past, opening the heavy oak door cut with a stained glass window.

"People like that exist in every kingdom," Jengo said, sighing.

Augum thought of the Pendersons and silently agreed.

They were in a crowded smoky tavern, its patrons holding tankards of slopping ale. People talked in loud voices, sang, and danced. A large hearth was set into the right wall, a bar counter on the left. Vine and wreaths of holly hung from iron candle chandeliers. Men of all races and creeds sat on rustic wooden stools. Some had sheathed swords, some pickaxes. Glassy eyes drifted their way as Augum noted no one wore a robe.

"You aren't trying to sneak some of that mead again, is you Jengo?" yelled a big man behind the bar wearing a greasy apron. His hair was black and his eyes almond-shaped.

When Augum saw those eyes, his heart squeezed. He wished Mya were here. He imagined secretly holding her hand at the Star Feast.

"That was only one time, Huan, and I did it because I was really sick."

Huan laughed. "You barely had a cough."

"I was dying of winter fever!"

"Everyone here's dying of winter fever. Look at them drinking to get well."

"Aye, I be sick unless I have me ale," said a rotund man on a nearby stool. His hair was so greasy Augum thought it'd light on fire if he neared a torch.

Huan cracked a grin at the man. "You be sick whenever your wife come in here and drag you off by that fat chin of yours."

"That be all too true. She don't much like the bottle."

"She don't much like you either." Huan turned back to Jengo. "So since when did you make friends? Spit me some names so I can pass on tall tales."

"Oh, uh—"

"—Jasper and Penelope," Augum interrupted, realizing it was safer to use false names.

"Penelope?" Leera mouthed.

"It's all I could think of," he said as the innkeeper reached under the bar and brought out four tin tankards.

"On the occasion of Jengo bringing friends in for the first time in living memory," Huan began, removing the stopper from a stone jug, "allow me to serve you some very special and very sweet almond mead all the way from Blackhaven. I've been saving it for the younglings because it'd take four of these here jugs to get you cross-eyed."

He began pouring. "Anyway, even your father should approve. Couple miners brought it in the other day. Hardly knew what they had." He wheezed with laughter, spilling mead onto the counter. "Traded them some horse ale, I did."

Jengo cleaned his tankard quickly before Huan poured him the mead. "Thanks, Huan, and Happy Endyear."

"Happy Endyear," Augum and Leera chimed in, clinking tankards with them.

Augum thought it tasted like sweet almonds mixed with thick molasses. It was actually quite good and he found himself taking a second sip, and then a third.

Jengo glanced around the tavern. He was the tallest and thinnest one there. Many a curious eye swiveled his way. "Busiest I've ever seen it. Is it safe to have all these people here? What if they burnt the place down?"

"Just the way I like it—rowdy, stinky and drunk. Keeps the coin rolling. How's your father anyway? Business good?"

Jengo shrugged.

"That man needs to come in here and drink my gutter ale more. All those specialty wines can't be good for his health." He raised his tankard. "Nonetheless, he's the most honest iron trader in town. To your father."

"To my father," Jengo said blandly.

Huan downed his tankard in one go and burped. "So you from out west then, Penelope?"

"Uh, yes," Leera replied.

Huan wiped his hands on his filthy apron. "Where from? Any news to share?"

"Blackhaven." She glanced to Augum, obviously wondering if it was a good idea to say so much. "No news though."

"Ah." Huan glanced at their robes. He looked like he wanted to say something else but instead tipped his tankard under a large cask behind him. "Time for some proper ale. So you're from Blackhaven, huh? Well you're not the only ones. Good deal of these drunkards would rather work in the mine supporting the war effort than actually be in the stinkin' war." He turned to grin at Jengo. "You saw how the place was as quiet as the grave when that herald swung through."

Augum glanced around the crowded tavern. Almost every man looked able enough to join the Legion.

"Fewer and fewer men come to the mines every month. Soon they'll be giving girls pickaxes, they will." Huan took a long pull from his tankard and grimaced. "Legion don't seem to realize you need big ugly men to dig out iron if you want to keep making swords and armor. Can't send everyone to war, you know, and damned if the place isn't empty every time that foul trumpet blares." A customer down the bar hooted for his attention. "It's that Abrandian drunkard again. Excuse me."

"What trumpet?" Augum asked, but Huan had already left to attend to a wobbly old man.

"There's always a lookout at the hill by the road," Jengo replied. "Every villager takes his fair turn. Soon as the lookout spots a Legion herald or Constable Clouds, they send up a blast and every man of age disappears. It's become a kind of game. Clouds knows all about it, but whoever he catches just has to pay a 'fine'. Only those that actually anger him get drafted."

"Who is this Constable Clouds?"

"He collects taxes on behalf of the Legion and is supposed to send men for conscription, but he's as corrupt a man as they come."

"So the Legion army hasn't actually visited here yet?"

"Not yet, but everyone knows it's just a matter of time. It's truly frightening, and of course we're all going to die horrible deaths when that happens. They raze villages to the ground."

Augum and Leera exchanged looks knowing just how true that was.

Jengo peeked in Huan's direction before helping himself to more of the mead. "Besides, I'm guessing almost everyone here broke one Legion proclamation or another. We're all doomed."

"How do we talk to Huan alone about, you know, the castle?" Leera asked.

"I'll ask Priya to cover the bar for a while." Jengo's head swiveled over the crowd. "There she is. Be right back."

They watched as Jengo pushed through the throng, a tree among shrubs. He met up with a slender woman with very long black hair and sienna skin, gracefully holding a tray of drinks and bread. She wore an indigo cloth wrapped around her waist and draped over one shoulder. Jeweled studs pierced her lips and nose. Jengo conversed with her before the pair made their way over.

"This is Priya," Jengo said, blushing as he presented her.

Priya made a small bow. "Greetings," she said in a slight accent. Her face was soft, brows perfectly trimmed. Several turquoise, amber and brimstone necklaces hung from her neck. "So you're Jengo's new friends. How many times has the world supposed to have ended since you met him?"

"She's from Tiberra," Jengo quickly added. "Her mother has a scribe shop in town—"

"My *crazy* mother," Priya interrupted with a radiant smile aimed at Jengo.

Jengo chuckled nervously. "These are my friends, Aug—"

"—Jasper and Penelope," Augum said. "Um, Happy Endyear."

"Happy Endyear to you."

"I like your necklaces," Leera said.

Priya smiled. "Thank you, and you have the prettiest face. Those freckles make you shine."

Leera twisted and fidgeted as if never having been complimented on her looks before.

"Right," Jengo began, "so Priya, think you could take over for Huan a little while? I know it's rowdy, but—"

"You're being silly, Jengo. Of course I can, but won't you tell me why?"

"Well, we need to talk to Huan. Private, uh, trading business, that sort of thing."

"So you've decided to take over your father's business after all."

"No—no, I mean, maybe, we'll see …"

Priya studied him a moment. Jengo cleared his throat and took a sip from his tankard.

"You are hiding something, Jengo," Priya said with a giggle. "But I will not press you." She paced around them, still holding the tray, and on through a small door at the end of the bar.

"Do you think she's prettier than me?" Leera whispered into Augum's ear.

Augum gave her a funny look. "I don't know, how in all of Solia am I supposed to tell?"

Leera's face fell as she gave him a half-shrug.

He shuffled his feet, feeling stupid. How else was he supposed to answer that? He wanted to say they were *both* pretty, but that probably would have been the wrong thing to say. And obviously Leera was way prettier, but verbalizing that would have been tantamount to … upon reflection, why *hadn't* he just said she was prettier?

They watched as Priya spoke with Huan, who at that moment was giving the old Abrandian a stern dressing down for vomiting all over the bar. She patiently pointed in their direction. Huan looked up and sighed. He angrily gestured at the defiled bar, but Priya placed a calm hand on his arm. He listened to her, rolled his eyes, and passed her his cloth, trouncing their way while brushing his hands against his apron.

"Jengo, I'm very busy, I don't have time for end-of-the-world stories again—"

"Yes, I know, Huan, but please, this'll only take a moment. It really is important this time, I swear."

Huan eyed Augum and Leera's robes once more before groaning and gesturing for them to follow. He tottered around the bar and pushed through the crowd, doling out quick-witted compliments or friendly jibes at his patrons. They exited through a back door and out into a snowy courtyard lit by torches decorated with holly and vine. A group of older men stood in a close-knit circle, smoking pipes and talking in low voices.

"Huan, we're looking for something," Jengo whispered, Augum and Leera crowding close.

"What is it this time, another banned spell book?"

"No, it's a castle," Augum said.

Huan sighed. "You should know where Eastspear is, Jengo, I hardly need to—"

Jengo shook his head. "No, another castle—"

"Oh, I see!" Huan winked and dropped his voice. "Want to go treasure hunting do you? I did the same when I was your age." He snorted and ruffled Augum and Leera's hair, much to their annoyance. "Well," he began in a conspiratorial whisper. "I happen to know of a very ancient, but dangerous castle, hidden in this very Ravenwood—"

Leera crossed her arms. "Does it sit leagues west of here and have black walls?"

Huan looked at her as if for the first time.

"Yeah, we know about that one," she said. "We're looking for a different one."

Huan placed his fists on his waist. "A different castle ... huh."

"It was built around the same time as that castle though," Leera continued, "but it's supposed to sit somewhere up in the Muranians."

Huan's almond eyes narrowed ever slightly. "I've heard dark stories of this supposed castle. The Occi call it Bahbell, which means 'gateway to hell'."

Jengo paled. "The Occi? Aren't they ... aren't they *cannibals*?"

"Oh, probably. Legend says the Occi are ancestors of Bahbell's king, the great Occulus, who was the most powerful necromancer to have ever lived."

"Where could we find the Occi?" Augum asked.

Huan looked over his shoulder. The other men glanced his way and he quickly turned back to the group. "The Occi don't like strangers. It's been rumored they boil them in broth, especially during long winters. Once a year, one of them, always the same one, straggles down from the mountains to do a trade run with the *Good Medicine* shop here. He's real ugly and buys all kinds of strange concoctions." He suddenly noticed how attentive Augum, Leera and Jengo were being. "Wait, you're serious about this, I thought you were japing me—!"

"Yes, of course we are," Leera said. "I mean, serious that is. We need to find Bahbell."

"I'm not," Jengo said. "No way am I going to look for some crazy cannibals."

Huan sighed. "Look, kids, I like you, you kind of remind me of me." He burped and pounded his chest. "Damn foul ale. Anyway, let me tell you something very honest." He spoke slowly and clearly now. "Every single person who I have seen leave to visit the Occi has disappeared. Every. Single. One. Nobody who visits them ever, and I mean *ever*, returns to tell the tale. Nobody. Think on that a moment." He slowly prodded Jengo's chest. "I hope that sinks in to that gangly Sierran skull of yours. I don't know what you lot are up to, but don't you go looking for the Occi unless you want to die a horrible, unspeakable death."

Jengo swallowed hard. "But I said I'm not going to go …"

"Then I don't want to hear about it again. Go find yourselves a cave to explore like normal kids." He glanced at Augum and Leera before waddling back to the bar.

"I don't feel well," Jengo said, placing a hand to his forehead. "Think I'm coming down with something really awful."

"Who owns the *Good Medicine* shop?" Augum asked.

"Could be winter fever again." Jengo tried to cough a few times. "Oh, the shop? Now that's a place I can't enter."

"Why's that?"

Jengo tapped at his scar.

"The boy that gave you that owns the place?" Leera asked.

"No, but his father does and everyone knows boulders don't roll too far away from mountains."

"Some do," Augum said, thinking of his own father. "Do you think we can find the owner?"

"Not here. He hates to mingle with the rabble. I don't really blame him—one can catch all manner of hideous disease from such close-quartered mingling. No, best thing to do is go in his shop, but you'll have to do it without me."

"We'll go tomorrow then."

The men smoking their pipes began to glance their way.

"We should go," Jengo said quietly. "They could be Legion spies."

They made their way through the bar, Jengo stopping briefly to thank Priya, before pushing past the front door, where they had to step over a sleeping drunk—turned out to be the man that had accosted them earlier, pipe still in his mouth.

They arrived back at the Okeke home, finding the living room arranged with blankets and pillows. Mr. Okeke had even prepared an evening snack for them consisting of warm sweetened goat milk and dried blueberries dipped in honey. Augum relayed what they learned while popping blueberries into his mouth. Bridget was glad to hear nothing had gone wrong and reported Leland was more than eager to learn about arcanery.

"And Haylee?" Augum asked.

"No change, the poor thing. Wish there was something more we could do for her."

Before long, Mr. Goss and Mr. Okeke herded their sons to bed. Mr. Okeke offered Mr. Goss Jengo's room, but Mr. Goss politely declined. When Mr. Okeke insisted, Mr. Goss told him he preferred to sleep on the floor. Further, he would not dare deprive such a tall young man of his own cozy bed.

Jengo and his father cleaned up the table, refusing any help, allowing for Augum, Bridget and Leera to change into clean nightgowns Mr. Okeke had provided. When they asked him where he had gotten them from, he replied that his wife would always have been the first to share her belongings with guests. It reminded Augum of when Mr. Goss allowed Haylee to borrow his own deceased wife's dress so that she no longer had to wear the necrophyte robe.

The girls giggled at Augum's nightgown, for it was one of Jengo's, and therefore much too large. When all but the fat Endyear candle were extinguished, and the fire stirred one last time, a very tired trio crawled under their fire-warmed Dramask blankets to rest their heads on silky pillows.

As worried as Augum was about Mrs. Stone and Haylee, he still managed to sleep better than he had in many days.

POWERLESS

Augum woke to the pitched beams whistling and creaking overhead. The shutters were open, allowing a clear view of swaying branches. A strong gust occasionally sent plumes of snow swirling past. Clouds had to be overhead because it was as gray as old stone. The scent of burning pine and tallow was in the air, the fire crackling merrily in the hearth, the Endyear candle ever-present on the mantel.

He heard the gentle clink of a cup coming to rest on a saucer and looked over to find Leland asleep at the table beside his father, who was mending the trio's burgundy apprentice robes alongside Mr. Okeke, the pair quietly gossiping like a couple of old village hens.

Leera was asleep beside Augum, her freckled face creased with pillow lines, while Bridget sat awake, back against the carved settee, knees covered with a blanket. Her eyes skimmed over the tiny hand-written text of the ornate pupil's encyclopedia.

She looked over at him, smiled, and whispered, "Morning, Aug."

"Morning."

"I'm going with you to that shop today."

"Good, we could use your help. Where's Jengo?"

Bridget checked over her shoulder before leaning closer. "His father insisted he go do business on his behalf today. There was a bit of a ruckus. Jengo really didn't want to go."

"He wants Jengo to take up the iron trade."

"And poor Jengo wants to become a warlock."

"Without an academy or mentor though …" He drew the blanket to his face, not wanting to get up yet. It was just too cozy. He nodded at the book. "Learn anything new?"

"Actually, yes—I've been reading up on 3rd degree spells."

"You think we're ready to move on?"

"Well, we're still rusty with Slam and Disarm, but all we have to do is practice them regularly and we should be fine."

It was true—what with the Henawa adventure, they've hardly had time to practice. "Maybe Nana will test us on our 2nd degree soon." He envisioned having two rings around his arm. It almost inspired him to jump out of bed and start casting Slam. He imagined the entire town waking up to the sound of thunder. "So what are the 3rd degree spells anyway?"

Bridget flipped back a few pages. "Mind Armor, Object Alarm and Object Track."

"What do they do?" A hand suddenly smacked him in the face.

"Oh, sorry," Leera croaked, eyes puffy. She stretched and yawned like a cat. "What are you two planning without me?"

"We're just talking about 3rd degree spells." Bridget listed them again.

"Neat, so what do they do?" Leera drew her blanket up over her mouth.

"Mind Armor defends you from all kinds of attacks of the mind—"

"Like Fear and stuff?" Augum asked, remembering that harrowing moment Vion Rames made him so afraid he thought he had wet himself.

"Exactly, but a lot of others too, like Deafness, Confusion, and so on. Object Alarm sets off an alarm in your head when someone other than you touches the enchanted object."

"That one's definitely going to be useful," Augum said. "Now I'll know when Leera sneaks my food—" he cringed as the expected punch smacked him on the shoulder.

"And Object Track," Bridget continued, ignoring their shenanigans, "allows you to actually track where your enchanted object is."

Leera snorted. "Would have been useful when a certain *somebody* lost the pearl."

Augum turned to face Leera, whose half-hidden face barely concealed her grin. "Hey, we got it back, didn't we?" he said.

"Only because we got lucky."

"I'll take what I can get." He turned back to Bridget. "Have you checked on Haylee yet?"

"Let me do that now." Bridget set the tome aside and dug into the rucksack, withdrawing a tightly wrapped bundle. She hesitated. "I almost don't want to look."

Augum sat up. "I'll do it."

She placed the bundle into his hands and he carefully unwrapped it, clenching the pearl in his fist. He closed his eyes and allowed himself to see through the Orb of Orion, sitting on a pedestal in a dark room.

Haylee hung in the same position as yesterday. A new candle sat before her, the only one lit in the room. His insides twisted seeing her like that.

He listened for a time before whispering, "Haylee. Haylee, it's me, Augum."

Her head stirred and she moaned.

He cringed. The last thing he wanted to do was draw Erika into the room. "You have to be very, very quiet." At least Mya had been spared from such torments. The thought made his skin burn though. He wanted to shout that they'd pay for what they'd done, all of them, especially Robin.

"Hey, it's all right," he whispered instead, trying to keep his breathing calm.

She looked up. "They ... they killed them," she blubbered, shoulders heaving silently. "Augum ... they *murdered* my parents ... my grandfather."

"Don't think about that right now, think about anything else."

"I can't feel my arms ..."

It was difficult seeing her like that. He hoped Mrs. Stone would return soon with a plan to save Haylee.

"Augum ..."

"I'm here, Haylee."

"I don't know how ... how much longer I can last ..."

"Just stay strong, I promise we'll get you out of there. You believe me, don't you?"

Haylee sniffed, but her head nodded just a tad.

Suddenly there came the sound of clacking. Erika Scarson strolled into the room and immediately slapped Haylee across the face so hard her hair bounced.

"I'm so sick and tired of hearing you whine all the time. 'My parents are gone, ooh, my sweet parents'. Ugh. Why don't you take it like a real woman and own up to your traitorous ways! You betrayed my nephew, didn't you, you little blonde vermin? Hey, I'm talking to you!"

She smacked Haylee again, but her body had gone limp. "Such a faker. You disgust me." Suddenly Erika turned around, eyeing the Orb of Orion. "Is anyone in there? Anyone watching?"

Augum didn't dare say anything, else she might abuse Haylee some more just to get a rise out of him.

Erika put her ear against the orb and listened, earrings jingling loudly. Back in Milham, Augum raised a single finger, indicating for everyone to be particularly quiet.

After a time, she grunted and trounced off. He watched a while longer, desperately wanting to ask if Haylee was all right but not wanting to bring Erika back in the room. Perhaps, to prevent the violence, it was wiser not to talk to her. He kept watching Haylee for any sign of movement, but there was none.

He withdrew from the orb and opened his eyes, shaking his head.

"Aug? What happened?" Bridget asked quietly.

He only kept shaking his head.

"You don't want to talk about it? Is she all right?"

"She's alive, but I don't know how much more she can take." At least he had spared Leera and Bridget from that awful sight.

They sat together silently, heads bowed. The worst part of it was he felt completely helpless. There was nothing he could do except watch. He slowly wrapped up the pearl and shoved it deep into a pocket.

Bridget shuffled over on her knees and hugged him. "I'm sorry you had to see that, Aug. Mrs. Stone will save her, you'll see."

An ebony-skinned veined hand gently squeezed his shoulder just as Bridget let go. He looked up to find Mr. Okeke holding a steaming plate of eggs and bacon with a side of jam and bread. Augum hadn't noticed the mouth-watering scent until now. Yet it almost made things worse, for Haylee was just on the other side of that pearl and she couldn't share the joy of Endyear breakfast.

"There is only so much we can change, Augum Stone," Mr. Okeke said. He walked off to bring two more plates for the girls.

"Thank you, Mr. Okeke," Bridget said quietly.

Mr. Okeke nodded. "Happy Endyear. Perhaps tonight the weather will be good enough for a Star Feast. I am sure Mrs. Stone and this poor young girl will join us." He smiled at them.

Augum ate his food, tasting nothing. When they finished, Bridget collected the plates and washed them in a basin, while Mr. Goss proudly returned their repaired apprentice robes.

"Thank you so much, Mr. Goss and Mr. Okeke," Leera said, giving Augum a worried sidelong glance.

"Since when did you get so polite?" Bridget asked, also giving Augum a sidelong glance.

They needn't worry about him like that. Augum snatched his robe and went to Jengo's room to change. There he sat on the oversized bed, staring at a painting of a youthful ebony-skinned woman in dignified dress. Mrs. Okeke, who had died of sickness. He stared past the painting and thought of Nana. How were her studies going? Did she need help? He wished she'd teleport and scoop him up so he could do something useful, anything at all, to help free Haylee.

"Hey Aug, you about ready to go to the shop?" Bridget delicately asked from the other side of the door.

The shop. Suddenly that seemed like such a waste of time …

"Aug?"

"Yeah, be right there," he finally said. He changed into his burgundy robes and neatly folded Jengo's nightgown. Then he exited the room, dropping the nightgown off on his pillow, conscious of them staring at him. He made his way over to the door. "You two coming?"

"Yes," Leera said, "but you have to let us get changed!"

They raced off to Jengo's room.

He waited by the front door, arms crossed, images of Haylee blackening his thoughts. It wasn't fair she was going through all this. It wasn't fair they murdered her family. There was so much unfairness it made his knuckles whiten.

Leland moaned.

"Not today, Leland, let us leave them to their adventures," Mr. Goss said quietly.

Augum felt worse. He should have said something, told Mr. Goss Leland was more than welcome to come along, but instead he remained silent, brooding.

Bridget and Leera eventually popped out of Jengo's room. "Ready!"

Augum opened the front door and stepped out into the wind, letting the girls scramble after him.

"Aug, you all right?" Leera asked, exchanging a tentative look with Bridget.

"Fine." He remembered Mya's throat being sliced, the way she fell into his arms ... so unfair. He should have loosed the Banyan beast on Robin when he had the chance. Why had he let him go?

"You sure? Cause you don't sound like it—"

"I'm fine, all right, what do you want from me—!"

The girls stopped.

Leera gave him a pained smile. "Nothing, Aug, we just want to make sure you know we're here for you. You know that, right?"

He rubbed his face. "I'm sorry, it's just—"

"—you don't even have to explain," Bridget said, Leera nodding along.

He looked at them, the pair standing side by side in the snow, the cold wind tearing at their hair and robes. "Don't know how you two put up with me sometimes."

Leera shrugged. "Ugh, it's incredibly difficult but we manage."

He smiled. "Come on then, we have a shopkeeper to talk to."

THE MERCHANT, THE SCRIBE

A bell tinkled as the trio entered the *Good Medicine* shop, its swept planks creaking underfoot. Glass jars sat in neat rows on shelves, full of herbs, powders, insects in fluid, and other colorful concoctions. Animal figurines carved from various tusks and bones sat on two opposite windowsills.

"What younglings want?" a voice called from the counter.

Augum looked over to find an elderly Henawa standing there. At first, he thought his eyes were deceiving him, but the man's skin was as white as snow, his hair like milk. He wore a blue silk tunic. Golden bracelets clinked on his arms. His eyes had dark puffy bags underneath, his skin as wrinkled as wet parchment.

"Chunchuha!" Augum blurted.

The man's snowy brows rose up his forehead. "How you know Henawa?"

"Because we were just with the Henawa—"

"You lie, maniye—you still have hair."

"Then how come I know that maniye means 'dark skin'?"

The man scowled. "Andava, you read mind. You nuliwi."

"Yes, we are nuliwi, sir, but we can't read your mind." Augum approached the counter with Bridget and Leera. "So how come you're here and not with your tribe?"

"You not see I old man? Henawa leave old, sick, injured to die. Keep tribe strong."

Come to think of it, Augum didn't recall seeing any old Henawa back at the farm.

"And I no 'sir'. I no metal man. You know Henawa words for 'honored elder'?"

Augum shook his head.

"Achishi Zafu. I sick. Tribe leave in wood. I survive. Come here. Have son. Make maniye coin. Now you buy or go."

"Please, Achishi Zafu, we just want to ask a question."

"You buy, I answer."

Augum turned to Bridget. "Do we even have any coin?" he whispered.

Bridget shook her head.

He glanced back to the old Henawa. "Will you barter?"

"You show."

"We'll be right back then." The trio left the shop.

"Not sure we have anything left to trade," Bridget said as they paced back to the Okeke home.

"Let's just have a second look anyway."

"We better find *something*," Leera said, "otherwise we might have to do chores for him."

When they entered, Mr. Goss and Mr. Okeke were in deep discussion about the intricacies of the iron trade, something Mr. Goss seemed to find riveting. The trio waved hello before taking stock of their inventory—arcaneology tome, burned yellow book on elements, and the Slam spell parchment.

"Can't trade any of this," Bridget said, putting it back.

Augum's eyes travelled to a rustic pine side table on top of which sat the folded Dramask blankets they had acquired in Evergray Tower. He held one up, letting the fine striped wool unravel.

"Yeah, but they're *so* warm—" Bridget said, grimacing.

"I think it's worth it," Leera said. She and Augum looked to Bridget, who finally surrendered a nod. He folded up the blanket and the trio returned to the shop.

"Achishi Zafu, we have something to barter—" Augum stopped as a muscular Henawa youth of about sixteen turned his way, holding a muddy pickaxe in one hand. His round face scowled like the old man, but his hair, unlike any other Henawa Augum had seen, was cut short. This had to be the man's son.

"Hi there," Augum said, approaching the counter.

The youth scowled. "You call my father 'Achishi Zafu'?" He had no accent whatsoever. "I've seen you with that stupid Sierran." He spat on the floor before Augum.

The old man immediately slapped the back of the boy's head. "Spudi sapinchay!" and unleashed a string of Henawa curses while gesturing at the planks.

The youth's milky forehead reddened. "Fine already!" He glared at the trio as he took his time removing a dirty cloth from his loose coat. He dropped it to the floor and squished it about with his boot. He then kicked it up to his hand, as if having done the motion hundreds of times.

"No respect," the old man said, shaking his head.

"Just croak already," the youth muttered.

Bridget gasped. "How could you, he's your *father*!"

The youth snorted. "Some father. Makes me work in the mine during Endyear."

The old man leaned forward on the counter, his face next to his son's. "Henawa no celebrate maniye nuliwi! You want shop when father die, you listen. You work."

The youth grimaced. "I'm Solian, not just Henawa! I've never even *seen* other Henawa before—"

The old man pointed at his son's snowy skin. "You sapinchay! Henawa forever!"

"The Henawa are weak and useless barbarians. All they do is chase deer, sit around a fire and grow fat! I'm sick of this!" The youth barreled past them and stormed out the door.

"Chaska, listen to Father—!" but Chaska was already gone.

The old Henawa closed his eyes and expelled a long breath. His gaze fell back on the trio. "What maniye want!"

Augum held up the Dramask blanket. "Achishi Zafu, we've come to barter for information. We would like to know where to find the Occi."

The old man's face darkened. He raised his chin, looking down on them in an appraising manner. "You wish death, maniye?"

"Of course not," Leera said. "We can take care of ourselves. We have someone helping us."

"Andava maniye," the old man muttered, shaking his head. He leaned closer, making a dismissive gesture at the blanket. "You say you see Henawa. Son no listen to me. You make son believe Henawa proud. You make son know Henawa brave. You teach him this, I help you, maniye."

"But how are we supposed to do that?" Augum asked. "We're not Henawa."

"You see Henawa, you know Henawa. You do this for Achishi Zafu."

The trio left the shop with slumped shoulders. Augum rubbed his face as the wind whistled through the branches.

Not only was Chaska a couple years older than them, he was rude *and* he was an enemy of their new friend, Jengo. How in all of Sithesia were they going to convince that youth, who had never seen another Henawa before, to even listen to them? And who were they to even tell a Henawa what the Henawa were like! They were only among them for a few days!

Leera rubbed her eyes and let out an exasperated sigh. "Maybe there's some other way to find the Occi ..."

"We could just wait until one of them comes to trade," Augum said.

"So you're saying you'd like waiting for, oh, I don't know, *forever*?"

Bridget gathered her robe close. "Why don't we just talk to Chaska?"

Leera threw up her hands. "And say what? 'Oh, hey there, we just thought we'd swing by to tell you about your people. They're so proud and brave.' Yeah, I'm sure he'd warm up to us right away."

"Well we won't know until we try." Bridget's head swiveled between their doubtful faces. "Fine, you two can find an alternate way to get to the Occi. I'm going to talk to him on my own." She wrapped the Dramask blanket around her shoulders like an old woman and marched off.

"Yeah, good luck with that!" Leera shook her head. "Ugh, she's so unrealistic sometimes. I bet the two of us can find out where the Occi are before she does."

Augum smirked. "I'm not waiting around behind some freezing bush."

Leera poked his chest with each word. "Don't. Be. So. Smart. Anyway, I have an idea. Come on."

They strolled to the center of town where a group of men and women jovially shot arrows at a hay target. It had begun snowing again. The wind kept a steady pace and the trees swayed along.

Leera stopped by the well, its sloped roof covered with a blanket of snow. "So what's in town here ..." She focused on a stall with a low awning, an anvil and a series of iron tools. A young man in a soot-stained sleeveless coat hammered at a horseshoe.

"There's the blacksmith." She pointed at another stall with a multitude of clay pots. "The potter."

"What are we looking for?" Augum asked.

"Don't know yet. Someone old and wise, maybe the town sage or something. Just look for a really long gray beard. Old men with long gray beards are always wise, aren't they?" She pointed at a closed stall with the words *Lordrick's Leathers*. "Leather worker there. And there's the weaver, the miller, the shoemaker—"

"If I had coin I'd buy a pair of winter boots." He was sick of his feet freezing in nothing but turnshoes. He had tried wrapping them in cloth but it only made walking more difficult.

"... engraver ... scribe ... Wait a moment, a scribe might know where we can find the Occi, right?"

"Isn't that the girl's mother we briefly met at the tavern?"

Leera glanced at him, one brow raised. "You mean Priya, the very pretty one."

"What?"

"Nothing," yet she kept gawking at him as if waiting for him to say something particular.

He snorted. "Oh for—she wasn't prettier than you, all right? Now let's go." He pinched the cuff of her robe in the direction of the scribe's house. Leera happily bounced along.

He hid it well, but that was one of the hardest things Augum had ever said. He had been thinking about it now and then since the tavern. Why had Leera asked him if he thought that Tiberran girl was prettier? What did it mean? Was she comparing herself to her to get Jengo to ask her to the Star Feast? Or did she just simply want to know if she was prettier?

They walked up to a sod house with a wooden sign depicting a quill, parchment and inkwell. Written underneath in the neatest hand was *Panjita the Scribe*. Leera opened the door.

"Close it quick lest Panjita freezes to death!" barked a shrill voice from the corner. Leera slammed the door shut out of surprise, sending parchment flying off a nearby desk the size of a bed.

"They shall pick those up," said an old woman with a gray ponytail, clunky spectacles, and crimson sienna skin. She limped forward, cane in one hand, quill in the other. She was short, only up to Augum's shoulders, and wore a very long cerise cloth wound around her waist and draped over her shoulder. Her face was bejeweled with tiny stud piercings.

Augum picked up the parchments and placed them on the desk, already strewn with scrolls, inkwells, and bronze animal figurines acting as paperweights.

The woman pointed her quill at Leera like a sword. "Does the freckled creature want to kill me? She leaves the door open that long and she might as well put Panjita's head under a guillotine." She waddled around the desk like an old bear, plopping down in a bentwood chair as worn as she was, one of its back supports broken. She hung her cane on its armrest, tossed the quill on the desk, and clenched her hands together.

"What do they want?"

Leera cleared her throat. "Hello, ma'am—"

"—Panjita Singh is her name, and if the boy and girl can't pronounce it they might as well get out now because Panjita doesn't have time for imbeciles." She leaned forward a little. "Panjita thinks the boy and girl indeed look like imbeciles."

Leera gave Augum an uncertain look. "Uh, hello, Mrs. Singh—"

"—it hasn't been *Mrs.* for thirteen years, now the girl better get on with it unless she enjoys watching Panjita melt with age before her eyes."

"Uh, right, sorry, *Ms.* Singh, it's just that we wanted to ask you a question."

Ms. Singh looked skyward and raised her hands. "Well thank the Unnameables, a question, a real question, how will Panjita ever answer? Perhaps she *would* answer if the simple girl would stop roving about like a mole and simply *ask* the almost certainly trivial question."

Leera gaped.

"Panjita is getting impatient, she's thinking she'll soon be hurling her inkwell and trinkets at imbecile brats that haplessly wander into shops drooling like brainless—"

"—we need to find the Occi," Augum blurted.

Ms. Singh pushed on her thick spectacles. They immediately began sliding back down her nose. "Ah, so the boy can get to the point." She stared at him with magnified eyes. "Does the boy have a death wish?"

"No, of course not. We just need to find the Occi." When Ms. Singh gave him a highly skeptical scowl, he added, "We'll be well protected."

"Does the boy think something about Panjita's appearance screams gutterborn? Is there something about her face, perhaps her oafish spectacles, that warrant such an unashamed bashing of her superior intelligence and worthy wit?"

"Not at all, we really *do* need to find the Occi."

"Oh? So the boy and girl blithely standing in Panjita's presence haven't been dared to steal an Occi horn by one of their foolish chums?"

"No, of course not. What's an Occi horn anyway?"

"Ah, feigning ignorance is a trick as old as time. That aside, have the boy and girl heard of the tales, legends and campfire stories told to children to scare them from going to see the Occi? Do the obtuse pair before Panjita know mothers and fathers tell their children that if they do not behave, the Occi will come in the night and snatch them away to hell?"

"No, haven't heard those," Leera said, "but it doesn't matter, we have a powerful protector."

"Oh, the girl must think herself ever so smart. Despite Panjita's wild protestations, said girl will of course continue to think this way until she wakes up slow-roasting in a cauldron with her insides hanging out over the edge while little Occi children gnaw on her fingers."

Leera swallowed. Augum thought she had finally met her sarcastic match. It was time to change tactics. "So your daughter works at the inn," he said in a conversational tone.

Ms. Singh looked Augum up and down as if eyeing a diseased mule she'd never purchase. "Panjita does not appreciate a know-nothing Solian delinquent—and not even a man—approach her in regards to her only daughter. She finds this terribly offensive, for he is not nearly noble or rich enough for Priya—"

"—no, that's not what I—"

"—Panjita is thinking of releasing the hounds of hell if the unsuitable does not remove himself from her premises."

"Think we better go," Leera said out of the corner of her mouth.

"The smartest thing the freckled Solian has said thus far. Panjita thanks the snotlings for wasting her precious time and asks them never to return again. If Panjita were younger, she would help their departure with a kick to the—"

They closed the door a little too loudly for Ms. Singh's tastes. There was a bang and then a rolling sound from the other side.

"Well that went well," Leera said in mock cheer as they strolled away.

"Guess we're back to looking for old men with long gray beards."

THE ATTEMPT TO SAVE HAYLEE

Augum and Leera roamed about looking for a sage while the snowfall thickened. The town slowly emptied as people disappeared inside their homes, leaving them to stand around an Endyear torch, rubbing their hands and stamping their feet against the cold.

"Wonder how Bridge is doing," Augum mumbled, trying to get his teeth to stop chattering.

Leera snickered. "Probably chased back to the house by that brute."

"Yeah. Guess I should check on Haylee." He retrieved the pearl from his pocket and slowly unwrapped it. Leera gave him a worried look as he closed his eyes to see through the Orb of Orion. Inside that dark room, lit by a single candle, a sandy-haired figure in a red and black striped robe crouched by Haylee. Back in Milham, Augum felt heat flash through his body.

"I'm sorry, Hayles, I had to do it," Mya's murderer said, feeding Haylee a spoonful of soup from a wooden bowl. She slurped it up, wincing, her head hanging.

"If we didn't teach you that lesson, what would stop the next traitor?" Robin raised her chin to look into her eyes. "Do you understand?"

She only glared at him.

"I know you're angry, Hayles, but I had no choice. They would have thought me weak if I hadn't sent the command. That's what commanders do, Hayles—they make decisions, important ones. They *command*. How am I ever to become one if I can't make those decisions? Stop being selfish and put yourself in my shoes, would you?" He shook his head slowly as if pitying a worthless peasant, hand still on her chin. "I'm important now. People look up to me, like they looked up to my father. You know he was a warlock captain in the army, Hayles. Everyone respected him. Even Mother—"

"—he beat you both daily!"

"Shut up! He did it because he had to teach me the ways of the world! He did it to make me a man." Robin's fist clenched, but then he sighed, letting go of her chin with a spiteful twist. "As for Mother ... she was always so weak, so pitiful. But his men ... they listened to Father. *I* listened to Father." He paused, studying her. "*You* should look up to me, you know. Do you still look up to me, Hayles?"

She spit in his face.

He dug out a fine cloth and proceeded to wipe his cheek. Something about the way he did it reminded Augum of the Blade of Sorrows—methodical, patient, and dangerous.

Robin folded the cloth, put it in his pocket, picked up the bowl of soup, and slowly poured it over her head. She hung there, taking it.

VALOR

Augum could barely restrain himself from yelling vile curses, but he knew that would make things far worse for her. If there was only a way to teleport in there, smash Robin's face in.

"You could have been right here with me, Hayles." Robin stood up, tossing the bowl aside with a crash. "Instead, you chose those weak gutterborn rats, and for what? Look at you. Look at what you did to your parents. Look at what you did to your grandfather. I'll give you one last chance. Tell me you're very sorry and you'll obey every single one of my commands from here on, and I'll consider having you released. I'll consider … taking you back."

Robin watched for longer than necessary to receive his answer.

"Fine," he said at last. "Have it your way, but when Auntie draws the knife across your traitorous neck, just remember that you had your chance. You better hope that crone gives up the scion instead." He walked out while Haylee whimpered.

Augum watched for a short while, conscious of his body growing colder back in Milham. When neither Erika nor Robin came back, he whispered, "We'll get you out, Haylee, don't you worry."

She began quietly crying.

"We'll get you out, I promise. Stay strong," but his words sounded as useless as a wheelbarrow missing its wheel. With a heavy heart, he withdrew.

"Robin was with her," he told Leera once the pearl was tightly wrapped and back in his pocket.

"What did that vermin want?"

"For her to apologize and say she'd obey every command of his from now on. He talked about his parents a bit too. His father was a warlock captain in the army. Beat him and his mother daily."

"I know."

"You … you do?"

"Yes. Everyone did. Robin used to come to school black and blue. But no one did anything because they were too afraid of his father. Even the teachers turned a blind eye." She twiddled her thumbs. "But any time someone tried to help Robin, he would lash out at them. Brutally. Just like his father. There are stories … too many stories."

"So he was made this way."

"You were bullied too, Aug. Do you go around doing the same thing to others? People have choices. He chose his path a long time ago."

They stood in silence for a while, lost in thought, until Leera shook her head. "I really hope Mrs. Stone pulls through."

"Me too. Me too …"

"There's Bridge. Look at her smirking."

They watched Bridget approach, blanket fluttering from her shoulders, hair gathering snowflakes.

"What are you so happy about?" Leera asked.

"Nothing, just made a new friend, that's all."

"You made friends with that brute?"

"He's not so bad if you just *listen* to him, you know."

Leera gave Augum a look as Bridget strolled by. "Hey, where are you going now?"

"To the *Good Medicine* shop."

"Wait up for us—"

"You two look like you need to sit by a warm fire," Bridget said as they caught up.

"We're fine," Leera replied, drawing her robe tighter. "So did you explain to him how brave the Henawa are?"

"Nope."

"Okay … so did you tell him how good they are at ambushing? Or hunting?"

VALOR

"Nope."

"I don't get it, what *did* you do?"

"I told you," Bridget said as she opened the door to the shop. "I only listened."

Leera rolled her eyes as the trio entered.

"Hello, Achishi Zafu," Bridget said with a bright smile.

"What maniye girl want?"

"Only to tell Achishi Zafu that his son, Chaska, is leaving."

"Andava maniye better not—"

"—he's leaving on his nemana."

The old man froze, watching Bridget a moment. Then he raised his chin and gave a proud nod. Augum and Leera exchanged perplexed looks.

"He's leaving tonight," Bridget continued, "after the Star Feast, if there is one. He is going to hunt the winged demon." She glanced out the window at the curtain of falling snow. "The weather is a bit bad right now."

The old man stared ahead with a small smile on his weathered face, as if reliving days of old.

Bridget quietly turned and left, Augum and Leera following in a daze.

"What just happened?" Leera asked when they stepped outside.

Bridget slowly led them back to the Okeke home. "I told him his son is going on a nemana, a spiritual quest. In the Henawa culture, a boy is not a man until he returns from one. Chaska knew a lot more about the Henawa than he let on at first. He said his father told him all the Henawa stories, and that his father always lectured him for not listening to those stories, but, see, Chaska *had* been listening—and he's determined to bring back the bones of a winged demon, which I'm guessing just means a large bird."

"But ... how did you make him talk to you in the first place?" Leera asked.

"I asked him if he'd come with me to the Star Feast."

Leera stopped mid stride, coughing. "You did what! You *like* him!"

"No, silly, not like *that*. Well, I mean, he's cute, but he's also lonely and just wanted someone to talk to. I honestly thought I could help him." She shrugged. "Besides, this opens the door for you two to ask someone."

Leera and Augum blushed, cheeks fire red.

"Well, I have a person in mind already," Leera said, suddenly skipping off to the Okeke home, nose in the air.

"Someone's in a good mood," Bridget said, nudging Augum with a playful elbow.

He forced a smile, but his insides prickled. Leera was going to ask Jengo to the feast, it was obvious—she was rushing to do it right now. Suddenly he didn't want to go in at all and stopped.

"Hey, want to see if, uh, if there are any games going on?" He glanced back the way of the village, the snow swirling in thick clouds.

"What? It's freezing. And aren't you hungry?"

He'd eat bark if presented on a plate. "No, not really."

"Well there's nothing going on," Bridget said as Leera disappeared inside the house. "I mean, look at it, it's miserable out." She stared at him a moment and sighed. "Just ask her."

"What? Ask her what, if she's hungry?"

Bridget gave him a sisterly look. "You know what I mean, Aug."

"I think I'm hungry after all." He marched off to the house, leaving Bridget to groan and catch up.

When he opened the door, Mr. Okeke, Mr. Goss, Jengo and Leera sat at the table. Leland played with a wooden

VALOR

puzzle toy while Leera held a private and giddy conversation with Jengo, who sat right beside her. It immediately confirmed Augum's suspicions.

Mr. Goss squinted. "Oh, hello, Augum! How was your morning?"

"Fine." He stamped his feet at the door to shake off the snow and proceeded to sit across from Leera.

Bridget settled at his side. He felt her eyes on him.

"Well now that everyone is here, let us begin lunch," Mr. Okeke said, standing. "Jengo, if you please."

"Yes, Father." Jengo flashed Leera a secret smile and got up to help. Mr. Okeke began lecturing his son on proper iron trading practices. Jengo dully nodded along.

Mr. Goss took a sip of tea. "So, Leera said we are one step closer to finding Occulus' castle."

"That all depends on whether or not Bridget's future husband gets his father to tell us," Leera said.

"Oh? And what could this be all about?" Mr. Goss asked in a playfully scandalized tone.

Bridget snickered. "Leera's just exaggerating as usual, Mr. Goss."

"Well, you *did* ask him to the Star Feast."

Mr. Goss set down his tea, brows traveling up his forehead. "An interesting development indeed! May I ask who the lucky fellow is?"

"His name is Chaska," Bridget said, face scarlet. "He's a Solian Henawa."

"Well that is just splendid. Congratulations, Bridget. I am sure he must be very honored to be going with such a pretty young lady."

Bridget shrank a little while curling strands of cinnamon hair behind her ear.

Mr. Goss glanced out the window. "Let us only hope the weather clears."

"Have you ever missed a Star Feast before due to weather, Mr. Goss?" Leera asked in an overly cheerful manner that made Augum suspicious.

"Only once, when I was your age. It was the worst blizzard I have ever seen. But you know what we did? Those of us with dates ran off to an abandoned barn and had the most marvelous supper anyway."

"Aww, Mr. Goss, that's so romantic!" Bridget cooed.

"Wonder how Mrs. Stone is doing," Augum muttered, hoping to switch topics.

Mr. Goss cleared his throat. "Yes, well, perhaps we should not celebrate too much. After all, there are people in great trouble tonight."

The table fell quiet.

"The castle is called Bahbell," Augum blurted. "It means gateway to hell."

Jengo swallowed hard.

Augum felt a kick from Bridget. "So, uh, think the weather will improve soon?" he asked in a forced jovial manner.

Bridget rolled her eyes as Mr. Goss jubilantly recounted an occasion when the clouds miraculously parted, allowing for a last-moment Star Feast.

Mr. Okeke and Jengo soon served lunch consisting of leftover leek soup, herbed salmon, buttered steamed carrot, and for dessert, Sierran custard pie.

After lunch, Mr. Goss and Mr. Okeke retired to the living area to have tea, while Augum checked on Haylee again. She hung sleeping as a quiet voice spoke nearby. He wondered if it was Erika or Robin. When he withdrew, it was to a silent table, everyone's face showing concern.

"Nothing new to report," he said after wrapping up the pearl.

"Time is running out," Bridget said. "It'll be sundown in a few hours. Hope Mrs. Stone hurries."

"Let's use the time to train," Leera said.

"An excellent idea," Jengo said, "as long as we do it safely."

Leland moaned loudly.

"Of course you can help us," Bridget said. She retrieved the yellow and blue books from the rucksack and paired off with Augum while Leera paired with Jengo. Leland scuttled between the two groups, moaning.

While rehearsing the 1st degree, Augum tried not to steal glances at Leera and Jengo. He had a harder time than usual casting the spells.

Mr. Okeke and Mr. Goss would occasionally stop their conversation to watch, commenting on the wonders of arcanery.

Later, Augum and Bridget switched to the 2nd degree. To his secret satisfaction, Leera had gotten nowhere with Jengo, who seemed far more concerned about dying than learning.

Leland lined up some pillows in a row for Augum and Bridget to send flying backwards with Push, much to Jengo and Mr. Okeke's delight. Leera kept telling Jengo to focus, but his eye would inevitably wander over to what Bridget and Augum were doing.

The pair eventually moved on to Shield. Augum asked for a volunteer. Mr. Okeke eagerly offered, using a carved ebony cane to attack with. Augum summoned his shield of hard lightning again and again, gradually feeling more comfortable with it.

At the third hour, Jengo was reading the blue book on arcaneology and Leland snoozed by his father on the settee, having exhausted himself. Bridget practiced wrapping things with her vine while Leera practiced brightening and dimming her palm. Augum moved on to Disarm, a spell he was not nearly as proficient at. Mr. Okeke once again volunteered to help, but Augum only managed to yank the cane from him once every three attempts.

Eventually, everyone decided to rest in case they needed their arcane energies to help Mrs. Stone. Jengo continued studying the blue book while Augum checked on Haylee. She now sat limp in a chair, unmanacled, the room still lit by that single dying candle. Two Legion guards in half helms stood behind her. There must have been more people nearby because he heard shuffling feet and quiet voices.

Sundown would come soon. Was Nana on her way there now? Had she failed in her studies?

"Anything new?" Bridget whispered when he withdrew from the orb.

"Not really."

"Let's take turns watching. You shouldn't be the only one burdened."

"I'd rather you didn't. It's ... disturbing."

"More disturbing than watching you tortured by Robin?"

He looked at her, bit his lip, and handed the pearl over.

The waiting and watching went on for a while. There were no new developments other than the doubling of the guards and the occasional appearance of Erika, who paced relentlessly, red robe fluttering.

Then, just as Augum was monitoring Haylee, he heard an implosive sucking sound back in Milham. One of the guards must have heard it as well because his head snapped to the orb. Augum felt a sharp tug and withdrew, stifling the pearl in his fist.

In the Okeke home, Mrs. Stone was being helped to a chair, back bent, eyes encircled by tired lines.

"We are so very happy to have you return, Mrs. Stone," Mr. Goss said.

VALOR

Everyone gathered close while Mr. Okeke set a pot of water over the fire for tea.

"I have not slept," Mrs. Stone croaked, "and I am late and quite tired, but I may have a solution." She withdrew two scrolls from within her robes, one large and one small. The small one was crinkled and yellow from time. She handed it over to Bridget. "Decide amongst yourselves who will be the one."

The trio crowded around the ancient scroll. It turned out to be a complex set of instructions on how to cast spells through the Orb of Orion. Near the bottom, it revealed a crucial piece of information—only someone who was tuned to the orb stood any chance of success.

"I don't understand, Mrs. Stone," Bridget said. "How are we to free Haylee with this? None of us know spells powerful enough."

Mrs. Stone handed over the larger scroll. "This may work."

Bridget unfurled it—it was a Group Teleportation scroll. They had used one before to escape the Legion.

Augum glanced between the two scrolls. "But ... how? We can't read inside the orb."

"The scroll must be cast within the orb."

"That makes no sense, Nana, how are we to—"

Bridget grabbed his arm. "—by memorizing it."

"Correct," Mrs. Stone said. "The spell will be triggered if spoken correctly. All you need do is have the scroll in hand while your attention is within the orb."

Augum gaped at the long set of instructions and the arcane phrase that would trigger the spell. The words were complicated but rang with familiarity. The plan seemed ludicrous and far-fetched.

"What about the tuning?" he asked.

"Looking into it—" Bridget said, skimming the yellowed scroll. "I'm guessing you're supposed to have spent a lot of time with the orb."

"Augum looked through it the most," Leera said. "You can do it, Aug. If anyone here can, it'd be you."

"Nana, maybe you should—"

"I spent the last half day teleporting all over Solia and beyond in a frantic attempt to track down this scroll. My arcane energies are spent, I have had no sleep and I am not tuned to the orb. I daresay it would be foolish for me to make the attempt."

"Don't worry, Aug, we'll help you prepare," Bridget said. "Give me the pearl."

Augum handed it over, throat suddenly dry. This was far beyond anything he had ever tried before. Memorizing a complex spell and casting it *while* peering through the Orb of Orion? Was she mad?

Everyone sat in tense silence as Bridget glanced through the orb. "There's a whole bunch more guards in there now," she said after withdrawing and wrapping up the pearl. "Erika's there too, and who knows who else. I think the best way to do this is to somehow get Haylee to touch the orb just as you finish reading the Teleportation scroll."

"But how's he supposed to do that?" Leera asked.

"I may have a solution to that problem," Mrs. Stone said. "My research has uncovered it is possible to move the Orb of Orion, as long as one is tuned to it."

Augum frowned. "Move it? But how?"

"I think I understand," Bridget said. "If we can *lock* it, we should be able to move it using the same principle, right? Maybe give it a command like *move* or something."

He sighed. "I can try. Give me a bit of time to memorize this." He began reading the instructions to Group Teleport. Nothing was sinking in though—there was just too much

VALOR

pressure. Leera sidled in beside him and began reading it aloud, which helped somewhat. The difficulty came with the pronunciation of the arcane trigger phrase. Luckily, Mrs. Stone patiently guided him through that part of the challenge.

"Unclutter your thoughts, great-grandson. Do not fear your training. Do not fear success. Remember, too, that you can cast other spells within the orb."

Augum looked up. Of course—Centarro! It was by far their favorite and most interesting spell. It was ancient and off-the-book, allowed for pure concentration, but also had a serious side effect upon expiring—the dulling of wit and slowing of reflex. It was risky, but probably his best chance.

They discussed various strategies some more, settling on Augum taking the time to figure out how to move the orb first before doing anything.

"It's almost sundown," Bridget said at last. "Think you're ready?"

"Think so," he replied, taking the pearl. "Let me just look a moment."

His consciousness dove through the orb. Augum counted no less than eight guards, of which two stood behind Haylee's chair. Erika Scarson stared at the orb, knife in hand.

He retreated to Milham, pearl tight in his fist. "If only there weren't so many people in there ..."

"Allow me." Mrs. Stone opened her palm and he handed the pearl over. "Prepare yourself, and remember—they are expecting me to show up at the gates." She closed her eyes and spoke in a firm voice: "I am coming!" Augum imagined the words booming on the other end. She opened her eyes and handed the pearl over, giving a slight nod.

Bridget gave his elbow a squeeze. "Good luck," she whispered.

SEVER BRONNY

He looked over the old instruction scroll and the teleportation scroll one last time before taking a deep breath. This was it—Haylee's life now depended entirely on him.

He closed his eyes and allowed himself to see through the Orb of Orion, taking in all the details— the stone block walls, wet from a leaky ceiling; the single mocking Endyear candle that sputtered, almost at its end; the four remaining guards positioned near Haylee; and Erika issuing commands to soldiers out of view.

"... and be sure to inform Lord Sparkstone of the crone's words," she finished saying, earrings jingling. She yanked up Haylee's chin. "Your wait is almost over, my sweet dove of a traitor." Haylee stared at her with distant red eyes. When Erika let go of her chin, her head fell forward limply.

Augum guessed the orb sat on a table.

Go forward, he commanded.

Nothing.

Fly. Go up and forward. Move. Then he realized he had to picture the orb doing that very thing. He commanded it to roll forward—and it worked! The orb rolled, falling off the pedestal. For a moment, Augum feared it smashing on the ground like glass, yet it bounced instead. Erika turned around just in time to catch it. She gaped at it stupidly.

"Your Ladyship," one of the guards said. "What is happening?"

"I don't know ... it has never *moved* before."

Augum ignored them. He had to get Haylee to touch the orb just as he finished the trigger words for Group Teleport. But would the spell work *through* the orb like that? There was only one way to find out ...

Erika's eyes suddenly widened. "We have to get this thing out of here!" But just as she began to move, Augum used his Shine extension—Shock. Erika yelped and let go of the orb. It bounced again. One of the guards caught it, but Augum was ready. He imagined himself shoving at the air.

"Baka!"

The guard was sent sprawling, the force sending the orb flying backward into a corner. Erika raised her palm and yanked at the orb using Telekinesis.

Lock, Augum thought, and the orb froze in midair. Erika tried jerking her hand but the orb stayed in place.

"Get in here and help me!" she screamed at the guards, never taking her eyes off the orb. This was it, Augum had to do it now or lose Haylee forever—

"Centeratoraye xao xen!"

The fluttering of the candle slowed. Every detail of the room stood out in sharp contrast—the unpolished surface of the floor; the arched doorway with its keystone; the splash of water on Erika's hide boots. His thinking clarified as if his mind had previously been working through fog. Everything became simple and understandable.

Unlock, he thought. The orb started to fall. Erika was moving her lips to cast another spell.

"Grau!" Augum yelled, making the motion in his mind. The room crashed with the sound of thunder. The puddles on the floor vibrated as the candle snuffed. The guards dove to the ground, hands over their ears, before darkness enveloped the room.

There was a cool moment of ringing silence.

"Shyneo," Erika said, hand erupting in flame.

"Haylee, get the orb!" Augum yelled, but one of the guards had grabbed her, soon joined by another. They picked her up and were about to carry her from the room.

Augum sensed he only had one chance at this. He remembered how the orb recoiled after casting Push and thought to use the same principle, this time with Telekinesis. He reached out arcanely and yanked the lead soldier dragging Haylee. The orb shot straight for him, slamming into his chest and falling right into Haylee's lap. She wrapped her hands around it just as Augum began reciting the complex arcane phrase that would trigger the Group Teleport spell.

Yet just as he neared its completion, another pair of hands encircled the orb, trying to yank it from Haylee's grip. He glimpsed the cuffs of a red robe as everything began glowing hot white. A wind kicked up as he felt himself being pulled away.

Then the air crunched and everything collapsed on itself.

THE SINGHS

Augum opened his eyes. He stared at the world with the mind of a simple child. Shapes and colors were all that interested him. Movement was too complex, but there was a lot of it. Sound was unknown and unintelligible.

As time passed, he slowly became aware he was lying on a wooden floor. The movement sharpened as did the pain in his head. He felt queasy and weak. Someone had their arm around his shoulders, someone with raven hair, dark eyes and freckles.

"Take your time, Aug," the girl said. "Everything's under control here."

There was the sound of a muffled struggle. "Help me tie her up, Jengo," an older ebony-skinned man said to a towering youth.

Augum rubbed his head. It throbbed along to the beat of his heart, a familiar pain he vaguely understood happened when he pushed himself arcanely.

Eventually the girl helped him sit up and fed him a cup of water, brushing hair aside from his sweaty forehead.

"What happened?" he mumbled. "Where am I?"

"You're just experiencing the side effects of Centarro," said a cinnamon-haired girl sitting across from him. "Everything's all right. She's restrained."

Who's restrained? What was she talking about?

The shapes in the room came into focus and began to look familiar and comprehensible. That was a statue over there; a chair over here; a settee; a hearth; two ebony-skinned men—father and son; an old woman—Nana—his great-grandmother. She was casting spells on another woman tied in a chair, wearing red robes. That woman …

That woman was Erika Scarson!

Things quickly became clear. Mr. Goss bumbled along helping Mr. Okeke and Jengo clean up the room, the contents of which lay strewn about as if a small tornado had barreled through. Haylee slept on the settee, golden hair matted with blood. Bridget covered her with one of their Dramask blankets. The pumpkin-sized Orb of Orion sat on a pillow on the floor—it had made the trip back.

Leera's gaze was locked on Augum. "You did it," she whispered, smiling.

"She is subdued," Mrs. Stone said at last, reaching for Mr. Goss. "Please take me to a bed, I must rest now."

"This way, Mrs. Stone," Mr. Okeke said, leading them to Jengo's bedroom.

Jengo stood behind Erika's struggling form, hands tied behind her to a chair. She was looking about with vacant eyes, mouth screaming silence.

"She's blind, deaf and mute," Bridget said. "Soon as she arrived, Mr. Okeke and Mr. Goss jumped on her, while Mrs. Stone cast some spells."

Augum glanced to Haylee's still form. "How is she?"

"Mrs. Stone put her into a healing sleep. She won't wake until tomorrow. Everything seems to have worked out."

"What do we do with Auntie Erika?" Leera asked, refilling Augum's cup from a skin of water. "Drop her in a deep well maybe?"

"You know we can't do that," Bridget said with an admonishing frown. "We have to keep her prisoner or something. Maybe conduct a trial, I don't know."

"I was kidding," Leera said, adding under her breath, "sort of."

Jengo brought a small basket of dried fruit. "Keeping her prisoner is extremely risky. It's already amazing we didn't all die in this skirmish. Besides, she's a warlock—there'd have to be safeguards." He examined a broken nail. "This is sure to get infected …"

Bridget made a dismissive wave. "You'll be fine. Anyway, there used to be warlock trials in the court of Blackhaven. Until the Legion took over."

Leera scowled at Erika's struggling form. "Well we can't drag her along with us."

"I'm sure Nana will know what to do." Augum pawed at the bowl, snatched a dried apricot, and popped it in his mouth.

"Can I at least slap her?" Leera asked.

Bridget gave her a disbelieving look.

Leera turned to Augum. "Come on, just once."

He chuckled. "Only if I can do the same."

"*Augum Stone—*"

"Uh-oh, she used your full name," Leera whispered.

"I was kidding." He shrugged. "Sorry, Lee. No slaps. Kicks, though—"

Bridget straightened.

"All right all right!" He sighed. "No kicks either …"

Leera pouted her lips. "Never get to have any fun!" She brightened almost immediately. "By the way, Aug, we heard everything you said, but we didn't see how you actually did it. Want to tell us what happened?"

"The memories are kind of vague, but I'll try." He relayed what he remembered.

"... so we *can* move the orb," Bridget muttered when he finished, tapping her chin. "That could really come in useful."

"Warlocks have such neat toys," Jengo said. "Just make sure it doesn't roll over your foot. Gangrene sets in real quick on toes."

Leera narrowed her eyes at him.

"What? It's *true*."

"Want to try looking through it?" Bridget asked.

"No way, I don't want it to possess my soul or anything."

"Are you sure you want to become a warlock?" Leera asked. "I think you'd make a better chandler."

"Do I hear talk of candle making?" Mr. Goss said, returning from Jengo's room, Mr. Okeke just behind.

"My honor is being maimed, Mr. Goss—they question my sincerity in becoming a warlock."

"As long as it is in good fun," Mr. Okeke said. "Humor is a great healer."

Leera shook her head. "The Legion must be *so* angry. Not only did they fail to get the scion, but we got Haylee *and* the orb back."

"And her," Augum said, thumbing at Erika. "Maybe she can be useful somehow." He gave Bridget an imploring look.

"No, we are not making her our slave," Bridget said. "She's not a puppy you can train."

Leera raised a finger. "Ah ha—a leash! Perfect, Bridge!"

Bridget gave her a look.

"No leash? Ugh, I can't live anymore." Leera pretended to choke herself.

"Dramatic," Bridget said tonelessly.

VALOR

"That's not what I meant," Augum said. "Maybe Mrs. Stone can interrogate her or something. You know ..." He grinned while making prodding and clipping motions.

"Augum Stone, I do believe you are getting to be as foul as—"

"—there's that full name again," Leera said, wagging her finger at him. " 'Augum Stone, if you don't start behaving'—"

Leland moaned loudly, hands over his ears.

Bridget put him on her lap. "All right all right, we'll stop." She tickled him and he squealed.

Mr. Okeke glanced out the window. "I do not believe it ..." He turned to them and smiled.

Everyone immediately scrambled for the door. Laughter ensued when the group got jammed in the doorframe, only to explode out into a pile of bodies.

Patches of dark red sky poked through quickly moving fluff. It had stopped snowing, though the wind was still shiver-inducing. It was only dusk, but if it continued like this, it meant the Star Feast was on!

The girls celebrated, but Augum had mixed feelings. He was looking forward to the feast yet dreaded seeing Leera dancing with Jengo.

"I shall go to the village and see what the elders say," Mr. Okeke said, retrieving his coat before striding off. Everyone else piled back inside where the girls danced with each other, singing *A Farmer's Daughter and the Heir*. Erika struggled feebly in the background. Mr. Goss stood beside her just in case, beaming and poking his nose, still forgetting he lacked spectacles.

When the song finished, Mr. Goss' face creased with worry. "I am not entirely sure it would be a good idea for you lot to attend." When the trio gave him horrified looks, he added, "Just in case you are recognized."

"Mr. Goss, you *must* let us attend," Leera pleaded. "Our spirits would be crushed, and we desperately need a bit of cheer in these hostile times."

Deftly done, Augum thought. Even Bridget looked impressed.

Mr. Goss rubbed his chin. "I suppose it is important to keep one's spirits up, and I do not recall hearing an objection from Mrs. Stone … Oh, all right."

The girls hugged him. "Thank you, Mr. Goss!"

"Surprised Haylee hasn't woken up," Augum said as the dancing and singing resumed.

"It's an arcane slumber," Bridget said, ponytail swinging. "She'd sleep through Slam right now."

"And how long will the blind and mute enchantments last on Erika?"

"Don't know, but I doubt Mrs. Stone would have left her with us if she remained a danger."

"Nice to have the orb back," Leera said, letting Bridget go with a twirl. "But now we don't have a way to spy on the Legion."

Bridget collapsed onto a bench at the table. "Wouldn't have done much good seeing as they knew we were watching."

Leland got up and prodded her, moaning.

"I'm too tired, little one," Bridget replied, blowing a strand of hair from her eyes, "you best find a new dance partner."

Leland groped along the table, fumbling with the big blue tome. He moaned again.

"You want to continue studying?"

Leland nodded.

"Jengo, want to join us?"

And so Bridget gave a lesson on Telekinesis, demonstrating again and again the motion and concentration required. Unfortunately for Jengo and Leland, neither was able to move the cup Bridget had placed as their target—Jengo because he feared dying in a horrible explosion and Leland because he was far too young. Nonetheless, she indulged both like a patient schoolteacher.

Meanwhile, Leera practiced her 1st and 2nd degree on her own while Augum rested in one of the pine armchairs. He had had enough training for one day, and besides, he was feeling conflicted. On the one hand, he had saved Haylee, but on the other, Leera was going to the Star Feast with Jengo. It hurt his feelings she was going with someone else.

At last, Mr. Okeke returned, beaming. "I declare the Star Feast to commence this very late evening!"

Everyone released a shout of joy, Augum only half-heartedly so.

"And now we must work," Mr. Okeke continued, "for there is much food to cook and prepare. I am afraid we are going to need all hands."

Bridget and Leera were more than willing to help with chopping and cooking, while Augum volunteered to peel and boil the potatoes. As he slaved away, chin on one knee, he noticed Leera had been shooting him tentative sidelong looks. He turned his body and ignored her. If she was wondering how he felt about her going with Jengo, she needn't bother.

Bridget gave him a pointed look as she handed him a wooden spoon for the potatoes. "Don't *forget*."

His brows rose. "Well I wasn't going to use my hands."

Bridget rolled her eyes and returned to mixing sauce for the chicken they were going to roast over the fire. Leera looked up from her job of cracking eggs Jengo had brought from the market. Augum saw a fleeting glimpse of hurt feelings there, before turning back to the potato pot. He gave it an angry stir. Why was *she* acting all hurt? Because he wasn't dancing joyfully the she chose Jengo over him?

A knock came at the door. Mr. Okeke wiped his hands on a cloth and walked over, beaming. "I wonder who this could be …" He opened the door only a crack, no doubt to prevent someone seeing a tied-up person in a chair.

"… Panjita thinks it rude Mr. Okeke does not allow her and her daughter entry on such an important evening."

Jengo suddenly scrambled out of the kitchen area for the door.

"Quick," Mr. Goss said to the trio, bolting over to Erika, "help me take her into Mr. Okeke's room—"

They dragged the kicking woman, chair and all, into the other room while Mr. Okeke stalled Ms. Singh and her daughter at the door. Jengo hovered over his father's shoulder, wringing his hands. Then they did the same for Haylee, who was much easier to carry. They placed her in Jengo's room with Mrs. Stone, on some cushions on the floor.

"Does Mr. Okeke want to murder Panjita with this cold?" Augum heard Ms. Singh say as the trio scurried back to the table. Mr. Okeke glanced back to make sure everything was all right before opening the door.

"Now, Mother, please don't forget to be kind," Priya said under her breath as her mother hobbled past, her cane "accidentally" landing on Mr. Okeke's foot.

"Please, um, this way," Jengo said, nervously gesturing to the living area. "I'll fetch some tea."

"Ah, tea," Ms. Singh said, "no doubt laced with some obscure Sierran poison to finish shivering Panjita off."

Ms. Singh stopped in her tracks when she spotted the trio gawking from the table. They immediately stood to greet her. She straightened an elaborately embroidered rose-colored silken shawl while glaring at Augum and Leera through thick spectacles.

"Panjita should not be surprised to find the young villains in the Okeke home. Though if a certain boy should look upon a certain daughter, Panjita's cane suffices as a wonderful weapon."

Augum's cheeks tingled. "How do you do, Ms. Singh," he said amiably, eyes anywhere but near Priya.

"Panjita does it well, whatever it is the youngling refers to."

Priya wore a long golden silk cloth wrapped around her waist and over one shoulder. A turquoise necklace hung around her neck. The jeweled studs in her lips and nose sparkled in the candlelight. Both women wore golden earrings and a great many golden bracelets.

Priya smiled at the trio, bowed her head slightly, and hovered by her mother, who had taken a seat on the settee, back rigid, cane on her lap.

"What honor brings Ms. Singh to my home?" Mr. Okeke asked. "I must apologize I am not yet dressed for the evening's celebration."

"Panjita believes Solian traditions are nothing short of superstition," Ms. Singh began, sighing. "However, her daughter, who is adamant on sending her mother to an early grave, demanded Panjita's acceptance. And so here Panjita and her daughter sit, in terrible agony of the question to come."

Mr. Okeke looked to the trio, no doubt as confused as Augum. What question?

"Father, I have invited Ms. Singh and her daughter here because I …" Jengo stole a furtive glance at Leera.

Here it comes, Augum thought miserably, he was going to ask Leera to the Star Feast. Though what that had to do with Panjita and Priya he hadn't the faintest idea.

Jengo cleared his throat for the third time. "Because I wish to ask … I wish to ask Ms. Singh for her daughter's hand in marriage."

Augum's stomach did a cartwheel. His face grew so hot he thought it would melt. Leera was staring at him and all he wanted to do was smack his forehead with his palm. He had been such a daft, clueless, stupid fool …

Ms. Singh, however, had an altogether different reaction. She immediately began choking as if having swallowed a large bug.

Mr. Okeke was not doing any better. "—I forbid it!" he kept saying, flattening his hand and slicing the air with it. "I absolutely forbid it. You are not old enough, Jengo, nor is the girl Sierran!"

Priya, who took hold of her mother and helped her overcome the sudden attack, kept her soft eyes on Jengo.

"No, not now, I mean, when I turn sixteen of course!" Jengo sputtered. "When I'm a man grown!"

"Jengo, son, have you completely lost your mind?" Mr. Okeke said, fingers pressed to his temples, eyes closed.

"This is absolutely unacceptable," Ms. Singh said, standing. "Panjita forbids her daughter to marry this … this young gangly demon. He is unfit, unworthy, *unsuitable!*"

Mr. Okeke straightened. "My son is hardly unfit, and it is Priya who is unsuitable—"

"How *dare*—"

Mr. Goss stepped in just as Ms. Singh began swinging her cane. "Now, Ms. Singh, please be reasonable—" but immediately took a whack to the stomach, buckling with a wheezing groan.

"Mother, stop! Now look what you've done!" Priya dove to Mr. Goss' side.

The trio only gaped while Leland moaned, one hand holding Bridget's.

VALOR

There was another knock on the door. Mr. Okeke, who was giving his son a furious look, strode to get it.

"Uh, hello, Mr. Okeke … is … is Bridget there?" asked a husky voice.

"She is, now please excuse me." He gave Bridget a perplexed look before continuing to berate his son.

Leera elbowed Bridget. "Is that …?"

Bridget stiffened, smoothed her robe, and strode over to the door, leaving Augum to stand awkwardly beside Leera.

Meanwhile, a scuffling noise came from the other room.

"Panjita demands to know what that infernal racket is! Do the Okeke's raise animals in their home like common peasants?"

"Now, Ms. Singh, you're just hearing things," Jengo said as politely as possible, while Priya waved at him not to say things like that.

"How dare the sun-blackened stilt walker insult Panjita!"

"Mother—"

"Jengo, I'm sorry about what happened between us," Chaska said, stepping through the doorway. He wore a finely woven royal blue tunic fringed with gold, and white-knuckled a bouquet of pine branches neatly tied with red and gold ribbon.

Jengo gave him a bewildered look while dodging Ms. Singh's cane.

"Oh, no, these are for Bridget." Chaska's hands trembled as he extended the bouquet to her.

"Thank you," Bridget mumbled, giving a small curtsy, blushing cherry red. She took the branches. "Just, uh … ignore the, uh …"

Augum had never seen Bridget tongue tied and couldn't resist exchanging a look with Leera.

"I'll just put these away," Bridget said quickly, setting the branches into a jar while the kerfuffle behind continued unabated.

"No one's given her flowers before," Leera whispered to Augum. "Or whatever you call ... *that*."

"Branches?" he asked.

They snorted a laugh together. When Chaska looked over, they pretended to be busy with the commotion. Soon as Chaska returned his attention to Bridget, Augum thought to take his chance.

He leaned into Leera's ear. "Will you go to the Star Feast with me?" desperately hoping she would say yes.

She gaped at him a moment, reared back, and clocked him in the shoulder. "What took you so long!"

"What! I thought you were going with Jengo! After all, what about that secret conversation you had with him at the table?"

"*That?* He told me he was going to ask Priya to the Star Feast—"

"Oh ... so ... are you going to come with me or—?"

"You can be such a ... Ugh, of *course* it means I'll go with you, I'm just so mad at you right now!" but her eyes sparkled and there was an upward twist to the corner of her lips. In that moment, Augum was the happiest he had ever been. For the first time ever, he actually asked a girl to go to the Star Feast with him—and she said yes! Well, kind of—she did punch him—hard—in the shoulder, but he knew what she meant, and besides, that's just who she was.

He was so full of joy it didn't even bother him to see Ms. Singh barrel into Mr. Okeke's room on sheer stubbornness, dragging everyone along with her, shouting, "Panjita demands to know why there is a woman tied up in a chair! What kind of demon house is this!"

THE STAR FEAST

It took a grumpy Mrs. Stone, having been unable to sleep through the chaos, to explain why a woman sat tied to a chair in Mr. Okeke's room. She tersely told Chaska, Priya and Ms. Singh that the woman in question was part of the Legion, and if loosed, would bring destruction to the entire village and everyone in it.

Muted introductions only came later, and although Ms. Singh initially expressed skepticism this was *the* Anna Atticus Stone, she fell quiet after seeing her cane float to the ceiling for trying to give Mr. Goss a final whack (for good measure of course).

When Mr. Okeke began yelling at his son anew, he found himself muted much like Erika, albeit for a short time, only so that Mrs. Stone could get a word in edgewise.

Mrs. Stone eventually succeeded in herding everyone to sit at the table, Chaska included. She stood at its head, glaring at everyone in turn, staff in hand. "I daresay some in this room have taken leave of their senses. I hope we can continue this discussion in a civil manner befitting our ages."

"Panjita thinks this most unusual, and to be treated like a child is—"

"Ms. Singh," Mrs. Stone began, flexing her jaw, "let us speak on the subject at hand. Now as I understand it, neither you nor Mr. Okeke approve of the marriage of this girl to this boy. Is that not true?"

"I forbid it—" Mr. Okeke said.

"It is simply out of the question—" Ms. Singh said at the same time.

"And am I correct in understanding that Jengo and Priya are both under the age of sixteen?"

Jengo and Priya both cast their eyes down as Mr. Okeke and Ms. Singh crowed in agreement, gesticulating to accent the point.

"Now, Jengo, what would stop you from marrying Priya when you *do* turn of age?"

Jengo looked up suddenly then stared into Priya's worried eyes. "Nothing, nothing in all of Solia. We'll run away together if we have to, we've already talked about it—"

Mrs. Stone raised a hand to silence Mr. Okeke and Ms. Singh's protestations. "And Priya, what would stop you—"

"—nothing in all of Sithesia!" Priya said, face flushed.

There was a marked silence as Mr. Okeke and Ms. Singh briefly exchanged a look. Mrs. Stone watched them a moment before continuing. "Is it worth losing your son and daughter to prevent their obvious love for each other, a love that, as it seems to me, shall continue regardless of your disapproval?"

Mr. Okeke cleared his throat and looked upon his son, sitting quietly, a great hope in his eyes. "Although I am not comfortable with the arrangement ... perhaps, in time, I will learn to ..." The man swallowed. "... to appreciate your choice, Son."

VALOR

Ms. Singh, too, looked at her daughter, who stared back in distress, wringing her hands under the table. "Panjita feels this a great dishonor to the family name—"

Her daughter covered her mouth with her hands, tears streaming from her eyes.

"*However*, Panjita also realizes we live in a distant land, with very …" she glanced around distastefully, "… *different* people." She straightened. "Whether Panjita likes it or not, Solia is now the Singh home, and as much as this match unsettles Panjita, she, too, will attempt to … understand it."

Priya melted. "Oh, Mother—"

"Good, it is settled then," Mrs. Stone said. "I can trust you to all keep the secret of what you have seen in the other room to yourselves, for we live in dangerous times, and I am sure none of us want the Legion razing Milham to the ground." She glared at them. "Now I will return to a much-needed rest, and if anyone wakes me for anything short of an apocalypse, I shall turn them into a goat where they stand." She stared a moment longer, making sure there was not one iota of dissent, before shuffling off to Jengo's room.

Jengo and Priya kept stealing furtive but victorious glances at each other, while Bridget gave the bulky Chaska a friendly smile. He returned it, face reddening.

Mr. Goss cleared his throat delicately. "Perhaps I shall return to fixing apple pie for tonight's feast. Leland, come along and help your father."

Leland moaned, got up from the table and pawed his way over to the kitchen.

Everyone else slowly stood, smoothing their attire or fixing their hair.

"Ms. Singh," Mr. Okeke began in a somewhat strained tone, "may I invite you to sit and have some tea?"

Ms. Singh looked about to protest but caught the eye of her daughter, who was making an imploring face. She sighed. "Panjita will sit with Mr. Okeke, but he is yet to prove he is not a demon."

Mr. Okeke seemed to accept that was as good as it was going to get right now and gracefully led Ms. Singh to the settee.

Now that the adults had gone off to chat or make food, the youths sat back down at the table.

"Chaska," Jengo began, towering over everyone even while sitting, "I didn't have a chance to say this earlier, but I accept your apology. My wound was grievous and I endured great pain but—oof!" (Priya had apparently given him a kick under the table), "uh, right, everything's fine now between us is what I mean."

Chaska glanced to Bridget quickly before dropping his eyes. "And I apologize for saying those things about your mother."

Bridget smiled before glancing at Augum. "You know, Aug, I love you like a brother, but you can be quite thick sometimes—"

"—yes, he can be." Leera nodded vigorously.

Augum rubbed his face. "I know I know ..."

"I hate to break up the occasion," Mr. Goss said, "but there is still quite a lot of work to do. I am sure there will be plenty of time to socialize at the feast tonight."

Everyone immediately scrambled to help, including Chaska, who gave Bridget a hand with the vegetables. Leera mashed the potatoes with Augum while Jengo and Priya worked alongside Mr. Goss, occasionally stealing glances at their parents, deep in strained, but polite, conversation.

The night moved along until at last all the food sat prepared before them. Everyone was starving for, as per tradition, they had all skipped supper. It took a lot of willpower for Augum not to sneak a bite. Leera repeatedly attempted to strip the honey-roasted chicken of one of its legs. "But it's got *honey*," she whispered when Bridget gave her a disapproving look.

Mr. Goss, meanwhile, made sure Erika remained tied. "Would not want her getting loose now, would we?" he said cheerfully, pressing the bridge of his nose out of habit.

"I will need assistance bringing our contribution of food, Mother," Priya said.

"Panjita's daughter is *not* to go unattended. I will—"

"That is hardly necessary, Ms. Singh," Jengo said," I will escort your daughter with the utmost dignity."

Ms. Singh scowled at him. "Should the young demon lay a single hand on Panjita's daughter—"

"*Mother*—"

"I promise to be most civil, Ms. Singh."

Ms. Singh sniffed. "Very well, Priya has her mother's leave to abandon her to this villainous and barbaric household."

Priya rolled her eyes. "Thank you, *Mother*."

Jengo opened the door for Priya and they left, suppressing giggles.

"Let us pack everything into baskets now," Mr. Okeke said. He fetched a bundle of them and laid them on the benches. The trio, Leland, Mr. Goss and Mr. Okeke then stuffed them with food while Ms. Singh sourly inspected the ebony nightmare carvings.

Bridget and Leera disappeared into Jengo's room, and when they emerged with their hair done up and pinned with white ribbon, Augum and Chaska stood gaping like fools. Bridget's was in a twisted ponytail, and there was emerald eyeshadow around her eyes. Leera's raven hair had a light curl to it and she had smoky eyeliner that somehow accented her sharp brows. Her freckles sparkled with what Bridget proudly called "pixie dust".

Leera twirled gracefully. "So ... what do you think?"

When Augum and Chaska couldn't get a word out, Mr. Goss and Mr. Okeke promptly stood.

"Marvelous—!"

"Most charming—!"

Both seemed to hint for Augum and Chaska to say something, *anything*.

Chaska swallowed. "Very pretty, Bridget."

Bridget reddened. "Thank you."

Leera looked expectantly at Augum.

"Nice, um, ribbon."

Leera gaped.

"Yes, a very nice ribbon indeed," Mr. Goss said, nodding along with Mr. Okeke.

Augum wanted to punch himself in the face. Nice ribbon? *Nice ribbon?*

Luckily, Bridget whispered something into Leera's ear and she brightened forgivingly.

Priya and Jengo soon returned carrying two covered baskets apiece. As tradition demanded, everyone assembled around the Endyear candle.

Mr. Okeke glanced out the dark window. "The council should have the tables ready by now. It is almost time."

"Shall we sing *The March of the Stars*?" Mr. Goss asked.

"A wonderful idea, Albert," Mr. Okeke said. "I shall begin. *Let all who dwell beneath the skies—*"

"I hate this song," Leera muttered as everyone joined in.

"*—gather round to feast and favor—*"

"Barely know it," Augum whispered, struggling with the words. Sir Westwood hadn't been very fond of singing and the Pendersons only knew vulgar tunes.

"*—duck and goose and chicken turkey pies—*"

"Kill me now," Leera muttered.

"*—every nuance will be savored, for the stars never cease marching—*"

"Here comes the fun part," Leera said tonelessly, readying to make the traditional gestures that went with the song. "*Not for you—*" She jabbed Augum in the chest. "*Not for me—*" She pointed listlessly at herself. "*No, they never cease marching ...*"

VALOR

The chorus was repeated, Augum even managing to poke Leera in the arm, always aware of his burning cheeks.

The group went on to sing some notable favorites, including *It's Beginning to Look a lot Like Endyear*, *All I Want for Endyear is Boar Pie* (Leera made sure to tell Augum how much she hated boar pie), *A Maiden's Love*, and *A Widow's Heart*. During the last two, Mr. Goss and Mr. Okeke's eyes watered while Leera stepped closer to Augum.

At long last, with less than an hour to midnight, the expected time of the feast, festive singing floated in from outside. Mr. Okeke opened the door, revealing a throng of people slowly walking by holding baskets, blankets, steaming covered dishes, torches, candles, and wreaths of ivy. They sang traditional Endyear melodies, the young belting out altered versions, the old singing with aplomb.

The group gathered their things and joined the procession, which wound its way past the Okeke home along a path through the towering snowy evergreens. A full moon made the great sagging branches visible and cast long thin shadows through the pristine forest.

Augum snuck peeks at the clear and starry sky, noting how the wind had calmed. He still had a hard time believing he was going to the Star Feast with a girl. With *Leera*, whose cheeks sparkled like the snow.

"Who are you looking for, Chaska?" Bridget asked, walking by his side.

"Oh, no one …"

"No one? Not your father?"

Chaska shrugged bulky shoulders. "Guess it'd be all right to see him before I went. Oh, here, let me carry that for you." He gently took Bridget's basket, which she had been lugging with both hands.

"Thank you," Bridget said, smiling sheepishly.

Chaska now carried two baskets and both seemed to defeat his posture, yet he instantly straightened every time Bridget glanced his way.

"Here." A grinning Leera dumped her basket into Augum's arms, giving little care to the fact he was already burdened with blankets *and* a basket brimming with vegetables.

We'll see about that, Augum thought, mustering his concentration. Soon everyone, Chaska included, was giving him admiring looks for the way he seemed to effortlessly carry such a large load.

"Now you're just showing off," Leera said, snatching the basket back, mumbling, "Cheater …"

"So where are you going, Chaska?" Jengo asked, trailing just behind with Priya.

"He's going on his nemana." Bridget then went on to explain what it meant.

"I know in Nodia a boy has to hunt a red bear," Augum said.

"In some parts of Sierra it's a lion," Jengo said. "What a horrible way to die. Wonder which one's worse …"

"Glad all we Solians have to do is turn sixteen," Leera mumbled.

"What, you mean the womanhood and manhood feasts aren't embarrassing enough?" Bridget asked. "I'd rather take the lion."

"At least we get presents." Leera made a face. "Then there's all the pressure to get married. I plan to be nowhere near a village when I turn sixteen. Year and four months to go."

"Year and a month for me, give or take," Augum said.

Bridget smiled. "Year, six months and a few days."

Leland moaned while holding Mr. Goss' hand.

"Seven years and ten months for my son."

That drew chuckles from everyone.

"But lest we forget," Mr. Goss threw in, "if you live in a Legion town, sixteen is the year of conscription."

That sobering thought silenced them.

VALOR

The trail narrowed and became rockier. It dipped and rose over steepening hills, until they walked single file, torches ablaze, the night filled with cheerful song. After climbing one last tall hill, they spilled out onto a hilltop glade surrounded by stubby evergreens, branches bent with snow. The vastness of the night sky presented itself like a great luminous canvas. The Muranians, dimly lit by the moon, curved around them like some distant but enormous half-finished wall.

People milled around long trestle tables and benches. Torches decorated with ivy and holly dotted the clearing. As tradition dictated, three large central fires burned in a triangle in homage to the ancient witch. The flames of each fire licked at a pig, four chickens and a boar, all slowly turning on spits manned by village youths dressed in fur coats. Folks placed their plates and flatware on the tables, already brimming with candles, ivy, and evergreen branches.

Mr. Goss, Leland, Mr. Okeke, and Ms. Singh all walked ahead to reserve a table for the group, while the youths stayed behind to gawk at the sky, baskets at their feet.

"Beautiful ..." Priya whispered, leaning close to Jengo.

"Everyone's dressed so pretty," Leera said, head swiveling to take in the gowns, doublets and cloaks. "And look at us—still wearing the same charred and patched apprentice robes ..."

Jengo smiled. "It's a mining town and it's Endyear, I don't think anyone minds. Besides, to them, they look like school robes."

Leera grimaced. "They kind of *are* school robes."

Augum mustered his courage. "I think you look nice," and immediately turned away, feeling her stare. He pretended to inspect the jagged outline of the Muranians.

Bridget, too, glanced at the looming rock, blacker than the night. "They look so close, yet they're so far away. It's scary to think we'll have to climb them soon."

"Is that what you were talking about earlier, that castle?" Chaska asked.

"Yes, Bahbell …"

" 'Gateway to hell'," Leera said.

"Why do you have to go there?" he pressed. "Is it some kind of nemana?"

"We have to find something to prevent a great evil," Bridget replied.

And find it before my father does, Augum thought.

Chaska scratched at his short milky hair. "If this Mrs. Stone is as powerful as you told me, why doesn't she just do it on her own?"

"Because she needs our help, Chaska," Bridget replied.

"She wants to train you in the old way," Jengo said, staring up at the stars. "The way before the academies, when apprentices learned by trial and adventure."

"How do you know that?" Bridget asked.

"It was in your book, the blue one, near the beginning in the history section."

"Ah, we've really got to read that thing …"

"I don't have two lifetimes to spare," Leera muttered.

Priya smiled and reached up to pinch Jengo's cheek. "My Jengo wants to become a warlock. How cute."

Leera scowled. "It's not 'cute', it's dangerous. Do you know how many apprentices—oof!"

Bridget had elbowed her, flashing a reprimanding look.

"Well, they deserve to *know*, don't they?"

"It's Endyear, Lee—"

Priya's face darkened. "Know what?"

"She's right, my sweet Priya. It's better for you to know. There is a great chance I shall die learning the arcane way—"

"*Slight* chance," Leera corrected.

"What's worse," Jengo continued, "is that nowadays warlocks are hunted by the Legion. When they're captured, they're given a choice—serve or die. The ones that serve are forced to convert to necromancy. If I do not perish in the training, I shall surely perish as a necromancer. I just hope it will be a noble death."

"Oh, Jengo." Priya looked up at the towering Sierran. "Then I shall be by your side every step of the way."

He met her gaze and smiled.

"Panjita is waiting for her ungrateful daughter!" Ms. Singh called from a distant table.

"We better go," Jengo said. He reached out to hold Priya's hand but she immediately withdrew, whispering, "Not in public!"

"Oh, right ..."

They joined a table consisting of innkeeper Huan, a woman with pale skin and dirty blonde hair, and a youth with a striking resemblance to both of them. Ms. Singh, Priya, Jengo and Mr. Okeke took a seat beside them; Mr. Goss, Leland, Leera, Augum, Bridget and Chaska opposite.

Everyone exchanged the requisite pleasantries and Endyear well wishes. The singing continued throughout, as did the steady arrival of villagers, petering out now to only a few stragglers. Finally, a dark-skinned old man with a short black beard wandered to stand between the three fires. He wore a full-length cotton-white robe cinched at the waist, a loose white headdress, and a golden sash across his chest. He held an ornate golden lantern, inside of which sat a fat candle, more than two-thirds gone. Augum surmised it to be Milham's official Endyear candle as every village had one.

"That's Mr. Hanad Haroun," Jengo whispered. "He's originally from Sierra, but now he's the senior town elder."

Mr. Haroun raised a hand and the singing died as heads turned in his direction. "Welcome to all who reside in our little mining village of Milham!" His voice was gravelly and travelled well. "And welcome to those passing through. On behalf of the other elders, I impart Endyear blessings upon you all."

"Happy Endyear!" the crowd chanted.

"I start my yearly speech, which I promise will be short—" some among the crowd tittered, "—with dark tidings." Everyone fell silent. "As many of you know, we have recently had a visit from a Legion herald." Many people hissed, those at the trio's table loudest of all.

Mr. Haroun raised his hand again. "All able-bodied men were to assemble in Eastspear. As you look around at your loved ones, your friends and neighbors, you will note many men did not heed this call. Help them be strong. Let us be united."

The crowd muttered in agreement.

Augum looked around at the rapt faces and realized this kind of talk was highly treasonous. He suddenly feared what had happened at Sparrow's Perch happening here.

"Regardless, the Legion grows stronger every day," Mr. Haroun continued. "This we know. They march eastward to Tiberra in search of war. This, too, we know. They promise us eternal life if we give them seven ancient artifacts. They call this the 'Great Quest'. Alas, this we also know."

Augum nodded solemnly. Eternal life was supposed to come from the Leyan plane, a place his father intended to conquer. Yet Thomas Stone—Augum's great-grandfather and Mrs. Stone's husband—left that plane only to age before their eyes, finally dying in Augum's arms. He did it to prove to them that the power of eternal life couldn't be brought into the mortal world. His great-grandfather had given his *life* to make a point, and Augum swore to himself his sacrifice would not be for nothing.

Mr. Haroun glanced down at the snow as he absently stroked his pointed beard. "But what we do not know, my dear friends, is how it will affect us. There may come a day when the Legion rides into our town to snatch men for their wars. They may also take our women to serve as unpaid servants—slaves, if you will. They may burn Milham to the ground for our impudence. Some of you have already born

VALOR

witness to such a thing." More nods among the crowd, including the trio and Mr. Goss.

"We send the Legion tokens of respect in the form of mead, gold and iron, but their thirst grows. Thus I say there may a come a time when we will have to decide our fate, for I know many of you would rather stand up for your neighbor than succumb to your enemy, and when a powerful force at last stands against the Legion, so, too, will we." At this, many cheered and whistled. Mr. Haroun let them go on a little bit, glancing around, the fire dancing in his eyes.

Augum suddenly recalled Lord Tennyson delivering a speech at the Sparrow's Perch naming ceremony. He remembered black-armored soldiers crashing through the woods riding great warhorses; crimson-armored death knights wielding great burning swords; his father in golden plate and sitting a deathly horse …

"Aug, you all right?" Leera whispered as Mr. Haroun went on. "Is there something in the trees?"

"I'm fine, thanks," he said, feeling the sweat on his brow.

Leera glanced at the same trees. "I remember it too."

He looked at her. There was fear in those dark eyes. "They won't come tonight," he said.

"How do you know?"

"They won't come …" but the truth was, he didn't know for sure, and now that he thought about it, those three fires acted like great beacons. He wanted to shout how dangerous this all was and that they should run back to town and arm themselves. As far as he knew, there were few soldiers here and no warlocks, and the only person capable of holding the Legion horde at bay lay sleeping back in the Okeke home.

"… and so I now conclude with heartfelt thanks. Thank you for your company, your spirit, your trust, and for such a prosperous year. Although it is not quite yet over, let us look back on it forever with fondness and gratitude before bidding it farewell." Mr. Haroun received a wine glass from a young helper. He raised it in the air. "In the tradition of those that came before us, let us play and let us eat! Happy Endyear!"

"Happy Endyear!" called the crowd. Glasses clinked and flatware scraped on plates; bowls were emptied and the roasted meat divvied up; blessings and well wishes were heartily conveyed. Musicians played their instruments as games began to take place at the tables—Cuppers, Pass the Present, Old Man Mule, and Piggy Run, the latter two very popular with the children. Tables competed against each other in trivia. Men challenged each other to drinking competitions while the elderly played dice or cards.

The trio ate their fill and then ate some more, laughing at jokes and exchanging stories. Everyone seemed merry, and throughout, the stars twinkled overhead as the moon crept across the sky.

Eventually, Mr. Haroun once again strode to the center, a hand held high to silence the somewhat unruly crowd.

"And now, my dear friends, I ask that everyone who brought a partner ..." He raised a finger in anticipation of what he was to say next, "start the Endyear dance!" He began clapping his hands in rhythm, the crowd quickly joining in. The musicians took up the pace, playing *The Swinging Lantern*, a spritely tune to get people moving. Girls exchanged shy and giddy looks while boys asked for their hands. There were giggles and chortles, laughs and even cries of alarm as some of the younglings asked their counterparts to dance, only to be promptly denied with the words "Icky boys!".

Augum had never danced before and thought he'd rather be wrestling Dap or one of the Penderson brats right then. Nonetheless, seeing Chaska leave the table with Bridget and Jengo with Priya, lent him enough courage to stand before Leera and extend his hand.

"Leera Jones, will you dance with me?"

Leera beamed, glitter-dusted cheeks shining in the light of the fire. She took his hand and shrugged playfully. "If I have to."

Augum gave her a light punch on the arm. "Of course you have to."

"Hey now, is that any way to treat a lady?"

"You have another year and four months before you can call yourself a lady."

Leera sucked in her breath. "Ouch," but she was smiling.

He led her to the center, where couples already danced, and awkwardly placed his hands at her waist. They avoided looking at each other, but managed to keep a rhythm somewhat close to the tune that played.

His main concern was not to step on her feet. The last thing he wanted to do was make a total fool of himself. His cheeks seemed on fire, his heart felt like it was going to explode, and a vaguely familiar butterfly feeling fluttered in his stomach. He was awfully conscious of himself; of the way her hands gently held his neck; of every sound and nuance, as if he was under the influence of Centarro.

Now if only there *was* a spell that made him into a good dancer ...

When the dance ended, he felt it was far too soon, but as was proper and as Solian tradition dictated, they were to choose new partners from those that had not danced yet. They glanced at each other one last time before joining the crowd.

Leera asked Mr. Goss, Bridget asked Leland, and Augum, who could think of no one else, asked Ms. Singh. He immediately regretted that decision.

"If this demon child who purported to have interest in Panjita's daughter thinks Panjita would dance with him, he would be better off running into the woods and freezing to death."

Huan slapped his knee with laughter, almost spilling his drink in the process.

"That is so very rude, Mother!" Priya said. "Come, Augum, I have someone for you to dance with." She led him to an ebony-skinned girl around his age with long tightly-curled black hair. She wore a square-neckline green dress and a thin golden necklace. Her dignified parents looked on—the mother smiling, the father glaring. Augum had to do a double take at the father, who was none other than the village elder, Mr. Haroun.

"This is Malaika. Malaika, meet Augum."

Malaika curtsied and smiled, and soon Augum was dancing for the second time in his life. She had a confident poise to her and smelled like vanilla and honey. Yet he was so nervous to be dancing with a stranger that he did not say a single word to her.

"You're an awful dancer," Malaika said with a giggle. Before Augum could die from shame, she added, "But I can teach you. Here."

"Psst, look at Leera!" Bridget said as she danced with Mr. Goss, who kept tripping over her feet and apologizing.

Augum used the opportunity to steal his attention away from Malaika—Leera twirled a moaning Leland like a maple seed. The little tyke tore free, stumbled and fell. She giggled, helped him up, pinched his cheek, and continued at a more leisurely pace. She seemed so carefree and ... pretty.

Augum wondered what she'd look like in a more formal dress like the one Malaika wore. The thought almost made him burst out laughing. He was so used to her wearing either a drab nightgown or the same apprentice robe he wore.

Leera happened to glance in his direction. When their eyes met, both quickly looked away.

Malaika gave up trying to show Augum how to dance—he was hopeless, mostly because his thoughts were so frazzled. After a change of song, Malaika curtsied and Augum bowed stiffly. Neither said a word, though she gave him a pleasant smile. Then he and Bridget joined up with Leera and Leland.

"She was awfully pretty, that girl," Leera said as they walked back to the table, Leland in her grip.

"Her name is Malaika," Augum said.

"Well she's a good dancer."

Suddenly, a miracle—Mr. Okeke somehow managed to convince Ms. Singh to dance with him. It was enough to get the entire table clapping.

"Panjita thinks her table ought to mind its own business!" Ms. Singh said. She then allowed Mr. Okeke to lead her to the dance area on the crook of his elbow.

Jengo danced with a quiet Bridget while Chaska danced with a chatty Leera. Augum's cheeks prickled every time he just "happened" to see her dancing in the big Henawa's arms.

Leera soon returned to plop down on the bench by Augum's side, full of smiles and giddy laughter. He recalled seeing maidens kissing knights in those old books of Sir Westwood's and wondered what it'd be like to kiss her.

She caught him staring and gave him a warm smile. He quickly looked away, mortified. "Wish we had more time," he mumbled.

"For what?"

"Oh, uh ... dancing." He wished everyone would arcanely disappear, at least for one dance.

She stood up and extended her hand. "Augum Stone, would you take this fair lady and dance with her?"

He gulped and leaned forward. "Are we allowed to dance *twice*?"

"That's just an old Endyear superstition." She gave a wry smile. "Besides, who's going to stop us?"

He took her hand. "In that case, my Lady, it would be a great pleasure," and he playfully led her to a more somber affair named *The Winds of Winter*.

Leera placed her hands on his shoulders. "This song's fit for a funeral. Who died around here?"

He could barely concentrate. She smelled faintly of blackberry and citrus. He thought his skin would surely burn through his robe. He even forgot to reply.

Suddenly she leaned back and gave him a troubled look. "Oh no, I'm so sorry, I didn't mean to—"

"—mean to what?"

"I mean, I wasn't referring to … you know …"

"Oh … Mya?" His stomach sank to his turnshoes. His grip loosened at her waist.

She stared at him stupidly before looking away, shaking her head. "I'm such an idiot—"

"No—" he said a little too quickly. "I mean, you're not an idiot at all." He wanted to say she was the cleverest girl he had ever met actually, and now that he had a chance to study the fineness of her raven hair, the way her mouth curled when she thought of something funny, the soft moonlight reflecting off her sparkling freckles, he realized she was the prettiest too.

But he dare not speak those thoughts aloud.

She looked him in the eyes as the song came to a darkly dramatic close. He felt his heart hammer, the blood rushing to his head. She was breathing very quickly too— her waist expanded and contracted under his sweaty palms, her skin almost as hot as his. Their faces inched closer together—

"Panjita thinks that most inappropriate!"

They recoiled apart—only to discover Panjita shooing off a large man with a slopping tankard.

"Just one kiss, m'lady—" the man garbled drunkenly.

"Panjita will give the mongrel the kiss of her cane!" She swung and this time her aim was true—*SMACK!*—right in the face. A tooth sailed out of the man's mouth, landing in his tankard. The table behind burst in laughter. Even the man cackled. Then to the crowd's amusement, he finished his ale in one gulp—swallowing his tooth.

"Panjita thinks this man a barbarian," she said, striding off as people howled with laughter.

"Well at least that was memorable," Leera muttered, looking a little dejected.

Bridget cleared her throat directly behind Augum. "Hey, are you forgetting something?"

Leera and Augum paled.

Bridget extended her hand. "Mind if I steal him? We haven't danced yet."

"Of course I don't mind," Leera said quickly, and wandered off.

No, wait! Augum wanted to say.

Bridget placed her hands on his shoulders as a new song began.

"Which one's this?" she asked.

"*Chivalry's Shining Armor*," he replied, remembering one of the few Sir Westwood enjoyed. "How is Chaska?"

"Good, he's preparing himself for his nemana." She looked down. "You're dancing too stiffly. Here." She adjusted his hands on her waist and kicked his right foot. "Lead with that one. And for the love of everything good, relax."

"I thought I *was* relaxed."

"Trust me, you weren't. There, better already."

Somehow he was able to follow Bridget's instructions through his frazzled thoughts.

"She looking over at us now?" Bridget asked.

He glanced past her shoulder. Leera immediately looked away.

"Yes."

"She likes you."

He wanted to say he liked her back, but it seemed impossible just then.

Bridget sighed. "I hope we make it through this …"

"It's just a dance—"

"No, I mean—" she nodded at the dark outline of the Muranians, looming in the distance.

"Oh ... me too." His heart constricted as he thought of Mya. If the same thing happened to Leera or Bridget ... He swallowed hard, feeling his hands sweat again.

"We have to watch out for each other," Bridget said quietly, looking off into the night. Then she smiled and composed herself, sniffing sharply. "And when this is all done, we'll go to the academy together!"

"Right, definitely," he said, nodding along and smiling.

They finished the dance in quiet thought, comfortable in each other's embrace. Augum thought of the dark path that lay ahead; of Bahbell, the seat of the first great necromancer and the gateway to hell; and of the Occi ... cannibals or demons or whatever they were. It was enough for him to wish the Star Feast had no end.

As the festivities continued and the night cooled, half-finished plates began to outnumber finished ones. The musicians played slower and slower melodies as the elderly, families and children began taking their leave. They waved their goodbyes and imparted Endyear best wishes. Tables began to empty as youths cleaned up. The trio helped, packing the baskets and blankets.

"Time to go soon, Leland, it's a long walk back," Mr. Goss whispered, but Leland was already snoozing on the bench, curled up in a Dramask blanket.

Duties done, Augum sat content, watching the stars twinkle overhead, moved by the delicate fading melody of a stringed instrument played by someone who has known loss ...

As the tired musicians announced the last song of the night—*The Dimming Fire*, Bridget suddenly grabbed Chaska by the sleeve.

"Look—"

They turned to the forest where a snow-skinned man in traditional Henawa dress emerged, a bow and quiver slung over his shoulder. He was old and stooped, his perfectly groomed long milky hair touching his waist. Fur accented his shoulders, trousers and boots. Bones hung on necklaces around his neck, and beads decorated a long hide shirt painted with animals and leaves. In one hand he held a sack and in the other a hide shirt.

The man stopped before them.

"Father," Chaska said.

"I not always treat Chaska with respect," the man began, "but today, I say goodbye in the Henawa way." He handed Chaska the sack. "Food and family charms for nemana." He then unfurled the shirt, holding it steady before Chaska. It was marked with slashes, intricate beadwork, and burnt-in silhouettes of boar, horses, bears and axes. "Henawa war shirt." He handed it over and unslung the bow and quiver. "Henawa war bow."

Chaska swallowed as he took the items. He put the war shirt on over his royal blue tunic. "Father, I don't know what to say …"

"Chaska promise to return. Chaska promise to grow his hair long like Henawa."

Chaska's lip trembled. "I promise, Father … Achishi Zafu."

The old man gave a firm nod. "Father promise treat Chaska with respect. Chaska will be man. Chaska always father's son." He turned his attention to the trio. "Youngling maniye see Achishi Zafu before go." His gaze wandered back to his son. "Now Chaska stand by fire with Father," and walked to the dying flames.

Chaska gave Bridget a stiff nod and jogged off to join his father.

"I hope he's successful," Augum said, watching the back of the muscled Henawa as he and his father bowed their heads by the low fire.

Bridget watched after him for a time. "Me too …"

DECISIONS

Augum woke to a light wind whistling through the beams of the cabin. All was quiet except for the gentle crackling of the fire and the slow breathing of those asleep nearby.

As he lay in the dull morning light, he replayed the highlights of the Star Feast—the music, games, singing, food, and of course the dancing—especially with Leera. He took his time enjoying the memories, each forever seared into his mind.

Until he heard a jar being quietly opened. He raised his head to find his great-grandmother sitting at the table, gingerly spreading honey over toast, blue tome open beside a steaming cup of tea. She lifted the dripping slice to her lips and took a slow bite. "Mmm ..." she toned, licking her fingers one by one like a child enjoying stolen candy.

When she finished, he sat up and whispered, "Morning, Nana."

"Crimson heavens, you startled me, great-grandson. Morning to you."

"Sorry, Nana." He joined her at the table, still wearing Jengo's oversized nightgown. "Where's Erika?"

VALOR

Mrs. Stone replied without looking up from the book. "I brought her in to sleep with me so that Mr. Okeke could get some rest."

He glanced to Jengo's closed door. "She slept beside Haylee?"

"I brought Haylee out here."

He looked about and discovered Haylee bundled in a Dramask blanket on the settee. He had thought it was Leera, but Leera slept on the floor near Mr. Okeke's door.

"Telekinesis?"

Mrs. Stone nodded as she flipped a page.

"How many times have you read that book, Nana?"

"One of the keys to greatness is review, Augum. Cleverness only gets you so far."

He thought about that. "I'm not very clever …"

"It is as wise to know one's weaknesses as it is to know one's strengths."

He chewed on his finger, wondering what his strengths were. Fearing a lecture, he decided not to ask. His thoughts drifted to Haylee and the way she had hung from those chains, her bruised face, and how much it had upset him to see her like that.

"Haylee's suffered terribly," he said.

"She has indeed. You all have."

"Do you think … do you think there's anything I can do to help her? They murdered her parents and grandfather."

"Compassion, Augum. Compassion heals." She scanned the pages with a bony finger. "There is much to be done before New Year's. We have a very dangerous journey ahead of us."

He poured himself a cup of tea. "Nana, can I ask you something?"

"Mmm?"

"Why are you taking us with you?"

"I have not decided who I am taking with me as of yet, in point of fact, but I suspect I will not have to. First, however, I

195

shall conduct a memorial ceremony. The Unnameables know how much death you have all endured. Then I shall explain the dangers that lie ahead. Those that still desire to join me may do so."

"Even ... Leland?" he whispered.

"Sometimes those that seem to have the least power or strength actually have the most." She glanced at him. "Did you not want to go, is that it?"

"No, it's not that at all, I know for sure Bridget, Leera and I want to go, it's just that—well, we're not ... we're not very powerful."

"Is that so?" Her chin rose. "Never underestimate the power of friendship."

"But friendship can't stop a fireball or a giant elemental—"

She leaned forward a little. "Oh, but it can." She watched him struggle with the idea before straightening. "That aside, there is a link between you and your father, a link that I believe you may be able to exploit in due time."

"What kind of link?"

"Your mother. She is the only person he truly cared for. I suspect some of what he loved in her he sees in you. If you understand that link, you may be able to save many lives."

"You think he'd listen to anything I say?"

"That I do not know." She paused to reflect. "What I *do* know is that although there is great danger in the coming journey, there is also great opportunity. I taught at the Academy of Arcane Arts for thirty-five years. Never have I witnessed three apprentices develop as quickly as you, Bridget and Leera. Why do you think that is so?"

"I don't know ..."

"Do you think it is because you are blessed somehow, or destined for greatness, is that it?"

He shrugged. "Maybe it's because we're learning outside the classroom."

She raised a finger. "Precisely." She flipped to the beginning of the tome and read. " 'For it has been found, through considerable loss and considerable triumph, that those bold souls who train by the side of their mentors, outside of rooms or walls, upon the trails, mountains and plains of the land, with willful spirits and daring hearts, ascend the greatest heights in arcanery'."

That's what Jengo was talking about, he recalled.

"Opportunity for growth, Great-grandson. You are learning much, but you still have much more to learn before you are ready to face your father. In all of Sithesia, I believe you may perhaps be the only person able to stop him. If there is even a chance of that, I believe it worth the risks." She leaned toward him a little. "Do you take my meaning?"

He blinked. "Yes, Nana." In point of fact, he didn't. Him, stop the Lord of the Legion? Yes, the man was his father, but he was still a 20th degree warlock with three scions and the might of the Dreadnoughts behind him. Perhaps Nana had a little *too much* faith in him …

Suddenly he remembered holding a dying old man in his arms. "Great-grandfather's last words …! He said something to me, something about how one day I'll face my father, that the meeting will be a 'mirror of my fears'. He told me to train hard. Then, just before he died, he said 'it has been this way for eons', and, 'the blood of kin can …' " He looked into her eyes. "What did he mean, Nana? The blood of kin can what?"

"Thomas was my husband, yet he was also Leyan, and Leyans are privy to information we ordinary mortals are not. Nonetheless, that last line rings with familiarity. Let me see if I can recall where it is from." She closed her eyes in concentration. "Ah, 'When thy fallen can't be slain, when lion children rise again, when fires burn from east to west, blood of kin can vanquish death'." She opened her eyes. "It is an ancient witch poem from the time of Attyla the Mighty. Some call it prophecy. Others say it was merely a testament to history long passed. I lean toward the latter. Our beliefs become reality, even if we have to delude ourselves to make them true."

Augum committed the poem to memory. They sat in silence for a time, drinking tea.

"Do you think we'll find Bahbell?" he eventually asked.

"I am afraid we must. If Lividius finds that recipe and creates a portal to Ley … well, let us just say that our odds of stopping him dramatically decrease."

"Huan said Bahbell meant 'gateway to hell'. He also said the Occi might know where it is."

"Is that so?" She steepled her fingers. "Legend says the Occi are the descendants of Occulus himself. They live high up in the Muranians and guard their location well. Finding them will be tricky, for few that have seen them lived to tell the tale."

And what makes *us* any different? Augum thought. He trusted Nana though, trusted her to keep them safe.

"And what do we do with *her*?" he asked, nodding at Jengo's door.

"She is dangerous. I shall have to teleport her to a Dramask prison."

He recalled the way Erika had slapped him three times, each time yanking his jaw so that he stared into her eyes as she did it again. "There's something … very wrong with her."

"What does it say of you that you can see that?"

He stared, having no response.

Mrs. Stone closed the tome. "On to other matters then. How comfortable do the three of you feel with regards to your 2nd degree?"

"Very comfortable, I guess."

"Do you believe yourselves ready to move on to the 3rd degree?"

"Yes, oh, of course yes!"

"So be it. I think it prudent we do some training before we go then."

"Does that mean you will be testing us on our 2nd degree?"

"If there is time. Now if you think I will go easy on you because of the circumstance—"

"—I would be sorely mistaken ... I know, Nana."

She watched him a moment, a slight smile curving her lips. "Correct. I expect you to work hard, Augum, for the spells become increasingly more difficult from here on. You will have to concentrate and help as much as you can. One day, you may find yourself the leader of many people. They will look up to you. They will follow your example."

Yet again, a hint at him becoming some great leader. Has everyone lost their mind? What did he know of leadership?

Mrs. Stone's eyes narrowed slightly. "What lies ahead will be far more dangerous than anything we have done thus far. Prepare yourself."

He nodded and took a sip of tea. The cup trembled slightly in his hand.

"Now how about you tell me all about the Star Feast ..."

He was more than happy to, going through the night in great detail—except for the dancing part—that he wanted to keep to himself.

Mr. Goss, Mr. Okeke, Leland, Bridget, Leera and Jengo eventually roused and groggily made their way over to the table, all still wearing their nightgowns—except for Mr. Okeke, who changed into red hose and a gold and blue tunic belted in the middle, explaining he needed to do some accounting of his iron ore business today. He, Jengo and Bridget worked together in the kitchen to make sunny eggs, leftover potatoes, and spiced leek soup.

Augum and Leera shared a single secret look before breaking out in grins. It was then he knew things wouldn't get weird or anything. Yet he still wished they had kissed ...

Much of the conversation was about the Star Feast of course. Bridget and Leera talked about the dancing, dress and music while Augum and Jengo mostly reminisced about the games.

"Oh, we're so sorry you missed it, Mrs. Stone," Bridget said in a dreamy voice, "You would have loved it."

"I daresay a few too many Star Feast memories cram this old mind already." Mrs. Stone glanced around at them. "I never did have a chance to commend you all for your outstanding work at the Penderson farm with the Henawa."

The trio blushed.

"I am proud of you. It was a difficult situation yet you managed it well."

"We can't take all the credit, Nana," Augum said. "Mr. Ordrid the healer saved you."

"And Augum saved the healer," Bridget said.

"Mr. Penderson too," Leera added. "After revealing his sca—"

"—I got lucky," Augum interrupted. "We all did our part though. Those ingredients didn't find themselves." He was uncomfortable talking about his scars, especially in front of Nana.

"It was a marvelous and frantic hunt," Mr. Goss said, and he went on a boastful and rather exaggerated retelling of the trio's exploits in those final moments before Mrs. Stone was awakened.

"I wish I could have been there," Jengo said, removing the empty plates with Bridget and Augum's help.

"It wasn't as fun as Mr. Goss made it out to sound," Leera muttered.

Jengo shrugged. "Well, probably good I wasn't there after all then. I'm sure I would have died a horrible death in that vortex."

Mr. Okeke stood and smoothed his clothes. "Please, Mrs. Stone, if there is anything I can do to help you gather those supplies, do let me know. Good day to you all." He put on his coat and departed.

Leera looked confused. "Supplies? For what?"

"I should think for the journey ahead, child."

Bridget and Augum exchanged amused looks.

"Oh, shut up," Leera hissed.

"Jengo Okeke, you wish to do some training," Mrs. Stone said.

The tall ebony-skinned Sierran gave a quick bow. "Yes, Mrs. Stone, very much so."

"Please understand my priorities lie with those that are serious in the arcane discipline."

"I'm serious, Mrs. Stone. I would do anything—"

"Anything? Is that truly so, child?"

"Well, no, not anything I suppose ... I don't ... I don't want to die ... or get hurt." He swallowed. "I mean ..."

Mrs. Stone merely observed him.

"I'm ... I'm just afraid—" Jengo blurted.

"You are afraid."

Jengo examined the plank floor, searching his mind. "I can't leave my father and my future wife. Maybe ... maybe I can learn arcanery here on my own."

"Train wild—?" Bridget asked.

"No, that's not what I meant ... well, if I had to, yes, but I was rather hoping to find a mentor that would be willing to train a whole bunch of us here in town, either that or find a book—" he nodded at the arcaneology tome sitting nearby, "like that one."

Mrs. Stone turned to Leland. "My dear child, do you still wish to become a warlock?"

Leland moaned loudly and gave an emphatic nod.

"Mrs. Stone, I have been giving the matter some thought," Mr. Goss said, pushing at his nose. "I am not sure it is wise to take us along with you on this dangerous journey. Shh, Leland, let your father speak. Now as I was saying, I was thinking it would be better for us to stay here in Milham." Mr. Goss pinched his son's good cheek, the one with the dimple in it. He turned back to Mrs. Stone. "Perhaps I could find work as a chandler again, that way I can put a roof over our head. I also need to spend time teaching Leland how to write without … without seeing his writing. And of course, all spare monies will go to pay for a mentor."

Leland moaned as Bridget scooped him up in her arms. "There now, little Lee, it'll be all right, don't you worry …"

"You are father to a boy with many challenges ahead, Mr. Goss," Mrs. Stone said. "I support any decisions you make."

"Thank you kindly, Mrs. Stone, and I very much appreciate the opportunity for adventure, but I must think of my son. Besides—" He smiled at Augum and Leera. "I know that I would slow you all down."

The trio made a show of protest, but Mr. Goss' smile only widened.

"My father and I will do everything in our power to help you and Leland, Mr. Goss," Jengo said. He crouched down beside the disappointed little tyke. "Maybe we can even train side-by-side, huh? Would you like that, Leland?"

Leland gave a reluctant nod.

"It's really for the best," Bridget whispered, giving the boy a delicate squeeze.

"Thank you so much, Jengo," Mr. Goss said. "We are most grateful."

Mrs. Stone used her staff to help her stand. She walked over to Haylee, laying a glowing palm on her forehead. Haylee's swollen eyes slowly opened. Her cheeks were bruised, hair matted with blood and dirt.

"Bridget, a cloth, if you will."

Bridget hastened to wet the cloth Jengo provided and hurried over. She gently dabbed at Haylee's face.

"Where am I?" Haylee's voice was weak.

"You are in the Okeke home, in the town of Milham, far to the east," Mrs. Stone replied quietly.

Haylee gaped a moment before closing her eyes tight, as if burdened by awful memories.

Mrs. Stone placed a hand on her shoulder and gave it a squeeze. "You are safe now, my child. Think on nothing. You have been through much."

Haylee's brows crossed and she winced. She hid her face under the blanket, shoulders heaving.

"Jengo, perhaps some soup might help."

"Of course, Mrs. Stone." He reset the pot over the fire.

"She shall require much rest and care," Mrs. Stone said.

"I'll help her wash and change," Bridget said.

"Good." Mrs. Stone watched Haylee another moment before standing. "Now, a warlock must learn how to pay their way with their craft. Therefore, Augum, Bridget and Leera—I would like you all to come up with ways to raise money using nothing but your arcanery. We will buy supplies with the coin you earn and leave the remaining for the care of the needy."

Bridget beamed while Leera scowled, muttering, "I hate chores …" Augum, on the other hand, thought it was a really good idea.

"I am sure I need not remind you discretion is essential. In the meantime, I will teleport Ms. Scarson to an arcane prison in Dramask. There I shall also discover the latest news and see if I can provide my arcane services to have a new pair of spectacles ground for Mr. Goss."

"Thank you so very much, Mrs. Stone, I really do not know what to say."

"No need to say anything, Albert." She glanced to the trio. "And later, I shall teleport you to a special location for new training."

They exchanged excited looks.

"If all goes well, maybe we can depart by New Year's day." She gave Haylee another pat before standing, allowing Bridget to take her place. "Good luck to you all."

"And you, Mrs. Stone," Jengo said as she paced to his room, closing the door behind her. There was a momentary struggle and an implosive sucking sound, then silence.

Leera groaned. "Time to get changed and start earning …"

WORK AND SORROW

It was a cloudless sunny day outside, the snow sparkling as it caught the light. Evergreen boughs wilted under the weight of frost, the occasional clump of snow cascading down from up high. A cold wind tickled the tops of the trees, filling the forest with gentle swooshing sounds.

Augum, Bridget and Leera had agreed to split up as they searched for ways to make coin, thinking to use Repair and Telekinesis, and sometimes Unconceal. Jengo volunteered to stay behind and care for Haylee, along with Mr. Goss. Leland wanted to come but was forbidden by his father, who felt the trio needed to focus on the task at hand. The boy moped in the Okeke home, pawing at some animal figurines Jengo had given him.

As they neared the center of town, they heard the sounds of children playing. A series of Endyear games and activities had been setup for the very young, with the adults supervising and managing the events. Many elders also took part. There was a hoop game, a horseshoe game, a throwing target game, and games of Old Man Mule and Piggy Run.

"I have an idea—" Bridget said when she saw the merry display. She ran off to the Okeke home, quickly returning with Mr. Goss and Leland.

Hanad Haroun joined the group. "Hello there, honored guests!" he said, arms wide in welcome. He was dressed in a very colorful women's frock and seemed to have been pelted with snow. A voluminous orange wig straddled his head awkwardly.

Mr. Goss chortled. "Oh, dear me, Mr. Haroun, I see the children have taken great advantage of the town elder."

"Yes, I am afraid they have. It is tradition in Milham to have the elder council member degrade himself with the younglings in a most unseemly fashion." A snowball smacked into the back of his neck, and a young child with chocolate skin raced off, chased by his parent.

"My my, now that is quite cold," Mr. Haroun said, squiggling about while the trio snickered. "And hello there, who is this?" He bent down before Leland, who hid behind his father.

"This is my son, Leland."

"Ah, Leland. A fine name. Well, Leland, how would you like to play some games with the other children?"

Leland moaned uncertainly.

"Don't worry, your father will be by your side the entire time. Now are you ready? Come along then!"

"Good luck, you three!" Mr. Goss called as he trailed his son and Mr. Haroun, the three of them waddling along to Leland's clumsy steps.

"Wish I was that young again," Leera muttered, watching a tiny girl plow into a snowman and bursting with loud crying. "On second thought, no I don't."

"I'm going to the tavern," Augum said. "Maybe Huan has some broken cups and dishes to repair."

"I'm going to try the mines," Leera said.

Bridget looked around. "Guess I'll hit the shops. And don't forget—"

VALOR

"Discretion, yes," Leera said. "We got it."

They parted ways, wishing each other good luck.

Augum stepped into the dim atmosphere of the Miner's Mule Inn, occupied by only a handful of patrons mostly gathered around a dark oak table, with a single straggler at the bar. Huan stood off to the side at a tall wine table, looking like he had been the last to leave the Star Feast— there were dark circles under his eyes and his apron was askew and full of stains. He stared at a worn book splayed open before him, quill in hand.

"Blast this infernal ledger," he muttered as Augum approached. "You again. What is it this time, you want to delve into the depths of the Black castle?" He bellied a laugh, throwing the quill at the parchment.

"No, sir, I just came by to ask if I could earn some coin repairing anything or moving things for you."

"You look a little thin to move the kind of stuff I need moved, my boy, and I throw out what gets broken—no sense in keeping it around now, is there?"

"What is it that you need moved?"

Huan snorted. "We need to replace two empty casks with full ones from the basement. Usually it takes two strong men, so we needn't talk about it."

"How much is it worth to you if I accomplish this task on my own?"

"I'll eat my boots before the entire town, my boy."

"Sir, I'm serious. We need the coin to purchase supplies."

"What did you say your name was again?"

Augum stared at him, drawing a complete blank. What *did* he tell Huan his name was? Leera was Penelope, but what was his false name again? Huan's almond eyes narrowed. Augum had to think quickly.

"What does it matter if I get the job done?"

It seemed to work because Huan didn't hesitate replying.

"You can't get the job done, it's impossible." The large innkeeper leaned closer, breath smelling of ale and roasted peppers. "Impossible, that is, unless you're a warlock ..."

Augum gave him a faint smile.

"I knew it," Huan said, shaking his head. "The moment I laid eyes on you, I knew it. You and that friend of yours wear the same matching robes. Years ago, a couple warlocks came through town with a gaggle of kids on some kind of academy excursion or whatnot. They, too, had the same robes, but different colors."

"Where were they from?"

"Some fancy southern desert school. They all had thick accents. Could barely understand a word. Had every custom of kid though. Seemed like one of them snotty, worldly kind of schools, know what I mean? Anyway, luckily the older warlocks spoke the common tongue, so we got along fine. Let me tell you, that man complained and complained about Solian wine, said it didn't compare to their vintage. 'Well', I says to him, 'and what vintage might that be?' And so he says—"

"Sir, can I get started?"

Huan made a grand gesture to the staircase at the back of the room. "You go ahead and try then, young man," and snorted another laugh.

Augum strolled to the staircase and down the steps, carved from the earth and planked with cedar. The basement was full of crates, candles, tools, and oaken casks, stacked on their side and banded with iron straps. They were smaller than a barrel but still looked very heavy. He wandered over to one and tried pulling on it. It didn't budge. He retreated a few steps, took a deep breath, and extended his arm, palm splayed. He envisioned the cask floating along and up the steps. It groaned and began to move, but the effort was immense—it was heavier than he thought. If he wasn't careful, it would smash into the ground and split apart. It teetered on the edge of the casks below it.

VALOR

"How's it coming down there?" Huan asked, and Augum had to run to prop up the cask else it would have fallen.

"Fine—"

"What happened to that magic, huh?"

"It's called arcanery, sir, and I don't mind you watching, but I just need to concentrate."

Huan threw a dirty cloth over his shoulder. "Right ... well let's see it then, I don't have all day to indulge youthful fantasies."

Augum shoved the cask back over the tipping point. He then stepped away and raised his arm again. This time, he knew exactly how heavy it was and how much concentration he needed, though his head had already begun to throb.

The cask began to grind towards the edge.

"I'll be a pig on a spit," Huan muttered.

Augum ignored him, using all his concentration to catch the cask as it dipped off its resting place and swung forward. Amazingly, he discovered he could use its momentum to kind of push it along, straining from the effort in its low position and relaxing when it was a little higher. He turned completely around, the cask under his spell but not in total control, and stepped along behind it. He had to be getting better at the spell, for the barrel was nowhere near as heavy as it should have been. Huan tripped and fell as it practically rolled over him on its journey up the stairs.

Augum settled it at the top before plopping down on the steps, wincing.

Huan stood beside him, shaking his head. "That was some magic trick. Where are the strings?"

"Wasn't a trick." Augum got up, determined to finish the job.

Huan grabbed him by the shoulder. "Wait, let's roll it together, I don't want my other patrons seeing a warlock in my establishment."

Augum helped Huan roll the cask around the tables and behind the bar.

"Tell you what, you get two more to the top of those steps, and I'll give you two silvers."

Two silvers! For that price, he'd do ten barrels. Augum kept his face smooth. "Deal." And so he performed the feat two more times. By the end of it, he was in so much pain he could hardly roll the barrel.

"Thank you," Augum croaked upon accepting payment, trying to keep his nausea at bay.

"That's more than the labor's worth, but it's Endyear and these old drunken fools couldn't move their behinds off the seats if I paid them to. Say, you look a little pale, boy, are you all right?"

"Just great ..." Augum said, stumbling out of the place, studying the coins. On one side, they had King Ridian's crowned head; on the other the Solian evergreen—a tall pine. He wondered what kind of coins the Legion was going to issue.

"Look, five coppers!" Bridget said when they met. "Got them by repairing Ms. Singh's chair, though if it wasn't for Priya, I would have probably been chased out of there. Wait, what happened to you?"

"Used Telekinesis to move a few casks ..." he showed her the two silvers.

"Aug—way to go! That's four times more than me—!"

"Keep your voice down please," he whispered, holding his throbbing head. "Huan was feeling a bit generous I think. Endyear and all."

"Well great job, Aug. Now I wonder how much Leera got ..."

"I'm going to lie down for a bit if you don't mind."

"You earned it. I'll keep looking for more work."

Augum returned to the Okeke home to find Jengo sniffing the contents of a bunch of jars filled with different colored powders.

"Oh hey, Augum, how did it go?"

"Two silvers," he whispered, still holding his head. It hurt more than usual, but then again, he *had* pushed the boundaries of the spell. Usually he had help moving something so heavy.

"What's in the jars?"

"They're supposed to be healing sands," Jengo replied. "You soak them in water and wash with them. I think I might be coming down with a dangerous northern skin pox, and one of these is supposed to stop it in its tracks." He glanced at Augum. "Are you all right?"

"Fine, just need to rest. Arcanery and all that ..." He didn't bother explaining and strolled by to one of the pine living room chairs.

"Hi," he said to Haylee, who was holding a spoon, staring at her soup. She didn't even look up. She was dressed in a simple light blue linen dress, her face and hair freshly washed, a result of Bridget's efforts.

"I'm glad you're all right," he added, still whispering. Talking louder hurt too much right now, though the throbbing was slowly retreating.

Haylee looked up with glassy blue eyes, seeing past him. "They should have killed me."

"Don't say that—"

"They should have killed me, like they killed my parents and my grandfather. No, not they—*he*. *He* did it ... *he* murdered them." Her eyes wandered back to the soup.

Augum didn't need to ask who she meant by "he". He remembered Robin slicing Mya's throat, that surprised look in her eyes.

"I'm sorry..." he said.

"Is that supposed to mean something?" she asked, voice rising. "Is that going to bring them back!"

He looked away, feeling smaller than a pebble.

"You should have left me there. I didn't ask to be saved." The words had a venomous sting to them. "You should have left me back in that snowy field when I ran away from you the first time."

Augum's throat felt dry and his headache had suddenly gotten worse.

Jengo quietly placed a cup of steaming tea before Haylee.

Her eyes narrowed. "Who is this giant reptile?"

Jengo stepped back, brows raised.

"Haylee, you don't mean that—" Augum began, but she shot him a withering look

"Don't tell me what I mean and don't mean, you don't get to tell me—"

"I understand that you're lashing out—"

"So what! What does it matter! They're dead, and I should be too—!"

"Forgive me for intruding," Jengo said. "I'll take my leave. I ... I need to cut some wood today anyway." He brought over two chocolate biscuits, delicately placing them between Augum and Haylee. She glared at them. He then quietly took his fur coat and departed, leaving the two of them alone.

Augum allowed silence to permeate the room, listening to the faint crackle of the fire and distant swoosh of the evergreens.

"I saw them crawling, you know ..." Haylee mumbled, closing her eyes. "He made them crawl to me, beg me for their lives. Mother said I was brave, that I deserved better. Father said I was his special little girl ..." She sniffed deeply. "He made them crawl, then he ..." a hand shot to her mouth and she shook her head, unable to say what happened next.

Augum reached over to a cloth Haylee had been using and gently placed it into her hand. She squeezed it in her fist.

Bridget and Leera suddenly spilled in through the door, laughing.

"… believe it when I see it—" Leera stopped mid-sentence, gaping at Augum sitting across from Haylee, who shrank beneath her blanket.

"Oh, sorry," Leera mumbled, giving Augum an odd look.

Bridget quietly closed the door and the pair sat themselves at the table, talking in low voices.

Augum returned his focus to Haylee. "Robin murdered Mya in front of me." He could almost smell the fire again; the thatch; the oil and flesh. "He'll pay for what he did. One day, he'll pay …"

He became conscious of Haylee watching him, but when he met her eyes, she looked down. Behind her, Leera stole a look his way.

"Mrs. Stone is going to perform a memorial ceremony soon," he said. "It'll help a little."

Haylee only sat there staring at nothing, spoon in one hand, cloth in the other.

Not knowing what else to do, he slowly got up and made his way over to the girls.

"How is she?" Bridget whispered.

Augum only shook his head.

Bridget nodded.

"Probably loves the attention," Leera muttered.

Bridget gave her a look. "*Leera—*"

"Just kidding, sheeze. So I hear you scored two silvers."

Augum smiled half-heartedly and withdrew the coins from his robe, placing them on the table.

"I don't believe it," she muttered. "I had to wash a filthy floor, didn't even get to use my arcanery, and all I got was a lousy six coppers."

Bridget swept strands of cinnamon hair away from her forehead. "Why don't we do some quiet studying for a bit."

Leera scowled while Augum shrugged. "Sure," he said, secretly relieved. He wasn't in the mood to talk anyway.

From the table, Bridget gathered the yellow book, the Slam spell scroll, and the blue tome on arcaneology. "Which of the three you want, Lee?"

"Scroll, I guess." Leera held it like a filthy cloth, shoulders sagging. She propped her head on her hand and began to read, eyes glazing over immediately.

"Book," Augum said. He fared no better in the mood he was in, the tiny scrawl of the ornate tome about as decipherable as dog scratchings.

Bridget, meanwhile, quietly turned the pages of the yellow tome, lips moving.

Eventually Leera placed her head on her arms and fell asleep. Augum soon did the same. Bridget did not protest.

THE MEMORIAL CEREMONY

Augum was startled awake by an implosive crunch. As he raised his head, the page of the blue book he was supposed to have been studying stuck to his cheek.

"Oh, hi Mrs. Stone," he said, peeling the page off his face and quickly repairing it arcanely.

Jengo dashed out of his room. "Has the apocalypse started?"

"It's just Mrs. Stone, Jengo," Bridget replied, rubbing her eyes. Augum thought she might have succumbed to an afternoon slumber as well.

Mrs. Stone glanced at Leera, who still snoozed, head lying on the Slam spell scroll. Augum jabbed her with his elbow and she shot up, scroll plastered to her forehead.

"There's only raspberry jam left!" she blurted. As it dawned on her where she was, she smacked the scroll aside and shrank, mumbling, "Sorry."

Mrs. Stone's lips thinned. "I see you have all been keeping yourselves remarkably busy."

"We gathered two silvers and sixteen coppers, Mrs. Stone," Bridget quickly said, trying to salvage some of their dignity.

Leera rubbed her sleep-creased cheek. "Bridget got most of the coppers, but Augum scored both silvers."

"Adequate—but only barely, and only because it was your first time. I look forward to hearing the details of what spells you performed and how much you charged, but right now, if you do not find yourselves too busy, I would like to know where Mr. Goss is."

"I think he and Leland are still taking part in Endyear activities with the other children," Bridget said.

"I see. Could you fetch him for me please?"

"Yes, Mrs. Stone." Bridget ran off.

"Any news from Tiberra, Nana?" Augum asked.

Mrs. Stone took a seat across from Haylee, who sat with a blank look on her face. "The Legion have advanced to the Tiberran border, numbering in the tens of thousands. King Bimal Pradeep has summoned every soldier and warlock in all of Tiberra, trying to raise an army powerful enough to stop them. Warlock emissaries have teleported to Canterra in hopes of brokering a pact. I daresay the common folk are terrified—shops have been closing; people are going into hiding; and towns are fortifying their gates. I expect battle to break out any day now."

Jengo sat beside Augum. "I didn't know they number that many …"

"This is only the beginning, I am afraid. Lividius will use necromancy, Dreadnought steel, and the scions to augment his armies. History further portends that he shall raise those he slaughters, making his armies stronger and ever more difficult to stop."

Jengo looked to Augum a moment. "Lividius—?"

"The Lord of the Legion."

"Right, of course." Jengo sidled away from Augum a bit, as if afraid of catching an awful disease.

VALOR

Mrs. Stone's cool eyes fell upon Haylee. "They took Erika Scarson as a hostage intended for trade."

Haylee's hair whipped up. "What! How could you—"

"I am afraid I had no choice, my dear child. I came as an uninvited guest to the king's court. I risked offending the Tiberrans if I did not accept their request with regards to the prisoner."

"You should have killed her then—"

"I understand why you feel that way."

"You don't understand anything! All this is your fault! If you'd only given them the scion in the first place, my parents and my grandpapa would still be alive!" Haylee's face dropped behind a curtain of blonde hair. Tears fell onto the blanket. "I never should have come with you ..."

Mrs. Stone watched her a time before standing up, leaning on her staff as if feeling three times her weight. She strolled over to Jengo, passing on quiet instructions.

"Yes, I've heard of that tea, Mrs. Stone. I'll get the ingredients ready."

The front door suddenly opened and in walked Bridget leading Mr. Goss, Leland, and Mr. Okeke.

Mr. Okeke's smile quickly faded upon spotting Haylee. "Is there anything I can help with?" he asked, removing his coat and hanging it on an iron hook by the door.

"I could use some assistance finding tea ingredients, Father."

Mrs. Stone turned to address Mr. Goss. "I was rather hoping to teleport you to Dramask to purchase you a new pair of spectacles, Albert, but I am afraid it will have to wait until this evening."

"I am most grateful, Mrs. Stone," Mr. Goss said. "Please take as much time as you need." He let his son go. A snow-splattered Leland pawed his way over to the table and sidled in beside Augum.

"I wish to perform a memorial ceremony." Mrs. Stone glanced at Haylee. "I believe now would be an appropriate time." Her gaze swept over them, settling on Mr. Goss. "As I understand it, Albert, you have not attended one since your wife's passing."

Mr. Goss nodded slowly.

"So be it. And you, Mr. Okeke, do you wish to attend the ceremony?"

"Thank you, but my son and I have long made peace with the death of my wife."

"Very well." Mrs. Stone came near and placed a hand on Mr. Okeke's arm, whispering, "May I trouble you then with a request?"

"Of course, Mrs. Stone."

"We require suitable black robes. If I were to—"

"I actually have just the thing, Mrs. Stone, no need to trouble yourself." Mr. Okeke strode over to a blanket box, withdrawing two large black cloths of heavy fabric. "These were meant to be used in the mines, but they were traded to me in exchange for iron. I was intending on making them into tablecloths. I know they are far from ideal, Mrs. Stone, but perhaps—"

"They will do just fine, thank you. Bridget, could you please grab a knife and cut the cloth into seven portions?"

"I'll help," Leera said.

Once the task was complete, Mrs. Stone solemnly dispersed them to Augum, Bridget, Leera, Mr. Goss, Leland and Haylee. Then, as they draped the cloth over their shoulders, she turned to address them. "Now all we require is a quiet spot."

"I think I know the perfect place, Mrs. Stone," Bridget said.

Mr. Okeke opened the door for them. "We shall have the tea ready upon your return."

Bridget led all the way to the site of the Star Feast. Although it had been dark in Milham, the Muranians still gleamed crimson to the east. The tables sat in the same

VALOR

arrangement, looking lonely in their emptiness. The three fires sat cold and black.

"A moment, if you please." Mrs. Stone paced to the woods. She pointed her arm and a series of branches rose from the snow. They shook in midair, discarding the frost, and floated to one of the fire pits.

Mrs. Stone repeated this process twice more before shuffling to the pit. She extended her palm and the branches began to steam and sizzle. She withdrew her hand just before the point of ignition and turned to them. "Please gather in a circle."

They did as she asked, fanning out. Augum recalled Mrs. Stone performing a memorial ceremony back at Castle Arinthian. This time, he would see new figures in that fire. So much death ...

Mrs. Stone raised her chin. "I call upon the spirits of the dead to listen to the cries of the living and to remember those they left behind, those that still breathe the air and eat of the earth. Dearly departed, allow us a final goodbye as we mourn your passing from this life."

The woodpile burst with tall flame that changed color, settling on a deep blue. Augum felt the heat on his face.

"Hear the cry," and as once before, Mrs. Stone began singing a primitive fragile tune that seemed to span eons of time.

Augum stared into the fire until it became a curtain of white, blurring with the snow. The first figure to emerge was One Eye, the befuddled but honor-bound old man who was once Mrs. Stone's friend. Augum raised a hand and gave a single wave, remembering his brave sacrifice that allowed them to escape the Blade of Sorrows. The old man winked with his remaining eye, raised his cane in acknowledgment, and faded away, allowing a large woman with a kind smile to waddle forth. Augum would never forget the face of Miralda Jenkins, a face that shone with peace. She had used the last of her arcane strength to lift the witch's curse off him, at the price of her life. For a time, she stood there, filling Augum's soul with warmth and quiet peace. Eventually, she closed her eyes, lowered her head, and faded into nothing.

The next figure he saw surprised him—it was Prince Sydo Ridian, the boy who had died in a state of confusion, perhaps madness even. Sydo had treated the trio poorly and betrayed them, yet Augum felt no ill will toward the boy anymore. His antics cost him his life, a harsher punishment than he deserved.

Sydo stood with a face creased with sorrow, as if wishing he were still alive.

"Goodbye, Prince Sydo," Augum said.

Sydo only dropped his eyes. His shoulders sagged in resignation before he too disappeared.

At last, the form Augum longed to see slowly took shape. Mya walked forward with a humble casualness he had forgotten, wearing a black servant gown. Her long silky jet hair was as straight as ever, almond eyes like two brilliant emeralds, porcelain skin almost translucent. She bestowed a radiant smile as bright as the sun, appearing so close, yet so very far away.

He slowly raised his hand in greeting, whispering, "I remember dancing with you. We were almost caught." He laughed gently. "Imagine the pair of us stuck in Ley together …" He sighed, watching her form ebb and flow with the bright white. "I would have been all right with that if you were there to keep me company …"

She continued smiling at him, head slightly tilted, hands softly clasped together before her. Somewhere in that great unknown, he heard the echo of a distant song.

"I think about you," he said. "I ask myself if I could have been faster. Could I have prevented Robin from … from killing you …" He stared into those smiling eyes. "Sometimes I try to think of arcane ways of bringing you back, you know. I can't tell anybody about it, but I can tell you. I know you'd understand …"

He was unable to speak anymore. They stood like this for a long time, watching each other. When his heart felt at its heaviest, she stretched out her hands and made a graceful gesture—that of a bird flying free. He swallowed hard, keeping himself from running to her and taking her in his arms, knowing he would never lay eyes on her again.

"Goodbye," he mumbled as she slowly walked backwards. She gave him one last radiant smile, a smile he'd never forget, and turned away, her steps silent. Her form began to blur and whiten, until it was one with all. Everything lost its importance in that whiteness—time, ambition, pain, happiness. It soothed his being and his aching heart like a warm bath after a long cold day.

After a time, it began to fade, bringing into focus a world of color and sound. The light in the west was now hues of purple, the sky to the east dark. The scent of pine and cedar mingled with smoke. When he looked around, he saw it was just he and Haylee now, draped in black fabric that fluttered lightly in the breeze. He must have spent a lot of time in that trance.

"I saw them again," Haylee said quietly, face wet with tears. "I saw my parents and my grandpapa. I got to say ... I got to say goodbye. I'll never see them again, will I?"

He watched the smoke curl its way skyward, a dance of infinite forms. "No, you'll never see them again."

Haylee looked off into the darkening mountains, hair streaming behind her. "What now? What is there for me now? I have nothing. I *am* nothing ..."

"Then you have nothing to lose." He had said it simply and without knowing why. They locked eyes. For a moment, they were one and the same, two souls knowing loss.

"I have nothing to lose ..." and she walked off, leaving him.

The cold began to bite, but he cherished standing on that hilltop alone, taking in the eternal view, the vast sky, the calming of his heart. He watched as the first stars appeared in the east, the purple faded to black in the west, and the near full moon took shape from behind wisps of cloud. Only then, with the night blooming in quiet but infinite glory, could he bear the cold no longer.

"Shyneo," he said, and returned to the Okeke home for tea.

THE SPIKES

The morning after the memorial ceremony went by quickly. Breakfast was a chatty affair, with Mr. Okeke and Mr. Goss trading stories on the intricacies of their professions. Mr. Goss, wearing a pair of newly ground spectacles acquired after the memorial ceremony, began giving his son lessons on how to write. Mr. Okeke took Jengo to the mines for a lesson in commerce, while Haylee resumed her place on the pine settee, covering herself with a Dramask blanket. She hadn't yet bothered putting on the brand new burgundy apprentice robe purchased for her by Mrs. Stone the night before. Instead, she stared at the fire, mug of untouched tea in her hands.

Leera leaned toward Augum, whispering, "Why'd you think she got a new set of robes? Is Mrs. Stone going to mentor her too?"

Augum only shrugged.

The trio barely had time to settle their stomachs before Mrs. Stone dispatched them to earn more coin with their arcanery. It was a challenge Bridget looked forward to but Leera hated, muttering something about it being a chore.

Augum didn't mind so much, though he did consider it more work than fun. He returned to Huan at the Miner's Mule Inn, receiving a silver for his efforts in moving a cask and three cots. Bridget and Leera each took in 12 and 7 coppers respectively, repairing pottery, tools and glass windows for people.

After lunch, Mrs. Stone had them practicing arcanery. Jengo had returned by then and took over teaching Leland how to write, while Mr. Goss departed with Mr. Okeke in search of work. Mrs. Stone looked on, occasionally remarking on how to perform a spell better. Haylee, who finally changed into her apprentice robe, sat at the table, head resting on her arms. No one bothered her, though Mrs. Stone did ask if she was interested in joining them for an excursion later. Haylee only shrugged, and Mrs. Stone did not press the matter.

The trio cycled through all the spells in their arsenal: Shine, Telekinesis, Repair, Unconceal, Shield, Push, Disarm, Centarro and Slam. For the last, Mrs. Stone enchanted the home to be silent from the outside. The trio's arcane display both awed and terrified Jengo, who repeatedly dove into his room for shelter, proclaiming their certain doom. Leland only moaned and clapped. Even Haylee looked on, though her face remained impassive.

"You have comported yourselves well," Mrs. Stone said at the end of it. "Now let us depart for a very special excursion." She glanced to Jengo. "Please inform your father we shall return for supper."

"Yes, Mrs. Stone." He hesitated. "Mrs. Stone, is it ... is it possible that I come too?"

"I am afraid you are not qualified, Jengo."

"Oh ... perhaps it is better I stay anyway. Someone needs to look after Leland. Besides, I'd probably get killed in a horrible arcane accident or something."

"I'll go," Haylee said without any emotion.

Mrs. Stone observed her coolly. "Have you at least achieved your 1st degree, dear child?"

Haylee stood. "No. I want to go though."

"Let her come, Nana," Augum said, feeling sorry for Haylee.

Mrs. Stone thought over it another moment before extending her veined hand towards her. "Please join us, child."

Haylee joined the circle between Mrs. Stone and Augum. She was cold to the touch and her grip was limp. The push and pull of teleportation forced Augum to hold Haylee's limp grip tighter. Unlike before, the sensation of tumbling and falling lasted far longer. It took a great deal of restraint not to vomit.

At last, they reappeared on solid ground. Everyone but Mrs. Stone fell to their knees, gasping and coughing. When Augum finally calmed his stomach, he looked around, discovering they stood amidst a sea of towering rocky mesas, like giant fingers extending from the earth. Theirs was only the width of a house; some had to be a league wide, while others wouldn't fit a bird nest. The sea of stick-like pedestals jutted from mountainous terrain that seemed to stretch infinitely in every direction.

It was almost warm, wherever they were, and the sky was clear, sun bright, wind mildly cool.

"Welcome to the Spikes," Mrs. Stone said.

Augum glanced over the edge he was closest to and instinctively retreated. The fall looked to be several thousand feet straight down. He swore there were bones at the bottom.

"How did you get up here, Mrs. Stone?" Bridget asked. "I thought you can only teleport to places you have previously visited."

"Very astute, Bridget. I had never climbed this spike, nor had my mentor who teleported me here. Yet at some distant point in the past, an ambitious warlock did climb it. This is one of a series of advanced training spots, called *Trainers*, handed down for generations from headmaster to headmistress. Each academy has its own series of Trainers, jealously guarded and only shared with those students showing the most promise and loyalty. Further, each Trainer is rated—the one we currently stand on is rated for the 3rd degree."

"Look, it's initialed," Leera said, finding a large granite stone scratched with a wide assortment of signatures. "Some of these go back hundreds of years!"

"The oldest Trainer, and also the most challenging, dates back to near a thousand years, when the Academy of Arcane Arts was founded. If you knew your arcane history, you'd find some interesting names—"

"My father!" Augum blurted, fingering the words *Lividius Stone* etched crookedly into the rock. "So he was here …"

"But if these are the academy's Trainers," Bridget began, "won't the Legion be using them?"

"Perhaps, but a proper headmaster or headmistress would never share these with those undeserving. It is a point of great school pride."

"But Augum's father knows about them."

"He does indeed, but I believe him too busy with the Great Quest and the coming war to occupy himself with such things. There is no reason for him to come here or suspect us being here."

Augum hoped so—the last thing they needed was his father suddenly showing up.

"Haylee, what are you doing!" Bridget cried out suddenly.

Augum turned to find Haylee standing on the very edge, toes curling over. She was looking forward, hair blowing in the wind, hands clenched.

"Haylee, are you crazy!" Leera called.

VALOR

Augum took a step forward but was held back by Mrs. Stone's sudden hand on his shoulder. He looked at her but her eyes were solely on Haylee.

"My dear child, look at me." The wind gusted as Mrs. Stone took a single step forward. "What possesses you to stare into the last abyss?"

"There's no point ..." Haylee blubbered, turning around, balancing on the knife-thin edge like a leaf in late autumn. "I want to join them ..."

"We all want to join those that pass before us, thinking we have been left behind."

"You can't stop me ..."

"This I know. Your life is your own to do with as you see fit, a burden we all carry. Should I stop you now, you will only attempt it at the next opportunity. Should I tie you up, you will wait."

"Your stupid memorial thing didn't work."

"It is a balm easily defeated by hopelessness."

"I have nothing, no family, no home, no place to be, and no friends—"

"You have us, Haylee!" Augum said, reaching out, voice strong and unwavering. "You have me. I'll be your friend."

Haylee locked eyes with him and bit her lip.

"We'll be your friends," Bridget echoed, but Haylee's eyes were only on Augum. As they stared at each other, bumps rose on his skin. He saw his five-year-old self toiling with the bucket at the well as the Penderson brats skipped up to him.

"He done look like a filthy mutt," said seven-year-old Garth.

"You is right, he done look like he gots fleas," said five-year-old Buck, checking to see that his brother agreed.

Garth made to spit like his father but ended up drooling instead. He gave a sharp nod. "Darn right."

"You is ugly and stupid!" Wyza cried, kicking dirt in Augum's face.

"I ain't done nothing wrong," Augum said, accidentally dropping the bucket of water back down its rope. It splashed at the very bottom of the well.

The brats laughed.

"You is dumb as a toad!" Garth said.

"Dumb as a toad," Buck echoed.

"Yeah, dumb as a toad—!" Wyza went to push him but he stepped out of the way. She stumbled and fell right into the well. Without even thinking, Augum's hand shot out and caught her ankle, holding her just long enough for her brothers to violently shove him out of the way and drag her back to safety.

"What you is trying to do, kill our sister!" Garth screamed.

Buck, meanwhile, ran back to tell. That day, Augum took one of the worst beatings of his life, acquiring the first of the scars that traced along his back like an unfinished painting.

He had forgotten about that, the memory buried under layers of bitterness and hurt. Yet as he stared into Haylee's eyes, another memory came, this one warped and strange. He saw himself as an eight-year-old blonde girl, happily running among friends. They were all girls around the same age. They were giggling and laughing and chasing another girl with red hair. She was crying and calling out, but no one on the dingy city street bothered to help her. She ran as fast as she could, yet the girls in the group kept up.

"We're only playing, Dora, stop running!" he heard himself shout in a girl's young voice.

Dora ducked into an alley and they followed. She bolted around a corner from which came a terrible shriek. When he had caught up with the other girls, they found a large round hole in the ground and water shooting past. The others screamed and ran off, but he didn't. He only stood there, staring into the darkness, blonde hair dangling before his face.

"You saved her," Haylee suddenly said, taking a step away from the cliff. She looked confused. "How did I see that?"

"What's going on here?" Leera asked.

"I saw you too," Augum said. "You ran after Dora …"

Haylee's hand shot to her mouth. She fell to her knees. "They never found her … it was my fault … they never found her …"

Bridget ran and embraced her, slowly drawing her away from the edge.

"It was my fault …" Haylee kept saying.

"What just happened?" Leera asked Augum as Mrs. Stone prepared to teleport Haylee back.

Augum slowly shook his head. "I have no idea. I … I was her for a moment there, and she was me, except … except we were younger …"

Mrs. Stone finished saying something to Bridget before teleporting away with Haylee.

Bridget walked over, face pale. "Mrs. Stone said she'll be right back. What … what did we just see there?"

Augum repeated what he had told Leera.

"But that's impossible … unless …"

"Unless what?"

"Do you remember how you used to cast lightning uncontrollably, especially when you felt cornered?"

"Yeah …"

"Well maybe you just did it again, except using some other wild arcanery …"

"So what are you saying, I can cast random wild spells?" There was a stigma attached to wild warlocks who learned arcanery on their own. They were deemed crazy and often killed themselves.

"I'm not sure, maybe Mrs. Stone will know."

"What did you see?" Leera asked, watching him closely.

Augum hesitated. He wasn't sure if it was appropriate to tell. Luckily, Mrs. Stone teleported back at that moment. She paced forward, using her sleek staff as support.

"Nana, I don't know what happened, but I was Haylee for a moment there when she was young, and she saw through me in the same way—"

"In times of stress, a warlock may subconsciously search for alternative solutions that materialize in the form of wild arcanery. Though it is rare and can fail disastrously, it does happen to those with sufficient ... *motivation*. If I am not mistaken, you may have just cast the healing spell *Empathic Transmission*."

"What element is that, Mrs. Stone?" Bridget asked.

"Healing, 4th degree." She gave a small smile. "When I was younger, I accidentally set a boy's tunic on fire. I discovered I had dual arcane inclinations, which later turned into multiple. I can selectively, though in a limited way, cast spells from some of the other elements. It takes a tremendous amount of practice and patience, for learning outside your primary element is very difficult, as it goes against the grain, if you will. Nonetheless, it *is* possible. I believe any warlock has the ability to do it, all they need is grit and a predisposition toward that element."

"Motivation ... so you're saying I can develop certain spells in the healing element?"

"Perhaps, yes, though not likely."

This was momentous news. What if he could heal their wounds when Mrs. Stone wasn't around? How amazing would that be! What else was he capable of—what else were they *all* capable of! The blood in his veins raced at the seemingly infinite prospects.

"I want to cast other elements too," Leera mumbled.

"Mrs. Stone, how is Haylee?" Bridget asked.

"She is resting. She has been through a lot in a short period of time. We must be patient and compassionate."

"Of course, Mrs. Stone."

"Now I must ask for your concentration." Mrs. Stone looked around at the bleak landscape. "It has been sixteen years since I came here last. Let us prepare." She let go of her staff. It stood straight, supported arcanely, while she stretched as if readying to exercise. First, her neck, then hands, arms, torso, and finally legs.

The trio followed her example. Augum wondered what they were going to do that required warming up like this.

"It was always my practice—excuse me, the practice of my mentors—to stretch before a Trainer session." She curled all the fingers in her hands." Ah, it is good to be back. All right, let us begin. Have you guessed what it is you are about to go through?"

The trio shook their heads. "No, Mrs. Stone."

She paced to the far edge and turned back around, watching them. Her staff stood in place where she had left it, like a spear jammed into the ground.

"What's going on?" Leera whispered to Augum.

"No idea …"

"There will be no idle talk from now on. Failure to follow my instructions will result in automatic disqualification. Nod if you understand."

The trio nodded, exchanging wild looks of excitement and fear. Augum now got what was going on—they were about to be officially tested for the 2nd degree!

"Please spread out."

As soon as they got into position, Mrs. Stone gestured at a rock—it hurled itself at Augum. He instinctively raised his left arm and summoned his lightning shield. The rock bounced off harmlessly, the shield disappearing before the rock even hit the ground.

"Bridget, return that rock to me using Telekinesis."

Bridget raised her arm, brows knotting in concentration. The rock picked itself up and floated over to Mrs. Stone. She snatched it out of the air before letting it drop from her hand. She withdrew a pottery cup from within her robes and tossed it at their feet, where it smashed.

"Leera, repair the cup then return it to my hand, all without touching it."

Leera swallowed hard before crouching. Her hands shook as she splayed them over the pieces. "Apreyo." At first, nothing happened and Augum was afraid she had failed, but then the pieces began to move, the cup reforming with an arcane glow. She took a deep breath, poised her hand over it, and guided it back to Mrs. Stone using Telekinesis.

Mrs. Stone caught it, making a quick gesture with her other hand. A rock hurtled at Bridget, who just barely blocked it by spawning a shield made of twigs and leaves. Mrs. Stone flicked her wrist again, hurling one at Leera, who also just managed to block it with her shield, made of pond leaves and water.

Mrs. Stone gestured at her staff and it shot into her hand. She held it out. "Augum Stone—Disarm."

It was strange hearing her address him by his full name. His heart thundered—this was the spell he'd been having trouble with. He shook out his hand before raising his arm, visualizing the staff flying from his great-grandmother's grip. "Disablo!" and he yanked arcanely—the staff twirled in the air and came clanging to the ground.

Mrs. Stone returned the staff to her hand telekinetically and repeated the test for Bridget and Leera, both of whom passed.

"Raise your primary hands please." They did so. "Now cast Shine."

"Shyneo!" Their hands lit up instantly—it was their most often-used spell, and the one they were best at.

"Extinguish." Mrs. Stone then tossed the cup at Bridget's feet where it smashed. When Bridget repaired it, she threw it at Augum's feet. He also repaired it. She then paced forward, again leaving her staff to stand perfectly balanced.

"Bridget Jones—Push."

Bridget looked beyond Mrs. Stone at the great drop and hesitated before making the shoving gesture. "Baka!"

Mrs. Stone stumbled a few steps and returned. "Leera Jones—Push."

Leera didn't hesitate and Mrs. Stone had to catch herself, else she would have fallen. "Augum Stone—Push."

He glanced past her to the great fall that awaited if he did it too well. "Baka!" He made the gesture but nothing happened. His stomach plummeted. Did he just fail?

"You have one more opportunity. Failure to perform will result in disqualification. Augum Stone—Push."

He was conscious of Bridget and Leera staring, but he wasn't about to let his fear get the better of him. "Baka!" and arcanely shoved Mrs. Stone. She stumbled right to the edge, but held firm without falling. A headache began to throb as he sighed in relief.

"Please turn around."

They faced the great expanse, wind clawing at their hair, while Mrs. Stone took her time walking behind them.

"You may turn back around now. I have hidden three objects amongst the rubble. Augum Stone—Unconceal."

He put out his shaking hand. The spells seemed that much more difficult under the pressure of a test. "Un vun deo." He waited to feel the arcane ether. Nothing happened. He felt his brow sweat.

"You have one more opportunity," Mrs. Stone said after a time. "Failure to perform will result in disqualification."

Augum felt short of breath upon hearing those words again, but forced himself to calm down and breathe. He closed his eyes and listened to the wind, feeling for that subtle pull, for that *intent* to obscure.

"Un vun deo." At last, it came, and he dared not let it go, nor did he dare think on anything else but where it led. At the end of that invisible rope, he found a sunflower seed hidden underneath a rock.

"Leera Jones—Unconceal," Mrs. Stone said as Augum resumed his place, silently thanking the Unnameables.

"You have one more opportunity. Failure to perform will result in disqualification," Mrs. Stone said when Leera hadn't moved for a time. Leera reddened. Augum stared at her, willing her to succeed. "You can do it," he mouthed. She saw him say it and made a thankful face. Then she took a deep breath and closed her eyes, palm outstretched.

"Un vun deo," she said, and stood for too long a time. Surely she'd be disqualified any moment now, Augum thought. Just as Mrs. Stone opened her mouth to speak, Leera began slowly moving forward, eventually finding a coat button. She squealed in delight and resumed her place.

"Bridget Jones—Unconceal."

"Un vun deo," Bridget said, finding a copper coin in moments.

"And now for your final test. Bridget Jones—Slam."

Bridget inhaled deeply before closing her eyes. Suddenly she gestured as if throwing something to the ground. "Grau!" she cried in an animalistic fashion. There was the splintering sound of a tree cracking in half. It was so real and loud Augum and Leera flinched. When the sound dissipated, Bridget was biting her lip and smiling, probably because she knew she had passed.

"Leera Jones—Slam."

Leera took a series of deep breaths. "Grau!" making the throwing gesture. The sound of a great volume of water crashing filled the air. When it concluded, she was grinning.

Mrs. Stone's eyes settled on him next. "Augum Stone—Slam."

This was it. He had to get it right. He took a deep breath and exhaled slowly, focusing on the intricacies needed to perform the spell. He made a whipping gesture. "Grau!" The air split with a crack of thunder, so loud the girls covered their ears. It wasn't his most successful casting of the spell, but it was enough.

VALOR

"I shall return in but a moment," Mrs. Stone said, face impassive. She disappeared with an implosive crunch.

The trio exchanged looks, not daring to speak. Was there one final test? What was going on? They waited and waited, until there came another implosive crunch.

Mrs. Stone reached out. "Join hands. We now return."

They did as she asked, soon appearing back at the Okeke home. When the teleportation sickness wore off, they found Jengo, Priya, Mr. Okeke, Mr. Goss, Leland, and even Haylee standing together, clapping.

The trio exchanged wild looks of excitement—they had passed their 2nd degree test!

Mrs. Stone set herself apart and cleared her throat. "Leera Jones, please step forward." Leera did so and Mrs. Stone raised her chin. "In accordance with the ancient traditions of the Founding, I, Anna Atticus Stone, having achieved mastery in the element of lightning, before these witnesses, hereby bestow upon you, Leera Jones, daughter of Matilda and Oscar Jones, the 2nd arcane degree. Please give me your arm."

Leera pushed back her sleeve and proudly extended her arm. Mrs. Stone's hand began to crackle and shine electrically as she touched Leera's wrist. The light moved from mentor to apprentice, spiraling around Leera's arm, before settling in a second glowing watery ring.

"Congratulations on achieving your 2nd degree. You may now step back in line."

"Thank you, thank you so very much, Mrs. Stone ..."

Everyone clapped as Leera returned, marveling at her two spiraling rings.

Mrs. Stone then repeated the ceremony with Bridget and Augum. When it concluded, the trio hugged while receiving hearty rounds of applause from everyone, including Haylee.

Mr. Goss removed his new spectacles and dabbed at his face with a cloth, telling Leland, "One day, my dear son, that will be you. I just know it."

"We've got our second stripe!" Leera called, showing hers off to cheers.

Everyone quickly gathered to congratulate the trio with handshakes and hugs.

"Well done," Mr. Okeke said, clapping Augum on the back. "Well done indeed."

"I feel so privileged to even be here," Jengo said, squeezing Augum's hand with both of his.

Priya gave small bows. "That was very interesting, thank you and congratulations."

Mr. Goss took each of their hands and looked them in the eyes. "I am so very proud of you all."

Leland only moaned and hugged each one of them in turn.

Haylee stood apart, only approaching Augum when he had a moment of freedom from the crowd. "Congratulations," she said softly, eyes at her feet. "Just wanted to …" She looked up, unable to finish.

He smiled. "It's all right, and thanks."

She nodded and suddenly squeezed him in a tremendous hug. He returned it, glad she was there.

THE 3RD DEGREE

Mrs. Stone took the trio back to the Trainer. She had given them a choice: stay and continue celebrating or train in the 3rd degree. Needless to say, it was hardly much of a choice—who'd pass up the opportunity to learn new spells under the famous Anna Atticus Stone?

"I shall return briefly," Mrs. Stone said, and teleported away. When it was only the trio upon that towering rocky mesa, Leera turned to Augum.

"So, um, what did Haylee say?"

"Just congratulations, that kind of thing."

"Oh, right ..."

Bridget thrust her glowing arm of rings between them. "Look, we have our second stripe! Can you believe it!"

Augum and Leera promptly lit their rings up, admiring what they had achieved.

"After everything we went through," he muttered, holding his arm up. "Who'd have thought ..."

Mrs. Stone soon returned. "And now back to the business at hand. Before we begin the training, let me remind you why we are headed to Bahbell."

The trio shifted where they stood.

"Inside is supposed to be an ancient recipe for constructing a portal to Ley *without* needing a scion. This recipe requires very particular ingredients, ingredients Occulus was no doubt attempting to track down. Lividius knows of the recipe's existence and the fact Occulus had failed. What he does not know is exactly where Bahbell is. I am unaware of who among his party is looking for it, but I can assure you the castle is being searched for as we speak. Therefore, time is crucially limited—we must find Bahbell and the recipe before Lividius.

"I need not say that should he get his hands on the recipe, he will use it to open a portal to Ley and raid it with his armies on the pretext of bestowing eternal life upon all. We cannot let this happen. The guardians of knowledge *must* be kept safe. Their destruction would obliterate our unifying past and doom us to repeat our mistakes, something we are already beginning to suffer from due to the Leyan withdrawal from the world. They will share that knowledge of their own volition. Everyone must be allowed to benefit, not just a select few."

"Can the Leyans not stop him?" Bridget asked.

"He is growing more powerful by the day, aided by three scions, Dreadnoughts, his Black and Red Guard, and the undead. If he succeeds in winning Tiberra, it will be a new source of wealth and power for him. The Great Quest for the seven scions will accelerate, as will his thirst for emperorship. When he turns his sights on the other kingdoms, we may see a war unlike any seen before."

"Is there any way of taking those scions away from him somehow, maybe destroying them?" Augum asked.

Mrs. Stone glanced at the clear orb embedded at the top of her staff. As if in response, it clouded over. "The scions are indestructible Leyan artifacts. Perhaps they could be hidden or removed from the world, but that assumes much. As the Legion gains momentum, Lividius will surround

VALOR

himself with powerful protections, though his trust in others will be limited by his ambition."

"Do we know where to start looking for Bahbell?"

"I have been making quiet inquiries about the Occi. It appears some of them may be warlocks. As to where they could be found, I have an idea of where to start looking, but after that, we will have to rely on luck."

"The old Henawa man said to see him before we left," Leera said. "He might be able to point us in the right direction."

"Then I shall leave that to you. Now let us move on to an essential 3rd degree spell I feel may help protect you from the Occi. Would anyone like to venture a guess as to which one I am referring to?"

Bridget winced. "Mind Armor?"

"Correct. Mind Armor is a reflex spell, much like Shield, that protects warlocks from spells like Fear, Deafness, Confusion, Mute, Sleep, and so on. Without it, you are at the mercy of any warlock miscreant that crosses your path. Be warned, however, that the spell is much more difficult to perform against warlocks of higher degree. Further, as their arcane energies drain while casting an offensive spell, your energies also drain while defending. It is a rather simple spell with endless complex permutations, as you will no doubt discover. Knowing how to defend yourself against each kind of attack is key. Is everyone following me thus far?"

The trio nodded slowly.

"I would like to hear 'Yes, Mrs. Stone' or 'No, Mrs. Stone' please."

"Yes, Mrs. Stone," they chorused.

"Good. This is not a game. Although you have rarely come up against other warlocks thus far, I assure you the time will come. You will need to be prepared. In the old days of the Arcaners, duels were relatively fair, but now, a warlock might not even show his stripes before attacking. A well-timed Mute spell at an unsuspecting victim is usually more than enough to achieve victory. A thorough understanding of Mind Armor will force your opponent to fight you evenly, and vice versa, of course."

Mrs. Stone's chin dropped as her eyes fixed upon Augum. "Allow me to demonstrate."

He felt a strange tingling in his throat.

"How does that feel?" she asked.

Augum opened his mouth to speak but no words came out. He tried to clear his throat but that didn't work either.

Mrs. Stone nodded and the tingling went away. "Remember that sensation. I am high enough in degree that I can cast these spells silently. Most warlocks will have a trigger word and gesture that will alert you to the attack. I shall cast the spell silently to better tune you to pay attention to what counts—the sensations. Train yourselves to block the spell, not the word. Now let us try again. This time, concentrate on shielding against the oncoming attack. Everyone's thoughts are different, so you will have to improvise until something works. And do not forget to play to your strengths."

Augum felt the tingling and concentrated on somehow blocking the effect. He failed.

"Again," Mrs. Stone said, and so it went on like this for about ten consecutive tries, tiring Augum out just trying to defend himself.

"It is all right that you are unsuccessful, Great-grandson. Now take some time and focus on *why* you have been unsuccessful and *how* you can change it." She moved on to Leera and Bridget while Augum ruminated on what she had said. The point she was making, he thought, was that the attack had an initial feeling he had to recognize immediately, before the spell took effect.

"Armor your mind," she kept saying, "so that even when you yourself are not aware, your mind is on guard, ever watchful like an owl in the night."

VALOR

Neither Bridget nor Leera were successful either. When Mrs. Stone returned to Augum, he thought himself prepared, but failed yet again.

"Unfortunately, the only way to protect your mind against any spell is by knowing its *signature*," and so they continued on, hour after hour, the repetition grating on the trio's nerves.

Only Mrs. Stone seemed unaffected by numerous castings. "You are not concentrating," she would say, or, "Focus like your life depended on it, for one day it will," but the trio only tired more, until Leera collapsed, panting.

"Can we please take a break, Mrs. Stone?" a gasping Bridget asked.

"We will not rest. Breakthroughs come with perseverance. We are not at the academy. You will not master this spell otherwise. You should consider yourselves extremely lucky I am as patient as I am. Pupils clamored by the bushel for such an opportunity back at the academy. Few received it. Now—again!"

Augum's head felt like someone had been kicking it for the last hour. He summoned his strength and returned to trying to block Mrs. Stone's Mute attack. He failed, along with the girls, for the next hour, until all three were lying in the waning sun.

"We need to rest, Nana," Augum croaked.

"You wish to rest, do you? Very well then. Perhaps you may also want to rethink the coming journey. Bahbell is not like Castle Arinthian—it is far more dangerous. Milham is safe, and I am starting to think you three are not up to the task after all. Much of your future rests on your decision. Think carefully."

There was an implosive crunch and she was gone.

"Did she just leave us?" Bridget asked, panting as if having run for leagues.

Augum and Leera were both too tired to answer. The trio lay on the ground, barely moving, while the wind increased and the sun dimmed, reddening the horizon. The place suddenly felt lonely and so very far from anywhere.

"Where do you think we are, anyway?" Augum finally asked when some strength had returned.

"Probably somewhere far south," Bridget replied, "because it's so warm."

"It could be another plane, like Ley," Leera threw in.

They glanced around anxiously; who knew what manner of creature was out here.

Bridget sat up when Augum and Leera hadn't spoken in a while. "Well, don't either of you want to talk about our performance?"

Leera shrugged. "What's there to say?"

"What do you mean, 'What's there to say?' We're about to lose our opportunity to go to Bahbell. What, you two *want* to stay in Milham? Who would train us then? What would we do, mine for iron? Wait for the Legion to find us?"

Leera waved the thought aside. "She wouldn't leave us behind."

Bridget scowled. "Do you really think Mrs. Stone would let us go if she didn't think us ready? She said Bahbell is *dangerous*. If I were her, I'd leave us behind."

Leera rolled her eyes. "I know *you* would, but Mrs. Stone knows how to have fun. She likes to challenge us—"

"—and she likes to keep us *safe*, too. She's right, this *isn't* Castle Arinthian. Bahbell is a hostile place we're going to."

"Well, what do you want to do about it? Can't you see we're exhausted?"

"Try *harder*, push yourselves!" Bridget stood up, dusting herself off. "This is our chance to show Mrs. Stone how serious we are. She won't take us if we just do what's required. Aug, help me out here—"

"Why are you asking him for help? He agrees with me!"

Augum sighed while the girls stared at him. "Nana told me something the other day, before everyone woke up. She said that we're learning at a really fast pace, faster than she had ever seen, because we're applying our arcanery in the field—or something like that at least. Anyway, I guess what I'm trying to say is ..."

He slowly got up and looked at Leera. "Bridget's right, Lee, we have to work harder. Nana *will* leave us behind if she thinks we aren't up to it. Thing is, if we don't believe in ourselves, how is anyone else going to?"

Leera glared at him and shook her head. "I knew it," she muttered. "So you want to just stand there?"

"Kind of, yeah," Bridget said. "Let's all stand in a line and wait for her. That way she knows that, although we've been beaten, we're not ready to give up. If she comes back and we're laying about, she *won't* take us. Besides, we can also contemplate how to better ourselves."

"*You two* can, I'm going to lie right here and sleep."

"Fine."

"Fine!"

Augum felt bad but he stood beside Bridget anyway while Leera lay on her side, her back to them. After a long time, she made an aggravated noise. "Oh for—*fine!*" and stood up beside them, muttering, "I really hate the two of you right now ..."

He gave her a light punch on the shoulder. "Do this with us—it's no fun without you."

She frowned and punched his shoulder back—much harder. "I said *fine* ..." though he thought he saw her cheeks redden a bit and the corner of her mouth curve upward ever slightly.

"Mrs. Stone thinks you're going to face your father one day," Bridget said quietly after a time.

Augum only nodded, raising his hood to protect against the increasing wind.

"The millennials said something similar," Leera threw in, raising her hood too.

" 'When thy fallen can't be slain, when lion children rise again, when fires burn from east to west, blood of kin can vanquish death'," he said. "Nana told it to me the other day."

"Wait—" Bridget said. "Those are Thomas' last words, aren't they?"

"Yes. It's an ancient witch poem. Might be a prophecy. Anyway, guess I'm destined to confront my father, or fight him, or talk him out of his insanity or something."

"Doesn't sound like you believe it."

"Nana said it's just a poem. *I* think it's just a poem too. But she did say I can maybe—just maybe—reach my father through my mother. Apparently he sees some part of her in me."

Leera shook her head. "You're not going to be able to talk him out of being crazy. He'd just capture you again and use you for ransom, or groom you into his own Robin."

He stared at the jagged horizon. "I know one thing—no way could I face my father without either of you."

"No way we'd let you," Leera said.

"Definitely," Bridget added, drawing her own hood. "Let's just hope we don't have to face him …"

They stood like this for who knew how long, the wind slowly increasing in strength, the horizon steadily dimming. Thick, low-hanging clouds rolled in, so close Augum thought he could touch them. Stomachs began to groan as suppertime passed, but no one complained, at least aloud. He used the time to go over in his mind what he thought he could improve on. At long last, when it was pitch-black, there was an implosive crunch.

For a time, Mrs. Stone observed them, staff in hand, scion flashing with silent lightning. They stood at attention.

"So I see. Do you realize how dangerous the coming journey is? I may not be able to protect you. Do you really wish to go?"

"Yes, Mrs. Stone!"

"You would not rather stay in the comforts of Milham, eating warm food and laying by the fire?"

"No, Mrs. Stone!"

There was a resigned sigh. "So be it. Let us begin again."

And so they trained long into the night, collapsing again and again from exhaustion. Each of the trio vomited at least once from the terrible nausea of pushing their arcane boundaries. On top of that, they had to do it in complete darkness with a powerful wind and a very long fall only steps away. Augum had never worked so hard at anything in his life, nor was his body even remotely prepared. His legs gave way numerous times as his mind failed to function properly. He began hallucinating, repeatedly thinking he saw great big flying things in the blackness above.

At some time in the middle of that awful night, there came a glimmer of hope.

"I did it!" Bridget shouted from the darkness, sobbing. "I did it …"

"Again," came the sound of Mrs. Stone's voice. There was a pause in which Mrs. Stone attacked Bridget's mind with the mute spell. "Good. Again!"

Bridget made an anguished cry but gritted her teeth and pushed as if enduring great pain.

"Excellent! You have discovered the spell's signature and are on the correct path."

It was the highest praise Augum had ever heard her give.

Bridget collapsed, crying with joy and grief.

Mrs. Stone moved on to Augum, whose hopes were buoyed by Bridget's success. She repeatedly attacked his mind, until he too finally struck upon the right combination of thoughts that prevented his throat from closing.

"I think I got it!" he shouted, wincing from the throbbing pain in his head and trying not to vomit again.

"Repeat!" and so he strengthened the thought pattern until it was written in stone and he was able to block the attack without fail.

"Excellent! Now, Leera—"

Leera took the longest, vomiting a third time, but she would not give up. Augum could hear her sniffing and sobbing but she persevered through it, until she too cried out in victory.

Mrs. Stone forced her to iron the pattern in with repetition. By the end of it, Leera was writhing in agony but successful.

"Congratulations. Historically speaking, you have achieved what only a handful of apprentices have ever achieved—you have learned how to use Mind Armor to block Mute, all in the space of an evening. Tomorrow, we continue."

Leera dry heaved. Augum and Bridget had to help her up, though neither were in much better shape.

"Let us join hands in preparation for Teleport."

When they arrived back in the Okeke home, the trio collapsed where they stood, nothing to throw up, no energy to move. The candles, including the stubby Endyear candle, flickered and settled.

Teleporting had finished Augum off. He could barely think, let alone stand. He had to crawl to bed while the girls had to be carried by Mr. Okeke and Mr. Goss, both of whom fussed endlessly about the state the trio were in.

"Is this really necessary, Mrs. Stone?" Mr. Goss asked, wetting a towel. "They are frightfully pale and weak, and they missed supper."

"I am afraid it is, Mr. Goss—it is the price they pay for competence. It may save their lives."

Haylee helped too. She seemed better now—her hair was clean and there was a bit of color to her cheeks. She crouched down beside Augum, smiled gently, and cleaned his face with a cloth. He didn't have the strength to say or do anything, however, except fall asleep where he lay.

PERSEVERANCE

The next day, the trio were treated to an enormous late breakfast of warm milk, eggs, potatoes, bread, roasted lamb, and beet soup—and they ate every single bit of it. Jengo found their hunger amusing, until Leera snapped at him, "Just you wait until you have to stay up all night training—"

Jengo knocked on the cover of the blue book on arcaneology. "As a matter of fact, I've been studying with Haylee and Leland. It was arduous. I'm sure I'll come down with something vicious—"

"—all in the comforts of home. It's a book, Jengo, about as dangerous as a pillow. I'd like to see you do it balancing on a cliff edge in the middle of the night."

Jengo shivered at the thought.

"Tomorrow is New Year's," Mr. Goss reminded them.

That's right, Augum thought as everyone exchanged excited looks, though he suspected Mr. Goss had said it more for Mrs. Stone, who ate quietly and sparingly. Perhaps Mr. Goss wanted her to take it easy on them today.

He snorted—they had better odds of finding the remaining scions in the next few hours. "Sorry," he mumbled when everyone looked up.

"Leland and I look forward to gathering the supplies today, don't we, son? All that coin will go to good use."

Leland moaned sadly.

"He wants to come along," Mr. Goss whispered.

"He wouldn't if he knew what we were doing on that mesa," Leera muttered.

Augum was definitely not looking forward to returning to the training ground. The novelty of it had long worn off. All he associated it with was horrendous throbbing pain and vomiting. Every muscle ached and his head *still* hurt from the night before.

"I'd like to come," Haylee said meekly.

Mrs. Stone looked up. "Is that so, child?"

Augum gave her a look, trying to pass on what horror awaited her should she want to train with them. She didn't seem to get it.

"I do, Mrs. Stone. I'm ... I'm ready."

"You'll regret it the moment you puke all over your new robe," Leera said.

"*Leera—*" Bridget whispered.

"What? She has a right to *know—*"

"I shall not go easy on you, child," Mrs. Stone said. "Are you sure this is what you want? It is a serious trial, a trial that may even cost you your life."

Augum suddenly realized she may be talking about *more* than just training. Maybe she was asking if Haylee wanted to come with them to Bahbell ...

Haylee swallowed but nodded. "I'm sure, and I realize it may cost me my life. But if I'm going to die, I want it to be for a purpose." She glanced at Augum. "I have nothing to lose."

"So be it, child. You will have to work very hard though. Prepare yourself."

"I will, Mrs. Stone."

After breakfast, Mrs. Stone ventured to the center of the room. "There is no time to waste. Stand in a circle and hold hands."

When Haylee took Augum's left hand, he noticed it shook. She had to be nervous hearing them talk about their experiences on the mesa, or at least from seeing the state they were in the night before.

Meanwhile, Leera squeezed his right hand extra hard. When he glanced her way, she pretended not to notice. He blinked, confused.

There was an implosive crunch. When the sickness of teleporting passed, they assembled before Mrs. Stone like lambs awaiting slaughter, each putting on a brave face. Mrs. Stone told Haylee to stand aside while she refreshed the Mind Armor lesson for the trio. They only failed a few times before successfully blocking her Mute attack.

"Mute is a 6th degree spell. I chose to start with it because it is one of the more difficult mid-range spells to block. This one, Deafness, is only 4th degree. Let us see how you fare against it."

And so the trials began again, but this time there was no vomiting and little nausea. Augum's head barely hurt, even though he failed to protect himself from the spell time and again. That same sensation he felt of intrusion into his mind and tingling in his throat now focused on his ears. It was easier though, and after only about a hundred tries, he finally managed to block it, Leera and Bridget following shortly after.

They exchanged grins and nods, for it had only taken them the better part of two hours as opposed to before, when it had taken them all night. Throughout, Mrs. Stone imparted instructions for Haylee on what she was to be doing—simple stuff mainly, mostly the basics on Telekinesis, Shine, Repair and Unconceal. Although Haylee was reasonably proficient, she had not mastered them near to the degree the trio had.

"Now let us move on to Confusion," Mrs. Stone said to the trio. "It, too, is a 4th degree spell. Prepare yourselves."

This one was tougher because upon failure Augum had a hair-raising sensation as if he'd just woken up from passing out. There was something absolutely terrifying in not recognizing where he was or who the gawking people around him were. Even ordinary words required more thought than usual. Further, there was the added danger of accidentally stepping off the mesa and tumbling to his death.

It took them well past noon to succeed. This time they had learned their lesson—no one whined for lunch, not even Haylee, who seemed determined to catch up. She was woefully behind, mostly struggling with Unconceal. Mrs. Stone remained patient with her though, hiding objects again and again.

Meanwhile, the trio moved on to defending against the 4th degree spell Fear, an even more difficult spell than Confusion, for it caused them to want to run off the Mesa in terror. More than once, Mrs. Stone had to pull someone back from the edge, much to the horror of the onlookers. It barely helped that Augum had once been subjected to a real attack of the spell. It was still like living his worst nightmare.

Eventually, though, they conquered that one as well, and at mid-afternoon, Mrs. Stone teleported off, promising to bring back lunch.

"How's Unconceal coming, Haylee?" Augum asked as the trio sat trying to catch their breath.

"I hate this spell, it's impossible ..."

"And that's why it's not working," Leera said. "It's your *attitude*."

Haylee gave her a pointed look but said nothing.

"Let me help." Bridget sidled in beside her. "Unconceal is about feeling the subtle fluctuations in the arcane ether—"

Leera elbowed Augum. "There she goes sounding like Mrs. Stone again."

Yet by the time Mrs. Stone returned, Haylee had actually smiled for the first time in recent memory.

"Mrs. Stone, I did it!" she said, biting her lower lip, blonde hair sparkling in the sunshine.

Mrs. Stone placed a basket before the trio. "Show me."

Haylee covered her eyes while Bridget hid an acorn. Bridget then sat down beside Augum and Leera. "Ready."

Haylee opened her eyes and splayed her palm. She found the acorn immediately.

Lunch consisted of water, fried salmon, yellow cheese and journey bread. Augum only hoped they'd be able to keep the food down.

Soon they were training again, Mrs. Stone switching tactics by randomly casting all the offensive spells they had trained against thus far. It proved immensely difficult to guard against unknown attacks, but they handled it in the end, blocking almost all.

In the meantime, Haylee had to repeatedly perform Unconceal, often ending up on her knees crying from the pressure and grueling strain. Yet each time, a look of determination would cross her face, she'd grit her teeth, and stand. Mrs. Stone observed but didn't let up, asking Haylee to cast all the 1st degree spells successively. This, too, sent the girl to her knees.

As for the trio, Mrs. Stone challenged them with a 7th degree spell—Blind, but after repeated failed attempts, it became obvious it was beyond reach.

"We now know your current ceiling," Mrs. Stone said, allowing them to stand back up after a bout of nausea. This time no one had vomited, but all were wincing from pounding headaches. "Four degrees above your level of knowledge is very impressive, you should be proud. A typical apprentice can usually block two degrees above her own. Great adversity brings great reward."

While the trio recuperated, she returned her attention to Haylee. The hours dragged on as they practiced all they had learned thus far, including the 1st and 2nd degree spells.

"That will do for today," Mrs. Stone finally said around suppertime. "It is, after all, the eve of New Year's." She gave a rare smile. This news was most welcome, as everyone dreaded working through this particular night.

"I had wished to begin training you on Object Alarm, Object Track, and your 3rd degree elemental spell. Alas, time is short, and tomorrow we depart in search of Bahbell."

"Tomorrow?" Augum asked. "So soon?"

"A reflection of the urgency of our quest, I am afraid."

The foursome exchanged weary looks. Augum felt there was no way they were ready, at least arcanely speaking.

"However, one of you has qualified to take the test for their next degree." She turned to Haylee. "Should you feel yourself ready, you may stay and await my return."

Augum felt his skin crawl—left alone, what if Haylee changed her mind and wanted to jump off again! Bridget obviously shared the same concern, for the pair of them exchanged alarmed looks.

Haylee took a bit of time thinking about it. At last, she brushed the hair out of her eyes and nodded. "I'll stay, Mrs. Stone."

Augum gave her an encouraging smile before grabbing the lunch basket and holding hands with the others. They teleported back to the Okeke home where they were greeted by the aroma of roast duck, spiced porridge, and chocolate pudding for dessert.

Mrs. Stone returned to the mesa as Mr. Goss came in, arms full of supplies.

"That should be all of it," he said, placing the items into an already large pile. "Rucksacks, tents, rope, warm clothing, a lantern, food, and other necessities ..."

"But Mr. Goss, we hadn't raised nearly enough money for all that," Bridget said.

VALOR

"That is true, but Mrs. Stone did not trade Erika Scarson for nothing, you know. How do you think I paid for my new spectacles? The Tiberrans yielded quite a large sum of coin, actually."

"Mrs. Stone *sold* Erika?" Bridget glanced to Leera and Augum and the trio cracked with laughter. There was something terribly funny about Erika simpering to the Tiberrans, earrings jingling.

"Yes, well, the Tiberrans insisted on compensating Mrs. Stone for such a prize, and since we were in such need of it, she did not turn it down. Speaking of Mrs. Stone, where is she? I wanted to make sure I bought everything she asked for."

"She stayed behind with Haylee to test her on her 1st degree," Bridget replied.

"How fantastic! I am sure she will prevail." Mr. Goss pushed on his spectacles and made his way over to the table. "Shall we wait for them?"

"Mrs. Stone told us not to," Augum said, eager to start digging in.

Mrs. Stone teleported back sometime after supper with a tired-looking Haylee. She told everyone to gather together before announcing that Haylee had passed her test. She then performed the ceremony that bestowed the 1st degree ring around her arm. Everyone congratulated her, even Leera, though mutedly.

"I would also like to say that I have spoken at length to Haylee, and she will be coming with us on our journey to find Bahbell." Mrs. Stone turned to the girl. "You have come a long way in a very short period of time, child, and have suffered much. I am proud of you."

"Thank you, Mrs. Stone," Haylee said, sniffing and gazing at her with adoration.

Augum only smiled as Haylee gave him an appreciative nod. Now they were Mrs. Stone's foursome. He was happy to see her spirits raised.

That evening everyone sat chatting, quietly recounting the year, talking little of what lay ahead. As midnight approached, Mr. Okeke gathered them by the hearth where the Endyear candle burned its last. He distributed glasses of white wine to Mr. Goss and Mrs. Stone and youngling ale to everyone else. They toasted to the 3341st year after the Founding and blew out the candle together.

Later, exhausted from the day, Augum fell asleep knowing that tomorrow he'd have to say goodbye to Mr. Goss, Leland, Jengo and his father. He wondered when they'd all see each other next.

They woke early the next morning, before the winter sun had even penetrated the evergreen canopy, and set to cooking and wrapping food and organizing their rucksacks. There was a sense of urgency in the packing, as if everyone was worried the Legion would reach Bahbell first.

"Let's go see Chaska's father," Bridget said after breakfast, and the trio sped off, leaving Haylee to help Mr. Goss with the sandwiches.

The bell tinkled as they entered the *Good Medicine Shop*.

"Chunchuha, Achishi Zafu," Bridget said. "We've come to say goodbye."

"Old Henawa waiting for youngling maniye," the snow-skinned man began as they approached the counter. "Chaska go on nemana. Youngling maniye go on nemana too. Younglings search Occi, but journey bring danger. Occi dark nuliwi. Younglings must be suala, must have courage."

"Can you help us find the Occi?" Augum asked.

"Old Henawa too old to journey with maniye nuliwi." He withdrew a small leather scroll from behind the counter. "Old Henawa once hear directions to Occi. Old Henawa remember and make map." He handed it over to Leera. "Luck to you, youngling maniye."

"Thank you, Achishi Zafu," Bridget said, cheeks reddening. "And when Chaska gets back, please tell him ... tell him we said goodbye."

VALOR

The old Henawa gave a nod. They waved one last time before departing.

Leera unfurled the map as they walked back to the Okeke home. "I can barely make anything out here …"

Augum glanced over and found the map crudely drawn, with only the most basic symbols. "Well, let's hope it's all we need."

They showed it to everyone else upon returning to the cabin, but the only helpful suggestion came from Mr. Okeke, who deciphered a cross as a meeting of two trails, about half a days' walk east. From the map, it appeared they were to walk north and then east before climbing the Muranians.

"Watch for bandits and bears," he warned as they dressed in their newly purchased fur-lined winter coats, mitts, and, finally, proper fur-trimmed hide boots. "You are going into wild and dangerous country," Mr. Okeke continued. "Few go there. Be on your guard." He gave Mrs. Stone a large cloth sack. "Please take this journey food we have prepared."

"Thank you kindly, Mr. Okeke," Mrs. Stone said, handing the sack to Augum, who threw it over his shoulder, already weighed down by a bulging rucksack. Everyone carried one rucksack, but he packed himself the heaviest, consisting of the Orb of Orion, the blue book on arcaneology, the yellow book, and a tent, among other things.

Mr. Goss took Mrs. Stone's hand in both his own. "Thank you for everything. Leland and I wish you all the best of luck and safe journey. We hope to see you soon."

One by one, those that were staying behind embraced those that were departing, saying their individual goodbyes. Augum made sure to give Leland an extra squeeze and a pinch on his good cheek. Priya even showed up at the last moment to wish them all the best, gifting a small parcel of chocolate as a farewell gift.

"Thank you for the hospitality, Mr. Okeke," Mrs. Stone said, stringing a small rucksack over her shoulder.

"Thank you for healing my son's arm, Mrs. Stone."

Jengo bowed, rubbing his arm. "Yes, thank you, maybe I won't die from infection now."

Mrs. Stone gave a courteous nod and turned to depart, staff in hand. "Oh, and before I forget, I have arranged for a special surprise for Jengo and Leland. Do not be alarmed when this surprise shows up tomorrow."

Everyone exchanged intrigued smiles.

"Good bye to you all!" Bridget said.

"Goodbye, Bridget! Goodbye, Augum and Haylee and Mrs. Stone!"

They waved as the group of five meandered their way through heavily frosted evergreens. It was a bright day, the sun making the rolling sheets of snow sparkle.

"What surprise is it, Mrs. Stone?" Haylee asked once they were out of earshot.

"I hired a mentor from Tiberra using some of the money we earned from Erika Scarson's handover. He has been to Milham before, so he can teleport back and forth for lessons."

"That's so kind of you, Mrs. Stone, and what a great idea …!"

"Considering there is a war on, I will think it lucky he makes an appearance at all."

"Well I still think it was a marvelous thing to do."

They followed the path that snaked through the quiet forest, dipping over hills and valleys, until arriving at the hilltop of the Star Feast.

Leera elbowed Augum upon spying the central area where they had danced. "I have to teach you how to move those feet better," she said with a secret smile.

"He did all right," Bridget said.

Haylee adjusted the rucksack over her shoulder. "Wish I could have come …"

Bridget gave her a kind smile. "There's always next year."

Just as they were about to exit the glade, Mrs. Stone stopped and stared at the scion on top of her staff. It had clouded over.

"What's wrong, Mrs. Stone?" Bridget asked after a time.

Mrs. Stone slowly glanced back westward and stared. "Let us go."

The trio exchanged fearful looks before following, but said nothing. No one wanted to talk about what could possibly have spooked Anna Atticus Stone.

They travelled onward down the other side and onto a path untrodden in some time. The snow lay thick around them, a great white blanket that deadened sound. It was like this for the better part of an hour, the path steadily declining until it crossed another path, only visible because of a dip in the snow. They consulted the map, concluding this must be the marked cross. They changed course as the map dictated, traveling northeast. After another hour or so, the path exploded onto a vast open valley strewn with boulders.

"Nice to see the sun for a change," Augum said, squinting.

Leera looked up. "Enjoy it while it lasts, those clouds look endless."

And they looked laden with snow too, Augum thought.

"Breathtaking," Bridget said as they began descending the valley. They were but five minuscule fur-clad figures amongst an ocean of white, the boulders looking like enormous eggs hurled at the ground by giants.

Leera allowed herself to drift back with Augum, who brought up the rear, constantly adjusting the two sacks. She nodded at Haylee. "Why is she coming, anyway?"

"I think Nana had a talk with her after her test, didn't she?"

"I know *that*, but exactly *why* is she coming?"

"I don't know, maybe Nana felt bad for her. Besides, what else is she going to do? She has nobody—"

She shrugged. "I'm just saying, she could have stayed in Milham with the others—"

Augum sighed, glancing far ahead to where Haylee and Bridget followed Mrs. Stone. "She doesn't know who she is anymore. Think about it, everybody she knew is gone. She has no home, no place to belong, and doesn't even have any friends—except for us."

"Oh, and everyone *we* knew isn't dead? Her grandfather gave us up to the Legion. Her *boyfriend* murdered—"

"—Mya." He stopped in his tracks. "He murdered Mya; he murdered Haylee's grandfather, the very man that betrayed us; *and* he murdered Haylee's parents—"

"Why are you always defending her? Do you *like* her or something?"

Augum gave her a look. "Why are you always out to get her? I mean, I know you two had problems before, but why can't you just let it go?"

" 'Problems'?" Leera's voice dropped dangerously. " '*Problems?*' She made fun of me every chance she got, even making up a song the class sang before the entire. Damn. Academy—"

"Oh, you mean back when *you* liked Robin?"

Her eyes narrowed to slits. "I knew it, you *do* like her—"

"What? That's not—" but she had already stormed ahead, drawing her hood. He groaned and plodded along, feeling the weight of both sacks.

After a long descent meandering around the boulders, he finally caught up to the others. They waited for him at the bottom of the valley by a frozen stream. Bridget and Haylee were examining the leather map while Leera stood apart, face averted.

"… what do you think, Lee?" Bridget asked.

"Oh, what?"

"We're trying to figure out what the map says here." Bridget tried to show it to her but Leera only shrugged.

"Whatever you think, I don't care …"

Mrs. Stone shaded her eyes with her hand. "There is a small hole in the forest on that ledge there. Let us try it."

They gathered their things and renewed the trek. This time, it was Bridget that hung back with Augum.

"She seems upset."

Augum glanced ahead at Leera marching as if the snow had done her wrong. "She doesn't like the fact Haylee came along."

"Is that really what it is?"

He gave a half-shrug. "I don't know, they have a past. But then …"

She allowed him to gather his thoughts, something he appreciated.

"She thinks I like Haylee," he finally blurted. "What should I tell her, that I *don't* like her?"

"It wouldn't really make much of a difference." Bridget sighed. "Let me talk to her, though you know how stubborn she can be." She eyed his sagging shoulders. "Just because you're a boy doesn't mean you have to carry most of the weight all the time."

Sir Westwood certainly would say otherwise, having hammered it into Augum's head how it was a knight's duty to be chivalrous and gallant to women at all times.

"I'm fine …"

"You're 'fine'? Really?" She smiled and shook her head before speeding up, catching Leera halfway up the valley incline. They talked all the way to the valley ledge, where everyone waited for Augum once again. The sun had succumbed to the torrent of gray clouds when he finally caught up, huffing and red-faced.

They entered a forest of densely packed evergreens laden with snow, the path barely discernible. There were occasional cries of pain as branches whipped across faces. It was the quietest forest Augum had ever entered.

The snow in these parts was waist high, making the walk much more difficult. The cold deepened and, as he predicted, it had begun snowing—fat lazy flakes they could catch in their hands like leaves. Augum drew his apprentice hood, thankful for the hide mitts and boots. They needed breaking in, but this kind of journey would be impossible without them.

As he plodded along, he felt a familiar sensation in his throat—and immediately fought it off. Just as he was about to raise the alarm, he spotted Mrs. Stone watching him from up ahead.

"Was that you, Nana?"

"Indeed it was. Let us move along."

"She tested us too," Bridget said as he caught up.

They stopped around mid afternoon under a great spruce. After digging out a sitting area, Mrs. Stone had them use Telekinesis to gather wood for a fire, which she started arcanely.

Lunch was a welcome affair, with little talking other than jabs at the map.

"Maybe it's a well of some kind," Bridget said, turning the wrinkled leather.

Augum tore a piece of journey bread and handed the rest to Leera, who took it, but held on as if hesitating to say something.

"Want to, uh, check out that tree there?" she said.

He glanced around, confused. "Tree—? What tree?"

"She wants to *talk* to you," Bridget whispered.

He reddened. "Oh, uh ... *that* tree. Right. Sure. I guess."

She led the way to a large spruce, behind which she suddenly turned around. "I'm sorry for ... earlier."

He swallowed. Suddenly speaking was hard. "It's all right."

"You know me, I can be ... emotional sometimes." She looked into his eyes. "Haylee's been through a lot, and she's different now. I need to be more ... understanding."

VALOR

He just gaped at her. For some reason, all he could think about was that moment they shared together at the Star Feast, just before they were going to kiss.

"So, uh, do you forgive me?" she asked.

He realized she had been waiting for him to say something. "Oh ... of course."

She smiled and turned to go, but he caught her arm.

"Err, just so you know, I don't *like* her in that way."

Her smile widened. "I know." She gave him a light punch on the arm. "Come on, let's study the map."

Augum caught a look from Bridget as they returned. He smiled and mouthed, "Thank you." She only winked.

They took seats beside her and got out the map. A big black dot indicated something was ahead. The path shot off northward from that spot. Problem was nobody knew what the dot meant.

"Could be a village or something," Augum said, tearing the bread with his teeth. "What do you think, Nana?"

"I am of the mind we shall see when we get there."

A distant shrill scream with a grotesque gurgling quality to it suddenly pierced the air. When it was silent again, nobody moved.

"What. Was. That?" Haylee whispered, watching the trees with wide eyes.

"I daresay I do not know," Mrs. Stone said, which unnerved Augum. Mrs. Stone's eyes flicked to the scion. "I suggest we stay vigilant."

Bridget, holding a piece of salted ham, sidled closer to her. Haylee did the same. They watched the forest. Eventually, one by one, they returned to the food.

Before departing, Mrs. Stone made them practice some of their spells, at least the quiet ones. Augum thought it a bad sign. Was she expecting an attack of some kind? He decided not to push himself, saving his arcane energies in case something should happen.

Just as they finished packing, a rancid smell filled the air.

"Stay close—" Mrs. Stone immediately said.

They held their noses, for the smell was the scent of death mingled with foul dung. A tree rocked nearby and piles of snow came falling. They heard the sound of flapping wings and then silence once again.

"Is it up there?" Leera whispered. "Can anyone see it?"

"Stay right here." Mrs. Stone made to stride off, but Haylee grabbed her sleeve.

"Don't leave us, Mrs. Stone—"

"I shall not go far."

Haylee reluctantly let go, taking a step closer to Augum. The foursome stood with hands out ready to cast a spell, while Mrs. Stone plodded behind a clump of trees. In the silence that followed, Augum listened to the frantic beating of his own heart and swore he heard the girls' too.

They stood absolutely still, backs to each other, eyes darting at any noise or movement.

At long last, Mrs. Stone returned with a vexed look. "Whatever it was, it is gone now." She picked up her rucksack, strung it over her shoulder, and stood thinking a moment. "Let us go," and strode forth. The foursome hurried to catch up.

Augum took up the rear as usual, preferring it to be him than anyone else. The group stopped often, allowing him to catch up. Sometimes Mrs. Stone would test one of them with a spell, or there'd be a noise nearby and a tree would lose some of its snow. Everyone would stop and listen, hearing nothing but their breathing and the soft falling snow, and nothing would come of it. It went on like this for the greater part of the day.

They traversed hilly forest that thinned and thickened in cycles, crossing long rolling hills and wide shallow valleys. The pristine path meandered like a great snake, lonesome in its quiet solitude.

When the sky began to darken, Mrs. Stone decided to set camp. They found a spot under an enormous fir whose gnarled trunk was the length of two horses. These giant trees almost exclusively made up the forest here, with hardly a shrub in sight. Perhaps they choked out the sun to such a degree nothing was allowed to grow below their sprawling boughs.

"It will be dark here faster," Mrs. Stone said, glancing up at the thick canopy. "Please gather some wood, and do not stray."

Nobody needed reminding—they hardly stepped twenty paces from the camp, using Telekinesis to float branches over to a pile. Luckily, the snow was only ankle deep here, swooning in wind-sculpted waves.

Meanwhile, Mrs. Stone set to wandering in a great circle casting an enchantment. When she finished, she once again used arcanery to dry the branches. They soon burst into flame, allowing the foursome to warm themselves. After that, they began erecting the small square tents, made of hide and sinew and held up by two notched sticks. The girls were to sleep in one and Augum and Mrs. Stone in the other.

Later, they quietly sat around the fire eating supper, watching the play of shadows on the gargantuan trunks. Augum thought the only thing lacking was a haunting ghost story. Instead, Mrs. Stone lectured them on the other standard spells in the 3rd degree—Object Alarm and Object Track. The former would alert them when their enchanted object was touched, and the latter would trace where it had gone. She went on to tell them of the varied uses, such as casting Object Alarm on a door handle or a gate.

"As for Object Track ..." She smiled. "Allow me to tell you a brief story. Back when I was in the academy, a certain unwelcome suitor kept appearing before me, interrupting my studies to talk about utter nonsense. After the tenth time this happened, I lost my temper and levitated him to the ceiling, inquiring exactly how he kept finding me despite my best attempts at keeping myself hidden with my books. He confessed that he had enchanted a small rock with the Object

Track spell, plopping it in my pocket without my knowledge. So you see, one can get up to all sorts of mischief with such a spell."

The girls chuckled.

Mrs. Stone winked at them. "I was once considered quite pretty by some."

"I'm sure he wasn't the only one following you, Mrs. Stone," Bridget said. "So are there counterspells to Object Alarm and Object Track?"

"Yes, but you must be able to sense a spell had been cast first, which requires which spell again?"

"Reveal," Bridget said.

"Correct, and what degree—"

"11th."

"Correct again. All counterspells are mere extensions of their original spell—"

"I don't understand, Nana—"

"Perhaps if you would let me finish, Great-grandson." There was a pause in which Augum mumbled an apology.

"So," Mrs. Stone continued, "for example, Augum's Shine extension is the ability to shock someone. Bridget's Shine extension is the ability to weave her vine around an object and grip it. But there are some spell extensions that simply counter the originating spell, such as *Slow*. *Slow* does not attack the mind, but rather the entire body, and thus requires the use of its own extension to counter it. Arcaneologically speaking, it is quite an elegant solution, for to counter such a physical spell, you need to know its signature, and therefore the spell itself. Performing a counterspell is quite tricky as well, for one has to pronounce the spell incantation and perform the gestures backwards."

Augum was confused but nodded anyway.

"All my Shine extension does is light up some water," Leera muttered. "Useless."

"Ah, but use is limited only by imagination."

"What's mine, Mrs. Stone?" Haylee asked.

"Well, since your element is ice, what do you think it would be?"

Haylee thought about this a moment. "I could freeze things?"

"Partially correct—more precisely, you could cool your hand down a great deal without suffering damage to your person."

"Oh, what's the point of that?"

"Well, let us say for example that you could pick up something very cold or very hot, or even snuff out a glowing ember with your fist. You must be careful to understand its limitations, however, for one can easily hurt oneself with arrogance. And again, it is only constrained by your imagination. Further, extensions can be far more difficult than the original spell. Some warlocks learn them many degrees later."

Haylee raised her hand a little as if in class, drawing an amused look from Leera.

"Yes, Haylee?"

"We don't need to know our extensions to pass our degree tests, do we?"

"Though I prefer otherwise, you are *not* required to know the extensions to your spells to attain the next degree."

Augum withdrew Priya's chocolate bundle and passed it around.

Mrs. Stone broke off a piece. "Haylee, am I right to assume you have undertaken some training in necromancy?"

Haylee dropped her eyes. "Yes, Mrs. Stone."

"We've seen her tell a wraith to go piddle off," Augum said, recounting the time she saved his and Leera's life on the way to Hangman's Rock, "and a bunch of walkers too."

Haylee blushed.

"And you trained at the academy, I take it?" Mrs. Stone asked.

"I did. It's … it's not the same anymore, Mrs. Stone, you wouldn't recognize it. All the hallways have dead things, and all the mentors do is focus on necromancy and standard arcanery."

"What about subjects like arcane history, arithmetic, astrology, or the written hand?"

"We were only taught what we needed, Mrs. Stone."

The lines on Mrs. Stone's face deepened. "So you can communicate with the undead, is that right?"

"Only a little bit. It's pretty much the only thing I know because Robin and I spent a lot of time on excursions. He trained a lot more than I did."

"That ability to communicate with the dead may one day be useful to you. Do not let it go."

"I'll try, Mrs. Stone. Oh, I also know how to arcanely appear dead and decomposed, want to see?"

"That is not necessary, I believe you."

"Leera and I saw her do it," Augum said, throwing Leera a friendly elbow. "It was very believable."

"It was, uh, convincing," Leera said. The look on her face gave Augum the impression she was surprised to be saying something supporting about Haylee.

"Are we going to need to setup watches?" Haylee asked, nibbling on the chocolate.

"That will be unnecessary. My enchantments should prove sufficient."

They all relaxed a little; apparently, nobody liked the idea of sitting alone in this cold, wondering what was out there watching them.

"Are you really 20th degree, Mrs. Stone?" Haylee asked.

"I am."

"When did you get your 20th stripe?"

Mrs. Stone sat back. "Let me see here, it was just before my encounter with Narsus underneath the academy, so I would say eighteen years ago or so now. It took me another ten years to achieve mastery."

"Who did the ceremony for you, Mrs. Stone?" Bridget asked.

"It is known as *The Sleeving*, and it actually happens on its own, as if the arcane ether makes the final judgment on proficiency. It is a strange, unknown thing. Some say the gods are responsible, others say the warlock achieves a heightened state of being and thus subconsciously knows when she is ready."

There was a pause, but if anyone hoped to see her sleeve of solidified stripes, they were disappointed.

"Is it true that you're the only living master, Mrs. Stone?" Bridget asked.

"I am not sure. That is what they say, but the world is quite large, far larger than most Solians think."

"What's the furthest you've ever been?"

"Now that is difficult to answer since I have visited the Leyan plane. Also, the academy Trainers are located in some … unusual and distant locations, as you have seen. The world is indeed quite large."

Leera prodded the fire with a stick. "Ley still reminds me of that brat prince."

"Oh, him …" Haylee said. "We didn't get along."

"Shocking," Leera replied, but she said it with a smile, and Haylee smiled back.

Mrs. Stone used her staff to stand. "We should get some sleep. We have a long day ahead tomorrow."

"Yes, Mrs. Stone," they all said, and snuffed out the fire, using Shine to see what they were doing.

That was one of the advantages of being a warlock, Augum thought as he went to sleep beside his great-grandmother—no need for candles or lanterns.

THE LONG MARCH

Augum woke suddenly in the middle of the night. He listened to the darkness but heard only Mrs. Stone's wheezing beside him. As he tried to go back to sleep, there was the faintest clicking, answered by another clicking from the opposite side of the camp. Curious, he stuck his head out the tent.

The cold bit at his face and ears. He could see absolutely nothing, yet his nose picked up the faint scent of rotten meat. Another noise came, this time a low hissing, as if a snake were speaking.

"Boy ..." he thought he heard it say.

"Die ..." came the reply from behind.

He froze. Both sounded about twenty paces away, but it was hard to judge in the dark. Should he wake the others?

Then the clouds moved just enough to allow the tiniest bit of starlight, and what he saw made his heart thunder—a great many plumes of frozen breath, as if a hundred mouths floated in the dark.

"Boy ..."

"Die ..."

"Blood ..."

Augum slowly extended his hand. "Shyneo."

The area lit up in electric blue. Scores of reflective eyes shone in a great circle around the camp, from the trees to the ground. His first thought was they were huge ravens, except with old woman faces. All had hooked noses and blotchy, wrinkled skin sprouting with boils, pimples and moles. The hair was long and frazzled like a witch's, the upper torso that of a hag, everything else a twisted bird of some sort. The ones on the ground would stand to his shoulder.

All of them hissed quietly, some clicking their clawed feet.

"Harpies," Mrs. Stone whispered beside him. He had not heard her wake over the beating of his heart. "They are known to torment their victims for long periods before eviscerating their bowels. They are very dangerous, and I have never seen more than one together."

"Can ... can they get us?"

"No. Do you see how they perch on the edge of a great invisible circle? They cannot pass my protective enchantments."

Augum watched as one of the harpies opened its nose, before realizing those were beaks. The predator eyes gleamed in his light, never wavering. Occasionally one of the things would stretch out its black wings like a great moving shadow.

"Where are they from?" he asked quietly.

"Summoned from the same plane as hellhounds. They are said to be undead, for no one has seen one die. Of course, few see a harpy and live to tell about it, let alone study them for great lengths of time. They have a master. We are being watched and followed."

"A master? Could it be the Legion?"

"Highly doubtful. It takes a lot of necromantic skill to command a harpy. I do not believe anyone, even Lividius, has the capability to command this many."

"So you mean there's a more powerful necromancer around than my father?"

"Your father is singularly powerful because of his combination of scions, lightning element knowledge, and necromancy. Combine that with control of the Dreadnoughts and you have a formidable opponent. But as to necromancy as a formal discipline, that, I believe, he is not as advanced with … yet."

"So … are they all under the control of one person?"

"This I do not know."

"Does that mean whoever they serve can see us?"

"This I also do not know, my knowledge of necromancy and its creatures is incomplete."

"But they can speak …" He hoped they had nothing to do with the Occi.

"Apparently so. Now let us go back to sleep, we have a long day tomorrow." Mrs. Stone retreated into the tent.

He immediately followed, extinguishing his hand. However, going back to sleep knowing those things were out there proved near impossible, especially since they'd routinely remind him of their presence by whispering, "Boy …die," while clicking their sharp beaks and claws.

Eventually his tired eyes got the best of him and he drifted off to sleep, only to wake to the tent shaking violently.

"Get up, sleepyhead!" Leera said, snickering.

He fell back with a groan, craving shuteye. The camp bustled with activity and there was the crackle of a fire. He changed from his nightgown and back into his apprentice robe, fur-lined long coat, mitts and boots, before getting out.

The first thing he did was peruse the perimeter.

"See the tracks yet?" Bridget asked, preparing bacon over the fire, hair tied in a ponytail. "Big, aren't they?"

"Harpies watching us …" Leera muttered, crouching by the flames and rocking back and forth. "You know, those giant baby-snatching things that we all thought were imaginary. Great, isn't it?"

"I know, saw them with Mrs. Stone," he said.

"They as scary as the stories say?"

"Not as bad," he lied. "But very ugly. Where are Nana and Haylee?"

"Doing a bit of quick training—they already ate."

"Ah." He then relayed what Mrs. Stone told him last night about harpies.

"Wonder if it means we're getting close to the Occi," Bridget said, removing crispy bacon from the fire and distributing it.

"Fantastic," Leera said. "Maybe we'll get there in time for supper. I'm sure we'll make a great broth."

Augum couldn't help but crack a grin. "We'll be fine, we're with Nana. Besides, just think of the adventure."

"I love adventure, but a village of cannibals is … different."

It was a bitterly cold morning, the sky once again overcast. They finished breakfast and began to pack camp. Mrs. Stone and Haylee returned shortly after, with Haylee constantly raising her left arm as if to block invisible threats.

"How is Shield coming along?" Bridget asked.

"It's *hard*—going to take me a while."

Augum unconsciously used Telekinesis to grab his rucksack. Haylee's blonde brows rose. "You do that a lot?"

"Do what?"

"Use your spells for everyday things."

"Not really, I guess. Didn't even notice I was doing it there."

"He's been doing it more lately," Bridget said, folding a Dramask blanket and packing it away.

"I encourage you all to practice your arcanery at every opportunity available," Mrs. Stone said. "In fact, from here on, I shall expect it."

Leera gave Augum a *Way to go, thanks for that* look.

Haylee began to pack her things using Telekinesis but gave up, as it proved too difficult and time consuming.

They were soon underway again in search of that black dot on the map, being careful to stay very close together. Anytime they drifted too far apart, Mrs. Stone would wait. They watched the trees with incessant anxiety as they walked, stopping now and then to listen.

As the slog of the march set in and the cold bit at Augum's face, he thought of Mr. Goss, Leland, Jengo, Priya, and Mr. Okeke sitting around a hearth enjoying the warmth. If he could teleport like Mrs. Stone, he'd never sleep in discomfort again. The idea made him wonder why they weren't teleporting somewhere warm and safe every night, and resuming their trek the next day. It bothered him so much that the next time Mrs. Stone stopped to wait for him, he asked her about it.

"Do you think it prudent to always take the easy path, Augum?" She replied.

"No, Nana, I just meant—"

"I know precisely what you meant, my dear child. I may be old, but I like to think I still have my wits about me. You must know hardship to appreciate struggle and reward. It is an old unspoken Arcaner rule that warlocks work to achieve their ends without relying on one another too much. It is considered weak, if you will. Now, never mind your weaselly ways and let us continue."

Bridget gave Augum a sympathetic look before following.

"Well *I* thought it was a good question," Leera whispered as she passed.

They walked the narrow trail all day, stopping at lunch, debating the map, and practicing arcanery. When they resumed, the day darkened due to heavy cloud cover that moved swiftly overhead. Snow tumbled as the winds raked the tree canopy, the shwooming noise making it difficult to pick out other sounds, forcing them to stick even closer together.

The march continued league after weary league. Sometimes one of them would spy a winged shape in the forest, though often it was an owl or raven.

Augum's feet ached and his shoulders were numb by the time they broke through the trees. Before them was an upward-curving lip of exposed rock and dirt. The path wound northward around this wide feature.

"This has to be it," Haylee said, blonde hair peeking out from within her fur-rimmed hood.

Bridget kept her distance. "What is it?"

"Let us see," Mrs. Stone said, scaling the lip, Augum and Leera following.

When he looked over, he saw a massive round hole the width of a small village, as if made by a gigantic worm long ago. He couldn't see the bottom without getting precariously close, however, something he was unwilling to do in these winds. Regardless, it was a sheer drop. Trees curled over the edge like rows of shark teeth.

Mrs. Stone retreated, staff prodding at the snow. "It appears to be an ancient sinkhole."

"As long as nothing comes out of there, I don't care what it is," Leera muttered so only Augum could hear.

Bridget withdrew the map. "Now we know we're headed in the right direction. The next destination is some type of rectangle."

Leera snorted. "The big black circle on the map turned out to be a big black hole. Maybe the giant rectangle will be ... a giant sarcophagus."

"I don't get it," Haylee said.

Leera slowly gestured a rectangle. "You know, because they're the same shape ...?"

Haylee blinked. "Oh."

"Never mind."

The path wound around the edge and dipped back into the forest, beginning a steady but gentle incline. Bare-branched mountain shrubs began making an appearance as the trees shortened until they were stunted versions of the behemoths left behind leagues ago.

Hours later, hungry, tired and cold, they stopped at a windswept rocky plateau offering little shelter other than a few giant boulders, one of which they setup camp behind. The clouds dipped so low here they often blew at ground level, zipping by with the unceasing winds.

"We are at the base of the Muranians," Mrs. Stone informed them, trotting off to encircle the camp with protective enchantments, robe flapping.

Meanwhile, the foursome erected the tents against the boulder and chipped out a fire pit from the ice. When it came to wood, the task was near impossible as the windswept plateau surrendered barely more than a few twigs. Luckily, Mrs. Stone saved them the labor by shuffling off into the swirling mists to arcanely gather more.

The foursome spent the time preparing the inside of the tents, making them as cozy as possible, until Mrs. Stone returned with enough wood to start a small fire. Supper consisted of roasted pork, rice, journey bread, and melted snow. By the time they finished eating, the wind had snuffed out the fire and they all retreated to their fragile hide homes.

Mrs. Stone peeked outside and shook her head. "Augum, please grab the blue book on arcaneology and let us join the girls."

He happily did so and the pair scuttled around the dead fire. Night had come early, the wind at a constant howl. Definitely not an evening for outdoor activity.

The girls' tent was larger, sparing just enough room for everyone to sit in a tight circle.

"This is a perfect opportunity to study and practice the arcane discipline," Mrs. Stone said once they had all settled in. "I considered taking you to the 3rd degree training ground again, but I thought you might find this a little more comfortable."

The foursome nodded, faces etched with relief. Nobody seemed in the mood for an arduous training session.

"First, let us quickly touch upon elemental arcanery. Historically, warlocks tended to war with each other often, much more so than today, which is why we can expect elements to be full of war-like spells. Of course, there were many more warlocks in olden times, but that is another matter altogether—"

"What happened to them?" Augum asked.

"Many killed each other off in duels, some were recruited for war, and some were sought for extermination, deemed as threats. It takes a long time for a warlock to advance in degree, and the great majority hit their ceiling early on. Combine that with commoner superstitions and you have reason for there being so few of us in number. But I believe the single greatest cause for the decline of warlocks is the Leyan decision to withdraw from the world. They shared their knowledge with our academies and allowed our apprentices to visit them in Ley for special training sessions. Since that stopped, our way has slowly been dying out."

"What about—"

"If you do not mind, Augum, I would like to continue my lesson."

"Sorry, Nana."

"Now, elemental spells are as arcanely malleable as standard spells. You will have noticed Shine and Slam are relatively the same for all warlocks, distinguished of course by the warlock's element. For Shine, your hands light up with different colors and there is variety in your extensions. For Slam, Augum's sound is lightning, Bridget's is the breaking of a massive tree, Leera's is that of water crashing, and Haylee's is the cracking of ice, like that of a great glacier splitting in half. As you progress in your degrees, however, you will become aware of your element branching further and further away from other elements. It is this individuality that becomes your strength. Embrace it and do not be afraid to experiment."

She motioned for Augum to open the blue book. "Since we are in close quarters, let us practice and learn standard spells that require no maneuverability—"

She abruptly stopped as the ground began shaking. Everyone exchanged anxious looks. The tremors got much worse in a very short time, followed by a terrible roar.

Mrs. Stone's eyes widened. She hurled herself outside, shouting an arcane phrase—just as the roaring reached them.

Everything instantly went black.

CHANGE IN FORTUNE

"Is everyone all right?" Bridget asked in the darkness.

Augum felt himself over, finding no injuries. "Fine," he said, quickly echoed by Haylee and Leera. "Shyneo." His hand lit up electric blue, revealing all as it was. But there was one thing that felt amiss—it was suddenly too quiet, when before there was a howling wind. The look they exchanged was one of utter bewilderment.

They quickly piled out of the tent to discover Mrs. Stone standing outside. Augum immediately understood why the silence—they were in a giant shimmering blue bubble preventing packed snow from crushing them to death. It protected both tents and part of the rock face.

"It must have been an avalanche," Leera said in an awed voice, approaching the bubble. Augum recognized the spell—it was the same one Nana had used to save the trio in Sparrow's Perch, only much larger.

"I am afraid it was," Mrs. Stone said, rolling her staff between her hands in thought. "This presents a bit of a challenge."

"What do you mean, Mrs. Stone?" Haylee asked, voice quivering a little. "Can't we just teleport out of here with our stuff?"

"Not through a Sphere of Protection, my child—but we have a greater worry."

They stood there gawking at her. What could be worse than this?

She turned to them. "If we do not find a way out, we will run out of air."

"So after everything we've been through," Leera muttered, "it's snow that ends up killing us …"

"All right, all right," Bridget began, flailing her arms as if they were on fire. "Nobody panic, let's just think our way through—"

Leera's brows rose. "Who said anyone was panicking?"

"It is best to remain calm," Mrs. Stone said. "Excitement will only hasten our demise."

Sounds like she's been through this before, Augum thought.

Bridget paled.

"Bridget's brothers once buried her in snow a little too long," Leera said. She grabbed Bridget's arms. "Here, just sit down and relax."

Bridget nodded. "Yes, good idea …"

"What if we dug our way out?" Haylee asked, aiming the question at Augum for some reason, as if he had all the answers.

He just shrugged, looking to Mrs. Stone. "Would that work, Nana?"

"Perhaps, but the spell mechanics trouble me. Let us say I dispel the sphere, what would happen?"

He glanced upward, the snow lit blue by his electric palm and the bubble. "The snow would come crashing down on us?"

"Indeed, we must assume that will be the case. Further, we do not know how far we have to dig. I can dispel the bubble, but will I have enough time to cast a spell before the snow overtakes us? Group Teleport takes too much time, so that is well out of the question. Only Battle Teleport has the speed necessary, but it only works on the caster."

"Battle Teleport?"

"It is an almost instantaneous and, for someone such as I, nonverbal extension of Teleport. The problem with Battle Teleport is the distance of travel is rather short. Further, one runs the risk of appearing inside an object if one does it in an unfamiliar area."

Bridget looked around like a trapped animal.

Leera crouched down across from her, placing her hands on her shoulders. "Bridge, how would you like to start packing the tents?"

She stared at Leera a moment before nodding slowly. "I … I can do that …"

"What about Telekinesis, Mrs. Stone?" Haylee asked as Leera helped Bridget begin. "Can you not move the snow out of the way?"

"We do not know how much snow is above us. Even I have my limits, and if the weight is too great …"

"What about melting it?" Leera asked from inside one of the tents where she was helping Bridget pack.

"It may be worth trying." She reached up to the sphere and her hand began to glow. After a short while, she stopped. "It is as I suspected—the Sphere of Protection prevents access to the snow."

They kept throwing ideas at each other until the tents were packed. Augum began to feel light-headed by then.

Haylee took a deep breath. "Mrs. Stone, what if we were frozen in animation or something while you dug us out? I know there's a necromancy spell that can make that happen, mostly used for sacrificial purposes …"

Mrs. Stone stopped pacing. "Now I daresay that indeed may work. I do know of an off-the-book spell called Loterain's Limbo, but I have not used it in some time."

"What would that do?" Augum asked.

"You would, if I am not mistaken, stop breathing and go into a kind of stasis. Mind that you would still be conscious, but to all outward appearance, have no sign of life. However, it can be quite ... uncomfortable ... to be trapped in your own body."

Bridget breathed rapidly. "You mean ... we'd be buried alive?"

"Essentially, yes. Hopefully not for long though—I would teleport to the surface and immediately begin using Telekinesis to dig you out."

Bridget shook her head. "I don't know if I can do this ..."

Leera gave her a gentle hug. "We've gone through worse, Bridge. You *can* do this."

"We don't have a choice anyway," Haylee said, "unless we think of something better." She began moving their packs against the rock. "Mrs. Stone, we'll stand here at the base with the gear. You can dig your way down using the face of the rock to find us."

"An excellent idea, Haylee."

The foursome lined up with their backs to the rock, holding their rucksacks, breathing quick shallow breaths.

Mrs. Stone gave a small nod. "Let us have luck in this endeavor." The scion hummed a little louder, as if sensing arcanery coming. She approached Leera first. "Close your eyes, child." She then placed one hand on Leera's forehead and the other on her chest. "Cunodeo val xen lotereano." Leera instantly went rigid while Mrs. Stone moved on to Bridget, who squirmed and shook her head, breaths coming in rapid bursts.

"I don't know if I can do this, Mrs. Stone, please ..."

"Close your eyes, dear child."

Bridget winced and shut her eyes tight.

"Cunodeo val xen lotereano." Bridget froze, still wincing.

Mrs. Stone moved before Haylee, who had already shut her eyes. Soon she, too, turned into a statue.

"Great-grandson, are you ready?"

"Yes, Nana." He closed his eyes.

"Cunodeo val xen lotereano."

It was very unusual to have all his senses dulled, as if he had become nothing more than pure thought. Distantly, he heard an implosive crunch and then felt a dense pressure squish him from all sides, until finally equalizing. That had to be the snow.

It was difficult to focus. His thoughts kept drifting as if in a dream. He wondered how Bridget was faring, and hoped Mrs. Stone would get to them soon. Time seemed irrelevant, and he couldn't figure out how much of it had passed. Centuries, perhaps.

Finally, he heard a distant scratching and felt his body move, but he couldn't tell in which direction. Feeling suddenly overcame him as if a dam had burst. He opened his weary eyes, shaking from the cold. There was a fire before him, a blanket draped around his shoulders. His thoughts were too slow for a world that seemed to move very fast. He tried to speak but his voice slurred.

Mrs. Stone finished waking up the others. They sat side-by-side against the trunk of a tree with low-hanging evergreen boughs that moved with the wind. Other stubby trees stood nearby, swaying. The fire was small but ample, the night dark.

"I am too tired from my arcane exertions to teleport you all to a sheltered place," Mrs. Stone wheezed. "You were buried deeper than I had imagined. I daresay it took me a long while to find the right rock even."

"Where … are … we?" Leera asked, teeth chattering.

"Not far from where you were exhumed."

That word caused them to fall silent a moment.

"So… cold," Leera eventually said.

"Concentrate on getting warm and try not to speak. I shall scavenge more wood." Mrs. Stone left them to sit by the fire, disappearing behind the tree they sat against.

Moments later, there came a distinct clicking noise straight ahead. A child-sized old woman with bird feet and wings waddled into view, haggard face hissing quietly, large hooked beak swinging back and forth. The harpy's head swiveled around as if looking for Mrs. Stone. It then steadily approached, testing one foot before the other.

"Mrs. Stone ... help ..." Leera mumbled while Augum, Bridget and Haylee moaned feebly.

They could now smell its putrid stench as it finally realized there were no protective enchantments. It shot forward like a child eager for its toy, crooked beak snapping, giving the fire a wide berth. Its black eyes focused on Augum as its maw opened up—only to bite down on Mrs. Stone's staff.

There was a loud electric crack and the harpy squawked as it flew backward, slamming against a tree. Mrs. Stone stepped between it and the foursome, staff at the ready, scion humming. The harpy picked itself up for another charge, but this time Mrs. Stone raised her palm and shot forth a bolt of lightning, instantly exploding the creature in a burst of feathers.

"Quite a nuisance they are," she said, adding a few more sticks to the fire.

Suddenly the scion flared with multiple bursts of silent lightning. She drew it close, level with her face. Her eyes narrowed. "It happened again. Something is wrong. It feels a pull of some sort." She scanned the trees. "But how can that be ...?"

"What's ... going ... on?" Augum managed to ask, finally able to move a little. He dragged himself closer to the fire so he could warm up quicker, Bridget, Leera and Haylee doing the same.

Suddenly there was a great implosive crunch. A hairless man appeared before them with shiny black skin that faded to matte almost instantly, and eyes like two chips of coal, fading to brown. He wore dark brown pants and a loose-fitting wine-colored shirt, unbuttoned in the middle, revealing a muscular chest. Two curved blades hung from each hip.

"Oba Sassone—" Mrs. Stone said.

Augum felt bumps rise on his skin. Oba Sassone was a Leyan and somehow he had teleported right to their location. Because Leyans lose their long life spans immediately upon setting foot back in the mortal world, he knew Oba would start aging over the next couple of days before dying before their eyes.

"Krakatos the Ancient use portal cube," Oba said in his deep voice. "To mortal world he send Oba."

Augum distinctly remembered Krakatos as the oldest and wisest Leyan. He also recalled that the portal cube had to be wielded by an expert warlock for it to have any precision.

"Short time is, Anna Stone. Message Oba has—"

"Oba, you must return—"

Oba shook his head slowly. "Exiled Oba is. Prince Sydo Ridian tell Lord of Legion Oba help younglings escape before his death. Discover this Magua did. Fate Oba accepts. Oba only ask Anna Stone to take Oba home to Nodia when time come. There Oba pass to the warrior lands in peace."

"I regret I fail to understand—"

"Only message Krakatos sends important—forge divining rod Magua did. Scions it find."

"Impossible …"

"Krakatos say you know scion feel different now. Scions Leyan artifacts, this Anna Stone understand—"

"—yes of course, but how can—"

"Magua teach Dreadnought how make special artifact—divining rod."

"No …"

"Together work Magua and Lord of Legion. Scions he not have, he find with rod."

"But surely Lividius knows he will be destroyed should he actually come to possess all seven—"

"This problem Magua help fix. Magua only witch ever receive Leyan invite. Evil she is. Fool Leyans she did—fool all but one."

"Krakatos ..." Mrs. Stone gaped at Oba as if all her plans had fallen apart, looking old and beaten.

Augum had never seen his great-grandmother afraid before. It made his skin crawl.

"Destroy last portal Anna Stone must," Oba continued. "To Castle Arinthian Anna Stone go."

She glanced to the foursome lying around the fire. "If Lividius can track the scion, he will be on his way here this very moment ..."

"Anna Stone must hurry—"

"No, Oba, there has to be another way—"

"Other way there is not. Anna Stone's scion Legion may find, portal to Ley they must not. Destroy it Anna Stone must."

"Oba, the Lord of the Legion can still get to Ley," Mrs. Stone said in a quiet voice. "There is a recipe hidden in Bahbell Occulus was working on, a recipe to make a portal to Ley *without* a scion. We are on the way there now to retrieve it before the Legion does."

Oba's jaw flexed. "Know this Oba did not." He bowed his great head and sighed. "Then destroyed recipe must be."

Mrs. Stone turned to the trio. Augum swallowed hard, knowing exactly what she was going to ask of them.

A SUDDEN GOODBYE

"Mrs. Stone, don't leave us, please!" Haylee said.

"I am afraid I must—you are in great danger in my company. Lividius will be tracking me this very moment with this divining rod. He will teleport to the closest location he has been to and ride the rest of the way with his entourage. I will have to constantly teleport to get away, but eventually I will simply run out of luck. You must find Bahbell on your own and destroy the recipe. If I go with you, he will know exactly where to find you—and the castle. All is not lost, however—we can continue to communicate using the Orb of Orion if you give me the pearl."

Augum immediately gave up the engraved control pearl.

"I will counsel you and continue to train you when possible." She turned to Oba. "It would be best for us to walk until I have fully recuperated my arcane strength. When my energies return, I shall teleport us to Castle Arinthian and destroy the portal. Of course, Lividius has been there before, so we must expect him to try and stop us. If we are successful, I shall then teleport you to Nodia."

"It be so, Anna Stone." Wrinkles had already appeared under Oba's eyes and on his forehead.

Augum gave his great-grandmother a warm hug. "Good luck, Nana. Please be safe."

"You must keep away from your father until you are ready. And I shall do my best to prepare you."

"I'll try, Nana."

"We'll miss you so much, Mrs. Stone," Bridget said, also hugging her.

Leera stepped forward. "Thank you for saving us from the avalanche ... and mentoring us ... and stuff."

Haylee swallowed hard. "Mrs. Stone ..." but she couldn't finish.

"It is all right. You will all do fine. Take care of each other and continue to study hard. I will watch over you from afar. Be wary of death, for it is real. Keep on the move—do not stay near here overnight, it is too dangerous."

"Yes, Mrs. Stone," they chorused reflexively.

Augum suddenly realized he'd never see the big warrior again. "Thank you, Oba—for everything."

"Oba see Augum in great beyond, land of the warrior. Oba tell Thomas Stone Augum say hello."

"Thank you," Augum choked out.

"Let us make haste, Oba," Mrs. Stone said.

The foursome slowly waved as Anna Atticus Stone disappeared into the night, the doomed Leyan alongside.

A hollow feeling settled over Augum's heart. It was so sudden, so quick. He had been preparing to spend a lot of time with his great-grandmother, learning and training with her ... and now she was gone. He exchanged the same slack expression of disbelief with the girls.

"Let's get out of here," he said at last, realizing he had no idea which direction they were supposed to go.

Bridget kicked some snow on the dwindling fire. "We can follow Mrs. Stone's original tracks back to the rock then follow the map from there."

VALOR

"Shyneo," Augum said, removing his right mitt. His hand sputtered to life, lighting the area in cool electric blue.

"Shyneo," echoed the others.

"Please let us stay away from those *things*," Haylee whispered, searching the dark trees, drawing her long coat tighter.

"I can't believe what just happened," Leera muttered as they strode quickly along Mrs. Stone's original tracks. "I can't believe it …"

Augum kept up the rear, the food bag slung over his back, the rucksack digging into his shoulder. "At first I thought it had something to do with those harpies—"

"Yeah, me too—" Leera said. "Now all of a sudden we're supposed to do this on our own? What makes her think we can even succeed?"

No one answered the question.

The wind kept up a steady pace as clouds shot overhead, so close they sometimes skirted along the ground. Augum still shivered a little from being frozen, but he worried about the harpies the most. What if they came back? How would they protect themselves? His eyes incessantly searched the darkness, ears focused on picking up the sound of beaks clicking.

The news they had heard rolled around his brain like frozen tumbleweed. His father now had the ability to track down the remaining scions while Magua worked on a way for him to be able to possess all seven without destroying himself, bypassing the only Leyan safeguard.

He hoped his great-grandmother could keep away from his father long enough … but long enough for what? Who could stop him now? Their sorry foursome?

The situation felt bleak. To compound it all, if his father tracked Nana down and she gave up the scion, she'd die! The thought was so unbearable he shoved it out of his mind.

He glanced ahead at the girls, fighting the wind. It was just them now. Sure, Nana could be reached through the Orb of Orion, but it wouldn't be the same ...

"This is it," Bridget said, stopping.

Augum caught up to a gaping maw in the snow. It shot down alongside the face of the giant rock they had camped under. Haylee kept staring into that abyss. "I don't like being back here."

"Can't even see the bottom," Leera said. "Could have easily been our final resting place."

"Grim," Augum said. "Let's move on."

Bridget turned her back to the wind and brought out the map. "I don't know about this—if we continue on from this point, we'll have to start climbing the mountain."

"In the middle of the night?" Haylee asked. "In *this*? We'd have to be out of our minds!"

Bridget nodded. "I agree, we need to get away from here, but climbing in this weather is suicide."

"We should hide somewhere safe and sleep," Augum said. "Somewhere away from the trail."

They looked about. The only for-sure location with trees was back the way they came, but that was far too dangerous. After all, there was a harpy's body there. Suddenly he realized whichever direction they went, if someone stumbled across their path, all they had to do was follow their footprints. Unless—

"We have to follow this plateau for a while," he said. "The wind will erase our tracks. Then we can find trees to camp amongst."

Nobody else had a better idea so Augum led the way, keeping a quick pace but constantly checking behind him. The wind bullied their backs, the gusts so strong they'd often trip. Suddenly he caught a putrid whiff. The girls noticed it too, for they all turned around at the same time, searching the night. He expected a harpy to come hurtling out of the dark any moment now. What was merely a nuisance for Mrs. Stone could easily be the end of them …

The girls extinguished their hands one after another.

"Won't help us, they can see in the dark," he said, remembering those twisted hag faces surrounding their camp. Except this time, there weren't any protective enchantments to keep them back. "Come on."

They increased their pace. Once in a while, there'd be the unmistakable scent of death and decay, making everyone run. Somewhere upwind, the harpies were searching for them.

They skipped over rocks and wound their way around giant mountain boulders, until he heard the sound of trees rustling in the wind. They veered off the plateau, finding stubby but wide evergreens.

They searched the slight incline, looking for a suitable candidate to camp under.

"No, this won't work," Augum said when Haylee suggested a dying hemlock. "Have to find somewhere more sheltered."

They continued on, hunting for anything large enough to hide behind and dense enough not to be seen from the air. At long last, they found a crop of fat pines, the trunks surrounded by thick winter bush.

"Perfect," he mumbled, plowing through the snowdrift that stood guard like a wall. Only ankle deep snow lay behind.

He kept his hand lit while they setup the larger of the two tents, the top of which dug into the evergreen. As soon as it was erected, they tumbled inside, too exhausted to do anything except cover themselves with blankets. There was only enough room for them to lie on their sides.

"Well this is awkward," Leera said, trying to push Haylee aside.

"Hey, I got nowhere to go!" Haylee cried.

"Then face Bridget, not me!"

"Stop it, Leera," Bridget said.

"Fine, I'll shove over this way." Leera pressed against Augum's back. His face suddenly prickled with heat.

"Think those things will find us here?" Haylee asked with a slight tremor.

"Only if the wind changes," Augum replied.

"I'd have slept better not knowing that," Leera said.

They listened to the wind and the shwooming trees.

"I can't believe it's just us," Haylee whispered eventually.

"Same here," Bridget said.

Leera sighed. "Tomorrow we have to find the Occi and somehow not get eaten. Then, to make things even more interesting, we have to get them to tell us where Bahbell is. After that, we have to get inside the place and destroy this so-called recipe—oh, and before the Legion finds it."

Augum dimmed his hand. "It does sound crazy when you put it like that." He wondered if she could feel the heat from his body. He tried not to think about dancing with her, and how they had almost kissed.

"Maybe we should just go back to Milham and sit around a fire," Leera added.

"Think of Leland though," Bridget countered. "He's blind and helpless and totally reliant on his father. The Legion has no place for a boy like that. What if they wanted to take Mr. Goss away?"

"They do—but probably only to use him as a hostage to get the scion," Leera said. "Not that they need hostages for that anymore …"

"All right, now what if we had the power to stop them from getting Leland and Mr. Goss? What if we could save others out there, the faceless ones, people we haven't even met?"

They pondered that for a while.

Leera snorted. "Sometimes, Bridge, you sound like someone much older."

"Well sometimes I feel that old …"

VALOR

Suddenly Augum felt a hand squeeze in underneath his arm and wind around his chest.

"Do you mind? I'm cold," Leera whispered nonchalantly.

He swallowed and shook his head, thinking she must surely feel the walloping of his heart.

"When I was training to become a necromancer," Haylee began quietly, "I saw things that cannot be unseen, things coming out of the ground that should have stayed dead. I was told not to let it bother me, that it was normal, that it was all for the 'Great Quest'—because in the end, those that were loyal to Lord Sparkstone would get to live forever. *Forever* ... like in those stories about Leyans. Forever, like the Nodians think about the great beyond, or the southern priests and the Unnameables ..."

She paused a moment. "My grandfather did wrong by handing over Sparrow's Perch—"

Leera shifted uncomfortably at this.

"—it wasn't his plan to have everyone *murdered* though. He was greedy—he just wanted to get his estates and titles back in Blackhaven. When the Lord of the Legion rewarded him and then murdered all those people, my grandfather—you wouldn't think it now—but he suffered for that. He used to be so strong and mean and sharp, but after that, he kind of shrank and sat at home and withdrew and just ... looked out a window.

"One day he put me on his knee like he used to when I was younger, and he said, 'Haylee my sweet grandchild, I want you to learn from the worst mistake I ever made. Never allow ambition to override your heart. Look at what I have done. I have misjudged the Legion and killed so many ... for nothing but gold and empty titles.' When he told me that, that's when I started to lose myself. And then Robin and I were on a training excursion and we found you, and I just couldn't take it anymore ..."

She took a deep breath before continuing. "There's something I haven't told you about my time hanging in that cell waiting to die. After Robin killed my parents and my grandfather, he ... he raised them as the undead to torture me."

"Haylee ..." Bridget whispered. "That's ... that's horrifying. I'm so very sorry ..."

"I know, and I'm sorry about your parents, I really, really am. When I was in that cell and Robin let my parents and my grandfather wander in there in their new form ... well, I knew then what the Legion really meant by eternal life. It ... it *broke* me, and I haven't been able to put the pieces back together since."

For a time, they listened to the wind as it moved the trees and pushed around the snow. Augum thought of everything Haylee must have gone through. She must have suffered terribly. And maybe she was right too—maybe being undead really was what his father meant by eternal life. He let that thought simmer.

"Haylee," Bridget at last began, voice croaking with weariness, "I didn't know there was so much to you ..."

Haylee made a tired laugh. "I didn't either ... once I was popular and clever and witty and smart and rich—I mean, I made songs about people in school and had the class sing them—"

"—and I haven't forgiven you for that," Leera chimed in. "But after what you said ..." Her voice faltered. "I think I can learn to."

Augum was proud of Leera for saying that. He pressed his hand over hers and squeezed. She squeezed back.

"I hope you will." Haylee sighed. "But now ... now I don't know *who* I am ..."

"I know who you are," Bridget said. "You're a survivor."

THE RIDGE

Augum dreamed of pacing a great steed in a quiet spring forest. Birds sang, deer danced, and trees bloomed with color. The scent of linden, cedar and orange blossom filled his nose. Sunshine warmed his face. Leera held his waist, head resting on his shoulder.

Then the forest began to decay and darken. The trees thinned and lost their leaves. Snow started falling and a harsh wind picked up. The birds rotted before his eyes, falling to the ground dead. Deer, rabbit and squirrel became fleshy carcasses. Flies buzzed. He tried to warn Leera that something was wrong but she remained blissfully asleep on his shoulder.

Suddenly all the dead animals began to struggle to their feet. It was then he realized he could see through the ribcage of the great stallion beneath them. It slowly turned its ugly head to look at him, eyes glowing crimson.

He startled awake, soaked in cold sweat. Leera groaned softly, arm still around his chest, his hand entwined with hers.

It was just a dream, a bad dream, that's all ...

He gently unclasped her arm and sat up, looking at her sleepy face. The sun, dimmed by the canvas and the boughs of the pine, softened her freckled cheeks. Her raven hair fell thick and tangled. He had the urge to push it aside from her eyes.

He turned away suddenly. What was he doing? It was a curse to like her that way. He'd only doom her, like he had doomed Mya. Death followed him wherever he went, even into his dreams …

Yet they were walking towards death. *Bahbell* … even the name sounded like pain and fear. This wasn't like before either, when they were running from something. This time, they knowingly headed into danger—without the help of Mrs. Stone. Every bone in his body told him it was a bad idea and they should turn back right away, turn back and run to Milham as fast as they could.

He sighed, knowing full well he wouldn't be able to live with himself if he turned back.

Heart heavy, he stuck his head out of the tent. It was a sunny but windy morning, the sky vast and azure. He stretched and spent some time clearing the entrance that had built up snowdrift, thoughts in turmoil.

Soon the girls stirred awake and readied breakfast without a fire, constantly on alert for harpies. He tried communicating with Mrs. Stone through the Orb of Orion, but there was no response. Everyone wondered whether she had been successful destroying the Arinthian portal to Ley, and if Oba Sassone was in a Nodian village, breathing his last as an old man.

"Maybe you three should turn back," he blurted in the midst of being served journey bread and Solian cheese.

Leera gave him a look. "Did you take a knock to the head yesterday? We already talked about this, *a lot*, and with Mrs. Stone too. Pretty sure everyone here knows what they're getting into. Stop trying to talk us out if it, it's annoying and insulting."

VALOR

Bridget nodded. "Have to agree, Aug, it's insulting."

He glanced at Haylee.

She smirked. "Nothing to lose."

"You do have something to lose though," he said. "Your lives." He looked at each of them in turn, gaze finishing on Leera. "What happened to Mya can't happen to any of you."

She gave a pained smile. "Then we better do our damnedest to make sure it doesn't. Now eat something!"

He forced a smile. "Yes, *Mother*."

After breakfast, they packed up and departed, Augum leading, map in hand. He stopped almost immediately, sniffing the air, smelling something foul.

"Oh no—" Haylee said from behind.

Augum surveyed the bleak terrain. "I don't see any—" but he caught movement—a shadow had formed on the ground! He jumped, tackling the girls just in time as a large winged harpy swooped over them, leaving behind a ghastly stench. It clicked its beak as it soared.

"Shyneo!" the group chorused as they got to their feet. Rucksacks were left on the ground as everyone fanned out in defensive stances.

"Now what do we do!" Haylee cried.

"Kill it," Augum said, though he hadn't the faintest idea how.

The harpie circled overhead. Suddenly something shot out of a clump of trees at it.

"That's an arrow!" Bridget shouted. "Someone's over there—!"

There was a familiar piercing war cry.

"It can't be—" Bridget said as they began running to the spot. Another arrow shot at the harpy, clipping its wing. The thing immediately dove, disappearing behind trees.

Augum and Bridget were the first to get there, finding a snow-skinned Henawa warrior rolling in the snow as the harpy ran after, beak clicking. The warrior wore heavy wolf pelt and his face was painted with streaks.

"Baka!" Augum and Bridget shouted at the same moment, shoving the air before them. The harpy squawked as it was sent tumbling, giving the warrior just enough time to find his bow, nock it, and loose an arrow. It missed by a hair, disappearing into the snow behind the creature.

"Hold it!" Augum yelled, reaching out a hand and concentrating on Telekinesis. Bridget, Leera and Haylee helped, their combined arcanery holding the thing in place long enough for the warrior to shoot another arrow. This time it struck true, piercing the harpy's chest. The thing struggled rabidly in their arcane grip. The warrior dropped his bow and ran at it while withdrawing a war axe. He promptly buried it in the creature's skull, silencing it once and for all.

The foursome dropped their hands, letting the harpy fall to the ground in a heap of feathers and blood.

The warrior turned around, shoulders rising and falling in time to his frosty breathing. Underneath a wolfhead hood was short milky hair.

Bridget took a step forward. "Chaska—"

"Bridget." Chaska secured the war axe in his belt. "You should not have interfered."

"What? What do you—"

"My nemana was to slay a winged demon. I was to do it alone."

"But you followed *us*—"

"—I was to do it *alone*!"

"Don't you talk to her that way!" Haylee said, chin rising.

Chaska flashed her a hard look. "What did you just say?"

"You heard me, you foul oaf. She's my friend, and you won't disrespect her."

"It's okay," Bridget said, staying Haylee with a hand. "This is our friend, Haylee. Haylee, this is Chaska. He's Henawa."

"Why *did* you follow us?" Augum asked. "And how did the harpies not find you earlier?"

VALOR

Chaska's fierce eyes fell upon Haylee before he strode past to reclaim his bow. "Father told me to watch over you for the first portion of your journey. Said it was part of my nemana. And as for the harpies, Henawa know how to remain hidden, keep their scent downwind."

Bridget sighed. "I'm sorry, we didn't know we should have let you slay it alone. I'm sure you would have succeeded—"

"—come on, Bridget," Haylee interrupted. "Thing would have torn him to shreds if it hadn't been for us. He was rolling in the snow for his life."

Chaska's painted face twisted with anger. "I could handle myself. I didn't *need* your help. Now I have to kill another one to complete my nemana."

Haylee opened her mouth to argue but was stayed by a look from Bridget.

"Come with us," Bridget said. "We can help each other. Mrs. Stone had to leave, and without any offensive spells, well ..."

Chaska glanced between the dead harpy and the mountains. "We should bury it, otherwise it will attract the others."

"Does that mean you'll be coming with us then?" Bridget asked.

Chaska gave a nod and started digging. Augum, Bridget and Leera held their noses while helping to bury the nasty thing.

"He's a barbarian, I'm not going near him," Haylee said when Leera asked if she was going to lend them a hand. "But I'll help move the—" she made an icky gesture at the harpy "—*thing* with Telekinesis."

"You think him barbaric because that's the way you were raised," Bridget said in compassionate tones when they finished. "He's not a barbarian. None of the Henawa are."

"A barbarian is someone who burns down a village of innocents," Augum said. He extended his hand to Chaska, who accepted it. "Glad you're with us."

"Thanks." Chaska frowned at Haylee. "I grew up with ignorance. Used to it. *I* was ignorant, and kind of still am in a lot of ways."

Haylee did not meet his gaze and said nothing.

They retrieved their rucksacks and resumed their journey, now a quintet.

The Muranians loomed above, snowy like the face of a Henawa warrior, the streaks of visible rock his face paint. Augum wondered how they were going to fare climbing them. Will the harpies follow them up so high? Will an avalanche sweep them to their deaths? Soon they'll be out of the reach of Nana's teleport, and if something should happen, there will be little she could do for them …

Bridget filled Chaska in on their quest as they crept along the rocky plateau before beginning the climb up the Muranians. It started as a gentle incline through waist-high snow, the occasional boulder providing relief from a bitter and unceasing wind. They kept their faces covered as much as possible, hoods drawn tight.

The map called for a trek to a spot marked by a black rectangle several mountains over. The question was which mountain was the correct one? The map had gotten them this far, but the crude illustrations made navigation a bit of a guessing game.

"Slow down there, Aug, we're falling behind—!" Bridget called from below a few hours later. He turned to find the girls and Chaska strung out a ways down the slope like scattered petals of a flower. The incline had steepened and somehow he had made it a personal challenge, just like when he was a boy confronted with a monstrous willow … except he had neglected to wait on everyone, a stupid thing to do. What if one of them got in trouble? How would he get to them?

VALOR

He plopped down to wait. At least it was one heck of a view—the sun beat sharply on the slope, making the entire range glitter. The Ravenwood sprawled to the west, a vast sea of snowy evergreens. Somewhere in that great forest sat Castle Arinthian. Was Nana there that very moment? Was Father pursuing her? He imagined a great battle involving arcane castle defenses.

He opened his waterskin, taking a sip. Then he realized something—they had long passed the tree line. From here on it was only rock and snow. Doubtful they'd stumble across a stream to refill their skins in the snowy mountains …

"Hey there, climber," Bridget said, gasping and plopping down beside him, purposefully keeping her back to the view. "What's the rush?"

"Sorry, got carried away."

She took a drink of water as they waited for Chaska, Haylee and Leera. "We're going to have to figure out a way to make a fire, you know."

"And how to get more water."

"We can make water by melting snow with fire." Bridget placed a hand above her eyes and scanned the slopes above. "We also have to keep an eye out for a place to camp, maybe a ledge or something." She paused. "I don't see anything yet."

She looked back accidentally and yelped, hiding her face.

"Is it the height?" he asked.

She nodded vigorously, trying to control her breathing.

"I hate to say it, Bridge, but it's only going to get worse."

"I know, I know …"

Haylee caught up at last, panting for breath. "Can … we … slow … down … please?"

"Of course, sorry about that," he said.

She slumped to a seat beside him. Chaska, who was right behind her, was about to take a seat when she placed her rucksack in that spot. He scowled and sat beside Bridget instead.

Leera soon joined them, too tired to even speak.

Augum shook his head dramatically at her. "Defeated by a small hill …"

She raised her arm to punch his shoulder but dropped it, grimacing with exhaustion. "Think we need a break," Augum said, trying to keep the mood light. "Anyone hungry?"

They looked at him as if the answer should be obvious.

Lunch was quiet and simple—journey bread, salted dry beef, cheese, and pemmican shared by Chaska. When they finished, they sat a little bit longer, enjoying the view, allowing the food to settle.

"You know," Haylee began, "if someone would have told me a year ago where I'd be right now and with whom, I'd have told them they were stupid fools."

Augum cracked a grin. "You saying we're bad company?"

She smiled warmly at him, a smile that faltered when she saw Chaska trimming his fingernails with his teeth.

"Do you mind?"

Chaska looked about before realizing she was talking to him. "Huh?"

"Could you please not do that?"

"Do what?" He finished off his thumbnail.

"Groom your nails like that. It's disgusting."

Chaska flushed, dropping his hand. "Oh."

"Thank you."

"Anything else?" he said.

"Anything else what?"

"Anything else you'd like to comment on, maybe change about me?"

Haylee's eyes narrowed. "Want me to start a list?"

"Stop it," Bridget said, giving them both a pleading look. "Please."

"Sorry," Chaska said, wiping paint from his face with a cloth. "I'm better than that now."

"Oh, so now he thinks he's better than me," Haylee said, turning to Augum to elicit a supportive remark.

But Augum exchanged a weary look with Leera instead. "We shouldn't be arguing," he remarked. "We've got more important things to worry about."

"Like how to survive up here," Leera added.

Haylee stood up. "Fine, let's go then," and began marching ahead.

"She's been through a lot," Bridget said to Chaska as they gathered themselves to follow. "Please try to be patient with her."

"I ... I will. For you I will."

The incline increased yet again, making the going more difficult, especially for Bridget. She slowed them to a crawl, sticking to the ground like a frightened cat. She almost began hissing when they found their way onto a knife-edge ridge with barely enough room to walk on.

"There's no way, absolutely no way!" she said, shaking her head the whole time and refusing to look. Chaska, meanwhile, awkwardly stood behind her, looking like he had no idea what to do with himself.

"Bridge, we have to do this," Augum said, "and I know you can make it. Look, we'll even tie everyone together with a rope, all right?" He gestured for Haylee, who took the hint and dug through her rucksack for the rope Mr. Goss purchased for them.

Bridget seemed to draw little comfort from the rope, even though she tied it around herself six times. Augum was glad for it, because a steep slide developed on both sides. Further, they were thousands of feet up now and the winds had increased dangerously.

The pace slowed further when Bridget began worming along on her stomach. Haylee frequently gave Augum looks to get him to persuade Bridget to hurry up, but he ran out of encouragement, and none of it worked anyway. The poor girl would whimper, drag herself forward, whimper again, suddenly clutch at the rope and scream even if it was only a gust of wind—and start the cycle again.

"We're going to have Chaska carry you if you can't be more of a woman about this," Leera said with a grin.

Bridget gave Chaska a ferocious look. "Don't even—"

"—I wouldn't unless you asked me to!" Chaska said, raising broad hands in defense.

She made a small effort. Nonetheless, Augum began to worry about the pace. It'd be dark soon and they had yet to find a spot to camp.

After another hour of this awful toil, Haylee pointed ahead. "What's that?"

Augum squinted to minimize the crimson glare. The ridge flattened for a small stretch. There, inset against the vast whiteness of the mountain, was a black dot. Was it a rock? A cave? It was hard to tell from this distance. At the pace they were going, he estimated they'd reach it after sundown, but being stuck on a knife-edge ridge in the dark, with the wind howling louder than Bridget, was enough for him to try encouraging her again to speed up.

It made no difference—she was simply too afraid of falling.

The delicate trek continued as the ridge became even more precarious. At times, everyone had to crawl on their hands and knees along with Bridget to get past a particularly thin area. Snowdrift piled on the leeward side like a long frozen wave. Augum's leg pierced it more than once, dangling through the other side and sending his heart to his throat. At those times, he would freeze, breathing rapidly, before slowly extricating himself. A screaming Bridget didn't help the situation, and more than once Leera had to calm her down by giving her a hug and whispering soothing words.

Bridget would only shake her head and mumble. "No, we're going to die, we're going to fall and roll and die ..."

VALOR

The frequency of wind gusts increased as they climbed. When one slammed them, they would hunker down and wait until it passed. Bridget held on to the ridge for dear life during these occasions, begging to be taken back down. Leera comforted her as best she could while Chaska looked on longingly. Augum had the impression the lumbering boy wanted to be the one to cuddle her. He smiled to himself, knowing that feeling all too well.

"Something moved!" Bridget suddenly cried, pointing ahead.

"You're being hysterical again," Leera said. Bridget almost forgot her fears with the look she gave Leera. "I'm *not* going crazy, something really did move!"

Augum squinted. She was right, something *was* moving, a white figure that disappeared almost entirely into the snowy background—but it did leave a long sunset shadow which gave it away. It hopped onto the ridge and came toward them. By then, everyone had seen it.

"It's on all fours," Augum reported, removing his mitts to make it easier to cast a spell. His hands began to numb almost immediately from the wind. "Wait, now it's not ... what is that thing?"

It was built like a snow bear but occasionally stood on hind legs, mostly using its arms to move itself along. Its face was as hairy as the rest of it.

"It almost looks like a white banyan beast," Bridget said, one hand on Augum's rucksack for balance.

He prepared to cast the Push spell, hoping to knock the thing off the ridge, should it come to that. Chaska, meanwhile, unslung his bow and nocked an arrow.

As it got closer, it quickly became apparent it was far larger than they anticipated, perhaps twice the height of a man.

"I don't know about this ..." Bridget said, retreating a step.

"Harpies to the north!" Leera suddenly shouted, pointing.

Augum looked up to see three harpies fighting the mountain winds to get at them. They were about two thousand feet down but closing fast, their wings beating frantically.

Haylee began shaking her head. "This is bad, this is bad, this is so bad …"

Augum stared at the beast. There was something peculiar about it—not only would it stop and examine them on hind legs occasionally, but there was also a rope around its chest, as if something was strung on its back. Was it someone's pet? Or … suddenly he had an idea.

"Hello there, can you help us!" he called to the white-furred beast.

"It wants to eat us, not talk to us—" Leera said.

The thing stood up on its hind legs and cocked its head. It was now only a hundred paces or so away.

"Looks like you have gained the attention of some harpies," it said in a casual, growly voice. "Perhaps you should get off the ridge."

The quintet exchanged incredulous looks.

"Did that giant wolf thing just speak?" Chaska asked.

Leera only nodded, mouth agape.

"Yeah, we'd like to," Augum called over the wind as the creature got a bit closer. He still didn't trust it and kept his hands ready. "Thing is," he added, looking down the sheer drop, "we, uh, we don't really know how to do that safely."

"Well you *could* jump, though I doubt you would survive the fall."

"Yeah, that's what we're thinking too." Augum shared a look with Bridget. Was this a strange conversation or what? He turned to the beast. "Think we can follow you to that cave there?"

The beast gave a growling chuckle. "Why am I not surprised that you want to invite yourselves over. You lowlanders always do. But since I have so few visitors, I suppose I shall allow it." He turned his great bushy body, revealing a rucksack strapped to his back, dwarfed by his great bulk.

"We might want to hurry," Leera said, leading with the rope. "They're gaining!"

But they couldn't hurry at all, for Bridget wasn't moving any faster—if anything, she seemed to have slowed, as if panicked by the urgency of the situation.

Augum, meanwhile, kept one hand on the rope and the other on the ridge for balance. He had dropped his mitts in the scuffle, but didn't care that his hands were going blue, all he cared about was trying to get off that ridge as quickly as possible. Come on, Bridge, he thought, *come on*!

"Stop pulling, you'll kill me!" Bridget yelled.

He glanced down the slope—there was no escaping the fact that the harpies would reach them long before they got off the ridge.

"Damn ..." he said under his breath, turning to the snow beast. It sat on its hind legs watching them, halfway to the cave.

Suddenly Bridget's knee broke through the snowdrift. A monstrous chunk of it began sliding down the slope, taking Bridget and Haylee with it, rucksack and all. Both clutched at each other and the rope while letting loose a gut-wrenching scream.

"Chaska, help!" Augum shouted, digging in his heels and leaning back along with Leera. Chaska grabbed it just as Bridget and Haylee hit the end of the rope and then slammed into the cliff face, yanking them hard. For a harrowing moment, Augum thought they were done for. Instead, he found himself standing on the very edge of the precipice, looking straight down, holding on for dear life and trying to stave off the awful vertigo sensation.

There was a piercing cry from below. "My leg!" Haylee gurgled.

"I'm slipping ..." Leera said through gritted teeth.

"Can't ... hold ... it ..." Chaska said, groaning. "They're ... almost ... here."

"Um, excuse me!" Augum gasped at the beast. "Can ... you ... help ... us!"

The creature cocked its head before dropping on all fours and pacing back to them. Augum glanced down the slope, realizing it wouldn't get to them before the harpies. Below, Bridget shrieked and flailed, completely out of her mind, while Haylee tried to calm her, though her face was twisted with pain.

"Bridge ... you're ... not ... helping!" Leera said, but she only screamed louder and kicked harder.

The quickest of the harpies dove at Bridget.

"Watch out—!"

Bridget never even saw the harpy but her flailing boot connected with its ugly face. The thing fell, slamming against the slope a thousand feet down, tumbling the rest of the way.

No one cheered because there were two more right behind it.

"Grau!" Augum said when the next one dove for her. The air crackled a bit, a far cry from the thunderous explosion he was hoping for. It seemed apparent he needed the gesture and all his concentration for that.

The second harpy dove in for the kill.

"Watch out!" Leera shrieked as the thing dug its claws into Bridget, who screamed, flailing like a panic-stricken bird. Haylee, holding on with one hand, began punching and smacking the thing with her free hand, causing the rope to swing wildly.

It was all the rest of them could do to hold on.

Augum desperately struggled not to slip. "Fight it, fight it—!"

Bridget connected a fist into the harpy's face and it let go, leaving her and Haylee to swing backward and slam against the slope wall, eliciting a painful yelp from Haylee. The other harpy was on Bridget almost immediately, tearing at her flesh like a hellhound. Blood began spraying as the second harpy dove for the girls.

"Pardon me," said a gravelly voice as a shadow loomed over Augum. A huge white-furred arm reached over his shoulder and grabbed the rope. He yanked on it with little effort, shooting Bridget and Haylee away from both harpies' jabs. They flew through the air, crashing onto the ridge.

One of the harpies circled and dove for Augum.

"Shyneo!" he shouted, now unencumbered by the rope. His hand lit up, along with his two degree rings. For a moment, he considered casting Centarro too, but it was too dangerous on such a knife-edge. He concentrated on his Shine extension. As soon as the harpy was close enough, he dodged, managing to grab one of its clawed legs. A current shot through him and the thing yelped, shaking violently for a moment, before falling out of sight. It recovered some ways below, soaring back around like an eagle.

Damn, the shock hadn't been strong enough.

The other one was making a pass, this time at Leera.

"Be careful now," said the white beast, and leapt into the air, catching the harpy by the throat, punching it in the face so hard its neck snapped. He flung it off the ridge before even landing.

At that moment, the one Augum shocked dove at Haylee, only to be pierced by an arrow from Chaska's bow. It twirled and slammed into the ridge at Haylee's feet. She screamed and began to frantically kick it with her good leg. Chaska grabbed her, whispering soothingly, "It's all right, it's dead, I got you."

"That is all of them I think," the beast said.

Augum snagged his mitts and shot over to help Bridget, who lay on the ridge bleeding, barely conscious.

"She's hurt bad," Leera said. "We need a healer."

The beast studied them. "Perhaps you five should not climb so high on your academy excursions …"

"Uh, sir, can you please help us with our friend?" Augum asked, trying not to be rude. "We can't carry her ourselves on this ridge."

" 'Sir' indeed." The beast sighed, sounding like broken bellows. "Untie her then."

They quickly did. Bridget screamed, holding her side, as blood flowed freely onto the snow. The beast reached down and effortlessly picked her up with one arm, walking off without another word, her blood staining its shiny white fur.

Meanwhile, Chaska slung his bow and gently lifted Haylee, who moaned with pain. The three of them followed the beast as fast as they dared while safely navigating the ridge.

THE SNOW BEAST'S LAIR

The cave was enormous, three times the height of a man, furnished with two tables, one much larger than the other; a chair; and a series of shelves, all carved into the mountain. Trinkets, parchments and over-sized tomes sat on the shelves. In the corner was a large fire pit; to the side, a massive cabinet made of rough timber planks.

Augum felt like a tiny child in comparison to these oversized things.

The beast set Bridget down on the giant table. Augum had to discard his rucksack and food bag to climb it, giving Leera a hand up. Chaska then hoisted a moaning Haylee up, helped by Augum and Leera.

"I think my leg is broken," Haylee said through gritted teeth. "Oh my word that hurts."

"Are you bleeding?" Augum asked, accepting his rucksack from Chaska and placing it under her head.

"Don't think so. Check on Bridget."

Augum raced to Bridget's side, already attended by a panicking Leera.

"Put ... hand ... on ... it. Pressure ..." Bridget mumbled, pale as snow.

"She lost a lot of blood," the beast said in a casual manner, taking a seat on a giant rock chair. He picked up a sharp tool and a stone carving of a human. "She will probably die. I would not even bother, if I were you."

The beast's words were poison to Augum's ears. "No, she can't, we won't let her—!" Augum placed his hands over the wound on the right side of her stomach. "Please, you have to help us!" Blood squished through his fingers, instantly reminding him of Mya. He felt like he was going to throw up.

"I already helped you." The beast didn't even look up. "You owe me as it is, lowlander."

"Other ... one ... too ..." Bridget mumbled, gesturing at a bloodstain on her left shoulder.

Leera carefully removed Bridget's coat and gasped at the large gash. She quickly pressed her hands on it while Bridget's eyelids closed halfway.

"What can I do, what can I do!" Chaska said in a frantic voice.

"You can sweep the floor," the beast said, holding up the figurine and inspecting it close. "Then you can make a fire, put some snow in my mug and melt me some tea."

"What—! No ... I mean, what can I do to help Bridget!"

"You can watch her die, Henawa. But be grateful, for the other one will live. Though painful, it appears the break has not pierced her skin. Keep her leg raised and cool with ice."

Chaska hesitated, glancing desperately between Bridget and Haylee.

"Go ahead, we have her," Augum said.

Chaska nodded and jumped off the table, soon returning with armfuls of ice. He raised Haylee's leg onto his rucksack while she howled in pain, and applied snow to the break.

VALOR

Leera's freckled cheeks were stained with tears. "Damn you, you ... you mangy ball of fur! Why won't you help us with Bridget!"

The beast glanced at her, and for the first time Augum had a good look at it. It had the face of a wolf but lacked the ears. Its body was that of a massive snow bear. Its paws had pink skin hidden amongst a nest of protective fur. It crossed its great legs and cocked its head.

"That was rude. It is no wonder you lowlanders die by the dozen. You have no respect for anyone, do you? I am particularly annoyed that you are warlocks that cannot even seem to help themselves."

Augum watched as Bridget's eyes closed. "Bridge, stay with us! Bridge—!" He turned to the beast. "Sir, please, we're too young to teleport, and none of us know how to heal arcanely! Please, we'll do *anything*!"

"*Anything*, you say?"

"Anything!" they cried in unison.

The beast slowly put down his figurine and sauntered over. He leaned over Bridget's limp form, towering above them, black snout glistening. "Hmm ... I would say it is not worth your time. She is very close to death indeed. Are you sure you want to go through all this trouble?"

"YES!" they shouted.

"My my, excited little creatures you are. Very well then, but I cannot make any promises."

"Just do something already!" Leera cried.

The beast turned to her. "I do not like this one."

Leera gestured wildly. "Fine, I don't care, just do something! HELP HER!"

"Please remove your hand then."

"What? Why—"

"Do it."

Leera hesitantly did so. The beast leaned near, closed his eyes and blew frosty breath at the wound—it froze over instantly. He then repeated this for the other wound.

311

"Now fix a fire," the beast said, going back to his chair.

"What, wait, this is only temporary—" Augum said.

"Of course it is, and you are wasting time. Make a fire so we can continue."

Augum, Leera and Chaska jumped off the table and rushed to the fire pit and pile of cut logs. They immediately began building a fire, tripping in their hurry.

"I have no idea what I'm doing," Chaska mumbled. "I can't think straight."

"There's lantern oil in my rucksack—" Leera said, knocking over some logs. The beast looked up from his carving and frowned.

"Right." Chaska ran off.

"Don't forget the flint and steel—" Augum called. Chaska, already returning with the sloshing oil lantern, skidded and doubled back. Meanwhile, Augum used an iron knife the size of a sword to shave off kindling, stuffing the bundle into the center of the logs.

"Go go go—" Chaska said, handing him the lantern. Augum opened it and poured out the oil all over the fire. Chaska struck the flint and steel, immediately igniting the logs.

"All right, now what?" Augum quickly asked.

"An awful waste of lantern oil." The beast's eyes narrowed as he carefully carved an intricate detail on his figurine. "Boil some water."

Augum rushed back to the table, climbed on top, and grabbed a bucket-sized iron mug. He heaved it over to Chaska, who laboriously carried the heavy thing outside, scooping in armfuls of snow. Then he hobbled back and placed it on the fire.

"How is she, Augum?" Haylee gasped as Augum readied to climb back down.

"Not well," he replied, continuing his descent. "Not well at all …"

The trio gathered round the fire, wringing their hands.

VALOR

"Do you know what your kind calls our kind?" The beast asked.

Augum wanted to say a troll, but didn't dare.

The beast blew at his carving, creating a small dust cloud. "A troll. Do you know how that makes us feel?"

"Pretty bad, probably," Augum replied, trying not to rush him by asking what the next step in the process was.

"Quite right."

"So … what's the next step?" Augum asked, willing the water to boil faster.

"The water boils."

"No, I mean after that."

"You make two Gurgan salves, or what you call poultices."

"What kind of ingredients do we need?"

"I have all but one—bread."

"We have that!" Leera ran off to her rucksack to retrieve some journey bread.

"What else then?" Augum asked.

"How impatient you are …"

When Augum gave no reply, the beast sighed and stood. He wandered over to his cabinet and opened the door, withdrawing four jars labeled in an unfamiliar tongue. The first had what looked like crushed pine needles, the second a brown powder, the third a gel, and the last looked like bran.

The beast walked over and placed them before Augum. He pointed at the lid of each jar as he spoke. "Since I am guessing you cannot read Wolven, it is one part this jar, one part this jar, two parts this one, and one half this one."

"Leave it to me," Leera said, shoving the bread at Augum.

"What do I do?" Chaska asked.

Leera's eyes never left the water. "You can find a stir stick—"

Chaska scavenged an oversized spoon.

The water finally boiled and Leera began pouring in the contents, mumbling portion sizes. "There, done! Stir, Chaska, stir—!"

"So now what?" Augum asked, unsure how to address the giant wolf thing.

"Must I do everything for you?" The beast paced over to his cabinet, withdrew some coarse linen, and, using his sharp teeth, neatly ripped it into smaller pieces. "Place the bread into two separate strips. Pour the salve onto the bread. Wrap them loosely and press them against the wounds."

Leera snatched the strips from the beast and the bread from Augum. Augum, meanwhile, climbed the table and positioned himself over Bridget. Her wounds were already bleeding again. "Ready when you are, Lee!" he called.

"Just a moment," Leera said, finishing the first one. "Got it—here!" She used Telekinesis to hover the poultice right into Augum's waiting hand. The beast watched from his chair, an amused look on its face, while Augum positioned the poultice with shaking hands. "Everything's going to be fine, Bridge," he whispered, trying to ignore the fact her skin was getting paler by the moment.

"Incoming!"

Augum looked up just in time to catch the other one. He promptly pressed it onto the other wound.

"All right, what next?" he asked.

"My, must we be so needy? Well, I suppose you could make blood soup."

"What's that?"

"It will help the girl replenish her blood, obviously. You are not one of the brighter lowlanders, are you?"

Augum didn't care how many insults the beast threw. "Just tell us how to make it!"

"You will owe me even more, are you sure you—"

"YES!" they shouted again.

The beast strolled over to his cabinet once again, reached for the top shelf and withdrew a golden vial. "This is a very expensive potion, you realize." He handed it to Leera. "One part Golden Vitae, ten parts blood."

"Where's the blood?" Leera asked.

The beast snorted a laugh. "Well it is not coming from *me*."

Leera gaped at him. "You mean ... fine, whatever it takes!" She used Telekinesis to send the vial to Augum.

He caught it. "And bring the knife!"

Leera grabbed the sword-sized iron knife while Chaska snagged a bowl.

Leera tossed the blade onto the table and proceeded to climb up. Augum didn't wait for her—he handed Chaska the vial and grabbed the blade, running back to kneel over the bowl. Leera shot over and snatched the Golden Vitae from a hesitant Chaska. She uncorked it and began pouring a measured amount into the bowl.

"All right, now we need ten parts—" but before Leera even finished, Augum sliced his palm open with the sword-knife. Haylee gasped, while Chaska turned as pale as Bridget and had to sit down, mumbling something about the sight of blood. Augum let the blade fall to the ground with a clang. The cut bled profusely—Leera snatched his wrist and held it over the bowl. As his blood dripped into the Golden Vitae, it began to smoke and bubble.

The smell was nauseating. He chanced a look at the cut. It was like a broken fountain the way it gushed, and far larger than he had intended.

"That's going to take a while to heal," Leera muttered. "And leave a big scar."

"Don't care," Augum blurted, head already spinning.

Chaska groaned.

"Hey, big lug, mind fetching a bandage?" Leera said without looking away from the bowl.

"Oh ... right." Chaska heaved himself to his feet, swayed a little, and ran off to fetch another strip of linen.

Leera smirked. "You'd think for someone so big he'd have a bit more ... what's the word?"

"Fortitude?" Augum mumbled, trying to fight nausea.

"Yeah, that's the one." Leera checked the bowl. "Almost there, hang on ..."

"Think I need to lie down ..." he managed to mumble as black walls began closing in on his vision.

Chaska climbed back up, holding a strip of linen. "I got him—!" he said, running and catching Augum just as he fell back. The last thing Augum remembered was the frightened expression on Leera's face.

Sometime later he woke to a quiet cave, hand bandaged. "How's Bridget?" he wheezed.

"We fed her the entire concoction," Leera replied. She sat beside Bridget, patting her forehead with a damp cloth. Chaska sat just behind, awkwardly wringing his hands.

Haylee lay nearby, smiling at Augum. "I think we saved her."

"Here, take over," Leera said, handing Chaska the cloth.

"Oh ... I don't know if I—"

"Stop being useless. Just be gentle."

Chaska swallowed and applied the cloth to Bridget's forehead with a shaking hand. Leera, meanwhile, inspected Augum's palm. "Bandage is holding for now." She turned her attention to Haylee. "How's the leg?"

Haylee winced. "It's going weirdly numb, but still hurts like a storm."

"Splint ..." Augum whispered, too weak from the blood loss to speak louder. Sir Westwood had taught him how to splint a broken leg, but it was obvious he would have to resign himself to being a passive observer for a little while.

Leera glanced at Chaska. "Know how to make a splint? Because I don't."

Chaska wiped his sweaty forehead with a beefy hand. "Uh, I think so."

"Let's switch again then."

VALOR

Haylee looked like she was going to protest but said nothing as Chaska kneeled before her, passing off the cloth to Leera.

"So, uh, where's the, uh, break?"

Haylee grimaced with a stab of pain. "You haven't been around many girls, have you?"

Chaska's milky face went pink. "'Course I have," he stammered.

"Chasing and beating them up doesn't count," she said.

"I would never—" but then Chaska saw the genuine but fleeting smile Haylee wore. "Oh, that was a joke."

"It's the right leg. Please don't do anything dumb, because it hurts. *A lot*."

"I'll try." Chaska hesitated. "I mean—"

Leera cleared her throat lightly. "Maybe you should fetch some wood to make the splint from."

"Right, of course." Chaska, cheeks still beet red, climbed off the table.

"You are silly creatures," the beast said, shaking his head. He was at the smaller stone table, butchering a goat for supper with a giant cleaver.

"Who are you?" Leera asked.

"Is that your way of asking my name?"

"Sure, I guess."

"It never ceases to amaze me how rude you lowlanders can be." He chopped off the goat's head in one slice. It fell from the table and hit the ground with a splat. "My name is Raptos."

"Our names are—"

"—Haylee, Bridget, Leera, Chaska and Augum. Contrary to what you lowlanders believe, we wolven *do* have ears."

"I didn't even know big wolf creatures existed," Leera replied. "Where are you from?"

Raptos almost dropped the cleaver. "Was that a serious question? What kind of paltry education do those academies bestow?"

"Solia is having a few ... problems right now."

"I imagine so if you do not even know where Wolven come from, and to answer your question, raven-haired lowlander, we are from northern Ohm, just like the Henawa."

"That's where my people come from," Chaska said, chopping some logs with his axe.

"'Your people'? But you are not really Henawa, are you?"

Chaska, chest heaving from the exertion, stopped chopping and glanced up at the wolven. "Of course I am—"

"You are Solian first. Tell me otherwise. Go ahead, lie to me."

Chaska hesitated.

"Indecisive, stupid, a little bit fat, shorthaired. But wearing a war shirt, possessing a war axe and a traditional Henawa bow. I would say you are most certainly not Henawa. Your people and our people may have relations in the north, but here, you are nothing more than a vagrant. A castaway. Perhaps the son of a thief, cast out from the tribe and forced to take care of his son in the idiot southlands—"

Chaska hurled the axe aside. "DON'T YOU TALK THAT WAY ABOUT MY FATHER!"

The wolven watched Chaska a moment. "You do not obey the traditional honor courtesies as observed by our peoples when meeting. Then you have the impudence to take my wood without asking. Listen to me closely, Chaska, so-called Henawa—if I hear you speak one more word in my cave, whatever that word be, I will mutilate you in the old way. Do you understand?" His great furry arm holding the cleaver flexed, bulging sinewy veins.

Chaska opened his mouth to reply but caught himself. He said nothing, fetched his axe, and returned to chopping wood, keeping one angry eye on the wolven.

"We are taught the lowlander common tongue from cubhood," Raptos said in a calm voice, returning his gaze to

VALOR

Leera, "whereas you lowlanders do not know a single wolven word. Somehow you breed on pure ignorance."

"Now who's being rude?" Leera said. She sighed. "Will the Golden Vitae work on broken bones?"

"Flesh only. The golden-haired lowlander will have to bear the pain."

Haylee whimpered.

Leera closed her eyes in resignation. "Can we keep the rest of the Golden Vitae?"

"If you want to pay for it, yes."

"Put it on our tab."

"As you wish."

Leera shoved the Golden Vitae into her rucksack. Half of the vial's contents remained.

Chaska dumped a pile of sticks onto the table and climbed up, face red with anger.

"You'll need a blanket," Augum whispered.

"Don't speak—" Haylee said quickly through gritted teeth.

Chaska, who had opened his mouth to reply, glanced at Raptos, who watched him silently. He nodded a thanks to Haylee, reached into his rucksack for a blanket, and began tearing strips off.

Haylee lay back, breathing hard. "This is going to hurt, isn't it?"

Leera left the damp cloth on Bridget's forehead and crawled over to Haylee, grabbing her hand awkwardly. "It'll be all right."

Haylee gave her a weak smile.

Chaska fiddled with the blanket a bit, as if unsure what to do next.

"Wrap her leg tightly," Augum said, making an effort to sit up only to experience a narrowing of his vision. He immediately lay back down. "Then tie sticks to it …" He made eye contact with Leera and mouthed, "Distract her."

Leera nodded. "So, uh, why exactly are you so far from your home?" She asked Raptos. "Are you in some kind of trouble with your kind?"

Raptos tossed a few logs onto the fire like they were twigs. "I am a scout for an upcoming invasion of Solia."

"What—!"

Raptos growled a chuckle. "A wolven joke, but I suppose I cannot expect you to partake in our humor.

Haylee screamed as Chaska began binding her leg. The wolven flinched and growled at her. Leera immediately placed a hand over her mouth. "Shh ... it'll be all right."

"I do not like you, raven-haired lowlander, but you seem to have some common sense." Raptos place a massive iron frying pan over the flames. "The real reason I am here is to gather information on your Legion."

"They're not 'our' Legion," Leera said.

"Are they from Solia?"

"Yes, but—"

"Then they are yours. The Legion has been choking off the Iron Pass, the most important supply route to the north."

"Why are you in the mountains then if you want to investigate the Legion?" Leera asked, holding a squirming Haylee. "Aren't you a bit far from the action?"

"Your lowlander ignorance continually astounds me. How is it your kind know so little outside of your borders? We wolven are a mountain people—highlanders. We come down only when absolutely necessary. We are far too honest and honorable for lowlanders, who we find treacherous and deceitful. My brethren monitor the pass and various locations among the northern peaks. I have been posted to the Muranians, along with two others. Besides, I would rather conduct all my research by interrogation. I have already subjected one Legion scout group to the question. I hope to find more."

"Where did you find the group?" Augum asked weakly. He wanted to say that all lowlanders weren't so bad, that there was hope for them still, but he didn't have the strength.

Raptos threw the chopped goat onto the frying pan. It immediately began to hiss and sizzle. "On the plateau, three of them were in search of Bahbell, or rather, what's supposed to be inside it. I gathered quite a bit of information before dispatching them to the great beyond. It appears I can confirm the rumors—a lowlander has awakened the Dreadnoughts somehow. Not only is he trying to acquire all seven scions, but he is also trying to find a way into Ley to bestow his followers with eternal life—or so he says. Lowlanders are, after all, notorious liars. Yet if he *is* telling the truth, he and his people must be fools, for every wolven knows that the Leyan lifespan is only for the Leyans."

Leera flashed Augum a knowing look. Haylee had ceased struggling in her arms, passed out from the pain. Leera gently pushed Haylee's blonde hair away from her sweat-sheened face and sighed. Chaska looked on with a worried expression.

"She'll be all right," Augum said weakly. "Finish the tying."

A delicious aroma filled the cave as the goat meat sizzled away. Augum's stomach rumbled.

"So what's supposed to be inside Bahbell?" Leera asked.

"Ever curious are the lowlander younglings ..."

"We're almost fifteen years old, and Chaska's sixteen—"

"Well you all look the same to me."

"So you don't know what's inside Bahbell?"

"The scouts were not given that information, therefore I do not know, but if the Legion wants it, then so do we wolven. We suspect their ambitions will eventually lead them to invade Ohm." He swirled the pan around and the goat crackled in its juices. "Since you are young and ignorant, I do not expect you to know that every faction in the north—the mountain monks and their seers, the Henawa, the wolven, and all the others—would be no match against a force led by a lowland necromancer wielding seven scions and an army equipped with Dreadnought steel. And that is even *if* said forces banded together. That is why I am interested in what is in Bahbell—we will need every bargaining chip possible against the Legion. Anyhow, we do not care what happens to the other kingdoms. We only care about Ohm, the source of all knowledge and reason."

"Then the kingdoms must band together," Augum said.

Raptos growled a laugh, sounding almost like he was panting. "Your naivety astounds me, lowlander. In all of known history, the kingdoms have never banded together. Even when Occulus threatened their destruction, they still bickered. It took Leyan intervention to save the mortal world, though to be fair, it was Ley itself that was primarily under threat."

"Why are you telling us this?" Leera asked.

"Because you will all be dispatched to the great beyond soon anyway."

"What! What do you mean—?"

"You will not survive your debts."

"What are our debts?"

"I have helped you three significant times. Therefore, you owe three debts. I have already thought them over. They will be impossible for you to acquire, so it is more a source of amusement for me."

Leera crinkled her nose and opened her mouth to reply.

"Leera—" Augum interrupted, sensing she wanted to say something sarcastic. When she glanced at him, he shook his head in warning. She swallowed and nodded, allowing the wolven to continue.

"The first is to procure an Occi horn, for I am in need of an aerial scout. And while you are there, you shall acquire bloodfruit, as its herbal properties are highly prized—it is worth its weight in gold in the north. The third is to discover how I can get into Bahbell. The two most injured lowlanders will stay here as hostages until the debts are paid."

"And what if the debts aren't paid?" Augum asked.

Raptos withdrew the pan from the fire, picking up a chunk of meat. "Then I shall enjoy dispatching the lot of you treacherous, rude lowlanders to the great beyond." He sucked the meat off the bone, licking his snout with a large pink tongue.

Augum, feeling a little better after smelling the delicious cooked goat, finally sat up. "We won't fail."

"Then you would be the first."

"We have a map, but it's hard to tell where to go from here," Augum continued, withdrawing it from his robe.

"Are you asking for another debt? Because I really think you ought not to."

Augum examined the map. "Never mind," figuring they could find the rectangle on their own. They just had to strike northeast from here and keep their eyes peeled.

While Raptos devoured his supper, Leera dug out some food from their rucksacks, distributing it between herself, Augum and Chaska. Haylee and Bridget remained unconscious.

"How are we going to get those things?" Leera whispered, keeping an eye on the wolven.

Augum shook his head. "No idea, but we'll have to pack light, take only what we need."

"You and I will go tomorrow," Augum said to Leera. "Sorry, Chaska, but we need someone to stay here and take care of Bridget and Haylee."

"Besides, we're trained arcanely," Leera added, "and where we're going, that will be crucial."

Chaska glanced down at his hands and nodded.

After supper, Raptos returned to his carving while Chaska and Leera tended to Bridget and Haylee. Later, Augum, having sufficiently recovered, joined Leera in quietly practicing their spells. After that, they secretly listened to the Orb of Orion, hoping for some word from Mrs. Stone. None was forthcoming. At dusk, they erected two tents on top of the table, for there was no door at the cave mouth, and it was cooling fast. When the sun touched the western horizon, they watched the red hues slowly turn to purple, then darken to night. The stars twinkled overhead in a vast sea, clearer and brighter than Augum had ever seen. Raptos eventually curled into a ball, allowing the fire to die, and everyone fell asleep.

THE FALL

Augum woke late to a damp and cold tent. Bridget slept on beside him. Raptos had already disappeared, leaving instructions with Leera not to be treacherous, for he would know. The thought did cross Augum's mind to call for Mrs. Stone's help, not that he'd be successful—she hadn't been paying attention to the pearl, either because she'd been too busy or simply unable.

After breakfast though, a quiet voice came from the orb. Augum and Leera scurried over and placed their ears to it.

"Hello, can anyone hear me?" Mrs. Stone asked, voice distant and muffled by what sounded like wind.

"Yes, we can hear you, Mrs. Stone!" Leera replied, smiling at Augum for the first time in too long.

"Good, I can hear you too. How are you making out?"

"We're all right, Nana," Augum replied. "Bridget and Haylee are injured, but we think they'll get better."

"Injured? How?" There was serious concern in her voice.

Augum explained everything that had happened up to that point.

"Be careful of the wolven, they can be quite callous. They are not like us."

"That's for sure," Leera muttered.

Augum was tempted to ask her to come save them. "How are you, Nana, is the portal destroyed?" he asked instead.

"Lividius tracked me to Arinthian Castle, but he was unsuccessful. The portal is indeed destroyed—"

Augum and Leera exchanged victorious looks at this news.

"—and Oba is back in his homeland. He will pass on today. Let us never forget his sacrifice."

"We won't, Nana, ever." He'd always remember the valuable training Oba administered in Ley.

They could hear a loud gust through the orb. "I am far away right now, somewhere it would take Lividius a long time to get to. I believe he thinks you are all with me. Be warned, however, for I hear they have sent an entire company in search of Bahbell."

"That's two hundred men—" Augum said.

"—and the commander has a speaking orb, so do not let them see you. It is impossible for me to help you at this time, but I will try to monitor the pearl often. I hope to do some training through it soon. Good luck to you all."

"Bye, Nana!"

"Thank you, Mrs. Stone, and we miss you!" Leera gave Augum a grave look. "We better go quickly."

Augum gave his palm a tender rub. "Agreed."

"How's it feeling?"

"Fine. Let's finish packing."

Chaska gestured that he'd help. Despite the wolven being absent, everyone agreed it would be safest if he remained silent.

"Inventory check," Augum said.

VALOR

Leera pawed through the rucksack. "Orb of Orion, two blankets, a tent, the lantern, flint and steel, rope, the remainder of the Golden Vitae, the map, and some rations."

"Goodbye, Bridge," Augum whispered to her sleeping form, squeezing her cold hand. "Get well."

Leera kissed her forehead and swept her hair away from her pale face. "Bye, Bridgey-poo, see you soon." She poked Chaska in the chest. "Take *good* care of her."

Chaska nodded.

"Good luck, you two," Haylee said in a weak voice.

"We're going to need it," Leera replied. "And take care of her too."

Chaska again nodded.

"Good luck to all of you as well," Augum said, feeling his chest tighten. Would this be the last time they saw each other? Would he and Leera live through this impossible quest the wolven had assigned?

"We'll be back soon," he said.

Haylee closed her eyes. "Promise?"

"Promise."

The pair of them climbed off the table and strode off, giving a final wave. Chaska, hunkering in his wolf hide, waved back, milky face grim. He looked small against the outline of the cave, small and lost.

"This is going to suck," Leera said, leading.

"But we *will* succeed," Augum replied, as determined as ever to make the impossible a reality. He had no idea what lay ahead, but he swore he'd do his best not to fail the others.

Leera gave him that familiar look of resolve. "Agreed," and marched ahead. Eventually she put quite a bit of distance between herself and Augum, who still hadn't fully recovered from losing so much blood the day before. He didn't mind too much, enjoying the tranquility of the epic view.

They avoided the ridge this time, walking horizontally along and around the mountain, two specks on a white vastness. The steepness steadily increased, but there was no point going higher since the marked rectangle was somewhere to the north and east of the mountain.

Augum placed a hand above his eyes and squinted, looking up at the peak. It stood clear against a vivid sky. Directly below it, an enormous snowdrift ledge cast a long shadow. He recalled being buried in the avalanche and quickened his step; Nana wasn't around to save them should it happen again.

The distance between he and Leera increased over the hours, aggravating him. He wanted to shout at her but feared starting an avalanche.

Mountains lay ahead as far as the eye could see, great behemoths with black windswept peaks that raked the sky. He consulted the map and realized Leera descended towards a massive glacier full of jagged seracs, instead of heading toward the side of another mountain that met up with this one.

"You're going the wrong way, Leera!" he shouted. She was too far to hear him though. He began to jog towards her, the rucksack bouncing on his back.

"Leera, you're going—" suddenly the ground beneath him gave way. He slammed against blue ice and fell straight down, eventually jamming between two sharp ice walls. Snow and ice smashed into his head from above.

"Oh ..." He moaned, wincing. Everything seemed to hurt. He tasted blood in his mouth. A bit of sun bounced off the walls above, casting a light blue glow. Below him, the fall continued into darkness.

Just great—he had fallen into a hidden crevasse in the ice, one Leera miraculously missed. The ice groaned. Was it moving? The thought made his heart thump. He listened. Sure enough, the ice was rumbling and cracking below him, in that deep darkness that beckoned for his life.

VALOR

"Leera, can you hear me!" he called, though his voice was weak because his chest was squished between the ice. He was wedged in so good he thought it'd take the wolven to get him out. His rucksack was underneath him, dangling on its strap, Orb of Orion, tent and everything else ready to fall into the void.

He tried to extricate himself but the movement only wedged him in further. Great, he thought. Got into a really good one now, and what timing too …

He resigned himself to wait, completely helpless.

"Augum!" came a distant voice.

Finally, he thought. Took her long enough … "I'm down here," he said, unable to shout.

"Augum, where are you!"

"Right … here."

"Augu—" suddenly she shrieked. A whole bunch of snow crashed onto him. He cringed, waiting to get hit by her body and fall to oblivion. Luckily, it never came. He glanced up. She had somehow managed to grab the ledge and hoist herself back up.

"Aug! Are you all right!" Her face was red, voice edged with panic.

He wanted to shout that this was her fault. If she'd only waited for him … "I'm great," he said instead. "Just taking a break. How're you doing?" Talking only wedged him in further somehow.

"This is no time for jokes, Aug. How are we going to get you out of there!"

He thought about it. She was right, and being angry wouldn't help. He struggled but again wedged himself in further. Nope, he couldn't move. There was nothing he could do. "I don't know …"

"What!"

"I don't know!" he repeated, but Leera only held up her hands.

"Hard to hear you, you're going to have to speak up!" She waited for him to respond, but the pressure of the ice prevented him from speaking. "Hold on," she said, rummaging. "Shoot, you have the rope!"

He groaned. He *did* have the rope. It was in his rucksack, except it was jammed beneath him.

She adjusted her position and placed a hand over her eyes. "You're going to have to somehow get the rucksack above you then get the rope out!"

Easier said than done, he thought bitterly. He wiggled to get at the rope, but it was impossible—his arms were completely jammed up against the ice.

"Use Telekinesis!"

"Fine," he said.

"What!"

Oh for—he closed his eyes, ignoring her, and focused his mind on the difficult task. He also tried to ignore the fact he had extremely limited experience casting Telekinesis gesture-free. First, he went through the motions in his mind. Then he opened his eyes and focused all his arcane energies on the objective. The rucksack strap slowly began to move. Leera was shouting something above, but he refused to let his concentration waver for a moment.

At last, the rucksack drifted above him, having twirled halfway around his body, before falling onto his side. The effort had pushed his arcane boundary. A dull familiar throb began at the front of his brain.

"Great job!" Leera called. "Now comes the tricky part—you're going to have to free the rope—"

Well, *obviously*, he wanted to say. If she'd only waited for him, they'd have walked in a different direction and avoided this whole mess.

The process of retrieving the rope was arduous and demanded great patience. First, he had to arcanely untie the rucksack. This was difficult on its own, but then he had to open it without spilling its contents, telekinetically reach

VALOR

inside without looking, and lastly pull the rope out with his mind. Luckily, he knew exactly where it was located in the rucksack.

An hour of this frustrating struggle passed, with many a near miss.

"You did it, Aug!" Leera shouted at last. "Great, we're halfway there."

The pounding in his head made him wince.

"Let me see if I can get it from here now!" She reached out. "Bear with me, never tried using Telekinesis so far away!"

The end of the rope finally began to snake its way up. She better not drop it—if that rope fell, he doubted he'd be able to catch it.

"Got it! Now you have to figure out a way to tie it around you!"

He had been thinking about this part. He had to use Telekinesis again to wrap the rope around himself and then make a knot. The knot would be the tricky part. He began, failing numerous times, until at last, another hour later, he managed to tie the rope awkwardly around his shoulder and waist.

"How are you doing down there?" Leera asked after a while. "You all right?"

"Yes," he lied, having completely exhausted himself from the effort.

"What!"

He didn't bother repeating himself.

"I'm going to dig in and start pulling," she said. "Are you ready? Here we go!"

He winced as the rope dug into him, but he didn't budge.

Leera cursed. "Again!"

Snow and ice slammed into his head from above, making the throbbing a hammering. All he could was close his eyes and hope a big chunk didn't knock him out.

"I'll see if I can use Telekinesis at the same time!" she said.

The rope bit into him for the third time. His body began to loosen slowly as he felt a force pull at him. Above, Leera groaned from the strain. He managed to get an arm loose and braced himself with it. Then he got the other one out and grabbed a handhold, righting himself.

He was free. Above, Leera collapsed, panting.

After a few gasping breaths, he shouted, "I think I can climb the rest of the way if you keep pulling!"

The pair of them struggled for the next half hour or so, until Augum at last pulled himself over the ledge with the last of his strength, wheezing for breath. Except for some bruising and a twisted ankle, he was remarkably unhurt. The two of them silently laid there in the afternoon sun, a light breeze blowing by, the sky clear of cloud.

THE OBELISK

As much as Leera apologized, Augum refused to hear it. He limped on in the *correct* direction, ignoring her protests.

"... you might have fallen into it anyway," she argued, keeping pace alongside. "Look, the path we're taking isn't far off from that crack at all." She waited for him to respond. "So, you're just going to ignore me the whole time now? Is that my punishment?"

"We should stop," he muttered, trying to quit hobbling.

"Wow, he speaks! And yes, let's do that because I'd like to take a look at that gash on your head."

"Just ... don't." It was a minor cut, hardly worth bothering about. He plopped down, stomach grumbling. Suppertime approached, they hadn't even had lunch yet and had only made it halfway to the other mountain.

"I'm sorry," she said for the umpteenth time. "I shouldn't have wandered so far ahead. It was stupid." She crouched in front of him and gave an exaggerated pout. "Will you forgive me? Hmm?"

He couldn't help but crack a grin at her silliness. "Damn it, you make it hard to be mad at you. Fine already, just … stop."

She flashed a self-satisfied smile and returned to sitting beside him. They ate quietly, deciding to treat themselves with dried and salted salmon wrapped in thin bread, with a side of dried green peas and nuts.

Augum watched the vast expanse with wonder. He'd never been to the mountains before, but remembered etchings he'd seen in Sir Westwood's books. The stories they told were always of heroic adventure and brave deeds, but none of them spoke of the intense cold that stiffened and numbed fingers, the long slog that burned the calves, the danger of hidden crevasses.

They were still up pretty high. Next they'll descend into a valley, cross over to the other mountain, and travel along its edge. On the other side of *that* mountain, they should find the rectangle as marked on the map.

Augum removed his foot from his boot and shoved it in snow to take the swelling down. By the time they set off again, the headache had gone away and the pain in his chest subsided. They even practiced their spells a bit, at least, the quiet ones.

The day moved along, the sun traveling overhead and edging toward the western horizon. Great circular disks of cloud appeared high up around the peaks, creating a strange halo effect. The trees of Ravenwood had completely disappeared behind them—their entire view was now composed of mountains, valleys, and the enormous glacier, the center so cracked it appeared a giant dagger had stabbed it repeatedly.

Augum pointed at a black dot on the glacier. "What do you think that is?" He'd been watching it for a while and swore that it was moving.

"I don't know, can't see from this far."

"Wish we still had the spyglass."

VALOR

They paced on, keeping an eye on it. It seemed to be going parallel to them in the same direction.

"Let's find a place to setup for the night, then eat," Augum said at dusk.

"Agreed."

They continued on, but the slopes here were as smooth as the cheeks of a Henawa child. There was no shelter anywhere. No trees, no rocks, nothing.

"Let's just stop here, I'm exhausted," Leera said.

"What if we get hit by an avalanche?"

She glanced up at the peak, its upper third painted by the remains of the crimson sun. "Wherever we go we're in danger of that."

"True."

The pair erected the tent, panting.

When they finished, Augum nodded at the dot on the glacier. "Look, he stopped too."

"Probably also setting camp for the night."

They crawled into the tent, making it as cozy as possible, before breaking out another delicacy—salted beef with rosemary. They also had dried apple and honeyed almonds for dessert. Mr. Goss and Mr. Okeke had done a marvelous job of finding them tasty provisions. Augum wondered how they fared back in Milham. He imagined them chatting idly before the hearth, cup of steaming tea in their hands.

After supper, they checked on the Orb of Orion. Amazingly, Mrs. Stone was there and waiting! They told her all about their day and how beautiful the view was, their ears pressed up against the orb. She admonished them for not taking sticks to poke the snow with, but overall was happy to hear they were all right.

"I would prefer Bridget, Haylee and Chaska with you, but circumstances are hardly ever ideal in such cases," Mrs. Stone said. "Let us conduct some training."

"Now? Here?" Augum said.

"Yes. It will not be easy, but we should be able to manage. Please take out the blue book."

"We didn't bring it—"

"Oh for mercy's sake—all right, I shall simply have to talk you through it. You do recall which two spells we are going to—"

"Object Track and Object Alarm," Augum and Leera chorused.

"Good, now let us begin with an explanation of exactly what each does—" and so there, on the side of a great mountain, so very far from the comforts of a warm hearth, with only each other and the sound of Mrs. Stone's distant voice to keep them company, Augum and Leera learned the fundamentals of the two spells. They had been unable to cast them yet, but after a three-hour lecture, they certainly had enough to start practicing on the morrow.

Exhausted from the day, they fell asleep soon after Mrs. Stone bid them goodnight, holding hands under their nest of blankets.

The pair set off again early in the morning, munching on salted pork and journey bread as they trundled through the snow. This time they attached to each other with rope, just in case one of them fell into another crevasse. The mountains threw long pyramidal shadows across the snowy landscape. For the third day now, there was no cloud, only an ever-brightening azure sky. The wind was light but steady and bitterly cold, forcing them to keep their hoods up and mitts on as much as possible. The person on the glacier remained, probably still asleep.

"Look—birds," he said, pointing at a small flock coming their way.

Leera stopped and stared, squinting. "You sure they're just birds?"

He placed a hand over his eyes. The hair on the back of his neck rose and his hands went clammy. They did seem kind of big. He quickly looked around—there was

VALOR

absolutely nowhere to hide on this great slope. An idea occurred to him. "Let's retrace our steps a bit and bury ourselves in the snow."

"They'll see us anyway."

"Got any better ideas?"

She shrugged. "We better hurry then."

They ran back about two hundred paces and began digging.

The flock continued coming.

"This is freezing," he heard Leera say beside him. "Can you see them?"

He left one eye uncovered by the stinging snow. "They're coming all right, and they *are* harpies. They're going to our last spot. Now they're headed this way." He gently used his hand to cover the remainder of his face. A moment later, they heard the swish of wings flapping as the flock flew overhead.

He swore he heard Leera's heart hammering as loud as his. After a long while, he chanced a peek. "They're gone, I think."

"Stupid things," Leera said through chattering teeth, uncovering herself.

"Probably can't pick up our scent through their own rotten stench."

Leera laughed.

They resumed their march, ever watchful, but the harpies didn't return. After warming up with some basic spells, they began practicing Object Alarm. Augum kneeled and placed both hands on the lantern, performing the necessary feat of concentration, visualization, and, in this case, setting an alarm in his head that would go off with someone's else's touch.

"Concutio del alarmo." He took his hands off.

"All right, here goes," Leera said, touching the lantern. She looked up at him. "Anything?"

"Nothing. You try."

"Maybe you're not using the gesture correctly." Leera picked up the lantern and they walked some more. They strategized how to get it right before trying again. This went on for two whole leagues, taking up the entire morning, until they had paced through a shallow valley and on around the other mountain.

They broke for lunch, disappointed neither had been successful. Augum set the Orb of Orion between them in case Mrs. Stone contacted them. The glacier steadily climbed ahead, curving northward away from them like a massively wide path nestled between two great mountains. The behemoth on the right was their destination. Somewhere on it should be the black rectangle as depicted on the map. And beyond ... the unknown.

"Hello?" they heard a muted voice say from the orb. "Anyone there?"

They placed their ears up against it. "We can hear you, Nana, go ahead!"

"I am in Tiberra helping evacuate villages, though I will not be able to stay long in case Lividius appears. The situation is chaotic and dangerous. I expect many casualties. Please continue with your studies and your quest. I shall attempt to check on you later today."

"All right, Nana, good luck!"

"Stay safe, Mrs. Stone!"

As they ate, they discussed the news and what they thought it meant. There was plenty to be concerned about, like how long could Tiberra hold out; how was the Legion going to occupy such a vast area; and were the people back in Milham still safe?

After lunch, they resumed their trek, still tethered together with rope.

"He's moving up the glacier northward," Augum said, hand over his eyes. "Wonder if he's going to visit the Occi, or maybe even Bahbell."

"Maybe we should be following *him* instead ..."

"Let's just stick to the plan. We should get there by nightfall."

They continued practicing Object Alarm, figuring they'd move on to Object Track once they got the hang of it. Much to their frustration, the spell continually eluded successful casting. Meanwhile, they had crossed yet another valley and moved onto the mountain that was supposed to have the rectangle. The map yielded no further instructions beyond that last mark.

"Maybe it *is* the Occi village," Augum said, glancing at the map as they rested.

Leera adjusted the rope around her waist, untangling the rucksack from it. "Or maybe it's a sarcophagus …"

"I don't get it."

She blinked. "You know, black rectangle … Occi … sarcophagus …?"

"Oh. Right," but he still didn't get it.

She glanced around at the vast emptiness. "What a lonely place. It's so … I don't know, spiritual I guess, as Bridget would say."

"Didn't know you felt that way about things." She'd always been practical and to the point.

She shrugged. "I'm just glad I'm here with you."

"Me too."

She grinned and gave him a light punch on the shoulder.

He had an urge to talk about the Star Feast and their dance together, but relented. This was a dangerous journey; best not to complicate things right now.

They sat in silence, snacking on raisins and various nuts and seeds before continuing the hike. The final hurdle lay ahead, a steep rocky incline terminating at a ledge. It seemed to circumnavigate the width of the mountain like a great ring. Overhead, the crimson sun threatened to disappear—and they hadn't even thought about a campsite yet.

When they reached the black wall, it turned out to be far steeper than it appeared from so far away. Walking around it would take them all night and was out of the question.

Augum consulted the map again. He glanced up, estimating a hundred foot climb or so. "Should just be right on top of that ledge there. What degree will teach us how to arcanely fly?" he asked half-jokingly.

Leera craned her neck and grimaced. "Don't think that kind of spell exists. I've certainly never heard of a warlock flying about like some bird."

He put away the map and untied himself—no sense in both of them dying if one lost their purchase, or if the harpies came back in the middle of their climb. "Grim thought."

"Huh?"

"Never mind. I'll go first—"

"Forget it, we're racing."

"What—? Are you crazy?" but she had already begun.

Augum chased after her. Both struggled at first, but soon were climbing capably.

"Bridget would never have gotten past this," Leera said halfway up.

"Just don't look down or you'll start screaming like her."

"Keep dreaming, scruffster—and I'm winning, by the way."

" 'Scruffster'?" He couldn't help but snort a laugh, which cost him precious race time—she was the first to reach the ledge and haul herself up. He made it soon after. She extended her hand and lugged him over.

"What do I get?" she asked, smirking.

He brushed the snow off his knees. Those freckled cheeks looked cuter than ever. What he really wanted to say was she won a kiss. Instead, he said, "You get to live," and strode past her, feeling stupid.

"How exciting …"

He turned, pointed at her with both hands. "Scruffbutt."

VALOR

She made a face. "That's just stupid," but smiled.

"Wit never was my thing."

"Then you should be taking notes from me."

Ahead was what looked like an obelisk surrounded by a circle of small boulders. Far behind, the mountain continued to rise, peak bloody in the failing sun. They neared cautiously. The obelisk was about eight feet high and made from black basalt. Runes marked its entire face.

Leera took off her mitt, running her fingers across them. "Some of these look kind of familiar, don't they?"

He nodded. "The bronze servant diagram in castle Arinthian." It was located in the castle cellar. He recalled having a lot of fun deciphering it. Seemed like years ago now.

"Damn," Leera said. "We don't have the blue book with us."

"But we do have the next-best thing." He dug out the Orb of Orion. "Nana, are you there?" There was no response. "Nana, can you hear me!"

Leera dropped her rucksack. "She's probably busy. Set it down on top, in case Mrs. Stone tries to look through."

Augum dropped his rucksack on hers and placed the orb on top. He strolled back to the obelisk. "Now let's see what we can make of these ..."

Leera pulled at something yellow in the snow. "What's this—?" She lifted what appeared to be a stick before yelping and tossing it away.

"What?"

"It's a bone—!"

"Maybe it's just an animal bone ..."

They exchanged doubtful glances before returning to the runes.

"Might be a code or something," Leera said, standing back.

"Shyneo." Augum's hand lit up. He touched one of the runes and was surprised to see it light up, fading a short time later.

They exchanged another look.

"Shyneo," Leera said, reaching for a rune. It began glowing as soon as she touched it. She touched another one in quick succession.

"Leera wait, maybe we should—"

The air split with the sound of an implosive crunch just after she touched a fourth symbol. They turned around to see a giant distorted skeleton, its head oversized, eyes childlike yet vacant and malignant. Strips of wet cloth hung off its decaying frame. It slowly raised its giant clawed hands and hissed.

A rotten stench filled the air.

PORTUS EA IRE ITUM

Augum just managed to summon his lightning shield in time to block the wraith's swipe. The force of the blow sent him tumbling backwards, head nearly smacking one of the boulders.

"Watch out!" he called as the thing raked at Leera. She rolled away, scrambling behind the obelisk. It turned its attention back to him as he got to his feet.

He shoved the air. "Baka!" but the Push spell had no effect on the hulking wraith.

Leera threw at the ground. "Grau!" There was the sound of an enormous volume of water crashing. The wraith looked up, but when it saw nothing above it, refocused on Augum.

"We really need to learn some offensive spells," Leera said, keeping the obelisk between herself and the wraith.

The wraith shot forward suddenly. Augum raised his shield and again was sent flying through the air, landing well behind the circle of stones. His arm hurt from the impact and he tasted blood in his mouth. The cut on his head he'd sustained falling down the crevasse had reopened.

"Mrs. Stone, can you hear us!" Leera shouted as she danced around the obelisk. The wraith made playful swipes at her that would have been deadly if they connected. "We really could use your help—!"

Augum thought he had no choice. Since Nana wasn't able to hear them, he had to try Centarro. Maybe it would show him a path out of this mess—

Except Leera beat him to it.

"Centeratoraye xao xen!" she said, dropping low like a cat poised to strike. Her movements became fluid and effortless. Instead of overreacting to the strikes, she barely dodged them, using just enough movement to avoid it.

Her brows scrunched as she studied the monster. It hissed and shook its arms, as if frustrated, before renewing its effort. At one point, she allowed its giant skull to get so close she actually slapped the thing. It reared back like an angry bull and began slashing wildly at her. She jumped and danced, always just out of its reach.

Suddenly she skirted through its legs, running along their path from the cliff. The wraith followed, hissing. Augum stumbled after, unsure how to help. She reached the cliff and turned around. "Get ready!" she called.

Ready? Ready for what? He ran as fast as he could to catch up. The wraith charged at her. This time, she feigned going through its legs before twirling aside.

"Now!" she called. "Baka!"

"Baka!" he echoed, making the push gesture.

The wraith was turning back to face them just as their spells hit it. The combined force was enough to send it over the edge, hissing.

Augum ran up to the cliff and looked down. He could see the thing slam into the bottom, sending up a great plume of snow. He watched a little while longer. It did not move.

"That was awesome—" he began to say just as Leera stepped into thin air right beside him. He instinctively snatched her hand and sent her swinging into his arms.

She looked into his eyes, a silly expression on her face. "Pretty," she mumbled, resting her head on his shoulders.

"I got you," he said, half-carrying, half-dragging her away from the edge. "Just relax. It's the after-effects of Centarro ..." He took her all the way back to the obelisk and sat with her, enjoying holding her. He made gentle soothing motions on her back to calm her. Eventually, she looked right at him and reddened. "What happened?" She asked, removing her arms from around his neck.

"Centarro."

"Oh, right ..."

"Guess we can't just press the runes randomly and see what happens," he said.

"Guess not ... sorry about that."

"Hello? Either of you there?" came a tinny voice from the orb. They rushed over and placed their ears to it.

"We're here, Mrs. Stone!" Leera said.

"I am glad to hear it. I do not have much time, but I notice you have discovered a portal pillar."

"Is that what it is?" Augum asked. "It almost tried to kill us."

"That is to weed out the unwanted. You must tap out the arcane phrase that makes up the Portal spell, tapping the destination rune last."

"What are the words of the Portal spell?" Leera asked.

"This is why arcaneology class is so important at the academy. You will simply have to remember the following: portus ea ire itum. The symbols are an oval; a square with two upside-down triangles facing each other; a square divided down the middle vertically *not* horizontally; and a letter 'T' with eyes."

"No way," Augum mouthed, pointing at his head. Memorize all that? How?

Leera nodded with a frown. "Mrs. Stone, wait," she said, "let me write that in the snow. Can you please repeat it one more time?"

"Merciful spirits, I shall only repeat it once more, there are hurt people here who urgently need my attention."

Of course, Augum realized—she's in Tiberra.

"All right, I think I got it," Leera said, finishing writing all the symbols. "Thank you and goodbye, Mrs. Stone!"

"Bye, Nana!"

The oval was the easiest to find followed by the square divided down the middle.

"It's getting dark, we should move this along," Leera said, checking the fading horizon. The wind increased, threatening to blow the symbols in the snow away.

"Here's the double triangle one," Augum said.

"—and I just found the 'T' with eyes, though they're just dots." She reached to press the oval, but Augum grabbed her wrist just in time.

"Forgetting something?"

"Oh, right, the destination symbol."

He let go and they examined the face. The problem was it was eight feet high, and there were a few runes out of reach up there.

"What would an Occi symbol look like …" Leera mumbled to herself, stalking the obelisk.

"What about this one?" He stabbed a finger at a group of skulls squished into a square.

"Grim, but promising … I see another one way up there." She pointed at a symbol of a skull with a triangular hat at the very top of the obelisk. "Kind of looks like a roof, doesn't it?"

He nodded. "Here's one." He pointed at a headless skeleton inside a square.

"And I see a fourth one near the very top again, other side," she said. "Getting too dark to see though …"

Augum squinted. "I can just make out a bunch of skulls under a roof."

"But which one of these is it …?"

VALOR

They examined the rest of the obelisk but found no others that fit their idea of what the Occi symbol would be.

"These two down here don't make sense," he said.

"I agree," Leera said. "That narrows it down to two."

"Right—we've got a bunch of skeletons under one roof or a single skull under one roof."

"Since it's a village, I'm guessing it's the bunch of skulls."

"Agreed. So now the question is, do we camp here for the night or see what's on the other end …"

Leera's eyes widened as she looked past his shoulder to the cliff, from which came a distinct hissing noise. "Looks like we don't have a choice …"

Augum reacted immediately by snatching their rucksacks and the Orb of Orion. "You trigger them and I'll boost you up for the last one."

"On it—Shyneo!" She began smacking the runes in order, lighting them up.

He brought his hands together and she stepped on them.

"It's almost here—" Leera said, looking over his shoulder.

He hoisted her up, but as he did so, the first rune went dark, quickly followed by the second. "Wait!" he called. "They're snuffing out."

She glanced behind him again and paled. "We've got to do something—"

"Quick! Step on my shoulders!"

She did, her boots digging the rucksack ropes in further.

"Shyneo!" he said. He smacked the first symbol, then the second, but the third was just out of reach—and the hissing was practically at his neck.

Leera suddenly gripped the edge of the obelisk and swung down to smack it, before shooting back up. Augum smelled the decay and heard the whistling swing of the wraith's claw just as an implosive crunch yanked the two of them away.

THE OCCI

Augum and Leera fell onto rocky ground, nauseous from the teleportation.

"You all right?" Augum wheezed.

"Yeah … you?"

He nodded, trying not to throw up, immediately noticing the air was thin and hard to breathe here. His heart palpitated wildly.

Torches burned a ways away and there was the sound of echoed chanting. The wavering light threw leaping shadows on the most gigantic cavern he had ever seen. It was cone-shaped, jagged top open to the darkening sky.

Leera quietly stood. "What is this, are we in some kind of mountain?"

"Keep your voice down. Looks like it. Those must be the Occi."

It was so cold here he shivered even inside his coat, yet there was no snow anywhere. Behind them was the portal pillar. The ground was strewn with sand, boulders, shrubs, and twisted trees with fruit that looked like bulging sacks of blood.

VALOR

"That must be the bloodfruit." He ran to one of the trees, yanked three squishy fruits, and quickly returned, putting them into his rucksack, hoping they wouldn't burst. "Now we just have to find the location of Bahbell and somehow get our hands on an Occi horn …"

"I think we lost our minds coming here," Leera mumbled, watching the distant fires. "Not that we had much of a choice …"

The chanting suddenly stopped.

"Uh oh," he said as torches rose in the air.

They sneaked behind a boulder as the mass of torches began bobbing in their direction.

"Great, now what do we do?" Leera asked. "Can't exactly outrun them with no exit …"

"Maybe we shouldn't hide—makes us look suspicious."

"So what, we should just face them?" She paused. "Well we better do it now then."

They stepped out from behind the boulder, awaiting the mob. "I think we *did* lose our minds coming here," he said as the crowd fanned out before them. There must have been over a hundred, all wearing the same crimson robes with an embroidered black skull over the heart, three dots in the shape of a triangle decorating the forehead of the skull. Knives hung in sheathes on hemp rope belts, along with carved ornate horns. Their faces were gaunt, some even deathly, as if melted by fire. Some were missing eyes, others noses or their lower jaw. Their hair, even the children's, was wispy, gray and wild. Bones peeked through their stretched skin, skin that ranged in tones from Henawa porcelain to Sierran ebony, and every color in between, including a few blues and reds.

A particularly tall chocolate-skinned woman with random tufts of silver hair pushed the crowd aside. She was the only one without a torch.

"Soiled unworthies …" she said in a dreamy voice.

"Soiled unworthies," the crowd echoed in monotone.

"They must be purified …"

The crowd nodded along. "They must be purified …"

Her arm slowly rose and a long crooked finger extended to point at Augum and Leera. "Into the pot they go …"

"Boiled and purified." The crowd stepped forward. "Into the pot they go …"

"Shyneo!" Augum said instinctively, Leera following.

The crowd hissed at their palms. Whispers abounded.

"Warlocks …" the tall woman said in that hypnotic voice. "Warlocks shall be given the gift …"

"Given the gift …"

"Come …" The woman gracefully extended her hand in the direction of the village behind her. The throng parted, clearing a path.

Augum and Leera exchanged anxious looks before stepping through. The crowd whispered as they passed.

"Come …"

"Unworthies …"

"The master awaits …"

Augum and Leera held their rucksacks close as these gaunt people followed with glazed eyes. The woman led, walking patiently, hands folded in front, entering a tiny village of stick huts loosely gathered around three central fires that burned a greenish hue. A giant cauldron sat on top of one fire, bubbling and steaming. A lumpy stake jutted from the second fire. As the pair walked by, they discovered a man impaled upon it.

"Unnameables …" Leera cursed.

"There will be no blasphemy …" the woman said quietly, her words repeated in whispers by the crowd. "Here, we worship the master, the one and only Lord of Death … You shall bow before him as we do … You shall be given the gift …"

"The gift …" echoed the crowd.

The woman pointed to a dark trail leading to the outline of a seated figure.

"'The master awaits …"

"Follow the path …" some in the crowd whispered. "Worship the master …"

Augum's heart wouldn't stop thundering in his chest as the question rattled around in his brain—who was the master?

The woman was now beside them. Her arm slowly rose and she flicked her wrist. A line of torches burst aflame, circling the figure, revealing an armored skeleton with a wide head, on top of which sat a crown of bone. One hand held a barbed scepter, the top of it an iron skull; the other rested on a glass globe. His throne was made entirely from bone, an elaborate, towering structure with a wide peacock-like fan on the back made from human leg bones, the feet and toes pointing out as if frozen in eternal agony.

"Kneel and say his name …" the woman said.

"Unworthies shall kneel … say his name," the crowd said.

Leera gave Augum an uncertain look.

"Kneel … or boil …" came the woman's silky voice.

"What's his name?" Leera mouthed as she kneeled alongside him.

It had to be Occulus, Augum thought, it had to be … or they were as good as dead.

"Occulus," he said aloud, taking the risk.

"Occulus," Leera echoed.

"Occulus," the pair of them chorused again in a louder voice.

The crowd dropped to its knees, including the woman. They bowed low, their heads touching the ground, before sitting up. The woman stood, gliding by them as if she hovered, red robe billowing gently. She turned to them and slowly backed up against the throne.

"All others are pretenders to the throne. There is only one Lord of Death." She opened her mouth and her tongue began to rattle. Her chocolate skin darkened until it was black, then lightened until it was bone white, finally returning to brown.

Fat white maggots with red snouts began to worm out of the skeleton from nooks and crannies. Two came out of the eyes as the women stared at them.

"Now ... *fear* the master ..."

Augum felt a tingling on the back of his skull. The sensation, so familiar because of Mrs. Stone's training, immediately triggered the correct response. He slammed the door on the Fear spell while the crowd behind them began shrieking and screaming.

Augum and Leera sat unfazed.

When she realized they hadn't been affected, the woman ceased her rattling, and the maggots oozed back into the skeleton. The terrified crowd stopped, some still whimpering, others crying.

"Impressive ..." the woman said.

"Impressive," some in the crowd whispered.

"Perhaps later we can play more games," she went on. "I like games ..."

"Games ..."

Augum was careful to keep his face stony. "Who are you?"

The woman gracefully placed her hands before her. "I am the master's wife ... Nefra ..." She gestured at the crowd. "They are his children ... from the many wenches he took ... We return again and again ... We are ... eternal ..."

A sickly over-sized child waddled past, red robe trailing. He glanced at them, revealing a rotten skull out of which worms crawled. He turned back to Nefra, gurgling, "Mommy!"

"My sweet, beautiful prince ..." She picked up the boy, captured a fat maggot, and fed it to him, the white juices slopping all over his robe.

Leera cringed. "I think I'm going to be sick ..."

Augum had to look away, feeling bile creep up his throat.

VALOR

A rhythmic drumming began in the village, tuned to the speed of their rapidly beating hearts. Augum and Leera's heads swiveled to see a gaunt Henawa man banging on a drum with a hide mallet. His silver wispy hair streamed to his waist, patches of it missing. His eyes were as bloodshot as his crimson robe.

"Peyas..." Nefra whispered, hissing the last syllable. "You disobey me ..."

"They are young, Nefra," Peyas said without a trace of a Henawa accent, crowd parting before him. "Let them go, Nefra ..."

Nefra put down her child. The boy continued chewing on the maggot. "The gift shall be given, Peyas ... They are warlocks ..."

"Warlocks ..." the crowd echoed.

Peyas stopped by their side, the drum never ceasing. "When will the gift be given, Nefra?" He spoke her name trance-like, trailing the last letter.

"Tonight, Peyas ... after the feast of the bloodfruit ..."

"Then they shall stay with me until then, Nefra ..."

Nefra's eyes narrowed and turned black. Her skin rippled with waves of color before returning to normal. "You are naughty, Peyas ..."

"Naughty ..." the crowd murmured.

"Do not make me punish you, Peyas ..."

"They shall come with me for now, Nefra ... You can give them the gift after ..."

"If you disobey me, Peyas ..."

The crowd hissed, leaving the threat unsaid.

Peyas spoke out of the corner of his mouth as he drummed on. "Stand and follow me."

Augum and Leera didn't need telling twice. Nefra's tongue rattled as Peyas led them to a hut separated from the village, beating his drum until stepping through its beaded bone curtain.

The hut was lit by a single torch and stank of rot. Shelves overflowed with stoppered jars of bones, pale pus, and maggots floating in murky fluid. The furniture was crude and made of sticks, as were the walls.

Peyas put down his drum and mallet. "You are childling fools. Do you know where you are?"

"We're in the Occi village," Leera said.

"Our harpies watched you for a time in the forest. Why would you ever come to this cursed place?"

"To save our friends." Augum decided it was best to be honest with this man. He lowered his voice and took a risk. "We need an Occi horn to trade for their lives."

"Then it is their fate to die."

"No, we won't let that happen—"

Peyas only observed him. His bloodshot eyes eventually wandered to Augum's bandaged hand, where he had slashed himself to save Bridget. "Do you need ointment?"

Augum glanced at a jar of pus. "Uh, I'm fine, thanks."

"Why did you stand up for us?" Leera asked.

"The flame of curiosity, although dimmed greatly over the years, nonetheless still burns."

She peeked through the curtain. "And what about that woman, who is she?"

"Nefra is our queen mother. We are the Occi, the undying children of Occulus."

"But you don't mean you're Occulus' *actual* children," Augum said.

"I do. Every cursed soul here is his real child, every single one but Nefra. The master took many women, but she is the only one who still unlives among us, having entombed the others long ago."

"*Alive?*" Leera asked. "How ghastly—"

"I prefer the term 'unalive'. And yes, those poor women are certainly beyond mad after all these centuries."

"Why would Nefra do such a horrible thing to them?"

"So that she would be the only queen when the master returns. She loved him greatly, and still does." He leaned closer, whispering, "Though he did not return that love. She is not his *beloved*, and never will be." He straightened, glancing at the beaded bone curtain. "She would have entombed me along with the others if she did not fear my father's wrath, for I am his firstborn. Time has made her crueler over the centuries. She plays ... *games* ... to keep herself occupied."

"I guess they're not fun games, are they?" Leera asked.

"I wish for you to never partake in them."

Augum shook his head. "His beloved? Firstborn? I don't understand …"

"Let me tell you a story. Over fifteen hundred years ago, a young Tiberran man met a young Henawa woman. They fell in love. The man's Tiberran family disapproved of the match, as did the woman's Henawa tribe. Yet their love was so strong that no one could deny it to them. A son was soon born, and the Henawa, their hearts warmed by their love, adopted the man and the boy into the tribe. The love blossomed, becoming so strong that it was said the sun brightened when they walked hand in hand; birds chirped in unison when they spoke; flowers bloomed as they passed.

"Then one day, the woman fell gravely ill. The man tried everything to save her, but could only hold her hand as she gasped her last, and he held it long after she went, even long after the tribe had moved along with the snow, taking his son with them lest he starved. Through an entire phase of the moon, he held his beloved, so stricken with grief was he.

"Or so the legends say.

"At long last, when the light was dark around him; when the birds were silent and the flowers wilted with frost, he rose and swore to the Unnameables that he would find a way to bring her back. A fever of his own making gripped him. He began a great search, spending endless nights studying old books. These books told of ancient forgotten places that harbored old arcanery, arcanery damned and sealed off from the world. And so he hid his beloved in a secret place, taking great precautions to keep her preserved, and began travelling.

"As the man aged, the path he tread darkened his soul. He slew scores of men, and took many women, all in an effort to forget *her*. He fathered many sons and daughters, though none out of love. He even built himself a great castle on one of those ancient forgotten sites, where he continued studying arcanery and necromancy. The dead rose around him in ghastly forms as he tried various ways to resurrect his beloved. Yet as gifted and determined as he was, all attempts resulted in failure, his creations grotesque shadows of their former selves.

"Then one day, frustrated and angry with the world, he came across an old legend about a mythic rock. This rock was said to grant audience with a witch—"

The hair on Augum's arms rose.

"—he travelled to this rock armed with an ancient but simple poem. Upon arriving, he performed a ritual hidden within its words. When the witch appeared before him, he begged her to resurrect his beloved. The witch told him she would do him one better—if he did her bidding, she would cast a powerful spell on every son and daughter he had ever sired, and every woman he had ever taken, and they would all live forever. Finally, if he completed a certain task, she would resurrect his beloved. When he asked her what that task was, she told him he was to conquer Ley for her father.

"To help him with this most difficult quest, he was to raise an army of the undead equipped with Dreadnought steel. She mentored him on the finer points of necromancy until he became a master and lord of many thousands of undead soldiers. He used this army to destroy the Lord of Dreadnoughts, taking his place as their ruler.

"The last ingredient to victory was a portal to Ley. The witch furnished Occulus with a recipe to build one. Yet the

Leyans, who still commanded great respect in the world, threw up a call to arms, bestowing seven artifacts upon the seven most powerful warlocks of the age."

"I know this part," Augum said slowly. "He was vanquished by Atrius Arinthian in the War of the Scions before he could finish the portal." Now his father was after that same recipe, trying to achieve the same ends ...

"I see history has not been forgotten by the young." Peyas' chin rose slightly. "Occulus slew six of the seven, but the last, the most powerful and gifted of the lot, indeed vanquished him in an epic battle."

There was a thoughtful silence. Augum wondered what Peyas would say if he knew Augum was a direct descendant of the man that slew Occulus, and the son of the current Lord of Death.

"A witch's pact is a terrible thing, a terrible thing," Peyas said quietly, shaking his head. "We should have died long ago ..."

Augum remembered his own pact with a witch—it had cost him his arcane powers just to send a message to Mrs. Stone. He wondered if she was the same witch Occulus once spoke with.

"Bridget would say it's all so tragically romantic," Leera whispered. "I mean, about the lengths Occulus went to in trying to raise his beloved."

Augum absently nodded along. Would he ever love someone so much as to go to those lengths to bring them back? Then he recalled once secretly thinking he'd find a way to raise Mya. He pictured standing before Hangman's Rock and calling upon the witch, begging her to bring her back.

No, that would be damnation. Look what it had done to Occulus ...

He turned to Peyas, feeling a cold sweat. "You mentioned the witch had a father ..."

"Her father is the Father of Demons, whose true name is unnameable, for He *is* an Unnameable." Peyas stared into the torch. "It is said all that is dark in the world originates from Him. All suffering, betrayal and death; every ill thought, every disease, every unkind word. It is said they are all his doing, and it will continue on this way until He lays claim to His old kingdom."

"But … why is Ley his old kingdom?" Leera asked.

"Now we speak of ancient things. Legend says that, in the beginning of time, two brothers were charged with the task of keeping knowledge for mortals. This they did, until one brother wanted all the knowledge to himself. The other brother forbade this. He wanted to stay true to their task and keep sharing the knowledge with mortals. There was a great battle. In the end, the selfish brother was damned to another plane, a plane of demons and fire. Some call it 'Hell', though it is known by many names. There this brother became the Father of Demons, forever questing to regain the Leyan plane."

"So this Unnameable, the Father of Demons, uses people," Augum said quietly, "to get Ley back …" He wondered if the other brother happened to be Krakatos the Ancient, that strange pink-spectacled Leyan man some thought immortal. If that was the case, and the witch was his brother's daughter, then she was also Krakatos' niece …

"I've always wondered though," Leera began, "do the Unnameables really exist, or is it just a bunch of old stories morphed into legend?"

"I have thought on this much. Who are the Unnameables? Are they real? If so, do they concern themselves in mortal affairs? I know nothing for certain, nor have I ever seen any sign or proof of their existence. Yet allow me to share a thought—an ordinary man appears powerful to an insect, but a 1st degree warlock appears powerful to an ordinary man. A 10th degree warlock appears invulnerable to a 1st degree warlock, yet a master appears mythic in proportion. But then, sometimes, a master learns new arts in a new plane."

Something clicked for Augum. "You mean if they get invited to Ley and study on?" Nana had once been invited to Ley, hadn't she?

"Precisely. Perhaps a master keeps learning and learning, until in the eyes of the insect they are a god. And so who is to say there are Unnameables? What if they are merely old powerful warlocks that never died?"

"This is surreal ..." Augum whispered.

"I just thought of something," Leera said. "We're now pretty certain that your fa—I mean the Lord of the Legion—made a pact with that witch, Magua, right?"

Augum nodded.

"Well, in his case, he'd ask for all the scions, wouldn't he?"

"Yeah, and so Magua granted him that divining rod to find them."

"Yes, but it also means she wants something *in return*—"

"You mean Ley? But then he had to have made the pact a while ago because he's been after Ley for some time now ..."

"Right. Now suppose he did make it a while ago and the witch promised eternal life for him and his subjects as part of the reward. She's probably been mentoring him in necromancy so that he can build his own army. Maybe she's even the one who told him how to regain power over Dreadnoughts. I mean, I don't know, but, history seems to be *repeating* itself—"

"It kind of *does* make sense that way, doesn't it? But I think there's more ..." A thought danced on the tip of his tongue. "What if ... I don't know, I mean ... what if the Lord of the Legion also wants to bring back his *own* wife—"

"The one he *murdered*?"

"Yeah, but—" He glanced at Peyas, who watched him keenly. He had to be careful here not to say too much. "What if he regrets murdering her? What if part of this whole thing with necromancy is Sparkstone trying to bring *her* back too, just like Occulus wanted to bring his beloved back?"

"It's possible I guess, except that I think the Lord of the Legion is just too … *evil* to want to do it all for a wife he murdered." Her eyes flicked to Peyas briefly as her voice dropped. "Remember what *Mrs. S* said about his past—that he was an evil little brat and cared about nothing."

"Except her, he cared about *her*."

"He murdered *her* because she wanted to leave him, and I'm sure she had plenty of really good reasons to leave an evil crazy man." Leera shook her head. "No, I think he wants the scions, all of them—and eternal life and being an emperor and stuff too."

"Yeah, maybe …" Yet Augum wasn't entirely convinced. He recalled seeing pain, although momentary, in his father's eyes when he mentioned his mother. Nana was right, there *was* something there, but how to discover exactly what?

"You younglings seem to know quite a lot about the pretender," Peyas said.

"Oh, it's common knowledge," Leera lied.

"So you've been here all this time?" Augum asked quickly lest the old Occi became too suspicious.

The gaunt Henawa fixed his bloody gaze upon him. "In the fifteen hundred years since the slaying of our father, the Occi have rarely left this place. Only I sometimes travel beyond the confines of these walls."

"Wait, you're the one …!" Leera said. "You're the one that travels to Milham for supplies, aren't you?"

"Yes, I am the one. Once a year, I visit an old Henawa man to buy medicine and trade. He helps me remember, for I have forgotten almost everything about my people." He gazed past them, eyes reflecting the torch. "We come with the snows from the north. We come from Ohm. We are hunters, gatherers and singers and warriors." He paused a moment, lost in thought. "He is my only friend, left behind because he was too old to take along. I was once left behind too ... Every year the old Henawa teaches me one Henawa word. I have been coming for ten years. I know ten words."

Leera smiled. "Chunchuha."

Peyas made an awkward effort to smile back, revealing a rotten mouth of missing teeth. It was as if he had forgotten the gesture across the centuries. "Chunchuha. It means welcome."

"So you don't ever dream of ... of running away or something?"

"Mortals look upon my flesh and see an abomination. They burn me, and fire hurts, as does the sun's touch, forcing me to travel by night. I am weaker than most mortals are in fact; I lack arcanery or the strength of the freshly risen. Yet I can command the dead. Among us, only Nefra is truly strong. She was a warlock in her day and continues to be one still. Besides, the further and longer we Occi stray from Bahbell, the weaker we become, until we wither and die. Yet regardless of the manner of our death, when the moon next becomes full, we wake here in the sands of this unholy mountain. No, one such as I cannot dream of better things, for this existence is nothing but damnation."

Augum scooped some of the fine sand from the ground and watched as it filtered through his fingers like an hourglass. "But ... why here? What's so special about this mountain?"

"I know why," Leera whispered, eyes dropping to the ground. "The castle ... it's below us, isn't it?"

"It is," Peyas said. "Hidden within this mountain is the great castle of Bahbell, built upon an ancient forgotten site, and here, at the top of this mountain, in this very cavern, is where the curse was cast."

Augum glanced down and felt a distinct chill.

Leera swallowed. "Don't suppose you know why Bahbell is another name for 'gateway to hell'? I mean, there isn't actually a *gate* down there, is there?"

"There is a great deal down there."

"Uh, right. Hope this isn't a stupid question," Leera pressed, "but, how do you know any of this stuff? Is it because you're so old?"

"Time does not necessarily bring wisdom or insight. Yet, back when my curiosity was stronger, I did travel often. Most of my knowledge, however, comes from my father's books. Bahbell has an ancient library. Once we were free to go there and indulge in learning, but the queen has forbidden it for some time now. We are not to soil the master's home with our rotten presence."

"So how is Occulus supposed to come back to life?" Augum asked.

"He will come back to life when the pretender to the throne is boiled alive, his blood and soul used for the ancient waking ceremony."

Augum didn't even wish such a fate upon his murderous father. Thankfully, he thought the chances of it happening highly unlikely—the last thing anyone wanted was the most powerful Lord of Death ever coming back to life and wreaking havoc.

"And what about this 'gift' we're supposed to get?" Leera asked. "Don't suppose it's a nice present of some sort, maybe a chocolate cake?"

"It is purification by cauldron, followed by rebirth as a harpy, forever at the beck and call of a horn. Each worshipper here has one harpy."

"Damn, I knew it …"

Augum wasn't surprised either. These were the Occi, after all. "Wait, so all those harpies were once … *people*?"

"Once, yes."

"Look, Mr., uh, Peyas," Leera began, "neither of us really feel like being boiled alive and, uh, turned into harpies, so how about we just *borrow* one of those horns and scoot on out of here through the portal pillar thingy?"

Peyas slowly shook his head. "Nefra would never allow you to leave."

VALOR

"But you've got to help us, our friend's life depends on it—"

"There is little I can do. Whenever I disobey the queen mother, she burns me, boils me, or impales me on the stake. The pain is not worth assisting you, not that there is much I can do anyway, for everything is pre-written in our fates."

"I disagree," Augum said. "I believe we always have a choice." It was something he had believed as long as he could remember, even when his fellow common folk proclaimed everything happened because the Unnameables wanted it to.

"Your fate is a difficult one then. I do not envy your path."

"So you won't help us?"

"I cannot."

"You mean you *will* not. Isn't that making a choice?"

Peyas frowned in thought but said nothing.

Augum sighed. "So who was that we saw on the stake?"

"Masius. He shall return from the sands after the feast of the bloodfruit, for tonight the moon will be full."

"Did he disobey Nefra?"

"He did, but he cannot help himself, having gone mad long ago after being tortured and buried alive by peasant farmers. He was gone for years, until one day, when the children of the farmers, having heard tall tales, exhumed him for fun. Masius crawled out of the ground and took his revenge, slaughtering them all in a fit of wild fury."

"Ghastly …" Leera whispered.

"My medicines are mostly for him, but they do not always work."

The villagers began chanting in the distance.

Leera peeked through the beaded bone curtain. "What's happening?"

"They are performing ritual worship, as done every night at this time for over fifteen hundred years."

"Doesn't that ever get boring?"

"There is no such thing as boring here. There is only suffering."

The chanting got louder. Peyas looked beyond them through the curtain. "Now you must stay silent or I will be punished."

"So we just sit here and wait to get ... turned into harpies?"

"Yes."

Augum and Leera exchanged determined looks—one way or another, they were going to get out of there with a horn.

THE SCOUT

It was very late, perhaps the middle of the night, judging by the dark sky-hole in the cavern, when Augum came to the conclusion they needed a distraction. Maybe they could somehow set something on fire and use the confusion to escape.

"Peyas …" Nefra's voice slithered in from outside.

"Peyas …" echoed the crowd.

"It is time. Bring the unworthies …"

Leera gave Peyas a pleading look but his gaunt expression did not change.

The ancient Henawa stood. "I am sorry. Come with me please."

"Oh, he's sorry," Leera said to Augum. "That makes everything all right."

Augum's mind raced for ideas as they slung their rucksacks over their shoulders and followed him out of the hut.

The crowd waited in a great circle, leaving space for them to walk through. Peyas bid them to stand between the three greenish fires, burning hot and bright. The single cauldron bubbled and steamed. Masius, the man impaled above another fire, had mostly burned away, leaving only charred husks of bone.

Peyas filled the empty spot in the circle while Nefra stepped before them. All the Occi, except for Peyas, held a bloodfruit.

Nefra raised the fruit above her head. "All hail the master."

"All hail the master," the crowd repeated.

Nefra began gorging on the fruit, watching Augum and Leera, her skin changing colors. The crowd followed her lead, filling the air with the sound of sloppy eating. The blood spilled down their robes.

Upon finishing, she raised her hands skyward. "Rebirth, Masius!"

"Rebirth, Masius!" the crowd chanted.

Augum felt something under his boot. He jumped back to find a hand with dark red skin poke through the sand. Another one soon emerged and a naked man hauled himself up, sand spilling off him. Half his face was skeletal, the other half handsomely chiseled with a strong jaw. His hair was wispy and gray like the other Occi.

Peyas walked to his hut and returned with a pristine crimson robe, draping it over Masius' shaking shoulders. The man hunched as if suffering from fever, even though the air was hot between the three fires.

"Can't you let me sleep for a while, hmm, can't you?" Masius asked in a shaking voice. "You know, maybe for eternity? Just a wee bit more of eternity?"

"You will behave and stay, Masius …" Nefra said, the words repeated by the crowd in whispers.

"Aw, come on … *come on*, Nefra. Gracious please, Nefra sweet, sweetest sweet?"

"Do not test my patience, Masius …"

Masius fixed his remaining good eye on Augum and Leera, hands writhing. "This time I got real far, I did I did.

VALOR

Real far I says. I saw lions. *Lions* standing on two feet! I'm going to go back, back I'm going—"

"Quiet, Masius …"

"Quiet, Masius," the crowd echoed.

Nefra's cold gaze fell upon Augum and Leera. "Are you ready to receive the gift?"

Before either of them could answer, there came a clicking sound. Heads turned skyward. Augum looked up to see a harpy carrying a black-armored man in its claws.

"That's a Legion soldier—" he said as the harpy let the man go. He fell like a sack of spuds, groaning when he slammed into the dirt.

Nefra's eyes narrowed. "Stand, Pretender …"

"Stand …" the crowd hissed.

The soldier wheezed and struggled to his feet. He looked in his mid twenties, with cropped nut hair, a weak jaw, and thick brows that connected. A sword hung by his side and his armor was studded black leather, not the usual plate. The emblem of the burning sword marked his chest.

"Unworthy …" Nefra said.

"Unworthy," the crowd echoed. "Pretender …"

The soldier frantically looked around as sweat began to bead on his forehead. "You're … you're *them* …!"

Augum felt a familiar tingling at the back of his brain. He shut the door on the spell immediately. The soldier was not so fortunate. He began screaming, looking about with wild eyes while retreating. When he reached the encircling crowd of Occi, they hissed and shoved him back to the middle. He howled and raised his arms to protect himself, nearly tumbling into the fire. Soon the entire crowd was screaming along with him, as if seeing a terrible horror. Even Peyas' gaunt face was slack with terror. Masius gripped his head and fell to his knees, rocking like a child.

Nefra made a graceful gesture and the screaming stopped. The soldier fell to his knees, weeping.

Masius looked up and smiled with half his face. "They're coming, they are! I finally did something worthy, I did!"

"Who is coming, Masius?" Peyas asked.

"The pretenders ... they'll destroy this place, they will. We can finally sleep ... I'll only burn one more time ... one last burning for me, yes."

Nefra grabbed Masius by the neck and lifted him from the ground, her skin tones flickering rapidly. "What did you do this time, Masius!"

"Told ... them ... where ... to ... find ... us ... I ... did ..." His hands feebly grasped at her arm. "They ... will ... destroy ..."

Her tongue began to rattle.

"No ... please ..." Masius said, but she brought him close and kissed him. He began writhing wildly in her grip like a rodent caught in the jaws of a snake.

"Nefra, no—!" Peyas said, but he did not move to help.

Augum and Leera backed away from Masius' flailing kicks, barely able to watch. The man began shaking violently and turning black, screaming and screaming until Nefra threw him into the boiling cauldron. He thrashed, splashing water that hissed in the flames, until suddenly becoming still.

The soldier, still on his knees, lay himself down, shoulders heaving.

Leera grabbed Augum's hand and squeezed. He felt her racing pulse and looked over. Her face was pale.

Peyas cocked his head slightly at them. Something about the look he was giving said he had not witnessed such a simple, human thing in a long time.

Nefra walked up to the soldier, jaw firm. "Pretender ... speak ..."

"Speak ..." the crowd said in an angry hiss.

The man raised a shaking arm defensively. "I'm just a scout ... that's all, I'm only a lowly scout ..."

VALOR

He must have been the one they had seen on the glacier, Augum thought.

Nefra's tongue began rattling. "Who comes this way?"

"Please don't! I'll speak! The Legion are coming—an entire company of two hundred. They're coming for the castle …"

"Unworthy pretenders shall not soil the master's home!"

"Unworthies …" the crowd whispered.

Nefra raised her head. "They will be destroyed in a grand war game!"

"Destroyed!" the crowd shouted.

She unfastened the horn at her hip and blew on it. A single note ricocheted off the walls, quickly joined by scores of others.

The sound was so loud Augum, Leera and the soldier covered their ears.

The Occi lowered their horns. Harpies soon began appearing from the hole in the mountaintop. The clicking of their beaks amplified as more and more dove in. They circled the cavern and came to hover, wings flapping, just above their respective villagers. The Occi grabbed their clawed feet and each pairing lifted off together.

It smelled as if someone had dumped a house full of rotten meat into the cavern. The soldier threw up while Augum and Leera tightly held their noses.

"You will watch them, Peyas, or suffer," Nefra said, gesturing at an Occi man to stay with them. She grabbed onto the claws of a particularly large and hideous harpy and flew away.

The man ordered to stay with them was huge, perhaps once a warrior. His skin was papery and a pale hue of blue. His muscles bulged through the crimson robe. His head was bald, parts of the skull peeking through; cheeks sunken and pierced, exposing rotten teeth. A harpy stood near, clicking its beak.

The soldier was still on the ground, breathing rapidly. "I don't want to die," he said, grabbing Leera's robe. "Please, don't let them boil me alive—!"

Leera jumped back. "Then fight! Fight him!" She pointed at the big Occi, who bared his teeth. His harpy spread its wings.

"You going to help, or just stand there?" She asked Augum, raising her hand. "Shyneo!"

"Shyneo," Augum said, hand crackling to life.

"You mustn't struggle," Peyas said. "He will kill you."

"Her mistake was leaving us here with only two guards," Augum said. This was their chance, and they weren't going to let it pass.

Leera took a step back as the large Occi approached. "We'll die anyway, won't we?"

Peyas said nothing.

The Occi warrior raised his arm at Augum. It ruptured with four dim rings that looked like they were made from smoke. "Voidus aurus," he croaked.

Augum at first reflexively summoned his shield—but the attack was against his mind. Luckily, Nana's Mind Armor training allowed him to block the Deafness spell.

The soldier gritted his teeth. "Give me courage, great Legion Lord!" and tackled the big Occi. The pair rolled in the sand, battling.

The harpy lifted off, circled once and dove at Augum and Leera. They barely managed to dodge out of the way. There was a splash followed by a gut-wrenching scream. They turned to find the big Occi looming over the cauldron. The soldier's head reappeared momentarily, but the Occi shoved him back under. The water thrashed as the Occi winced, his own muscled arm boiling along with the soldier.

Leera got to her feet. "Peyas, help us—please!"

Peyas glanced at the cauldron that held the soldier. It had resumed its quiet boil. "Our fates are pre-written. There is no use in struggling."

VALOR

Augum wanted to cast Centarro but thought better of it—taking on a large Occi *and* his harpy was too risky, considering the after-effects should he fail. Instead, he focused his mind and shoved the air before him.

"Baka—!"

The Occi saw the attack coming and summoned a shield made of smoky wind, but was sent sprawling, barely missing one of the large fires. It was Augum's single most successful casting of Push.

"Watch out, Aug—!"

Without looking, he jumped aside just as harpy claws whistled by his head.

The Occi got back on his feet and threw at the ground. "GRAU!" There was a monstrous noise like that of a sudden hurricane. Augum and Leera flinched and ducked, costing them precious time. Despite knowing the spell, Augum still expected to get swept off his feet, even if by the sheer noise of it.

The Occi warrior made a shoving gesture. "Baka!" and sent Leera tumbling.

Augum saw the horn bounce on the man's hip. He raised his hand and visualized it coming to him with Telekinesis. It lifted but remained clipped to the belt.

The Occi slammed his wrists together toward Augum. "Annihilo!" A fierce blast of ripping wind shot at him. Augum barely summoned his shield in time. The force of the blast still knocked him back. Not a moment later, he had to summon the shield again to block another harpy dive attack. The claws made a scraping sound across the hard lightning shield.

"Baka!" Leera shouted, but the man blocked with his own summoned shield, only stumbling a step or two. Leera then used Telekinesis to send rocks flying, but they did not have enough velocity to do anything—she was not advanced enough with the spell to cause damage yet.

Augum scrambled to his feet, cursing their lack of training. This was quickly getting out of control. They were going to lose the fight if they didn't change tactics.

He had no choice now—he had to try Centarro. He focused his mind, which had already started throbbing from so much quick casting, and shouted, "Centeratoraye xao xen!"

The glorious spell quickened and sharpened his perception instantly. The fire was mesmerizing; the sands soft under his feet; the air crisp and cool on his cheek. This was it, he had one objective now—*get the damn horn*.

He twirled away from another wind attack, simultaneously ducking a harpy dive—this time though, he reached out and grabbed its scaly claws, hitching a brief ride, letting go at the optimal moment and launching himself at the Occi, feet first in a flying leg kick. The warrior summoned his shield, but the force of Augum's kick sent both tumbling. Augum, whose reactions and senses were quicker than the Occi's, judged that he could rip the horn from the warrior's waist at the expense of suffering a vicious claw attack from the harpy.

He did not hesitate and tore the horn free, evading the Occi's clumsy attempts to grab him—luckily, Leera shoved the harpy with Push at the last moment and it missed him by a hairsbreadth.

Augum fluidly rolled away from the man's furiously pawing hands and blew on the horn, enjoying the distant echo. "Attack him!" he yelled, pointing at the warrior. The harpy dove and plowed into the Occi just as he was scrambling to get up.

Augum tried to stand too but the fog quickly began to set in. Leera sprinted to him and helped him up. "Go go go—!" she shouted, but his thoughts quickly devolved—they were hurriedly going somewhere. Then his consciousness knew only impressions. Falling. Sand. Walking. Running. Something cold and black and tall. Someone was shouting at him. His cheek suddenly stung. The words slowly took shape.

"Augum—!" A hand raised to slap him, but he blocked it instinctively.

"Aug, are you back? Come back to me, Aug! Hurry!"

"Huh …?"

"We're at the pillar! The pillar, remember!" Leera was quickly inspecting the black stone. "Damn it, you don't happen to remember which runes we're supposed to press, do you?"

He gazed at the pillar, mind blank.

Leera saw the look on his face. "We're in serious trouble here …"

She hurriedly unpacked the Orb of Orion. "Mrs. Stone, are you there? Mrs. Stone!" but there was no response.

"There is no use resisting fate," Peyas said, walking up to the circle of stones around the obelisk. Far behind him, the big Occi wrestled with the harpy.

"Peyas, help us—" Augum said, getting back on his feet, shaking the confusion off. "All we need is the correct symbols—"

"There is no use—"

"But there is! You can make a choice—you *can* help us." He stepped close to the gaunt Henawa. "You are suala sapinchay."

"What does that mean?"

"It means 'brave snowskin'."

Peyas watched him a moment before glancing back to the struggling Occi. The man was winning against the harpy.

"Please," Leera whispered. "We don't have much time—"

"I know of only two places for you to go," Peyas said at last. "The glacier from which you had come—or Bahbell."

Augum glanced up at the obelisk. "The skull with the roof over its head—that's Bahbell, isn't it?"

"It is. Is that where you want to go?"

"No, we need to get back to our friends—" Though now he knew how to get into the castle when they had to return …

"Then pay careful attention." Peyas stepped before the obelisk and touched the corresponding runes. They lit up in succession, despite the fact he had not used Shine. Instead of triggering the last rune that would have triggered the spell, he only pointed at it.

"Got it," Augum said as the runes faded. He looked back at the village and saw that the big Occi man was now free of the harpy and racing for them.

Leera grabbed Peyas' hand in both her own. "Goodbye, Peyas, and … thank you."

He gave a slight nod.

"Shyneo," Augum said as Leera took his other hand.

"Hurry, Aug, he's almost here—"

"Working on it …" He tapped out the correct pattern, gripping her hand tighter. "Here we go—" He smacked the final rune with his lit palm and was immediately yanked with an implosive crunch.

THE JOURNEY BACK

The portal spit Augum and Leera out at the base of the obelisk. It was the middle of the night but the sky was completely clear, lit by a field of the sharpest stars Augum had ever seen. The wide pale face of the full moon made the Muranians glitter, as if trying to rival the stars.

"Wraith's gone at least," he said after taking a good look around. That was a relief—he did not have the arcane strength for another battle.

Leera nodded at the glacier. "That must be the Legion company." A black line of troops snaked along the distant ice. Flashes of steel and armor occasionally reflected the moonlight. "They're in for a nasty surprise …"

Augum's hollow stomach groaned a complaint. They had missed supper, but there was hardly time for that now. "Let's put as much distance between us and this pillar as we can before setting camp. Nefra might come after us as soon as she discovers we're gone."

"Agreed."

They strode away at a rapid clip, heads swiveling back to the pillar. The unliving man had not followed them either. Augum wondered if Peyas had something to do with that.

The cliff took them twice as long to climb down as it had to climb up, and it was twice as hazardous at night, for the ice had grown more slippery in the harsh cold. Nonetheless, they managed it without incident before undertaking the long trek back toward the wolven cave.

"Did you slap me back there?"

She shrugged. "Maybe."

"Didn't help my headache."

"Kind of helped mine."

He glanced at her.

"What? It was sort of ... therapeutic. I should be slapping you more."

"Really?"

"Uh huh."

He stopped on the pretense of fixing his boot, grabbed a handful of snow, and playfully dumped it down her back. She squealed.

"You evil little—" and immediately began chasing him. He let her catch him and the two rolled in the snow, giggling and wrestling, relieving the tension of the battle.

"We ... should ... be ... walking!" Leera shouted as Augum, who was on top, kept trying to smear her face with snow.

"But wait, your face is dirty, let me just clean it—"

"GET. OFF!" She finally managed to shove him aside and the two lay in the snow, gasping for breath. He got up, smiled at her, and offered his hand.

"Jerk," she mumbled, taking it.

"We really do need to go though," he said. "Truce?"

"Pfft."

Some hours later, the eastern horizon began to blush with the first hint of dawn. The stars slowly disappeared, leaving only the ethereal moon. Deciding they were still too close to the portal pillar, they continued walking until midday, when exhaustion, hunger and thirst overcame their will. They broke for lunch in a wide valley between two mountains.

Augum squeezed the last of his waterskin into his mouth after eating salted and dried salmon steak. "I'm out …"

"Me too," Leera said, stuffing her waterskin with snow. "Should have refilled our skins in the Occi camp."

"With what, bloodfruit? Don't think the Occi even eat or drink." He nodded at her water skin. "And that's not going to work."

"What? Why not?"

"I tried it once with Sir Westwood on a long hunting trip. Snow didn't melt and only made me colder."

"I don't believe you," she replied, grabbing more snow and stuffing it in to her mouth. He did the same but found it only made him shiver, and did little to quench his thirst.

She glanced skyward. A bank of gray cloud moved in bringing light snow flurries. "Weather's turning and I'm too tired to go on. Let's camp here."

"All right, but we have to camouflage the tent with snow, in case the harpies fly by."

They did just that, erecting the tent and building a wall of snow on the north side where they figured the harpies would most likely be coming from. Then they crawled inside, hoping to catch a few hours' sleep before continuing on.

"What do you think our little harpy is doing right now?" she asked as they got comfortable.

"Probably waddling in circles or something."

She snorted, and found his hand under the blankets.

Augum woke some time later to a distant voice saying, "Hello? Can anyone hear me?" The wind blew and the tent was dark. He reached into his rucksack and brought out the Orb of Orion, placing his ear against it.

"Nana? Is that you?"

"Yes, Augum. I am most glad to hear you are well. I tried contacting you earlier but received no response."

"We were sleeping, Nana. We got out of the Occi camp but had to walk all night. We have everything the wolven asked for, including a way to get into Bahbell. Oh, and Nana, we learned a lot from the Occi—"

"—that is all very well and good, Augum, but I have precious little time to banter, and your training is more important right now. Is Leera there by your side?"

"She's sleeping, but—"

"Please wake her."

"Yes, Nana." He supposed he could tell her about what he learned later. He gave Leera a gentle shake.

"Ugh ... tired ... leave me alone ..."

"Wake up. Training."

She rolled over and opened puffy eyes. "Now ...?"

"—are you both paying attention?"

"Yes, Nana," Augum replied as Leera put her ear to the orb.

"—I was just asking how the spell casting of Object Alarm and Object Track went."

"Um, we haven't been able to cast either successfully yet."

"Not a single casting?" There was an audible sigh. "Considering your circumstances, I suppose I should not be too cross. Now tell me exactly what you were doing."

Augum and Leera proceeded to inform Mrs. Stone all about their many failed attempts with Object Alarm. After trying to cast it a few more times for her, Mrs. Stone diagnosed the problem—although their visualization of the object was fine, they weren't assigning a sound to the trigger.

"Think of a very specific sound," Mrs. Stone went on, "a sound powerful enough to wake you in your dreams and loud enough to be heard in conversation."

"How about a bell?" Augum asked.

VALOR

"That works just fine. Let us try again."

They continued casting the spell until Leera shouted out joyfully when Augum touched the lantern. His own successful casting came soon after.

"Good, you are well on your way to learning your first enchantment. There are complexities to the spell but we can discuss them later. I want you to continue practicing it often; I expect great progress on *both* Object Alarm and Object Track in the coming days. It is how you will guard the orb and your possessions. Now continue to work and study hard."

"We will, Mrs. Stone," Leera replied. "Have you checked in on Mr. Goss and Leland by chance?"

"I dare not endanger Milham and its residents with my presence. Lividius has put together a party of warlocks to help him find the scions, warlocks with seasoned travel experience, thus I am always on the move. So far, I have been able to stay a step ahead of them, but unless I find some way to stop the search, it is inevitable they shall find me. Luckily, the Tiberrans are proving quite the distraction, for they do not succumb easily."

"Oh and about what we learned from the Occi—I think my father made a witch's pact with Magua." He had to say *something* about it, even if it was something obvious.

"Yes, I believe so too—"

"I think it's the same one Occulus once made—" There was more to it of course but he didn't want to drown her in detail.

"What makes you so sure, Great-grandson?"

It all tumbled out in a rush. "All the pieces fit. Occulus was promised eternal life for all the women he had taken and the children he had fathered—they're now who we call 'the Occi'. Then he was taught how to raise an entire army of undead, which he used to take control of the Dreadnoughts. The last thing the witch wanted was for him to capture Ley for her father, the Father of Demons—"

"That is quite enough, Augum," Mrs. Stone said. "A preposterous tale told by a self-serving Occi, no doubt. I would have hoped you to possess better sense than to believe such a yarn. The histories are clear—Occulus was a mad man bent on destruction and power. He wanted eternal life and knowledge from the Leyans for himself. Besides, the Occi cannot have possibly lived so long—eternal life cannot happen outside of Ley, as you have seen with your own eyes."

"But Nana, they're walking proof of—"

"—of necromancy, nothing more. There are arcane illusions powerful enough to accomplish such feats."

"But—"

"Let us talk no more on the subject. I have a great many people to help here."

His shoulders slumped. "All right, Nana. Please be safe."

"And you, Great-grandson. Take care of each other."

"Bye, Mrs. Stone," Leera said.

Augum began folding his blanket. "She didn't believe me …"

Leera gave him a sympathetic look. "Well she did come from an academy, and history books are unquestionable in places like that. Besides, you know she can be a little stubborn sometimes."

"I'm worried. What if my father catches up to her?"

"She'll be fine, she's Mrs. Stone. I'm more worried about us. We have to get inside Bahbell without being killed by the Legion *or* the Occi." She shoved the Orb of Orion into a rucksack. "Not to mention, as was made so damn obvious last night, we can't really go toe-to-toe against warlocks without offensive spells."

He sighed. "I know … I thought we'd have learned them by now. We're almost 3rd degree!"

"It's that way on purpose with offensive spells. Imagine a bunch of 1st degree kids running around blowing each other up. Happens anyway sometimes at the academy."

VALOR

"I guess. Doesn't help us though, does it?"

"No, but I'm pretty sure that offensive spell the Occi used back there is the one we get to learn next."

"Then maybe I can talk Nana into teleporting us to a Trainer or something to learn it."

It was late afternoon and windy, the sky overcast. They packed up the tent and continued on their journey, stuffing snow into their mouths and practicing spells as they went. It had snowed the entire time they slept, but not enough to cover their tracks, which they used to retrace their steps.

"I'm thirsty …" Leera said a few hours later as they climbed towards their old camping spot. "What do you think bloodfruit tastes like?"

"Blood …"

"Think it's poison?"

"Probably … let's just keep eating snow. All we have is one more day of hiking left."

But snow wasn't enough, and it was making them colder. Their pace slowed as their thirst increased. Spell practice petered out. Leera withdrew the waterskin only to find it frozen solid. He refrained from saying I told you so.

They finally stumbled across their old campsite just as the sun dipped below the horizon. Tomorrow they would only have to climb down the other side of this mountain, cross a valley, and climb up another mountain to the wolven cave. The prospect seemed daunting without water though.

They used up the majority of their remaining energy setting up the tent. They tried rigging the lantern to melt snow, but the fire from the lamp was too small.

"Your eyes are glassy," Leera said quietly as she struggled to free her blanket from her rucksack.

He helped give it a tug until it came free. "Yours too …"

They lay quietly, breathing tired breaths, the Orb of Orion by their heads. There might be some way for Nana to melt snow for them through the orb, Augum thought, but she never did check in.

When sleep came, it was restless and inconsistent. All thoughts and dreams involved taking liberal gulps of fresh water.

By the time they departed in the morning, Augum's throat and tongue felt like sand, stomach a great cavern. His muscles were sore and achy and his head hurt as if he had been pushing arcane boundaries. Every step felt like it took twice as long as it needed to. Spell practice was out of the question.

The day was cloudy and windy with sharp snowdrift attacking their faces. They skipped breakfast but sat for lunch, nibbling at the last of the journey bread.

Leera's head rested on her knees. "Parched …"

Augum didn't even have the strength to nod along. Besides, he was too busy envisioning himself swallowing a great pool of clear water. He tried focusing on the distant glacier, but his eyes wouldn't stay on the same spot. He thought he saw black dots there. Sometimes there was one, sometimes many.

"You … see something … on the glacier?" he finally managed to ask. Talking was an awful struggle that sucked his energy now.

Leera didn't even move her head. "No …"

"Just … look."

She squinted at the great winding ice sheet. "Imagining … things." Her head fell back to her knees.

Augum kept his gaze on the glacier, swearing something was there, yet the dots kept appearing and disappearing like visual afterglow. Wherever he looked, he saw these dots appear, sometimes along the snow, sometimes in the air. "Must be … harpies …"

"Nothing … there … Aug …"

He fought his aching knees to stand. Even shouldering the rucksack was a challenge. "Let's go …"

"Need … rest …" She stood with a tortured moan, her movements that of an old woman's. He helped her place the

VALOR

rucksack over her shoulder. Her eyes were half-closed and dreamy and the look on her face worried him. He recalled how she had crumpled the night they had been caught in the blizzard together, outside the Penderson home.

And they still had a ways to go …

Augum brought her to him in a warm embrace. Her arm reached around his back and weakly hung on. They stood like that for a bit, gathering snow on their hoods, until a sudden gust almost knocked them over. He decided it would be best to tie the two of them together, not because he feared the wind, but because he feared them drifting apart in their tired stupor. If they lost sight of each other in this …

He dragged out the rope, aching hands making the task take far longer than it should.

Step by dreary step, they plowed on over their old tracks, now barely visible under the fresh snowfall. The flakes began getting fatter, but at least the wind slowed a touch.

At suppertime, they were on the northeast face of the mountain housing the wolven cave. Augum figured that at the pace they were going, they'd make it back to the cave after midnight, if they managed the final steep climb, that is.

His rope went taut. He turned to find Leera lying in the snow. She had fallen numerous times along the way already, as had he, though usually they'd rest sitting up.

He labored back to her. "Leera … we've got to … keep going …" He gave her a gentle shake, but she didn't move. "Leera …" There was a sick feeling in his stomach. He quickly turned her over, resting her head in his lap, and swept matted raven hair aside, revealing a frosted face, cracked lips, and closed eyes.

"Leera … wake up …"

His heart pounded as he placed his ear to her mouth, feeling the gentlest of breath. He glanced at the desolation around him. "Help us … somebody … help us …" but there was only the wind and the soft pad of snow, patiently entombing them under its eternal blanket.

The sky was darkening. Should he setup camp and rest or go on ahead and return with help? No, he couldn't leave her. He laboriously unstrapped his rucksack and dug at the Orb of Orion.

"Nana ... you there? Nana ..."

No response.

He spied the three bloodfruits. What if they each had one, leaving one for Raptos? He thought about it. He didn't have the strength to carry her, or even to setup the tent at this point. What choice was there?

He looked around at the immensity of the slope. There was nothing but mountains in every direction—mountains and snow and ice and cold death. He withdrew one of the squishy red sacks and adjusted Leera's head to a better position, then pierced a hole into the skin of the fruit with his teeth. It was awfully bitter on the tongue. That wasn't good—bitter almost always meant it was bad for you.

"Please ..." he whispered, opening her mouth with his other hand. "Please ... let this work ..." He slowly tipped it into her mouth. She began to drink it weakly, finishing the contents. He threw away the peel.

Her eyes opened. He watched as her pupils slowly dilated like saucers. She seemed to stare past him. "I'm ... Leera ..."

"Yes ... are ... you ... all ... right?" He was so tired.

She gave him a peculiar look and sat up. Suddenly she shoved him back. "You're *him*!" she yelled, standing with renewed energy.

"What ...?" It took effort to sit back up.

"You murdered them—"

"No ... it's me ... Augum ..."

She looked around as if lost. When her eyes focused back on him, he saw a wild animal there. Suddenly she lunged at his throat and began choking him.

"Leera ... stop ... it's ... me ..." Black walls began closing in. He tried to unwrap her fingers, but in his condition, he was no match for this rabid new strength of hers. An old familiar electric stirring began in his chest. No, he couldn't let that happen—yet the wild arcane energies he had thought he learned how to control began to pulse weakly. A spark shot out of his hand, a spark he hadn't intended. Leera's eyes snapped to where she had seen it and she let go, quickly pedaling back. She was breathing rapidly. "Don't hurt me," she mumbled. "Please, don't hurt me …"

Augum finished gasping, hand on his throat. "Lee … it's all right … it's the bloodfruit … I'm sorry … had to do it …"

She drew her knees in. "I'm so scared …"

"We're almost there … nothing to be … afraid of …"

"Where's mum and dad?"

"Lee … you've got to … concentrate …"

She began rocking, mumbling to herself.

"Leera … all we have to do is … follow this path …" He limply gestured at their fading footprints. If they didn't keep going, their old tracks would soon vanish altogether and they'd be lost.

"Aug … I don't know what's going on. Help me …" Her voice sounded so small and distant.

"Just follow the path … we're tied together … I'll keep up …"

"The path?"

"Yes …" He didn't have the strength to gesture again. "Please …" By her reaction, he knew he couldn't take the bloodfruit as well; who knew what would happen if both of them were in such a state.

She stood up, staring at their footprints. The snowfall obscured everything but their immediate vicinity. Perhaps that would help, Augum thought. Keep things visually simple …

Suddenly she began to walk and he had to scramble to his feet. The movements were very painful now, his muscles burning, feet numb. Leera walked a few hundred paces along the path before abruptly stopping. She stood there letting the snow accumulate on her shoulders and hair.

"We've got to ... keep going ..." he said, panting.

"My ears are cold ..."

He painstakingly drew her apprentice hood over her head and then her fur hood. She continued on as soon as he was done. After about an hour of marching, with him struggling to keep up, she stopped again.

"It's too dark, I can't see ..."

Augum took off his right mitt. "Shy ... neo," he said, wheezing for breath. His hand didn't light. "Shyneo ..." Weak lightning began crackling along his palm. He hoped it was enough for her to see by. His vision began to blur as his eyelids kept freezing together. He could no longer tell if they were on the path or not. He began to fall; the rope would go taut and then it would stop as she waited for him to get back up and re-light his palm. She would only continue when he reassured her everything was all right.

The snow was swirling thickly now, bringing night with it. He estimated they were only a couple hours away from the cave as the slope began to steepen. Suddenly his hand extinguished. Leera stopped immediately.

"Shyneo," he said, but he couldn't even feel his hand anymore. He laboriously put his mitt back on. "Leera ... you've got to ... you've got to try Shine ..." There was no response and it was too dark to see.

"Augum ... I'm scared, there's something out here with us ..."

He swallowed and listened, hearing only the gentle swoosh of snow. "There's ... nothing ... there ..." Every word was agony, his throat parchment dry. "Cast ... Shine ... Leera ..."

"It'll see us ..."

"Leera ... there's ... nothing ... there ...!" A bit of anger welled up with the frustration.

She whimpered before progressing to a shiver-inducing full-throated scream.

He shot forward and embraced her, whispering, "It's ... all ... right ..." but he was so tired he collapsed with her still in his arms, the pair tumbling to the snow. "Shh ... it's ... all ... right ..."

Her screams subsided to weeping. "I don't know what's happening. Who am I?"

"You're ... Leera ... Jones ... and ... we're ... almost ..." He could not speak anymore. He didn't even know if he had the energy to stand. They lay like that for some time, the snow slowly burying them alive. He knew they had to keep going. Only death awaited them out here. Cold, detached, eternal death ...

"There's something there," Leera whispered.

He was unable to respond. All he wanted to do was sleep. Even keeping his eyes open was an immense struggle. Yet as he listened, he realized there *was* something out there. It padded along in the snow. Leera stiffened in his arms as whatever it was stopped just ahead. Was it his imagination though, perhaps triggered by her saying it? It was impossible to tell.

"You could be heard for leagues. Is this your way of skimping on your debt?" came a deep voice from the darkness.

Leera began screaming again but Augum squeezed her with strength he did not have.

"Help ..." he only wheezed. He was gasping now, scavenging for any hidden reserves of energy. "Promised ... you ... one ... blood ... fruit ... will ... give ... another ..."

"I know a good bargain when I hear one."

The wolven scooped the two of them up in the darkness. Leera howled and struggled. All Augum could do was hold her hand, too weak to speak. It didn't help much.

The wolven snarled. "I have half a mind to leave her. Her wailing is trying."

Familiar black walls began closing in. "I ... blood ... fruit ..."

"You fed her bloodfruit? Lowland fool ..."

The blurry outline of a cave came into view, dimly lit by a fire within. At last, the walls mercifully closed, but not before Augum glimpsed three figures silhouetted against the entrance, one held up between the other two.

ANNIHILO

Augum woke inside a tent on rocky ground, covered with blankets. His body tingled with shivers and his breath labored along. A fire crackled nearby, the comforting sound bringing warm memories, and there was the delicious scent of hot potato soup.

"Morning," Bridget whispered, smiling.

"Morning."

"Here, have this." She offered him a bowl of soup. He took it with a grateful smile. "You have a fever and need to rest. You were in an awful state last night; wouldn't even let me put you into your nightgown. Barely managed to change your bandage."

Augum struggled to lift his hand. Sure enough, there was a new linen bandage there. "Thanks. How's Leera?"

"Sleeping right beside you, silly. She's all right, but also has a fever. She went a little crazy, thought we were strangers—"

He glanced over. Her face was a little pale. "I gave her bloodfruit."

"I know, Raptos said as much. He fed her some kind of wolven tea at no charge, though I think it was to shut her up more than anything. Took a while, but she eventually fell asleep."

Haylee dragged herself into the tent with a groan.

"Hi, Aug," she whispered, brushing blonde hair out of her eyes. "Leg doesn't hurt as much, but I won't be able to walk for who knows how long. I'll need a healer at some point to make it right. But we can talk about that later. We were really worried about you," she went on as he slurped away at the soup. "About both of you, that is. Bridget only completely recovered yesterday, you know. We spent most of our time training."

He felt stronger with every mouthful. The soup tasted divine, thickly flavorful with added goat meat and spices.

"That was a close one, almost didn't make it back," he said.

"I knew you'd make it," Bridget said.

"How's Chaska?"

"Raptos made him search for firewood," Haylee said. "Poor soul has been struggling staying silent. Probably hollering his frustrations in some valley right now."

Augum smiled. " 'Poor soul'? So he isn't a barbarian anymore?"

Haylee reddened. "I'm learning, aren't I?"

"They've been getting along swimmingly," Bridget said. "Now tell us about your trek."

As he ate, he recounted their four-day-long adventure. There was so much to tell he found himself out of breath by the end.

"Does Mrs. Stone know about the Occi?" Bridget asked.

"I told her last time we trained but she didn't believe me. She said eternal life wasn't possible in the mortal world and that I should know better having seen my great-grandfather pass away. She said it was an illusion; that Peyas was just telling a 'self-serving' tale. Then again, maybe I should have told her they were unalive or something, or undead—or whatever the word is."

"Aww, how could she not believe you, Augum?" Haylee's face creased with sympathy. "It's a witch's curse—maybe it follows different rules."

"Well Mrs. Stone might be right," Bridget said. "Maybe that Occi man *was* lying. Though if it is all true—that is, if the same thing's happening again—maybe our knowing what happened in the past can help us somehow."

"Maybe. Peyas also said the Unnameables might be really powerful warlocks that just kept increasing in strength and knowledge, till we're like bugs to them."

"Now that's just rubbish," Bridget said. "Gods aren't warlocks, they're ... gods."

"If they even exist," Haylee muttered.

Bridget sighed. "If the story *is* true about Occulus ... well, how tragic that his beloved died."

"Leera said you'd say that—about how tragic it was." He finished the soup, sorely tempted to lick the bowl clean. "Now I wonder if my father also wants to resurrect my mother, and only Magua can help him. Maybe he feels guilty about what he's done."

"I'm not sure your father is capable of such a thing," Bridget said.

"There's no way he is," Haylee added.

Augum took a final lick of the crude wooden spoon before setting the bowl down. "How do you know?"

Haylee shrugged. "He's the Lord of the Legion, the Lord of the Dead, and the Lord of Dreadnoughts. He's razed villages and personally slain ... I don't know, hundreds at least. Trust me, he doesn't have a bit of pity."

"And remember what Mrs. Stone said about his youth," Bridget threw in.

Augum wished the bowl filled itself up as it had done in children's tales. "I know, I know, I remember ..."

They thought about it a moment.

"I wonder what ended up happening between the Legion and the Occi," Bridget said.

Haylee picked up the empty bowl. "Maybe they destroyed each other out on that glacier …"

"We can only hope," Augum said. "Where's Raptos anyway?"

"He usually leaves in the mornings," Haylee replied. "Sometimes he doesn't come back until late. Bridget made a fire and this soup, but I had to trade the last of the chocolate for the potatoes. Wouldn't even give us goat meat. He really doesn't give anything for nothing. Bridget and I repaired what we could for him arcanely, and that got us some stuff, but he didn't have much to fix, mostly a few figurines that had fallen from the shelves."

"We're going to need more provisions to make it to Bahbell," Augum said. "Takes two days to get to the portal pillar. After that, it's just a teleport ride away." He groaned. "I really don't want to be sick right now. What if they beat us to the recipe?"

Haylee adjusted her splinted leg with a wince. "Neither of you can travel while you're sick. Maybe Raptos has something that'll help."

Bridget absently polished the Orb of Orion with a cloth. "We don't have anything left to trade for food or medicine, really. We need everything we have."

"Raptos still doesn't know what's—" he paused to cough, "—what's inside Bahbell, does he?"

The girls shook their heads.

"Good. All right, here's the thing—it takes arcanery to activate the portal pillar, so I don't think he'll be able to get in without us—" He'd been thinking about this during the trek. "And since he trades for everything, maybe we can purchase provisions that way."

Bridget stopped polishing. "That might actually work …"

Haylee frowned. "Must you take him? Couldn't you trick him or something and leave him behind?"

VALOR

Augum watched her a moment. "You're not coming, are you?"

Haylee dropped her eyes, absently tugged at her splint. "You know I can't."

He sighed. "I know. I'm sorry."

"We discussed it at length while you were gone," Bridget said, giving Haylee a sympathetic look. "Chaska volunteered to carry her."

"But Nana can teleport—"

Bridget shook her head. "I spoke with her last night. She can't take the time or risk walking all the way here. It would only draw more of the Legion this way and to Milham."

"It's all right," Haylee said. "I promise I'll make that big lug stop often. And we're not completely defenseless—he's got his bow and I've got—"

"—your 1st degree only," Augum said.

"We'll be fine," Haylee said. "It's already settled. We'll leave as soon as you two are well again. And don't look so worried—just focus on what you have to do next."

Bridget resumed polishing the orb. "I don't know if taking Raptos with us is a good idea. What if his interest in what the Legion wants actually ends up in him getting the recipe before us?"

Augum laid back, body achy from the fever. "We'll just have to get to it before anyone else."

"Mrs. Stone's told me a bit more about how they're pursuing her," Bridget continued conversationally. "They track her by having the warlock who visited a place closest to where she is teleport the entire group. Means those warlocks are very high in degree as Group Teleport is a 17th degree spell …"

Augum nodded, closing his eyes. He was very tired and just wanted to rest. He hoped it was a chill, not a fever—they couldn't afford to spend time wasting away here while the Legion fought its way into Bahbell. He wondered who'd win—two hundred Legion soldiers or a hundred Occi and their harpies. If the Legion had warlocks, the Occi might be in trouble, though that depended on Nefra's arcane strength.

He drifted off to sleep with those thoughts swirling in his brain, until woken by a sudden scream.

"It's all right, Lee, you're safe," Bridget was saying. "Just a bad dream ..."

"Is Augum all right?" Leera asked feverishly. "I did something awful ... I tried to kill him ..."

Bridget stroked Leera's head. "He's right here, he's fine, don't you worry."

"Augum, I'm so sorry ... Aug ..." Leera kept mumbling.

"It's all right," he said. "I'm right here and I'm fine," but she didn't appear to hear him.

Bridget furrowed her brows. "Raptos said bloodfruit is a powerful hallucinogen. It may have made her fever worse."

"I wish I hadn't given it to her ..."

"Don't be silly," Haylee said, "you had no choice."

He knew she was right but still felt guilty. "Hallucinogen ..." He recalled Sir Westwood lecturing on some of the more deadly fungi. Apparently, assassins use them in the Sierran deserts.

"I wonder if that's why the Occi have gone crazy," he said. "All they eat is that stuff."

"They're Occulus' children," Haylee said. "*Of course* they're crazy—they've been alive for over fifteen hundred years!"

"Shh, keep your voice down," Bridget said, checking on Leera. "We don't know if any of that's true."

"Sorry ... I know my leg's not doing so well and all, but ... think you can give me some pointers on those spells before I go, Augum?"

Bridget gave her a disapproving look. "He's sick, Haylee, and besides, you're not ready for a 3rd degree spell."

"Well, *I* think I'm ready. People learn spells ahead of their degree all the time. I mean, isn't Centarro 3rd degree?"

VALOR

Bridget sighed. "Yes, but the Standard Spell structure hasn't changed for over three thousand years for a reason—it works best to learn the spells in that order."

"I suppose you're right," Haylee said, glancing down at her leg with a wince. "I have other things to worry about."

"I'm going to go back to sleep," Augum said, feeling another wave of shivers come on.

"I'll wake you for a late lunch."

He slept peacefully, knowing they were safe, at least for the moment. He dreamed of Castle Arinthian and its cozy canopy bedstead, its hearths and long red carpets, until Bridget woke him as promised around mid-afternoon.

He stretched. "I'm going to get some air." It was stuffy and damp inside the tent.

"Take the blanket with you and stay warm. Lunch will be ready in a moment."

He crawled out of the tent, blanket wrapped around his shoulders, breath steaming in the frigid air. The tent sat at the cave entrance. Too close for his comfort, that was for sure. He made a mental note to move it later.

Chaska was near the fire chatting with Haylee, or rather her chatting at him—ceaselessly. About her life, her family, what she'd gone through. Augum had heard her even while he slept. Chaska saw Augum and gave a nod and smile. Augum waved casually. Haylee did not stop speaking, but Chaska didn't seem to mind, stirring the fire with an air of contented patience.

"Told you they're getting along," Bridget said, exiting the tent.

Augum tightened the blanket around himself. "But I thought you two ... I mean, you and Chaska—"

"—don't be silly," Bridget said, suppressing a giggle. "I like him, but not in *that* way. Besides ..." She glanced at the pair of them just as Haylee let out a giggle, smacking Chaska on the shoulder for a skeptical look he had flashed her. "... I think they're cute together, don't you?"

Augum shrugged. What did he know about such things? But he was glad for her. Besides, they had to trust each other to attempt the journey he proposed—carrying her all the way back to Milham. Though he wondered how they'd get along when Chaska could speak again.

A shadow formed at the cave entrance.

"The battle is lost for the Legion, but they shall return with reinforcements," Raptos said, stepping inside and removing his rucksack. Haylee immediately quieted down as the wolven took a seat at his carving chair and began withdrawing assorted legion weaponry—daggers, short swords, swords, maces and axes. Every single one had the emblem of the burning sword. "It is important to study the weapons of your enemy."

Augum retrieved his rucksack from the tent and withdrew the horn and remaining two bloodfruits. He placed them before the wolven on the table. "Our debt."

Raptos paced over and picked the objects up. "This is indeed an Occi horn, and these indeed are bloodfruits." He placed the squishy fruit into his cabinet before stepping to the entrance of the cave and blowing on the horn.

A shriek came from within the tent. "They're coming! Run, Aug, run!"

"It's all right, Leera," Augum said. "Raptos is just testing the horn."

They waited for some time. At long last, a single harpy could be seen a ways off, flapping hard to gain altitude in the thin air.

"It appears your debt is nearly paid," Raptos said.

"Our remaining debt to you was to discover how to get into Bahbell," Augum said, watching the distant creature slowly near. "I can tell you how to do that, but you'll need to use the Shine spell to touch the runes, unless you have some other arcane way. Anyway, I'll write out the shapes for you and the order to touch them in."

VALOR

Raptos gave a low growl. "There will be no point to writing them out for me if I cannot use the portal pillar."

"Well, I suppose we can help you get inside, but only for a price."

"Learning, are we? But why would lowlander younglings want entry into Bahbell?"

Augum shrugged. "To explore …"

Raptos studied him a moment. "I sense you are being treacherous, lowlander. You are not as cunning as you think you are."

"Fine, we want to get inside for our own reasons."

"Hmm. And what is it that you want in exchange for gaining me entry?"

"Twenty days' provisions for myself and my three friends, and a Legion blade, since we lost our own."

Raptos thought about it a moment. "Agreed." He chose the smallest blade in the pile—a dagger in a black leather sheath—and handed it to Augum.

The harpy landed before them, bringing with it the stench of rot and decay. One of its crone ears had been ripped away, the area black with congealed blood.

"It has seen battle," Raptos said.

Augum spoke while holding his nose. "We had to use it to attack a big Occi man."

Raptos grunted and turned to the harpy. "You will scout the glacier for me. Return to report when you see the lowlanders in black armor or the Occi."

"Master …" The thing clicked its beak and took off.

"I shall gather the provisions now." Raptos dropped onto all fours and ran after the harpy.

Augum and Bridget watched him go before joining Haylee and Chaska at the fire.

"That thing is disgusting," Haylee said, stirring the contents of a steaming pot. "He better not bring it inside later, it reeked."

"I thought you're used to the scent of death and decay," Augum said. When she gave him a look, he quickly added, "as a former necrophyte and everything."

"I'm not. It's *disgusting*."

Lunch consisted of salted beef, rice and oats. Augum ate what he could, feeling the fever strengthen despite the warm food. After lunch, he rested, coughing and shivering, preferring the cold fresh air to the dampness of the tent. Leera stayed inside, one flap open for ventilation. Haylee and Bridget eventually resumed their spell studies while he listened, too sick to take part.

Mrs. Stone checked in a couple hours later, passing on the latest news from Tiberra—that the Legion had sacked and razed the town of Erlina, somewhere east of the Tiberran border. She had helped some of the people escape, but many did not make it. It was apparent helping the villagers was difficult for her as she could not stay in one location too long.

Once they told her how they were doing, she proceeded to continue their training. Augum opted out, choosing to rest by the fire, leaving Haylee and Bridget to partake. It was difficult and slow doing it through the orb, but at least the girls had the blue book, something that hindered Augum and Leera's progress on the slopes. Bridget learned the fundamentals of Object Alarm and Object Track while Haylee listened in. After Mrs. Stone assigned Bridget practice tasks, she told Haylee to focus on the 2nd degree. Haylee complained that she wanted to learn along with Bridget, but Mrs. Stone was unimpressed and gave a stern lecture on why it was important to learn the spells in historical order.

After an hour of remote training, Mrs. Stone broke off communication, leaving arcane exercises for Bridget and Haylee. Haylee had an awful time trying to do anything with a broken leg, however, and gave up shortly after starting, choosing to tell Chaska all about the colorful dresses she used to wear back in Blackhaven. Chaska promptly excused himself, gesturing he had to do something outside. Bridget practiced on, frequently checking in on Augum and Leera, until suppertime. Leera began shivering again, so Bridget and Chaska took her to sit by the fire. They then boiled rice and a few dried peas, the very last of their food.

Augum slumped down beside Leera, who huddled in two blankets. Her eyes were glazed and unfocused.

"How are you feeling?" he asked.

She only moaned.

Bridget stirred the small iron pot, one of those necessities the girls had not traded for food. The wind whistled as Augum watched it boil, basking in the warmth of the fire.

"Lucky you got back last night," Bridget said. "Looks like a storm's coming."

Augum glanced through the gaping maw of the cave entrance. It was darkening fast. Snow swirled by in twisting sheets, the sight reminding him of the rain he had witnessed as he tumbled high over the Tallows. That was so long ago now ... so much has happened since.

"No way would we have survived had it hit us on the mountain," he said.

"The wolven must have really good hearing because neither of us heard you."

"Well I thought even the Tiberrans could hear her scream." He gave Leera a playful elbow. She only grunted.

Soon the food was ready. "I'm surprised he doesn't want anything for the wood," Haylee said, feeding the fire before sitting down to eat. "Must be tough carrying it this high."

Bridget spooned some rice into a bowl and handed it to Augum. "Don't give him any ideas."

Time passed. They finished supper, gathering closer around the fire as the air froze and the winds increased to a howl. Raptos eventually returned with two sacks of pilfered weaponry and provisions, all of which he kept for himself.

The cave entrance began collecting snow, some of it pushing in as far as the table. Haylee and Bridget continued training while Augum and Leera sat motionless, conserving heat. Eventually it got so cold the tent had to be moved near the fire. They went to bed early that night.

The next few days were spent resting, waiting for the blizzard to pass. Augum and Leera slowly got better, while Chaska became irritable, long tired of his forced silence. With a subtle hint from Bridget, Haylee stopped talking his ear off. Training continued via the orb, though Haylee, due to her inability to concentrate past the pain of her leg, was unable to participate. Raptos, when not hunting and surveying the area, quietly carved his figurines or observed the group. He rarely spoke, and the group kept their distance.

In the early afternoon of the fourth day, Augum and Leera were finally well enough for Haylee and Chaska to depart. Mrs. Stone had been unable to fetch them, but Chaska was confident he could make the journey. Provisions were gathered and the group met a little ways outside the cave, where Chaska was able to speak freely.

"You sure you'll be able to manage her?" Leera asked, squinting from the sun.

Chaska gave a playful smile as he adjusted Haylee's grip around his neck. "Now I can just tell her to shut up."

"Then I'll squeeze," Haylee said, face scrunched from the pain of her leg, which dangled uselessly.

"And you'll lose your ride," he shot back.

"Better hold that tongue, Haylee," Bridget said with a smile, wrapped in an extra blanket that flapped in the mountain wind. "Besides, you'll need your energy."

Haylee swept the bleak landscape with her eyes, settling her gaze on the far east, where the trio had to travel. "I did try, didn't I?"

"You did," Augum said. "And we'll see each other back at Milham." But when, he did not know. He reached out to Chaska and they shook hands. "Good luck."

"And you," Chaska replied. "I've watched over you. I've killed winged demons. Now I'll bring word to your friends. It will complete my nemana. When I return to Milham, it will be as a Henawa man."

"Thank your father for the map he supplied us," Bridget said as she and Leera gave Chaska a light hug, careful of Haylee's splinted leg.

Leera gave Haylee the lightest punch on the shoulder. "Hey ... I'll see you."

Haylee smiled and nodded. "See you, and ... good luck." She swallowed as if fighting back tears. "Be sure you make it back."

Chaska gave them one last lingering look, nodded, and walked off, Haylee bouncing along on his back.

The trio stood watching until the pair disappeared from sight, then they silently plowed their way back to the cave.

Augum's heart felt heavy as they sat around the fire. Bridget picked at loose hairs on her fur coat, while Leera poked at the logs with a stick, chin resting on a knee.

Later, Mrs. Stone checked in to say she would like to begin lecturing on their 3rd degree elemental spell, something the trio had been looking forward to, especially since Augum and Leera mentioned how poorly they fared against a warlock. "This lesson is long overdue," Mrs. Stone said as the trio crowded about the orb, pressing their ears to it. "So we must therefore try to squeeze in as much training as possible prior to your departure. First of all, can anyone tell me the name of the spell?"

"I know!" Bridget said before Augum and Leera could reply, already holding the burnt yellow book on elements. "It's called the *First Offensive*."

"Correct, and it is exactly that—the first offensive spell in your arsenal, but also the most difficult and draining one you will be learning thus far, particularly because I am not able to be there in person. The First Offensive combines Shine, Telekinesis and Push all into one spell. It requires massive concentration but also sacrifice, for it drains your arcane energies at triple the rate. You will therefore have to learn to use it sparingly. The spells you have learned thus far have taken relatively little of your time. This spell, however, usually takes months of rigorous training before a warlock has their first successful casting. Needless to say, we do not have that kind of time. You will have to focus and work hard, much harder than ordinary apprentices. Am I making myself clear?"

"Yes, Mrs. Stone," they chorused.

"Augum, can you tell me an example of why this spell is dangerous to the caster and those around him?"

"Um, because it can drain your energy completely?"

"Incorrect. The spell is dangerous because it directly taps into your wild arcane energies. If you are not careful, it can lash out of control, injuring yourself and those around you. You must therefore pay strict attention to the energies involved. It is not a spell to be taken lightly, even during training. Are you all listening? Am I making myself perfectly clear?"

"Yes, Mrs. Stone," they chorused.

"Good. Now who can tell me the arcane trigger word for the spell?"

Bridget looked at the yellow book in her hand but resisted opening it. She closed her eyes instead. "Wait, I know this one ... I just read it—"

"Anyone else?" Mrs. Stone asked.

"—Annihilo!" Augum said, remembering the Occi speak it so articulately.

"No need to shout, I am not quite deaf yet."

"Sorry, Nana."

"In any case, you are correct. 'Annihilo' comes from the ancient witchery word 'annihilate', meaning 'to utterly destroy'. Now, how many of you consider yourselves proficient at your Shine extension?"

"Shyneo," Bridget said, attempting to wrap vine around the book in her hand. Instead, she dropped it. "I still haven't got the hang of mine …"

"I haven't even tried mine yet because it's useless," Leera muttered, coughing.

"I feel all right with mine," Augum reported. After all, he had shocked Vion Rames, a hellhound, and more recently, a harpy.

"Well you will all have to practice your extensions before you can even hope to cast the First Offensive successfully; and make no mistake—if you lack proficiency in either Shine, its extension, Telekinesis, *or* Push, you can expect to fail at casting the First Offensive. Many warlocks hit their ceiling at this point, lacking the discipline to follow through on the requirements to cast this spell successfully. Leera, what will First Offensive look like in your element?"

Leera blinked and coughed. Then she forced another cough.

"Remember, Leera, I can still *see* you through the orb, even if it is a curved image."

Leera turned red and swallowed. "I … I don't know …"

"I rather guessed that much by your protracted acting. Augum—what will your First Offensive look like?"

"Um …"

Bridget rolled her eyes. "Oh, come on, you two …"

Mrs. Stone sighed on the other end.

Augum winced. "Lightning …?"

"Correct, and it should have been rather obvious. Now, Bridget—"

"—mine's a vine, Mrs. Stone," Bridget said with a proud smile.

Leera flashed Augum a *she's such a goody-goody* look.

"All right, let us get into the details. Please open to chapter three of the yellow book on elements," and Mrs.

Stone began lecturing on the intricacies of the spell. They were forced to memorize and repeat back much of what she said, for they lacked parchment and quill. Bridget commented she missed her old writing book for just such a purpose, eliciting a disgusted look from Leera.

After four straight hours, Mrs. Stone finally explained the gesture, which involved putting both hands together and shooting them out, opening one's palms in the final moment—and that was the easy part. Combining four spells into one quick motion was much harder.

"And we still have to practice the other spells today," Leera muttered as she stood to practice the gesture.

It was an exhausting day, second only in difficulty to the time Mrs. Stone teleported them to the 3rd degree Trainer, and made harder by the fact Augum and Leera were still recovering from that bout of fever. At one point, she began casting mind spells *through* the orb, forcing them to defend themselves with Mind Armor. She worked them on every spell they knew as if their lives depended on it, which, they were all too aware, they did.

At least Nana was tuning to the Orb of Orion, Augum thought, realizing that would be incredibly beneficial in Bahbell.

Leera was the first to collapse, and this time there was no feigning involved. Augum was the second. Bridget was the only one with the stamina to remain on her feet.

Mrs. Stone left them to it before supper with the expectation they were not to go to bed until achieving twenty successful castings of each of the following requisite spells: Shine, their Shine extension, Telekinesis and Push. On top of that, she expected five successful castings of Object Alarm and three of Object Track. Luckily, she did not expect anyone to achieve a single successful casting of the First Offensive. Regardless, nobody completed the homework she had prescribed, not even Bridget, though they did their best.

VALOR

"I must say I am almost impressed by you lowlander younglings," Raptos said near midnight, sitting at his tall chair while carving a warlock figurine. He did not look up, but it was the first time he had uttered anything resembling a compliment. Not that anyone took much notice, lying around the fire, panting from exhaustion.

Because they had the provisions and because Mrs. Stone wouldn't let them leave otherwise, they trained like this for ten straight days, from the crack of dawn until dusk. On the seventh day of their grueling regimen, Augum finally struck the cave wall with a successful casting of the First Offensive. The trio immediately celebrated, jumping around in a group hug until almost landing in the fire.

Seeing that it was possible for one of them to actually cast it probably gave Bridget and Leera a boost, for both had their first casting of the spell within hours: a vine snapped out of Bridget's palm, punching and ensnaring a rocky outcrop in the wall; and a thin but focused jet of water shot out of Leera's hand. Because the water was arcane, it disappeared shortly after, much to their disappointment (could have made great drinking water in hard times).

No one was in any doubt as to why so many warlocks hit their ceiling at this spell, for it was the first great leap in difficulty, and only one of many, as Mrs. Stone had warned. In fact, when they reported their success to her, she actually breathed a sigh of relief, as if worried one of them might have hit their ceiling already.

After those ten grueling days, they were now able to cast every single spell in their arsenal on command, including their extensions, Object Alarm, Object Track, and the First Offensive. Mrs. Stone proudly told them they had squeezed about three month's worth of academy work in ten days, but at the sacrifice of learning arcane history, astronomy, arithmetic, the spoken and written word, and other essentials of a solid academy education.

"And when this is all over," Mrs. Stone added, "do not presume for one moment I will not expect you to study that which you have missed."

Leera only shrugged while Augum nodded in agreement, preferring to have a chance to learn so many interesting subjects. Only Bridget seemed depressed about the matter, actually petitioning Mrs. Stone to begin teaching those disciplines through the Orb of Orion. Much to Leera's relief, Mrs. Stone declined, explaining they had to focus on their greatest needs during this perilous time.

Raptos, meanwhile, kept them abreast of happenings on the glacier. A second Legion company had marched on the castle, though the Occi managed to repel their assaults. The wolven did not gather any supplies this time, nor did the trio ask him to. Still, he did not demand they hasten to take him to Bahbell. Augum suspected it was because Raptos was actually interested in the warlock process, maybe to report his observations back to his homeland.

When he asked him if wolven learned arcanery, the towering creature said they only had three innate talents—frost breath, ice armor and ice weapon, apparently making them formidable warriors. Of course, the wolven took great offense when asked to demonstrate these abilities, complaining bitterly about lowland manners.

Throughout their training, Mrs. Stone reported on the Legion's advance into Tiberra. Village after village fell, until the great horde had advanced to only two towns away from Dramask, the capital. She expected a siege to take place and resolved to help the Tiberrans in any way she could. Augum's heart went out to the Tiberran people, for he knew all too well what it was like to have one's town razed to the ground.

Yet most of their thoughts were on one thing: the journey into Bahbell, for the day had finally come when Mrs. Stone deemed them ready.

SETTING OUT

The next morning was cool and bright, frosting breath into icy plumes. The trio stood at the cave entrance wearing winter furs, rucksacks bulging with supplies, waiting for Raptos to finish packing.

Augum's eyes travelled the jagged Muranians, glittering in the morning sun. He felt fresh and rested. He had gained back the weight he lost from the journey to the Occi; had shaken off the fever and the cough that seemed as if it would never go away; and his palm no longer needed a bandage, though the scar was quite prominent. He probably should have chosen a better location to draw blood, but what was done was done, as Sir Westwood used to say.

Augum reflected back on the long days of training. He now knew fourteen spells: Shine and its extension, Telekinesis, Repair, Unconceal, Centarro, Shield, Push, Disarm, Slam, Mind Armor, Object Alarm, Object Track, and the First Offensive. Learning the last one had been a brutal struggle, but knowing he had passed a point where warlocks frequently gave up filled him with pride. He hoped he didn't have a ceiling to hit; he hoped he'd learn all twenty degrees like his great-grandmother, and maybe even attain mastery.

Leera glanced back at the cave. "What's taking that earless wolf so long?" She elbowed Augum. "What are you looking at?"

"Just ... admiring the view."

"That all?"

He shrugged. "Guess I'm wondering if we'll come back here."

"We've already seen more places than most common folk do in a lifetime," Bridget said. "We are very fortunate."

The wolven stepped out into the sun, a rucksack dwarfed on his back, his long fur waving like grass in the wind. "I shall lead the way."

"You know where the portal pillar is?" Leera asked.

Raptos stared down at her as if addressing a petulant child. "You insult me once again, raven-haired lowlander, this time by assuming I do not know my own territory." He dropped onto all fours and began pacing through the powdery snow.

Augum and Leera's old path had long snowed over completely. Raptos took a new route anyway, a sharper one with steeper inclines. He had to stop frequently, waiting for their comparatively tiny legs to catch up. Bridget, scared of tumbling to her death, asked to be tied to someone. Augum volunteered, though he almost regretted it. Sometimes she clawed at him like a cat if her foot slipped even one iota. At other times, she'd shriek, suddenly yanking at the rope. Leera didn't help matters by making jokes of her predicament.

The day eventually settled into a rhythm as the slopes gentled. The trio diligently practiced their spells as they went. They stopped throughout the day for quick meal breaks, but kept up a good pace until late in the evening, when they setup camp on the side of a mountain. The wolven dug a hole and curled up in it, undisturbed by the

VALOR

winds or cold, while the trio setup the largest tent, having left the other behind. Thoroughly exhausted from the day, it wasn't long until everyone was asleep.

The morning proved windy, the sky filled with fast-moving gray clouds. They ate breakfast, packed up the tent, and continued. By early afternoon, they were at the bottom of the rocky wall, now encrusted with ice and snow. The obelisk was only a ledge above.

"Blizzard had a good go at it," Augum said. "Going to be a trickier climb."

"The wraith fell right here." Leera pointed to a slight dip in the snow. "You should have seen Augum and I—" she made the Push gesture, "—whoosh! And over it went."

"How did you two climb this thing anyway?" Bridget asked, looking peaked as she glanced up.

Augum shrugged. "We just climbed—"

"—we *raced*," Leera corrected.

Bridget had to steady herself against the wall.

"I find little interest in your lowlander drivel." Raptos dug his paws in and began climbing the wall as if it was nothing more than a minor obstacle. It was the first time since they departed that he spoke to them.

Leera made a face as she watched the wolven climb. "Do we really have to take him along?"

"Yes," Augum said. "We promised." He turned to Bridget. "So how are we going to get you up there?"

"I'm not climbing it. No way, not ever. In fact, I think I need to sit down a moment …"

"What if we used Telekinesis?" Leera asked. "We're much better at it now, and if we combined our power, maybe we could get her all the way up."

They glanced skyward. Raptos was already halfway to the ledge, scaling the thing like a squirrel zipping up a tree.

"Would you be willing to try that, Bridge?" Leera pressed.

Bridget swallowed but nodded, her breaths coming fast. "Since the rope's too short, we have no choice, do we? Just don't drop me …"

"So now we have to decide if we pull her up from the top or push her from down below," Leera said.

"I think pulling her from up top would work better," Augum said, unable to fathom doing it the other way. "Let's go one at a time then, and if one of us slips, be ready to catch that person with Telekinesis."

They began the hundred-foot climb, Leera first, later followed by Augum. This time, they didn't race. In fact, Augum couldn't imagine why they had done it in the first place—seemed needlessly reckless now.

Augum finally joined Leera at the top. A ways off, the wolven studied the obelisk.

"No help at all from him," Leera muttered. "Useless mountain goat …"

"Hey, he's big at least," Augum said. "Probably be good in a fight."

Leera scoffed. "We'd have to trade our souls for him to help us."

"Let's concentrate here," Augum said. They stretched out their arms near the edge of the cliff. Suddenly the bottom looked a great distance away. He visualized Bridget being picked up, but after a few moments of intense concentration, nothing was happening.

"I think we're out of range," Leera said, glancing back at the wolven, who was now pacing towards them on all fours.

"You lowlanders are slower than Canterran molasses."

"Well you're more than twice our height," Leera said, "and you scale like a rat."

"One more insolent remark like that and I shall put you on the frying pan, lowlander."

Leera retreated a step and said nothing more.

VALOR

Raptos watched her with his wolf eyes while removing the horn from his belt. He put it to his snout and blew. The note echoed distantly.

"Not *this* thing again," Leera muttered.

"I see it," Augum said after a while, pointing northwestward. A harpy flew straight for them, fighting the winds.

Leera snorted a laugh. "You're going to get that thing to bring Bridget up, aren't you?"

"At no charge. Although it would be amusing to watch you struggle with the problem at hand, it is not worth enduring the wait."

Augum glanced down at Bridget. "I'm not sure she's going to appreciate this very much …"

The harpy landed before the wolven, bringing with it the stench of death and dung.

"Bridget's going to kill us," Leera said. "It's almost safer to leave her down there …"

Augum gave her a look.

"Well I was obviously *kidding*."

Raptos pointed at Bridget while talking to the harpy. "Pick her up and bring her to us."

"Here we go." Leera elbowed Augum. "You can tell her."

Augum cupped his mouth. "Uh, Bridge! Bridge! We're, uh, sending a harpy to pick you up!"

There was a shriek.

"She sounds enthusiastic," Leera said.

"A harpy, Bridge! Just let it pick you up!"

"Are. You. Mad! I'm going to—GET OFF ME YOU FILTHY—" Bridget began screaming and flailing wildly.

Leera tried to keep a straight face. "It'll be fine, Bridge! Just, uh … relax!"

They watched as harpy feathers flew.

"Wow, she's actually putting up quite the fight," Leera noted as Bridget wrapped the harpy's neck with her vine extension. Eventually though, the ugly thing began flying their way, Bridget still flailing and screaming in its claws.

"Don't fight so much or it might drop you!" Augum called, feeling awful for the whole affair but also trying not to laugh at the spectacle.

The harpy unceremoniously dropped her on the ledge.

Leera winced. "You all right, Bridge?"

Bridget, hair disheveled and face apple red, calmly brushed herself off before yelling at them at the top of her lungs, not a single word distinguishable. Augum couldn't remember ever seeing her so angry; she was a hornet. They all had to take a step back.

"—SCARRED FOR LIFE!" Bridget finally finished, making a rude gesture before marching off to the obelisk.

"Wow, didn't think she had it in her," Leera muttered.

"That was most intriguing," Raptos said, as if nothing had happened. "The harpy even picks up those it once considered enemies."

"Is that thing going to follow us around everywhere now?" Leera asked, still pinching her nose.

"It *is* kind of putrid, Raptos," Augum said, holding his own nose.

The wolven made a bit of a show of sniffing the air with his snout. "I consider my sense of smell to be far superior to your lowlander one. Yet note how I am unperturbed. Self control is a source of pride in the highlands."

"I shall do as I please, lowlanders." The wolven walked off to the obelisk.

The harpy flapped its wings at Leera. "Die …" it hissed.

She kicked snow at it. "Shut up."

It clicked its beak a few times before waddling after its new master.

"They make a fine pair," Leera muttered, watching the backs of the two creatures. "We better make sure Bridge is all right."

VALOR

"If she'll ever speak to us again," Augum replied as they followed along.

When Bridget saw the harpy approach, she ran away screeching like an offended owl.

"I don't think she's going to come until you get rid of it, Raptos," Augum said. "And if she doesn't come, none of us go."

Leera nodded in agreement.

"So be it, lowlander." He turned to the harpy. "I want you to fly over the glacier and report what you see when I call on you."

"Master …" It unfurled its wings and took to the air. After a few more moments, they were finally able to take a normal breath.

"It's safe, Bridge, come on!" Leera called.

Bridget walked back, arms folded, eyes slits.

Augum gave an unsure wave. "We hope you're not too—"

"—don't even *think* of talking to me." She stabbed a pointed finger at both of them. "Either of you." She marched past and waited by the obelisk. "Well?"

They exchanged glances before making their way over, joining hands. Augum, who had taken Bridget's hand, felt her nails.

"Ouch, Bridge—not so hard," Leera said.

She only tightened her grip.

Raptos ended up taking Leera's hand at the end of the chain. She hesitated but took his great furry paw.

"You do it, Aug," she said.

Augum studied the portal pillar, locating the runes. "You'll have to lift me up to hit the last one," he told Raptos.

The wolven flexed his jaw but said nothing.

"Everyone ready?" Augum asked. "Because we're about to enter a very old and dangerous castle."

Bridget gave a terse nod, while Leera grinned. The wolven stood still.

"Shyneo." Augum began tapping out the correct runic sequence. "Now!"

The wolven, one paw holding the others, wrapped the other arm around Augum's waist and boosted him up. Augum smacked the final rune, a skull with a triangular roof over it, and felt his body get yanked.

SURPRISE

They appeared in total darkness, coughing and groaning from the teleportation. Even the wolven yowled in sickness. A fiercely cold wind was shooting past them, oddly, from below. The sound was an echoing roar, as if they were in a gargantuan tunnel.

"Shyneo," Augum said when he had recovered enough. His blue light revealed they stood on a circular pedestal only about thirty feet across, made of smooth black stone, with the obelisk in the center.

"Shyneo," Leera said.

Bridget clung to the portal pillar. "Please tell me we're not up high again …"

Augum crept close to the edge. If there were walls, his light could not reach them. The wind ruffled his hair and hood as he stared down into that unfathomable depth. It reminded him of the well in Castle Arinthian's cellar, except much larger and darker. Guardrails absent, nothing prevented the wind from snagging him and pulling him over, so he took a step back.

"Uh, best you not look down, Bridge," he said.

"It floats!" Leera said. She was on her knees pawing underneath the pedestal, hair flying. "There's nothing underneath us—we're floating!"

"I can see cavern walls about four hundred paces in every direction," Raptos said.

Leera sat up. "How can you see that far in this darkness?"

"Your hands provide enough light for my superior night vision to see that far." He paused as he glanced around. "This is a most peculiar cavern. I cannot see the bottom or the top, but there is a great door in the wall." He pointed. "It has a mark in its center—a skull inside a circle. Its forehead has three dots in a triangular pattern."

"That's Occulus' mark," Augum said. "Now how do we get to it?"

"This I do not know. I would think that as warlocks, you would, however."

Augum shrugged. "We're just apprentices."

Leera crawled away from the edge before standing. "There's got to be some arcane way to get there. Maybe there's a secret password or something."

"Occulus was a very powerful necromancer," Bridget said, still clinging to the obelisk. "He had to have some kind of system so only those that he wanted to come in actually got across."

Augum bent low, hand shining over the polished black basalt. "Maybe there's a secret sign." But after much examination, they found nothing. He plopped down against the obelisk alongside Bridget, rubbing his head in frustration.

"Try the orb," Leera said.

He dug it out of his rucksack and put his ear to it. "Nana, are you there?" but heard nothing. She didn't wear the pearl openly as Erika had, so he couldn't hear what was going on. Maybe she was helping wounded Tiberrans and didn't want them to hear their agonized cries. He wondered how many villages had burned by now, and how many souls his great-grandmother had saved.

"Yes, Augum?" came the late reply.

"Nana, you're there, great! We've made it to the entrance to Bahbell, but we can't go any further."

"Let me see."

Augum walked about with the orb, explaining their situation.

"Place the orb on the ground. I shall try something."

He did as she asked, securing it on his rucksack. They stood around waiting until the floor abruptly lit up with a circle of blue runes running along the edge of the floating island.

"It is as I thought. These are instructive runes. Show me all of them."

Augum slowly walked the circumference of the platform with the orb. When he finished, he and the girls gathered around the orb and placed their ears to it.

"I am afraid this entrance requires a live sacrifice in order to gain entry. You must—" but she was cut off by an implosive crunch. The platform suddenly mushroomed with five black-armored soldiers—a squat balding man in a black robe fringed with gold; a man wearing sleek steel armor with a horribly burned face and scalp; and two boys and a girl wearing necrophyte robes.

"There!" someone cried, pointing at the Orb of Orion. Before anyone could react, the right arm of the rotund man exploded with eleven glowing ivy rings. He raised it and sniped an incantation.

Augum was startled by a strange sensation in his hands. He dropped the Orb of Orion, now enclosed within a shimmering green globe. He recognized the spell as Sphere of Protection, the one Mrs. Stone had used to trap them in a bubble back in Sparrow's Perch, and, more recently, save them from an avalanche.

And just like that, they were cut off from her.

Meanwhile, Raptos' fur frosted over with a thick layer of ice. A frosted mace fogged into existence in his paw. He gave a guttural growl at the nearest Legion soldier, but the fat warlock pointed his arm threateningly at the wolven.

Augum made eye contact with one of the boys, instantly recognizing him. He saw Mya's throat being slit, her body limply falling into his arms. Without thinking, he lunged at Robin Scarson, only to be caught by the sleek-armored soldier.

"Augum, stop!" someone shouted, but he was beyond reasoning, thrashing and cursing and spitting.

Robin, startled by Augum's sudden madness, swallowed hard. "Kill him for me, Commander. Do it now—!"

"The great lord demands his son alive, I am afraid." The voice was a garbled hiss, as if the windpipe had been scalded.

Robin spat on the floor, seeming to recover his courage. "Too bad. Then just don't let the gutterborn near me. He must have spent too much time with those Henawa savages; turned him into an animal."

Augum tired himself out. Panting, he gave Robin the blackest stare he had ever given a living soul. "Scum ... gutless murderer—"

"Control your monkey,," Robin said to Bridget and Leera with a mocking chortle.

"But you *are* a murderer *and* gutless," Leera said. "We should have killed you when we had the chance with the banyan beast—"

Robin pointed at her. "Him we have to keep for now, but you—you we can kill—"

"Enough—" The burned man threw Augum back at his group with unnatural strength. Augum slammed into Leera, sending her tumbling over the edge of the platform. Luckily, Raptos' reflexes were sharp—he snatched her arm and yanked her back.

VALOR

"He will pay by seeing his precious crone impaled on my new blade," the burned man said.

Augum met the gaze of those pale eyes, hidden behind folds of rotten flesh. Suddenly it dawned on him who this man was.

"Tridian ..." Also known as the Blade of Sorrows.

"*Commander* Tridian to you, boy. That crone of yours left me with quite the gift, though I was never quite popular with the ladies anyway. Consider me reborn, if you will, by the grace of our mighty lord. My years of loyal service to His Lordship overcame my failures. I am his first *revenant*."

"Damn," Augum heard Leera mutter behind him, but he was unfazed. New courage flowed through his veins. He squared his jaw at Tridian. "Come along to teach your little brat some more tricks?" He remembered the iron room and the cold way the Blade of Sorrows had directed Robin's questioning.

The pale eyes narrowed ever slightly. "Unwise of you, boy. You are greatly outmatched. I can break that ugly mutt's arm without any trouble."

"An empty threat, lowlander."

"So you think, earless wolf." Tridian's eyes flicked back to Augum. "Besides, just because I cannot kill you, does not mean I cannot do great harm or worse to your friends. Or have you forgotten that little lesson?"

The words caught in Augum's throat. He recalled how Tridian and Robin held Leera hostage in the iron room, threatening her life. They *were* capable of torture, and it was best to hold his tongue.

"Mr. Spigot!" Bridget abruptly cried out, grabbing the encapsulated Orb of Orion and holding it protectively. "What are you doing with ... with *them*?"

"Bridget—" The doughy man was old, with blotchy skin and sunken eyes. His squat frame protruded with an ale belly, and his balding scalp had a silver crescent of tired hair. "My girl, I am ... I am no longer your mentor. I am now a faithful servant of Lord Sparkstone." He moved his left shoulder to draw attention to his arm, and it was only then that Augum noticed the sleeve hung empty—the man was missing a limb.

Bridget's hand shot to her mouth. "Oh, Mr. Spigot ..."

"Shyneo," Mr. Spigot said. His remaining hand lit up with glowing leaves. "Now I must ask you to extinguish your palms."

They did as he requested.

"Can I slap Leera around for you later?" the girl in the necrophyte robe asked Robin. She had curly, fiery hair, a crooked smile, hammy fists, and a bullish body that reminded Augum of Dap. She appeared a couple years older than the trio, and much stronger.

Robin flexed his fingers. "Definitely."

Leera's head tilted, voice faking a sense of loss. "Aww, guess you're someone else's pet now, *Temperance*."

"It's *Temper* now," the girl said. "Temper!"

"As it was when you were Haylee's toad. Nothing's changed I see—still as thick as oak."

Temper growled like an angry hound and took a step forward, bulbous fists curled.

"All right already—!" Mr. Spigot raised his arm to get everyone's attention. "Let us concentrate on the matter at hand. Robin, Temperance and Garryk—I expect you to behave as if we're back at the academy. I will be submitting a report directly to our lord when we return, and it will weigh heavily in his consideration for leadership positions."

Robin thumbed at Augum's group. "And what about them?"

"They will be our prisoners," Commander Tridian replied.

"Raptos is no lowlander's prisoner."

"We shall see soon enough."

Robin and Temper glared at the trio while Garryk unstrapped three dusty old tomes, plopping them on the ground. He was a stunted boy with olive skin, a large birthmark on one cheek, and clunky spectacles that routinely slipped down his nose.

Robin spoke through his teeth. "Wart, what are you doing?"

"I think I read about this entrance, Honored Necrophyte. Legend says the pit is bottomless, and that if you fall, you fall all the way to hell. It was used to intimidate guests, especially foreign dignitaries that came begging to keep their kingdoms safe and—"

"I brought you along to get us inside, Wart, not to bore us to death with history."

The boy looked up, pushing on his spectacles. "But I thought you said I'm here to help you find the reci—ouch!"

Robin smacked the boy's head, sending his spectacles careening across the floor to Augum's feet.

Mr. Spigot immediately took out a little black book. "That's a mark against your record, Robin Scarson. When I say I expect you to behave like we're back at the academy, know that I mean it."

"Just like you had too many marks against your record, *Mr.* Spigot?"

"You *dare*. Another mark! A few more and you can kiss that future command goodbye, boy, not that anyone would follow you the way you treat your subordinates!"

Robin turned to Temper. "They cut off his arm so he could live up to his name."

Temper laughed.

Robin glared at Mr. Spigot while removing a stone from his pocket. He held it up—it was something One Eye had given him. "I *will* become commander one day, it's my *destiny*—"

"That is quite enough, Apprentice," the Blade of Sorrows said in his harsh voice. "Learn to hold your tongue. Spigot is right. I have said it before and I shall say it again—you have much to learn before earning command."

Augum picked up the heavy spectacles. They were smudged and greasy. He walked over to Garryk, wiping them with the sleeve of his robe. No one said anything as the boy took them from Augum, mouth hanging open in surprise.

"Do you see how he has won the boy over with one simple gesture, Apprentice?" Tridian asked as Augum strolled back to his group. "Have a gander at my soldiers. Not one has uttered a peep since their arrival. *That* is discipline. *That* is respect."

Heads swiveled in the direction of the five Black Guardsmen. They ranged in ages, from a middle-aged man with a hard jaw and gray stubble for a beard, to a thin boy no older than sixteen. There was a woman among their ranks too, face smooth but stiff, eyes alert and cold.

"You are quite right, Commander," Robin finally said, face red. "Though out here—"

"—you will do as your teacher tells you," Tridian interrupted. "Our fine lord personally gave me the instruction. All necrophytes are to respect their mentors on and off the field of battle. There have been ... too many incidents, it seems."

Robin gnashed his teeth at Augum, but said nothing.

Augum, for his part, watched Robin closely. All he needed was one moment to cast Push when that idiot wasn't paying attention—

"See the way he watches you, Apprentice? Like a wolf stalking his prey. You need to mind yourself around other warlocks."

Robin raised his hands in a defensive posture before dropping them in a hurry, as if afraid of appearing scared. "He wouldn't dare."

"Not if he wishes his friends to live, no, he would not dare."

Augum gestured between himself and Robin. "You and I have unfinished business." Tridian was right, but that didn't

VALOR

stop Augum from opening his mouth, even though he knew he should stay quiet.

"Shut it, boy—" Tridian growled. "Do not try my patience. Your mentor is not here to protect you this time." He turned to Mr. Spigot. "Speaking of which, if anyone should forget their place when it came to military matters …"

Mr. Spigot straightened and cleared his throat. "Let us not lose sight of why we are here."

"You want the recipe—" Leera said. "We all know it. You might as well stop pretending otherwise."

"How do you know about that?" Mr. Spigot asked.

Robin pinched Garryk's ear and the boy squealed. "Because *this rat* just told them."

"No," Leera said, "actually we already knew. You want to make a portal without a scion because your dumb lord doesn't know how to make one otherwise—"

Weapons were drawn and a series of shouts rang out.

"Halt!" Tridian said. Everyone froze. "You *dare* defile Lord Sparkstone's name?" The Blade of Sorrows' voice was filled with quiet fanaticism.

Leera gave a pandering smile. "Oh, no, not at all," she said sweetly. "I merely meant the lordship of the council at Blackhaven."

"The council has disbanded itself. There is only *one* Great Lord now."

"Ah, but I didn't say 'Great Lord', I only said 'lord'. Obviously I didn't mean *him*—"

"Leera, that's enough—" Bridget said in a terrified whisper, gripping her by the arm.

"She meant nothing by it, I'm sure," Mr. Spigot said nervously. "Now Garryk, you were brought along for a very specific purpose. Need I remind you how important a recommendation is in the lord's army? Use that marvelous mind of yours, if you will."

The blades steadily lowered as the boy fumbled with his books.

"Yeah, Wart, get moving," Robin chimed in, much to Temper's amusement.

"Yes, Mr. Spigot, of course, Mr. Spigot." Garryk quickly flipped through one of the books. He shook his head after reaching the end and shoved the book aside, opening up another. Augum was able to read the spine of the first—*Solian Legends, Myths and Lost Histories.*

"It's got to be in here ..." Garryk muttered, as everyone looked on.

One of the soldiers spoke up. "Sir, the rest of the company—"

"Will have to make do without us, Lieutenant," Tridian replied. "Let us hope they eventually make their way in, if the damned Occi do not pick them apart in the meantime."

The wolven stirred on his haunches, the ice armor still thick, mace held tightly in his paw. Some of the soldiers pointed their drawn weapons his way, as if sensing an attack.

"You lowlanders do everything so slowly and inefficiently."

"Yes, well, you *highlanders* are going to enjoy our slow march into your hovels one day," Tridian replied.

"You have no idea of the strength of the north, tin lowlander."

"This is no ordinary tin, dog. This is Dreadnought steel." Tridian drew his blade, a razor thin longsword that seamlessly flowed from tip to pommel, with not a line to break the smoothness. "And one of the finest Dreadnought blades ever forged."

"Before this is over, insolent lowlander, we will quarrel."

"I look forward to it. I have been ... *dying* ... to test my new strength."

Robin laughed forcefully. "Well said, Sir!"

Tridian flashed his apprentice a stern look.

VALOR

Robin cleared his throat. "Hurry up already, Wart!"

"Yes, Honored Necrophyte, I almost ... yes, yes, here it is!" Garryk lifted the big book while fumbling to push up his spectacles. "The servants of the old kings and queens that used to pay homage to Occulus wrote about the entranceway. It says only the death of an unworthy may bridge the divide."

Robin smiled. "Well that should be easy, got a whole bunch of them right here. Now which one to choose ..."

Augum raised his arms protectively before Bridget and Leera. "You're not taking a single one of us."

"You can't stop—"

"*Yes, I can,*" Augum snarled, and he never meant anything more.

"Well this is quite the conundrum," Tridian said in a voice that once would have sounded light under the circumstance. Now it sounded like a broken bellows.

"Garryk, what does the text mean by 'unworthies'?" Mr. Spigot quickly asked.

Garryk flipped back a couple pages, struggling with the awkward size of the book. His bony frame looked like it might collapse under its weight. "Unworthies are ... anyone who has not sworn allegiance to the Lord of Death."

"Well that settles it," Robin said. "Everyone on our side has sworn allegiance—"

Garryk turned to Robin. "Pretty sure it means Occulus, the other Lord of—"

Robin shoved his face into Garryk's. "Shut. Up."

"Y-y-yes, Honored Necrophyte."

Mr. Spigot brought out his little book.

"I didn't touch him, did I!" Robin said.

Mr. Spigot ground his teeth but did not strike a mark in the book. "I shall solve this dilemma easily by teleporting out and bringing back an animal to sacrifice." He made the gesture and spoke the arcane words, but nothing happened.

"Excuse me, I must have misspoken." He tried once more, but again nothing happened.

"Mr. Spigot, sir," Garryk began, flipping pages, "I'm pretty sure the castle has counter-spells against teleportation and the like. It's one of its defense mechanisms. Also, I don't think they meant animals to count, sir."

Robin smiled as if it was his birthday. "So back to the original plan." He nodded sharply at Augum's group. "One of *them*."

"I tire of this—" Tridian said, taking a step forward.

"Mr. Spigot, please, do something—!" Bridget shrieked, but Mr. Spigot only swallowed, his eyes on Tridian's Dreadnought blade as it pointed at Raptos.

"Let us settle this now, cur!"

BAHBELL

Raptos bared his teeth as everyone quickly scuttled out of the way—Augum, Bridget and Leera to one side; the soldiers, Garryk, Robin, Temper and Mr. Spigot to the other. The portal stone loomed between the two adversaries as they readied to battle.

"Come on, Raptos, you can do it," Augum said.

"I do not need your counsel, lowlander," Raptos said.

Tridian flexed, swinging his sword smoothly. It hissed neatly as it sliced the air. "If one of the brats interferes, kill the girls."

"With pleasure," Robin said with a malicious smile.

Augum made sure to stand in front of the girls. Bridget somehow clung on to him, Leera, and the Orb of Orion like a shivering squirrel.

"Hang on to us, Bridge," Leera whispered, "and don't look down."

Tridian raised his chin and taunted the wolven with a gesture of his left hand. "Come, dog."

"That word is a great insult to wolven, lowlander. It betrays your ignorance." Raptos' towering body seemed even larger with the ice armor. Yet there was not a hint of fear in what remained of Tridian's face.

"Then come teach me a lesson."

Raptos leapt on top of the giant pillar and swiped at Tridian's chest with his giant frost mace. Tridian actually stepped *into* the strike. The mace thunked off the armor, leaving no mark.

Raptos roared and swung to the other side of the pillar, scratching at Tridian's exposed face.

Tridian caught the huge paw with his left hand. For a moment, there was a match of strength. "I could have sliced it clean off, dog," Tridian said, before shoving the wolven back.

Raptos roared and flexed, revealing enormous veined muscles beneath his icy fur. He opened his jaws and blew cold breath at Tridian. The Blade of Sorrows' face immediately began to frost up. He shook his head and tried to step aside, but Raptos, with his pillar height advantage, kept aim. There was nowhere for Tridian to go.

"He's blind—" Leera said in hopeful tones.

"Commander—!" Robin shouted in warning as Raptos lunged.

Tridian rolled forward as Raptos' paw scratched along his sleek armor, again leaving no mark. The sword clanged against the ground as he recovered, quickly rubbing his eyes with his left hand.

"Is that all you got, mangy hound?"

"You lowlanders cannot help but cheat. The boy warned you. He should pay *the price*."

Robin paled as Raptos bared his teeth at him.

"You go near him and you will be cut to ribbons," Tridian said, pointing his blade. "Fight on."

Raptos growled, prowling low towards Tridian.

"Now you shall feel a sting." Tridian sprang. His Dreadnought blade sizzled through the air so quickly and thinly it appeared invisible. Yet as he finished his stride past the towering wolven, a thin line of red appeared beneath the ice armor, quickly blotching.

The wolven backed away and blew on his wound, freezing it.

"Neat trick," Tridian said. "I wonder if you can still do it without a head." He leapt again, but this time the wolven was ready, jumping back onto the pillar and swiping. His claws connected with Tridian's head, tearing a chunk off.

"Commander—!" Robin called, but Tridian only surrendered a grisly smile, for there was no blood. Even as they watched, the scalp seemed to mend. Tiny white things seemed to crawl from within his scalp, giving the impression maggots were doing the work.

"What dark sorcery is this ..." Raptos said.

"Ah, but it is *precisely* that." Tridian swung the Dreadnought blade to his left and to his right before aiming for the wolven, but Raptos jumped over the blade. It sank deep into the portal pillar in a shower of sparks. The wolven used the occasion to tackle Tridian. The pair rolled over the ground, coming precariously close to the edge, while the Dreadnought blade, still wedged in the pillar, wobbled stiffly like a saw.

"They can't fall—" Garryk said, "or it won't count!"

"It has to be blood!" Tridian said from underneath Raptos as another battle of strength ensued between them. This time the wolven clutched Tridian's gauntleted arms in his claws. The man looked like a doll next to Raptos' giant body, yet he did not yield. In fact, he smiled as Raptos bit his scalp. When the wolven tore off a rotten chunk of flesh, Tridian seemed to tire of the game and flung him back. Raptos slammed against the pillar, chest bleeding again. It appeared impossible someone so under matched in size could perform such a feat of strength.

"The blade, take the blade!" Augum shouted.

"I told you, lowlander," Raptos said as he blew frost on his wound, "I do not require your counsel!"

"Yes but it could pierce the armor!"

"Now who's cheating!" Robin called from the other side.

Raptos growled at Augum before reforming his ice mace. "Take your blade, lowlander!"

Tridian's forehead rose, though there were no brows to accent his surprise. He strode around Raptos, poised for a leap that did not come, and yanked his Dreadnought blade from the pillar. "That was a mistake, dog."

"I was born in honor, and should I die, it shall be in honor, lowlander."

"So be it." Tridian began whirling the longsword as he approached. It sliced from right to left in a butterfly fashion, zipping cleanly through the air. Raptos retreated a few steps before lunging forward, mace swinging. Tridian made a final backhand stroke that connected just as the ice mace splintered against his Dreadnought armor. The wolven fell in a heap at his feet, gasping.

Tridian paced around the stricken wolven.

"Be done with it, lowlander," Raptos growled.

"You fought well." The Blade of Sorrows' pale eyes briefly fell upon Augum, before he raised his sword and beheaded Raptos.

Bridget yelped and began silently crying in Leera's arms. Leera held her tight.

Tridian wiped his blade on the wolven's white fur before standing up and looking around. "Well? Why is nothing happening?"

Garryk frantically rifled through the books.

"Find the answer, Wart," Robin said, "or you're next—"

"Wait!" Mr. Spigot said. "Look there!" He pointed into the darkness. Hovering stone blocks began to silently appear from all around them, perhaps detaching from the walls, lining up neatly in a flat bridge that led directly to the door. There was a momentary grating sound as each stone locked into place.

VALOR

The display was mesmerizing. When Augum looked back to Raptos' body, he noticed it was almost gone, having somehow sunk *into* the platform, leaving only his rucksack and belt, horn still attached.

"Seize his possessions," Tridian said. The female soldier marched up to the rucksack and hauled it over her shoulder, kicking the belt into the abyss without a second glance.

There goes the horn, Augum thought. "Goodbye, Raptos," he whispered, stomach feeling hollow. Despite the wolven's aloofness, he had been a great help to them, and died with honor.

"Bring them, Lieutenant," Tridian said, turning to cross the bridge. Mr. Spigot and Garryk quickly followed, the latter fumbling with his books.

The gray-stubbled soldier made quick gestures. "Raina, take the freckled one. Spiller, the crier. Boots, you have the lord's son. Squeaky, Fatface—you're with me in the rear."

"Yes, Lieutenant," Fatface huffed. Augum could see why they called him that—his face was wholly out of proportion to his body, as if stung by bees.

The one called Boots sheathed his broad sword and prodded Augum's shoulder. "Go on then." He was a youngish man with a bored-looking face.

"What about their possessions, Sir?" Squeaky asked, voice high-pitched like that of a tiny mouse.

"Later. Move."

As Leera passed by, Temper slapped her so hard she fell to the ground, gasping. Then she spat on her. "That's for talking dirt."

"Told you it would feel good," Robin said as the pair strolled off.

Mr. Spigot hadn't seen and the soldiers did nothing.

Augum glared, wishing Robin had to walk past so he could deck him. One day, he knew they were going to duel as Tridian and Raptos had. One day ...

"You all right?" he asked, helping her stand.

Leera rubbed her tender cheek. "I'll get her for that—"

"Move along," the old lieutenant said.

"Sir, was I supposed to intervene—"

"Shut up, Squeaky."

They were herded to the other side of the bridge where an enormous iron door awaited them.

Garryk was already rifling through books, shaking his head. "I read the eyes to this door would light up as strangers neared. Then they would open ... I don't understand why it hasn't happened."

"Maybe because there's no one inside to let us in?" Temper said, voice oozing with condescension.

"Temperance, that's enough now," Mr. Spigot said. "Let the boy concentrate."

Augum saw the other two books Garryk carried were titled *The War of the Scions* and *The Mad Necromancer, A Tale of Horror*.

Tridian hissed an impatient sigh. Garryk's hands began trembling.

Leera lightly cleared her throat. "There might be a door rune or something."

Raina yanked on Leera's hair. "Who said you could talk?"

"Really now," Mr. Spigot said. "They're just students! That's hardly necessary. Commander—"

"You forget yourself, teacher," Tridian said. "They are traitors, nothing more, and are subject to military authority. *My* authority."

Mr. Spigot swallowed as he absently tugged at his empty left sleeve.

"I think they should be punished for opening their mouths, sir," Robin said.

Mr. Spigot straightened. "Although they may not be under my supervision, Robin Scarson, *you* are. Mind yourself."

Robin scowled.

VALOR

They waited as Garryk's forehead began to glisten with sweat. "I ... I ..."

"Oh for—" Tridian gestured at the door. "Check the damn thing already."

The younger soldiers—Squeaky, Fatface, Spiller and Boots—ran to inspect the door and surrounding wall.

"Found something here, Sir!" the one named Spiller called. He had an unfortunate freakishly bulbous chin and a matching bulbous nose. Augum pictured him earning his nickname spilling drinks as he tried to bring them to his lips.

"See what it is, Lieutenant," Tridian said with a bored gesture.

The old soldier marched over and inspected what they had found. "I can't make it out, Sir. Some sort of symbol."

Augum exchanged looks with Bridget and Leera. It had to be a rune. They had studied some back in Castle Arinthian. Would this one be in Mrs. Stone's blue book on arcaneology? It was quite the problem, for if they drew attention to the book, it would surely be confiscated.

"Why did we bring him along if he can't figure anything out?" Temper said to Robin.

"I'm asking myself the same question. Come on, Wart, what have you got for us already?"

"I ... I ..."

"Permission to slap Wart, sir."

"Don't be smart with me, Robin," Mr. Spigot said. "Let him study it. He'll come to the correct conclusion, I am sure."

Garryk looked up from his sitting position and shakily pushed his spectacles up his nose, from whence they immediately began to slide back down. "Study it ... right." He stumbled his way over to the rune, the soldiers reluctantly standing aside. "Uh ... yes, uh ... it appears to be a castle rune, sir. Except ... except I don't ... I don't have ..." He winced.

Robin threw up his hands. "You forgot to bring the right book, didn't you, Wart?"

Garryk began breathing rapidly.

"What a moron."

"Permission to slap Wart, sir," Temper threw in.

"Aug—" Bridget hissed as Mr. Spigot admonished Temper. But Augum was on it. "We can help," he blurted.

Heads turned his way.

"We have a book we can lend Garryk."

"Search them," Tridian ordered.

"Hey, but we gave it up ourselves—" but Leera was silenced by another sharp yank from the female guard.

The soldiers began rifling through their possessions, tossing everything to the floor, including the Orb of Orion.

Tridian perused the objects with his foot, stopping before one of note. "A Legion dagger. Care to explain?"

"Raptos gave it to us," Augum said.

"Is that so? Hardly seemed as if you were ... *friends*."

Robin and Temper chuckled in the background.

"You did not, by chance, murder a hapless Legion soldier for this blade, did you?"

"No."

"He's lying, Commander."

Mr. Spigot raised his only arm. "Stay out of this, Robin."

The Blade of Sorrows' pus-engorged face showed no emotion as his pale eyes studied Augum. "He is not. I am disappointed you still cannot tell the difference, Apprentice."

Robin gnashed his teeth at Augum.

The Blade of Sorrows resumed kicking their belongings, stopping at the Golden Vitae vial. "And this?"

"Don't know what that is," Augum lied.

"That so?"

"Commander, we don't have time for a questioning," Mr. Spigot said in a somewhat braver voice that betrayed itself with the tiniest waver. "The great lord requires this recipe most urgently."

Tridian's mangled jaw flexed as he studied Augum, before glancing to their scattered belongings on the polished basalt floor. "Confiscate it. All of it."

"You can't!" Bridget cried. "That's all our food! And ... and our blankets!"

"Then refrain from going hungry or getting cold."

"Commander, this is highly inadvisable, they're young—"

A mere look from the Blade of Sorrows was enough to silence Mr. Spigot. Augum wondered why the teacher was so afraid of Tridian. The man had to be an advanced warlock to cast Sphere of Protection—surely he could defend himself if things got ugly. Was it something to do with his missing arm, or did Tridian possess unrevealed revenant powers?

Augum glanced at Bridget, trying to draw out a clue from her. Mr. Spigot, after all, had been her mentor once. What did she know about him? Why would such a man, who seemed to have a kind nature, submit to the Legion? Yet her eyes reflected only sadness.

"Spigot, you get the orb," Tridian said. "I think I need not remind you how important it is to keep it enclosed."

Mr. Spigot tugged at his empty sleeve before picking up the enclosed Orb of Orion and stuffing it into his own rucksack.

"Someone tell the crone I want my aunt back," Robin muttered.

Tridian ignored him. "And get the boy to pick up the books."

"Go ahead, Garryk."

Garryk pushed on his spectacles before hesitantly making his way over.

"It's in the blue one," Augum whispered as Garryk picked up the burnt yellow tome and the blue pupil's encyclopedia.

"Check the index," Bridget said when the boy was having trouble finding the right spot.

No soldier admonished her for helping, perhaps because everyone was impatient for the process to move along. Garryk brought the book over to the rune and cross-referenced, flipping pages as he went. "I think I found it," he said at last.

"Sure you don't want to take a little more time, Wart?" Robin said. "Hold everyone up a day or two?"

Garryk squeaked an apology. After some more study, he began to chant the word "Entarro."

Augum immediately knew he was doing it wrong—Garryk had to pronounce the word exactly, not chant or sing it. Further, he probably had to visualize the doors opening.

The boy finally stopped the failed repetitions, body shaking. "I ... I d-d-d-don't think I can p-p-p-pronounce it."

"Great, his stut-t-ter has c-come on," Robin mocked.

"Mr. Spigot ...?" Bridget said quietly. "May I?"

Mr. Spigot looked to Tridian, who waved idly. "Just get us inside, my patience is at an end," said the Blade of Sorrows.

Bridget glanced over the text and whispered a set of instructions to Garryk, who nodded fervently along.

"Entarro!" he said at last in a strong and confident voice.

The eyes of Occulus' mark glowed red as the behemoth doors began rumbling inward. Inside was cool darkness.

"We require more light," Mr. Spigot said to Robin and Temper.

Robin raised his right palm. "Shyneo." Temper did the same. Their hands lit up with orange arcane fire. Mr. Spigot entered first, followed by the Blade of Sorrows and everyone else.

Robin, Temper and Mr. Spigot swept their palms in wide arcs as they walked, revealing rows and rows of towering stone warrior statues in identical armor and swords, the design from a bygone era. The soldiers faced each other like two opposing armies, leaving a path in between for the group to walk through.

"What is this place?" Robin asked.

Garryk riffled through one of the books as he walked. "This is called the sentinel room. Occulus had it built to instill fear in guests while projecting his strength. Legend says it's also supposed to be the place where he would teleport an entire company into battle."

Robin scoffed. "No one can teleport more than a dozen people at once. Two hundred's impossible."

"But the history books are clear," Garryk pressed. "That's how Occulus won so many battles. He'd teleport an entire company to a strategic location and—"

Robin checked to make sure Mr. Spigot was busy. "Just shut your sniveling face already." Then he approached one of the giant statues. "Do they do anything or just stand here?" He turned back to Garryk. "Well, Wart? Answer me when I speak to you."

Garryk fumbled with his tomes. "Oh, uh, I am not sure, Honored Necrophyte, the book doesn't say."

"Why don't you leave him alone already," Bridget said.

Robin's eyes widened. He was about to say something vile when Mr. Spigot returned to the group.

"Quite the place I must say," the man said. "Imposing."

Augum glanced up. High above them was a vaulted ceiling, its arched tresses looking like the ribs of a gigantic monster.

The doors began to close behind them. Everyone turned to watch. The sound of the wind from the pit died the moment they shut.

No one said anything as the group carefully continued on.

Suddenly they heard a rattling sound from ahead. "Soiled unworthies ..." came a hissing voice out of the darkness.

Everyone stopped.

"It's her," Augum said.

The youngest soldier, Squeaky, drew his short sword. "Who?"

"Nefra," Leera replied. "The Occi queen …"

Nefra's voice echoed in the darkness. "Pretenders … you will be … purified."

"What does she mean by that?" Robin asked, voice trembling slightly.

"She means you're going to be boiled alive in a cauldron and turned into harpies," Leera said.

"Pretenders … where is your master, the one who dares to name himself the Lord of Death …"

"Lord Sparkstone is busy tracking down the scions that rightfully belong to him," the Blade of Sorrows called out. "He is the true Lord of Death and Lord of Dreadnoughts. Now show yourself to us."

The rattling briefly increased in volume. "Scions … I remember …" The rattling grew so loud some of them covered their ears, before again subsiding. "Call on your pretender master … Bring him to face me with his lies …"

She wants to sacrifice him, Augum remembered.

"We will do no such thing, hag," the Blade said into the darkness.

"You *dare* …" The rattling surged. "Then you will amuse me until you do … the doors will not open but for a price … two of the black armored pretenders must duel to the death." The rattling ceased, echoing to nothing.

The grizzled lieutenant glanced at Squeaky, whose face had lost all its color.

That's right, she likes games, Augum recalled.

"Let us investigate before making any decisions," Tridian said coolly, striding forth into the darkness, the group quickly trailing.

They soon found themselves before another set of doors. Nefra was nowhere to be found.

VALOR

Robin shoved Garryk. "Well don't just stand there, Wart—open them."

Garryk closed his book and cleared his throat. "Entarro!" but nothing happened. "Entarro!"

"Entarro!" Bridget chimed in, but she also failed to open the doors.

Squeaky's breathing increased in pace.

Mr. Spigot turned to look back. "The door behind us—let us try it."

"It will be no use," Tridian said. "Let us be done with it."

Raina's cold gaze settled on the commander. "Cull the weak."

"No ... please, you can't ..." Squeaky's voice was a whimper. The sword shook in his hands.

"Please don't—" Bridget began to say but was met with a backhanded slap from Raina. The soldier's jaw squared. "Remain silent, prisoner."

"Surely there are other means—" Mr. Spigot said to Tridian.

The grizzled lieutenant also turned to Tridian. "Just give me the word, Sir."

Squeaky began backing away. "No ... please ... you can't do this ... I'm a Legionnaire!"

The Blade of Sorrows nodded at his Lieutenant. "Make it quick."

"But Sir—he's one of our own!" Fatface said, yet when Tridian's gaze fell upon him, he dropped his eyes.

"This is wrong," Garryk muttered, shaking his head. "So wrong ..."

Squeaky ran backwards into the darkness, disappearing beyond the light of their shining palms. Somewhere down the corridor between the stone armies, he tripped and fell, weeping and blubbering to himself.

"I shall help you find the coward, Lieutenant," Robin said.

"I forbid it—" Mr. Spigot said.

"Apprentice, you will help the lieutenant find Squeaky," Tridian only said, turning his flat gaze upon Mr. Spigot. "That is an order."

Robin's face lit up with a malicious smile. "Yes, Sir!"

"I'm coming too," Temper said.

Mr. Spigot could only watch as they ran off with the lieutenant.

"Come out, you coward, and face your fate—" Robin called.

Garbled pleading, crying and begging was heard from the darkness. There was a clanging.

"See, I've even thrown my sword away!" Squeaky's voice echoed, whimpering. "You can't strike down an unarmed boy!"

"You are a man grown!" Temper's voice echoed. "Die like one!"

"I can't listen to this," Bridget said, burying her face into Leera's shoulder. Leera held onto her tightly.

Augum thought he'd take a chance. "Mr. Spigot, we can take them if we work together." The expected smack from a soldier did not come, however. Instead, Tridian smiled gruesomely. "Why don't you tell the boy why you will not be switching sides, Spigot."

Mr. Spigot closed his eyes.

"Answer the commander!" Raina said.

Mr. Spigot raised his chin and stared coldly at Tridian. "They have ... they have my wife and two daughters hostage."

"Oh, let us not exaggerate now, my good man," Tridian said. "They are in the service of the Legion."

"Monsters," Leera said, rocking a whimpering Bridget. "Monsters ..."

"Found him—!" Robin's mirthful voice called from the other end of the room. Two fiery lights converged somewhere amongst the forest of stone warriors.

"Please, no ...!" Squeaky's voice was a terrified yelp now.

VALOR

Augum glanced around at the guards, contemplating his options. Was there a way to save the young soldier? Maybe get some of the older soldiers to fight each other instead?"

Raina saw him looking around and drew her blade. "This one is planning something. I see it in his eyes."

Tridian focused his steely gaze upon Augum. "If he does anything, kill one of the girls."

Boots drew his broad sword and positioned himself behind Leera, who still held onto Bridget.

"Hold him, Temper!" Robin's voice echoed from the darkness.

"No …! Unnameables save me!" Squeaky wailed.

"I'm sorry, son," the lieutenant said.

There was an agonized cry and a blubbering. "Momma …"

Robin cackled. "Look at that, he's calling for his mommy!"

Bridget kept shaking her head while covering her ears. "Make it stop … please just make it stop …"

"Papa …" then black silence.

Augum and Leera exchanged a dark look as the doors groaned open. Nefra's rattling laughter echoed in the darkness.

GAMES

The group reformed before the open doors. Robin had a victorious look on his pinched face. Temper was still breathing quickly.

Mr. Spigot took out his black book. He tried writing in it but his hand shook so much he only ended up putting it away.

"Let's see what the hag has for us next," Robin said as they paced through the doors, footsteps echoing.

They entered a massive room with an ornate gold and crimson wool carpet. The air here was sharply colder, frosting their breath.

"Garryk, do you have any information on this room?" Mr. Spigot asked.

Garryk flipped through the pages. "Pretty sure this is the Hall of Ceremony, sir. It is the center of the castle. To the left is supposed to be the soldier and servant quarters, the training ground, the arena, the dungeons and cellar. Ahead is the throne room, the royal dining hall, the library, the royal quarters and guest quarters. To the right is the smithy, laboratorium and spawnery."

Augum hoped not find out what the spawnery was.

"The recipe, Wart," Robin said. "Where is it?"

"I ... I don't know, perhaps the library. Bahbell is supposed to have the greatest—"

"And in exactly *which* direction is that again?"

"The map here is old, but ..." Garryk struggled with a foldout in one of the books. "It's to the right of the throne room, which is straight ahead."

They walked along on the sprawling carpet, footfalls softened by the ancient, stiff wool.

"So quiet," Fatface whispered.

Raina gave him a hard look.

They came upon an even larger pair of doors, these ones made from bronze. On the face of them was a powerful figure, standing tall, fists clenched, a cape billowing in an invisible wind. His face was chiseled and stern, eyes two black orbs staring off at an unseen enemy. Mr. Spigot, Robin and Temper's shining palms cast moving shadows on the raised bronze, giving the figure a squirming depth, as if ready to come to life and attack.

Skull-shaped torch sconces protruded from the walls, protected by cages of human ribs. Adorning strips of human spines ran vertically in between. The bottom trim looked to be made of bony fingers and toes.

Mr. Spigot slowly shook his head. "Ghastly ..."

"I think it's great," Robin said. "I want a castle like this. Well, open it already, Wart."

"I'll try." Garryk took a deep breath. "Entarro!" but as Augum expected, nothing happened. No, Nefra wanted to play her twisted games ...

Sure enough, the echoed rattling came again, this time from the darkness behind them.

"Unworthies ... Each door has its price ..."

"And what is the price on this door, hag?" Tridian called. Augum noticed something odd about the Blade of Sorrows' breath— it did not frost in the frigid air.

"An ancient test of cunning …"

Robin's face twisted. "What does that mean?"

"I've read about this somewhere," Garryk said. "An ancient test of cunning is answering three riddles."

"And what if we get them wrong?" Fatface asked, voice quivering.

No one had the answer to that.

Tridian's soulless gaze fell upon the trio. "*They* will answer."

Robin and Temper exchanged gleeful looks while the trio exchanged anxious ones.

The rattling returned. "I am a coil, sometimes woven … a traitor's neck is best broken … what am I?"

Augum, Bridget and Leera huddled close.

"This one's easy," Leera said. "It's got to be rope."

Augum nodded. "Agreed, but let's pretend we're having trouble with it and talk about our situation. Look, I think if we separate ourselves along with Garryk and the books, we have a chance of finding the recipe first."

"Just what I was thinking," Leera said.

"Yes but we'll have to do it in a way that forces Garryk to come," Bridget said. "Otherwise they'll take revenge on his family for changing sides. Either that or we steal the books."

"Both work," Augum replied. "And the Orb of Orion?"

"I—" Bridget began, but she was cut off by Tridian.

"Enough already. Your answer."

"Rope!" Augum called into the darkness. "The answer to the riddle is rope!" His palms sweated waiting for the reply.

"Correct, Unworthy."

The trio breathed an audible sigh of relief as the rattling returned.

"I end lives, wither mountains, move the sun and moon, am never now but always soon … what am I?"

The trio again conspired together.

"Death," Leera blurted.

Bridget shook her head. "Is death always soon though?"

"In this place it is …"

Augum shrugged. "This time I have nothing." To him, the riddle was gibberish.

"Wait, that's it!" Bridget said. "*Time*. And what I tried to say earlier before Tridian cut me off is that I managed to cast Object Track on the Orb of Orion when Raptos battled the Blade of Sorrows."

"Excellent," Augum said, "but will it work with the Sphere of Protection spell on it?"

"Guess we'll find out when there's enough distance between us and the orb."

"Enough already," Tridian's voice cut in. "Give us your answer."

"Time!" Augum shouted into the darkness. "The answer is time."

"Correct, Unworthy." The rattling surged before calming. "And now the last. I am soft under my miniature sun, but hard when I am completely done. I emit no sound and hate to drown but wind and breath are often death."

Once again, the trio converged.

"It's some sort of bright … something," Leera said.

Bridget absently tapped her chin. "What's soft under a miniature sun?"

"A head?" Leera offered.

"But how's a head hard when done?" Augum countered.

They thought about it some more.

Leera crinkled her nose. "I'm stumped."

"Answer," Tridian said.

The trio quickly threw around some more ideas, but nothing felt right.

"Answer. Now!" Tridian said.

"A candle—!" Garryk suddenly cried out into the darkness.

There was a quiet moment before the great doors began to rumble inwards.

Robin slapped the back of Garryk's head, again sending his spectacles flying. "Wart, what are you doing!"

"Couldn't help it, Honored Necrophyte, I knew the answer, and no sense—"

"Well yeah, obviously everyone had the answer except for the stupid gutterborns, but you forget you're on *our* side."

Temper stepped on the spectacles, grinding them underfoot. "Oops."

Mr. Spigot immediately withdrew his black notebook. "What did I say? A mark on both of your records!"

"Whatever," Robin muttered.

Garryk fumbled around for his broken spectacles. When he found them, he held both hands above the wreckage. "Apreyo." Once mended, he put them back on his nose.

"Thanks," Augum mouthed to Garryk when he had a chance. The boy quickly averted his eyes.

The group moved into the throne room. There was a stale rotten smell in the air, reminding Augum of Castle Arinthian's crypt, except much stronger. The source of the stench was soon explained when Mr. Spigot's light fell upon a skeleton, then a second one, and soon a third and more, until they stood before a field of them.

"So it's true—" Garryk whispered, dropping to his knees and rifling through *The Mad Necromancer, A Tale of Horror*. He cleared his throat before reading. "… 'and so it was said that the Deathlord's faithful had been so overcome with grief upon their master's passing that they entered his throne room and sacrificed themselves, so they could follow him into death'."

Mr. Spigot raised his shining leaf-covered palm. The bodies piled higher and higher the further the light crept. "A monstrous thing, this is …"

"They call it *loyalty*, Spigot," Tridian said.

"Idiocy if you ask me," Leera muttered.

VALOR

"Let's go see the throne," Robin said, kicking a corpse aside. The bones rattled and fell apart.

"You will respect the dead, Robin Scarson," Mr. Spigot said.

"I'm a necrophyte, *sir*," Robin replied mockingly.

"Then it holds doubly true for you."

Robin curled his lip but stepped over the next body. But soon there were so many that it was impossible to move forward without stepping on an ancient skeleton. Before them rose a great podium, the steps littered with corpses. An enormous and elaborate chair loomed in the darkness, with a gigantic fanned backrest made entirely from bones and skulls. Augum imagined what it had been like to come here and face the Lord of Death at the height of his power, when kings and queens came begging for mercy ...

"Beautiful," Robin whispered.

There was a garbled tinny voice coming from somewhere in Tridian's direction. He reached into a leather pouch on his belt and withdrew a small orb. Augum immediately recognized it as a seeing orb.

"I can barely hear you," Tridian said.

"Can't ... Occi ... cut-off ..."

"Yes, I know. It seems the Occi hag has allowed only a few of us entry. Keep trying, maybe there is some other way in."

"The castle must be interfering with the orb, Commander," Garryk said. "It has ancient and powerful arcane enchantments beyond current unders—"

"*Obviously*, Wart," Robin said. "Why don't you stop boring us with your blubbering and just point us in the direction of the library."

"Right, sorry. Uh, this way, Honored Necrophyte."

"Ugh, why does he have to call him that?" Leera whispered to Augum. "Makes me sick."

Fear is why, Augum thought. Plain old fear. He saw a bit of himself in Garryk. Back in the Penderson farm, he'd say

"Yes, Mr. Penderson," and "I'm sorry, Mr. Penderson," but no matter how polite he was it hadn't mattered, Mr. Penderson always treated him the same—with contempt.

The group moved away from the bodies, past a series of ornate benches and chairs and on to another bronze door, this one adorned with images of books and an engraved phrase.

" 'Nosiquos ani enitrios'," Mr. Spigot read, raising a gray brow. "Garryk?"

"Back when I was studying to become an arcaneologist—" Garryk glanced at the Blade of Sorrows and adjusted his spectacles. "That is, before I completely devoted myself to becoming a necrophyte, I studied the mother tongue. I believe it's ancient Tiberran, Mr. Spigot. Occulus himself was Tiberran, his wife a—"

"He's asking what it *means*, Wart, not Occulus' entire history."

"Oh. Right. I think it means 'Knowledge is Forever'."

"Typical," Robin muttered. "Just like in the academy, where everything has to be 'knowledge this' and 'wisdom that'. Why can't they write fun stuff?"

"Yeah, like directions to ancient treasure," Temper said.

"Exactly."

Leera rolled her eyes at Augum, mouthing, "Idiots."

Augum would have thought that funny under a different circumstance, for he and Leera had once gone treasure hunting in Castle Arinthian. Except the way that treasure hunt ended was not exactly their proudest moment …

"Shall I try opening the doors, Mr. Spigot?"

"Please, Garryk."

"Entarro!" but as expected, nothing happened except for Nefra's tongue rattling again.

"A price, hag, we know," Tridian said to the darkness. "What is it this time?"

A dim form briefly appeared in the darkness before them. The head squirmed as if made of snakes. There was a hiss and a green cloud suddenly shot at them. Everyone but Tridian coughed. The vapor felt harsh and bitter upon Augum's throat, like overripe lemon. It made him feel lightheaded and nauseous.

There was laughter behind Nefra's words. "You have been poisoned ... those that will not eat the antidote ... will die a most painful death ..."

Robin's face was as green as the cloud, while Temper smacked a hand over her mouth to keep inside whatever was trying to come up. Fatface already fell to his knees, retching.

"Well where is the damn antidote already?" Tridian shouted, but Nefra's form had disappeared. Instead, there was a metal shuffling sound. A squat suit of dented armor materialized out of the darkness, carrying a covered basket. The helmet was made in the shape of a pointed skull. Secured to its waist was a wooden practice sword.

"He's just like Fentwick," Leera said, gasping for breath.

Robin couldn't stop coughing. "What ... is that ... thing?"

The voice was a steamy whistle, as if garbled by eons of time. "Mine name doth be Horrick, foul unworthies." He plopped the basket down. "Eat thou shalt, or perish."

"The cloth—!" Spiller gurgled, pointing at the covered basket. "It moved ..."

Fatface went purple. "Gods, no ..."

"Thou shouldst best quicken," Horrick wheezed, "lest thee poison runs its course."

Tridian, the only one unaffected by the poison, strolled forward and uncovered the basket. What squirmed inside were giant white maggots with red snouts.

Bridget, Robin, Fatface and Spiller immediately retched.

Raina marched over to the basket, grabbed a maggot, and immediately ate it, hard face unchanged, as if it was nothing more than biscuit beef.

Augum grit his teeth and ran to the basket. He picked out three squirming maggots and hurried back to Bridget and

Leera. "Make it quick," he said, shoving one in his mouth. It rolled around on his tongue and he immediately expelled it, along with the contents of his stomach.

Leera's eyes watered. "Graaaargh!" she shouted to boost her courage, before biting one in half. She chewed on it as if her jaws were made of steel.

Meanwhile, Mr. Spigot finished his maggot and was helping Garryk. Boots and the lieutenant finished theirs without too much trouble. Temper finally managed to get one down, but not without retching first. Robin was about to hurl when Tridian came up to him and closed his hand over his mouth.

"Eat it, Apprentice, or you will die." Robin's face went from green to purple to blue. His cheeks expanded, then contracted and expanded again. Tridian held the back of the boy's head while pressing his mouth harder. Robin kicked and moaned, eyes watering.

"Eat it, boy!"

Meanwhile, every time Augum brought the squiggling maggot to his lips, his stomach would start writhing. The poison certainly wasn't helping either.

"You can do it, Aug," Leera said, wiping her mouth. "Think of it as a sweet but squishy treat."

"Not ... helping ..." Augum managed to blubber. The dizziness increased and he dropped down to one knee, the maggot squished to juice in his fist.

Bridget yanked on Leera. "Help ..." She shoved the maggot into her hand. "Force it in ... I can't ..." Leera didn't hesitate. She placed the maggot in Bridget's mouth and helped her clamp down. Bridget's face turned every shade of color. Her body shook.

"Come on, Bridge, you can do it, just swallow," Leera was saying, voice edged with panic. "Swallow, damn it—!"

Augum glanced around. Everyone had managed to eat the maggot except for himself and Fatface.

VALOR

Leera rushed to the basket and brought Augum another maggot. "Come on, Aug, I know you can do this. You *have* to do this."

Fighting off a dizzy spell, he took the maggot from her and shoved it in his mouth, snarling and groaning to pump up his courage, much like Leera had.

"That's it, Aug, you're doing it, keep going …"

The texture was what made it most difficult—it was like eating crunchy snot. He fought through it though and immediately started to feel better. His stomach settled and his dizziness faded. Yet the repugnant nature of the ordeal still left him drained.

"Come on, Fatface!" the lieutenant was shouting, a hand over the soldier's mouth. "Do you want your poor ma to get a letter from me? Hmm? How her own son couldn't swallow one measly maggot!"

Fatface was on the floor, armor strewn with chunks of vomit, face purple and leg twitching.

"Come on, son!" but Fatface had gone still, and the doors rumbled open.

THE LIBRARY

They sat recuperating for some time. Augum hoped to never have to endure something like that again. Maggots ... even the thought of it made his stomach churn. His eyes travelled to the still form nearby. Fatface—another corpse for the ancient pile. The poor man. His poor mother ...

"What was his real name?" Augum asked.

The soldiers glared at him. Only four remained now—bulbous Spiller, bored Boots, hard Raina, and the stubbled lieutenant.

"Mind your tongue, rebel," Tridian said, "lest they carve it out of you. He wasn't one of yours. Now, everyone up. Let's move."

"What about that thing?" Robin asked, nodding at Horrick.

The ancient suit of arcanely enchanted armor turned its skull helmet. "Wouldst thou care to duel, unworthy cur?"

Robin laughed. "Did you hear that? The little rust bucket called me a 'cur'!" He brought his hands together, aiming them at Horrick. "Annihilo!" A jet of fire shot forth, plowing

452

into the armor, but all it accomplished was a charcoal stain. "Damn. The iron goat is immune ... Huh."

"Thou canst do Horrick harm with such weak arcanery. Horrick thinks thou needst a smack in thy jaw from thy master."

"You little—"

Tridian gave a grunt. "Leave it be."

Augum exchanged looks with Bridget and Leera. Robin had caught up to them—looks like he was studying his 3rd degree too. Not to mention any necromantic spells he might know ...

They entered the library, walking onto old ornate carpeting, encountering rows and rows of great black oak shelves that towered out of sight. Each was as wide as a man lying on his side, and exquisitely carved with serpents, snakes and demons. The spines of the tomes were ridged and had symbols or words written in a mysterious language. Some were plain, some ornate; some green or blue, but most were the color of blood or night. It smelled strongly of ancient parchment.

"There must be tens of thousands ..." Garryk whispered, clutching his own tomes to his chest.

"An arcaneologists dream," Mr. Spigot added.

Tridian looked up. "We will have to search it."

"That will take some time with only the lot of us," the lieutenant said.

Tridian glanced around at them all. "Spigot, you will mind the traitors here. Kill them if they try to escape. Everyone else, join one of the youngling warlocks. We will need their light to search by. And see if you can find some working torches. Blast this infernal darkness."

Those that were leaving dropped their rucksacks and books by the doors, while the trio settled against the stone walls, near an immense tapestry depicting a swarm of dark soldiers taking a fortified hill. Beside the tapestry, Augum spied a small bronze plaque with a torch emblem and a rune underneath. He leaned up against it, obscuring it from view. No sense helping the enemy with light …

Mr. Spigot pulled up a rickety old chair.

"Where's Horrick, Mr. Spigot?" Augum asked, hoping to strike up amiable conversation with the man.

Mr. Spigot's chair creaked as he shone his palm through the doors. "He's standing in the same place." He nervously glanced around. Three lights wavered distantly. "Look," he began in a whisper, "I'm awfully sorry about all this. I wish I could help in some way, I really do, but they have my wife and daughters—"

"Mr. Spigot, we understand," Bridget said. "It's all right."

They nodded along. Hostage taking was a favored Legion strategy.

"Robin killed …" Augum swallowed, recalling Mya. "He murdered a friend of ours."

"But … no, he is just a boy! He could never—"

"I saw it with my own eyes, sir."

Mr. Spigot tugged on his empty sleeve, refusing to meet their gaze.

"Sir, can I ask …" Bridget glanced at the missing arm.

"Oh, this—a most awful thing it was. A messenger was apprehended carrying a letter to my wife and daughters. We were supposed to run off together to a secret village of refugees in the woods near Blackhaven. Many others were outright slaughtered for such intransigence, but because I was a teacher at the academy …"

"We came from a village like that," Bridget whispered. "The Lord of the Legion razed it to the ground and murdered almost everyone there."

Mr. Spigot kept absently playing with his hollow sleeve. "Yes, I have heard … stories. Sometimes I think it may have been worse for us had we actually escaped." He raised his round chin and looked at Augum. "It seems the Lord of the Legion's son is not like the father at all." His voice dropped

VALOR

to a whisper. "I am so very glad. There is a hope in you, my boy, a daring hope ..."

Augum thought to take the chance that presented itself. "Mr. Spigot, we need to find that recipe before they do ... and destroy it. If my father gets a hold of it, he will open a gateway to Ley. He *will* conquer it and his power *will* grow. He'd become unstoppable. Please, I know there's nothing ... *obvious* ... that you can do, but ..."

The color seemed to have drained from Mr. Spigot's face as he quickly checked about. "I ... I really shouldn't, I oughtn't ... If they—"

"Mr. Spigot, please—" It was Bridget this time. "At least some food. *Please* ..."

The ale-bellied man's brows softened as he looked at the girls. "You remind me of my daughters." He glanced over his shoulder. The lights could hardly be seen among the mass of shelving and books. "All right, all right, perhaps a bit of food, yes, it's the decent thing to do. But please, *please* don't try anything. I cannot permit you to—"

"Of course, Mr. Spigot," Bridget replied quickly, "we'd never risk your wife and daughters."

Mr. Spigot left them in the cool darkness as he tiptoed off to the rucksacks.

Bridget sighed. "Poor Mr. Spigot. If it wasn't for his family, I'd say we should run."

"Even so, where would we go?" Leera said. "Nefra would pick us off one by one with her dumb puzzles and games—if those morons didn't find us first."

"Maybe we can somehow use the Orb of Orion," Augum said, "get a message out to Nana—" He stopped talking as Mr. Spigot made his way back, holding a small bundle.

"I brought you some food, but you must be quick and quiet. Oh, and also this ..." He handed them one of Garryk's books, the one titled *The Mad Necromancer, A Tale of Horror*. "In case they take a long time, perhaps you could find some way to the recipe in here ..."

Bridget accepted the book. Leera took the food. "Thank you," they all said.

It was nothing but journey bread, bars of nuts and dried berries, and some stiff dried salted beef—but it went a long way into combating the leftover acid in their stomachs. Augum was hungry for more.

"Oh, and here's a waterskin." Mr. Spigot detached a leather bladder and handed it over. Everyone had a greedy fill. When they finished, they moved on to the book.

"Seems it was written by visitors only," Bridget said as she riffled the pages.

"More like written by other people who heard stories from visitors," Leera chimed in.

Indeed, the writing was long-winded and somewhat melodramatic, citing demons and the walking dead at every turn. There were entire chapters devoted to what Occulus' armies had done to the countryside, not to mention castles and their defenders. Whole cities were laid to waste by his armies of Dreadnought-armored soldiers. It made Augum wonder where all that armor and weaponry went.

"Wait, there—" Leera's hand shot to a section titled *Servitude in Bahbell, a Most Unfortunate Occupation*. She discretely tapped at a particular passage further down the page. They read in silence.

The castle had its typical minders and servants, all tortured souls, though one is worthy of a note in history. Horrick, they called him, was a suit of armor arcanely enchanted. This suit was particularly interesting because it had the ability to talk. It was used primarily to train the young princes and princesses of the castle—Occulus' children—in the art of the blade, but could also be commanded to defend them, lift heavy objects, open doors, and act as a frightful guide to visitors. Many kings and queens ...

Leera circled the part that said "open doors" with her finger.

"Have you found something there?" Mr. Spigot asked, removing the Orb of Orion from his rucksack. Augum was disappointed to see it was still enclosed within its green sphere of protection.

"Nothing much, sir," Leera lied. "Just some historical stuff."

"Ah." Mr. Spigot went on to recast Sphere of Protection. "There, that should do it for another few hours."

"Will you have to keep that up all night, Mr. Spigot?" Augum asked.

"I am afraid so. Can't have the crone—err, excuse me, Anna Stone—teleporting in now, can we?" He smiled at them. Seeing that no one returned the gesture, he cleared his throat and put away the orb.

"What's going to happen to us?" Bridget asked quietly.

"I ... well, my dear, to be perfectly honest, I haven't given it any thought. I'm sure, being so young ..." But then he stopped and ran a sweaty hand over his balding head. "I just don't know ..."

"Mr. Spigot, you can't let them murder us," Bridget pressed in a pleading whisper. "Mr. Spigot—"

"Hush, girl! We shouldn't even be talking. Please, all of you, return to the book and keep occupied. I'm sure everything will turn out just fine. In fact, if you find out where the recipe is, it'll come to an end quicker."

They exchanged knowing looks but went back to the book. Augum stared past the page though, mind buzzing with thoughts. He concluded they eventually had to escape, and sooner than later, lest Nefra whittled them down to nothing, or the Legion murdered them. They needed a break, and when it happened, they had to be ready. An idea occurred to him, but he had to wait to voice it for another hour, when Mr. Spigot got up to stretch his legs. The others still hadn't returned, but that wasn't surprising considering the immensity of their task.

"Shyneo," Augum said. "It's so we can see, Mr. Spigot. You don't mind, do you?"

Mr. Spigot surrendered a reluctant nod before wandering about, stretching his stubby legs and only arm. The moment he turned his back, Augum began talking in a soft whisper.

"After they get back, soon as we get the chance, we take Horrick and run, using him to open and close the doors behind us. Agreed?" They had to do it without Spigot taking the blame.

The girls subtly nodded their heads, all the while pretending to be immersed in the book.

"Wasn't there a map in one of these books?" Leera whispered.

Bridget gave a slight shake of her head. "Yes, but it's not in this one."

"Well we need that map too."

"And we'll have to choose our moment wisely—" but Bridget was cut off by Mr. Spigot's return. They resumed perusing the book.

"Wait, go back one," Leera said. "Thought I saw something. There …"

" 'The laboratorium is a place of great mystery'," Bridget began reading aloud, " 'a room where Occulus conducted many horrifying experiments in the obscure element of necromancy. It was even rumored that, in the months before his death, he worked on something grand that would have changed the face of Sithesia. Unfortunately, the author of this glorious compendium has been unable to track down anyone actually having gained entry into this shadowy room to confirm such a story, for Occulus forbade access even to his servants. Further attempts after his vanquishing have also proven futile, for, as discussed in previous chapters, the castle closed itself to the outside world, perhaps succumbing to some strange curse.' "

" 'Strangely,' " Bridget read on, " 'soldiers and wanderers continue to disappear whilst trekking near its grounds. Stories of cannibalism, witchery and demon worshipping have become entrenched in local folklore. Few wish to speak

VALOR

of what transpires in those mountains. Fewer still actually know. As time passes, it is the opinion of this author that the castle's location will slip from living memory, for the weight of its curse is great and dark'."

They sat in silence for a bit, contemplating those words. Could the recipe be in there?

"Where is the laboratorium?" Mr. Spigot finally asked.

"We don't have the map, sir," Bridget replied. "It's in one of the other books. May I get it please?"

"I suppose so, but please don't try anything."

"Thank you, sir, I won't. Shyneo."

Bridget padded off to where the Legion stashed the rucksacks. Mr. Spigot tried to eye her and Augum and Leera at the same time. After she had been gone a while, he made to stand.

"Mr. Spigot—sir—" Augum began quickly, trying to stall him. "Is there, uh, any news from the front? From Tiberra?"

Mr. Spigot craned his neck toward Bridget whilst trying to answer. "Yes, well, you know, I don't rightly ... excuse me a moment I have to—" but Bridget wandered back just then.

"I found it here, sir." She splayed the map out before them on the old carpet. It was neatly drawn in ink on old wrinkled vellum.

"I really don't think it a wise idea to let you look at that," Mr. Spigot said, nervously glancing around.

Meanwhile, Augum concentrated, committing as much of the map to memory as possible.

"Laboratorium is here," Bridget said, ignoring Mr. Spigot. "The entrance is from the Hall of Ceremony."

"And the spawnery is right behind the laboratorium," Leera pointed out with a forced laugh. "Not that we need to see anything there." Obviously, the girls were stalling too.

"Really now," Mr. Spigot continued, "perhaps you should give that back before—"

"Do you think the Occi queen will let us out alive, Mr. Spigot?" Bridget asked.

"I ... I really don't—"

Augum sensed they were running out of time and focused entirely on the map. What to do, where to go? There was a dungeon in the training yard by the arena—who knew where that went. No, what they needed was ... *an emergency escape portal!* Of course ... Bahbell *had* to have one just like Castle Arinthian—all arcane castles had one, didn't they? But where would it be? Occulus wasn't the kind of man to allow anyone else out, except for himself ...

Augum glanced down the map to a spot on the very end, beyond the throne room, titled *Occulus' Royal Quarters*. There. If there were any escape portals in the castle, they'd surely be in his personal quarters, deep in the mountain. It only made sense—

"Really now, this is most inappropriate—" Mr. Spigot suddenly yanked the map from under their noses. He took the book too. "I don't know what I was thinking ... so dangerous ... if they should ..." he kept muttering to himself as he waddled back to return the items.

"I memorized it," Augum whispered quickly.

"I think I did too," Bridget said.

"We have to find an emergency escape portal. I think Occulus might have one in his quarters—"

Leera gripped his arm. "Augum, that's *brilliant*—"

"But it's all the way at the other end of the castle, deep in the mountain—"

Bridget adjusted something within her robe. "I also grabbed—"

"What are you lot conspiring about over there?" Mr. Spigot asked, returning in a huff. "I heard you whispering."

"Nothing, Mr. Spigot," Bridget replied. "We're just hoping to survive this, that's all."

"But you want the recipe too. That's why you came here, isn't it?"

"We have to destroy it, Mr. Spigot—"

"*Don't* talk about that! It's high *treason* to even suggest it—"

"But Mr. Spigot—"

"Enough!" Mr. Spigot's face had reddened and sweat formed on his brow. He wiped it with the back of his good arm. "Just sit there and be quiet! And extinguish that damn hand, boy."

Augum did as he was told and the trio quietly sat against the cold wall, huddling close for warmth.

"Don't know what I was thinking …"

THE PRICE

The Legion group returned to the trio and Mr. Spigot hours later.

Mr. Spigot paced as they approached, hands writhing. "Well? How did it go?"

"It'll take an army to search this place," Robin said, dragging another chair near and slumping into it. "Temper, fetch me something to eat, I'm starved."

"I have already spoken to His Lordship," Tridian said as Temper strode to the rucksacks. "Took some effort to get through, but he is on his way."

"My father's on his way *here*?" Augum asked. This could ruin everything.

"Yes. I warned His Lordship about the hag, but he insists. Three reasons—the first is you, my boy. Seems he is most anxious to bring you to his side. The second is this library. It is an invaluable source of necromantic knowledge. The third is rather obvious, is it not?"

"The recipe ..."

"Sharp, this one is," Robin muttered.

"When will he get here?" Augum pressed.

VALOR

"Don't you worry about that," Robin said. "He'll get here soon enough." He turned to Tridian. "Why are we talking to this rat again?"

"We are done talking to the lord's son, actually."

Robin scowled. He didn't seem to like being reminded who Augum was.

Augum couldn't resist sniping at Mya's murderer. "Careful, *Robbie*, because one day you might just be under my command." He felt the look from the girls, but he wanted to hurt Robin—he had no intention of ever joining the Legion.

Robin only smirked, appearing to see through the ploy, and turned to Tridian. "Can we practice the art of the question on them a little?"

"Now is not the time, Apprentice. Perhaps when His Lordship arrives."

"Has anyone seen the map?" Garryk asked, wandering back from the rucksacks.

Mr. Spigot reacted a little too quickly. "I ... I actually took it out to inspect it."

"You did now, did you?" Tridian's voice was cool.

Mr. Spigot dabbed at his forehead with a cloth. "Yes, of course I did, I wanted to see if I could find the recipe somehow."

"And?"

"And—? And what, Commander?"

"And did you find the recipe?"

"Oh, no, of course not—"

Tridian only stared at him.

"But I *do* think I may know where it is."

"Do you now?"

Mr. Spigot's eyes flicked to the trio a moment. "Yes, uh, it may be in the laboratorium."

Augum and Leera met each other's gaze, silently communicating the same thought—Mr. Spigot couldn't be trusted while his family was held hostage.

"And how did you come to that conclusion, if I might inquire?" Tridian seemed to enjoy watching Mr. Spigot's mind race for an answer. When the tension became unbearable, Tridian adjusted his Dreadnought armor. "Very well, we will rest and then visit the laboratorium."

Mr. Spigot's shoulders relaxed.

The Blade of Sorrows took a sudden step closer to the man, voice dangerously low. "But if I find this is nothing more than an attempt to whittle our forces down using the hag's game ..."

Mr. Spigot tugged at the sleeve of his missing arm. "Not at all, Commander, not at all. I'd never jeopardize my girls ..."

"I don't trust him," Robin said outright. "He's got lying eyes."

Mr. Spigot fumbled for his black book. "You are not to talk to me that way, Robin Scarson, I am your teacher," but his voice wavered. "Another such infraction and I shall address the lord myself."

Robin shrugged. "Then I'll just tell the great lord you tried to secretly help the traitors. You stayed here all this time, counseling them on what to do."

"I never—"

Augum saw where this was going. "He did no such thing. We asked for the book and he wouldn't show it to us. We asked for food and blankets and he gave us nothing." He piled it on thick now. "When we tried to talk to him he told us to sit down and shut up."

Mr. Spigot nodded along. "Yes, yes that's right, I did. I told them to sit down and shut up."

"Enough already." Tridian waved the matter aside as if already bored. "Spigot, is the orb secure?"

"Of course it is."

"Good. Make sure it remains that way until our lord arrives. When the crone sees her brats under threat, she will have no choice but to come for them."

VALOR

"A most diabolically clever trap, Commander," Robin said.

Tridian grunted and strolled off to the rucksacks, where Raina, the lieutenant, Boots and Spiller milled, and where Temper awkwardly stood casting Shine for them while holding Robin's food.

Augum gave Mr. Spigot a look, trying to communicate with his eyes that he had said those things for his family's sake. Mr. Spigot only dropped his gaze, red in the face.

"Wart, bring your books and that map."

"Yes, Honored Necrophyte." Garryk hurried off.

"And bring me something to eat!"

Garryk soon raced back with his books and a small bundle Temper had shoved at him.

Robin promptly unwrapped a chunk of dried salted pork and began chewing loudly. "You three must be starved."

Every time Augum looked at Robin's face, he saw Mya's pale face. The urge to lunge at him rose to the point he had to look away. He could spoil everything if he did something that stupid now. He settled on envisioning his fist pounding Robin's face instead.

Crumbs sprinkled Robin's necrophyte gown. "When all this castle business is done with, gutterborns, we're going to continue where we left off."

"That's enough now, Robin," Mr. Spigot said. "Eat and rest up. There's great danger ahead. That Occi queen is no jest."

That seemed to wipe the smirk off Robin's face. "Wart, read up on the laboratorium and report your findings to me."

"Yes, Honored Necrophyte." Garryk pushed on his spectacles and began rifling through his books, reporting any relevant information as he went, including what Bridget had read aloud—but he had missed the part about Horrick being able to open doors. Eventually Robin grew bored and told him to shut up.

465

After some time, the soldiers gathered the rucksacks and led everyone back to the Hall of Ceremony. Along the way, Augum whispered, "Horrick, follow us," not actually expecting it to work. But Horrick shuffled along behind them without a word.

"That rusted blob is trailing," Temper said.

Robin glanced back. "Whatever, it can't do anything."

They reached the closed bronze doors to the laboratorium, adorned with a mortar and pestle.

"I am not sure this is such a good idea, Commander," Mr. Spigot said. "Perhaps we should wait for His Lordship—"

"His Lordship demanded we make as much progress as possible before his arrival. We will continue."

Boots and Spiller exchanged uneasy looks, as did Temper and Robin. All had to have been thinking the same thing—what would the Occi witch have them do now? Two of their number had already perished.

Mr. Spigot reluctantly nodded at Garryk.

"Entarro!" but once again nothing happened, other than the return of Nefra's hissing voice, this time with a hint of laughter. "Persistent in your follies, unworthies ..."

"Duty unto death," Tridian said.

Nefra's voice rattled with amusement. "Your false master ... He is coming ..."

"He is coming and he will annihilate you, hag."

"You think you know suffering, revenant ... You do not ... The true master and I made hundreds of revenants ... *hundreds* ..."

Tridian watched the darkness. "Play your little games."

"Indeed I shall ... The price of *this* door is great ... There shall be three duels ... Horrick will choose ..."

"Oh no, please don't make us face each other ..." Leera whispered.

"Then we simply won't fight," Augum said.

VALOR

Horrick slowly shuffled between them. Augum felt his heart rate triple as the armor neared ... and stopped before Leera.

"Thou shalt prove thyself in single combat."

Leera groaned. "Against who?"

Horrick moved along, stopping before the lieutenant.

"Thou shalt prove thyself in single combat."

"Oh no ..." Leera murmured.

The lieutenant eyed her and smiled.

"Easy as eggs, Sir," Spiller said.

"This is going to be fun to watch," Robin said. "Leering Leera about to leer her last. That has a nice ring to it. I should have been a minstrel."

Temper laughed supportively.

Augum gripped Leera's arms. She was shaking, her breathing rapid. "You can do this," he whispered. "Use the First Offensive and Centarro." His eyes focused on her soft lips. He wanted to kiss her, but instead gave her a hug. She placed her arms around him and squeezed, while Robin and Temper cackled in the background, sharing jokes.

Bridget quickly joined in. "I love you, Lee, please be careful. Augum's right—you can do it. Don't forget to use Push and Shield if you need to."

"They're saying goodbye to her," Robin said. "They know she's a goner!"

The grizzled lieutenant stepped forward, reaching to his back and drawing a double-sided battleaxe. He deftly twirled it in his hands.

"Make it quick, lieutenant," Tridian said.

"Give her a weapon!" Augum called.

Tridian looked him in the eye. "No."

"It's all right, Aug." Leera forced a smile before cautiously stepping forward, hands out. "Shyneo."

Augum thought himself crazy for allowing this to go on. He had to stop himself from shouting for the duel to come to a halt. He simply *had* to trust her.

Robin snorted. "Careful, lieutenant, or you might end up being shined to death."

The lieutenant suddenly shot forth and swung his axe. Leera wasn't quick enough to get out of the way, but she did manage to summon a shield made of pond leaves. The axe smacked into it, sending her flying back. As soon as the shield disappeared, the lieutenant swung again, forcing her to repeat the spell.

Everyone began cheering their side on. Augum's hands were curled into tight fists, stomach a knot. He was ready to jump in if need be, damn the consequences. "Come on, Lee! You can do it—!"

The axe whistled by Leera's head. She jumped back. "Disablo!" but the lieutenant yanked on the shaft, preventing the Disarm spell from completing.

Leera shoved the air before her. "Baka!"

He was thrust back a few paces, but she was not proficient enough with the spell to knock him down. He recovered quickly and charged.

Augum was shouting, "Do it now! Cast it!"

Leera dropped low. "Centeratoraye xao xen!" She yelled as the axe screamed through the air, aimed for her neck. She made a graceful movement and it missed, but only by a hair.

The lieutenant continued his swing all the way around, bringing it back for a second strike. This time Leera jumped *over* the axe and shoved the air before her, shouting, "Baka!" aiming at the great steel head of the weapon, propelling the man into a faster spin. As the axe came around a third time, Leera gave it a deft underhanded smack on the shaft as she stuck her leg out. The lieutenant tripped on her foot while the axe freed itself from his grip, twirling directly above him. He slammed into the ground, coming to rest face up just as the axe plunged into his neck like a guillotine, beheading the man.

Silence rang along with the steel twang of the axe.

VALOR

Leera stumbled back to their group, falling into Augum's arms, panting. He held her tight, knowing the side effects of the spell were upon her. "You did good, you're all right," he kept whispering as she muttered unintelligibly.

Robin was sputtering. "What ... what just happened ... how did she do that?"

"She must have cheated," Temper said.

"What spell was that?" Garryk asked in a quivering voice.

"I don't rightly know," Mr. Spigot whispered, watching Augum and Leera with grave eyes.

Raina glared at Augum. "He shall be avenged, that I promise you."

Leera began squirming in Augum's arms.

"Don't let them see the side effects," Bridget whispered, hugging the both of them, holding her in place.

But the Legion's attention had diverted to Horrick, who resumed his creaking shuffle, stopping before Robin.

"Thou shalt prove thyself in single combat."

"Me? Why me? What have I done!"

Horrick ignored him and moved on, stopping before Mr. Spigot. "Thou shalt prove thyself in single combat."

"But ... but ... I've never dueled before, I've never fought anyone in my entire life ..." Mr. Spigot's brow began to sparkle with sweat. "And he's just a boy ...!"

"You can't choose him," Robin said. "That's completely unfair! He's *11th degree*!"

"I won't duel a pupil," Mr. Spigot said, shaking his head, "I won't."

Horrick's skull helm tilted slightly. "Thou shalt duel or thou shalt both perish, contemptible malingerer."

Robin stepped forward, shaking like a tree in a storm. He withdrew the Destiny Stone from within his robes.

"Mr. Spigot ..." Garryk's eyes were wide with terror.

"Dost thou refuse, Unworthy?" Horrick asked.

"Face him or you'll both die," Boots said.

469

"But this is so unfair!" Temper called.

At last, Mr. Spigot trundled forward, only to be stopped by Tridian's gauntleted hand on his shoulder. The two exchanged a meaningful look, before Mr. Spigot gave a solemn nod.

Augum, still holding tight to Leera, instantly knew what had transpired between the two men.

"He threatened his daughters ..." Bridget said in a horrified whisper.

Mr. Spigot raised his only arm, still lit with Shine, but did not light his rings. His lower lip trembled slightly as his eyes fell upon Robin. "I am ready," he said in a barely audible voice.

"Kill him, Robin!" Temper shouted, but no one had joined her. It was total silence as Robin's arm flared to life with *three* fiery bands—somehow, to Augum's total dismay, he had leapt past them in study! It also meant he was now studying the 4th degree!

Robin reached out. "Vikari Vikarei!"

Mr. Spigot's right hand began to blacken and rot. He winced but stood his ground.

Robin pointed at the air and made a swooping gesture at Mr. Spigot. "Itak oos iu azim!"

A small ghostly specter appeared from up high, yielding a dagger. It swooped down and slashed at Mr. Spigot's neck. Blood began to spurt. Still, Mr. Spigot held his ground, though his eyes watered and his legs shook. His palm light began to flicker.

"It's some kind of necromancy," Augum whispered.

"No!" Garryk cried. "Please, stop it, just stop it!"

"Damn you, finish it!" Augum cried. "Can't you see he's not resisting!"

"Finish it." Boots offered his sword hilt first, but Robin smacked it aside. He brought his hands together, opening his palms at the last moment. "Annihilo!"

VALOR

A jet of fire shot out, slamming into Mr. Spigot's chest. The man started screaming as it burned through his black and gold robe. He fell to his knees, shaking, mouth open, eyes tightly closed, flames licking his chin. "I love you Mary, Lisa, Cathy ..."

"Finish him already, you coward—!" Augum shouted, but Robin only stood there, a malicious smile on his face. "You ever see something so funny, Temper? Look at him writhe around like that."

Not even Temper laughed this time. "Maybe you should kill him already, Robbie."

Like his teacher, Garryk had also fallen to his knees. Tears streamed down his cheeks, dripping onto the book in his hands. His thick spectacles barely hung onto the end of his nose.

Bridget covered her eyes. "What horror. I can't watch."

Leera, now cognizant again, let go of Augum and drew Bridget into an embrace. "It'll be over soon."

Boots shook his head. "Commander, this isn't right—" but Tridian said nothing. Boots strode forth. "I've had enough—" and impaled Mr. Spigot with his blade.

"No! He was mine to kill!" Robin snarled.

Boots yanked his sword. "Then you should have done it already."

Mr. Spigot's lit palm flickered out and he fell back, clutching his ale gut.

"Shyneo." Robin's palm lit up with fire, casting the area in orange light.

Nefra's tongue rattled in the darkness. "Unworthy ... I shall not be deprived ..."

There was a quick scuttling sound. Something small charged from the darkness and pounced before any of them could do anything. Soon there was another and another, until Boots was on the ground, screaming.

Temper backed away. "Gods, giant rats ..."

Raina and Spiller began frantically slashing at the things with their daggers, but by the time they killed them all, Boots lay dead.

A thick silence fell upon them as they stared at the grisly body, until Horrick resumed his dreaded shuffling, stopping before a weeping Garryk.

"N-n-no p-p-please n-n-not m-m-me …"

"Thou shalt prove thyself in single combat."

"Not him!" Bridget called. "Please, anyone but him!"

Robin smiled. "Your turn, Wart …"

"Monstrous …" Leera murmured, shaking her head. "This is all so monstrous …"

Horrick stopped before the Blade of Sorrows.

"Thou shalt prove thyself in single combat."

Tridian gave a derisive snort. "Prove myself …"

"Take mercy!" Bridget flailed in Leera's grip. "Please, this is so horribly wrong!"

Tridian stepped over Mr. Spigot's gasping body. The man was still alive, though barely.

"N-n-n-n-n-n—" Garryk couldn't form even a single word now. He sat frozen, staring at the Blade of Sorrows' sleek Dreadnought blade, at his looming and grotesque presence.

"Sacrifices have to be made for the betterment of the Legion, boy. Do not worry, I shall make it quick."

"N-n-n-n-n-n—"

Bridget suddenly stopped struggling. "The vial …" She frantically dug around in her robes and brought out the rest of the Golden Vitae.

"But where did—" Leera began.

"I grabbed it along with the map, but never mind that, we can save him after; we'll just have to be quick—"

"Face me, boy!"

"N-n-n-n-n-n—"

Horrick shuffled near Garryk. "Dost thou refuse, Unworthy?"

VALOR

"Face him or you'll both die!" Temper said.

"N-n-n-n-n-n—" Garryk was shaking head to toe now. His books slipped from his clutches and his spectacles fell to the floor.

"Just lop off his head, Commander!" Robin called.

"Thou shalt duel or thou shalt both perish, feckless loafer."

"He's choosing not to fight ..." Leera said in an incredulous voice.

"Face me or we both die!" Tridian roared.

"N-n-n-n-n—" Suddenly Garryk stopped shaking and gave Tridian a serene look. "No."

Nefra's tongue rattled. "I shall not be deprived ..."

"Stupid boy!" Tridian raised his blade.

At the same time, Augum shot his hand out. "Disablo!" The blade yanked itself from Tridian's grip and came clanging to the ground between them.

Tridian shot Augum a murderous look.

Temper screamed and began jumping from foot to foot.

"Rats!" Spiller called. "Everywhere!" They streamed in from the darkness, squealing and sniffing at the air.

Robin sent a rat flying with a kick of his boot. "Commander—watch out!"

Torrents of them lunged at Tridian and Garryk, though the vast majority fell on Tridian. The trio ran to help, using kicks, punches and every spell in their arsenal to get them off Garryk. Robin, Temper, Raina and Spiller did the same for Tridian, who in a rage had begun running blindly into the darkness, his entourage in pursuit.

At last, they managed to clear Garryk of the rats, but he had been bitten all over his face, neck and hands, and was gasping, eyes unfocused.

Augum jumped into action. "Put pressure on the wounds!"

"He's losing blood fast," Bridget said. "We have to be quick. Here's the Golden Vitae. Leera, find a dish. Aug, grab me that dagger, I'll slice my hand like you did—"

She froze. "Mr. Spigot, did you say something?"

Mr. Spigot lay near in a bloody mess, still clutching his belly. His voice was barely audible. "You have ... Vitae?"

Bridget quickly nodded, hands pressed tightly on Garryk's neck. "Yes," Mr. Spigot, we have it right here, but ... but we do not have enough to save you both."

He winced and offered his blackened arm. "For ... Garryk."

Leera shot over with a wooden bowl. "Are you sure? This'll mean—"

"Do it ..."

"Thank you, Mr. Spigot." Leera lined up the bowl underneath and sliced his arm with Boots' dagger.

"Hurry, hurry ..." Bridget said, blood gushing between her fingers. The sight instantly transported Augum back to holding Mya's throat, trying to prevent her lifeblood from draining. Concentrate, he told himself. He tore strips of cloth from a linen shirt sticking out of one of the rucksacks and began binding what wounds he could find on Garryk's body.

"Stay with us, Garryk, stay with us!" Bridget yelled.

"Almost got it, Mr. Spigot, hang in there!" Leera said.

"My ... girls ... I'm ... sorry ..." Mr. Spigot's eyes remained open, but he was gone. Behind them, the doors remained closed. Apparently, Nefra needed one more death for them to open.

"His heart stopped pumping—!" Leera said. "I don't know if I have enough!"

Bridget used one hand to quickly unstop the vial with her teeth. "Bring it, bring it quick! Augum, help—"

As soon as Leera hurried over, Augum poured the Golden Vitae into the bowl.

VALOR

"Hurry, feed it to him!" Bridget said, holding up his head while pressing on his wounds. Augum placed the bowl to Garryk's lips and slowly tipped it.

Leera readied more strips of cloth. "I think they're coming back—"

"This is it," Augum said. "This might be our only chance. I say we take Horrick and destroy that recipe—"

"Agreed," Leera said. "I'll get the orb and the books."

"Hand me those strips, Aug," Bridget said once she was done feeding Garryk the concoction. She hurriedly began binding his wounds, starting with the boy's mangled neck and face.

"Go go go—!" Leera said as she grabbed what she could.

Augum and Bridget hauled Garryk up, putting his arms around their necks and dragged him along.

Horrick!" Augum called. "Open that door!"

"As ye wish, vile usurper."

"Hurry ..." Leera was saying, running ahead to the closed bronze doors.

Horrick shuffled along.

"Quickly, Horrick!"

"As ye desire, useless unworthy," but his pace barely changed.

Augum looked back to see two shining hands in the darkness moving quickly toward them.

Horrick stepped up to the doors and waved them aside. They immediately began to rumble open. Leera squeezed in first followed by Bridget and Augum, Garryk hanging between them.

"Get in here, Horrick!" Augum called. "And close the doors!"

Horrick stepped inside as a blast of fire hit his back, doing no damage. The ancient armor turned around and waved the doors closed. Augum lowered Garryk to the floor and pointed his wrists at the opening. "Annihilo!"

SEVER BRONNY

The soldiers, Robin and Temper jumped aside as a lightning blast shot through the crack of the doors. Just before they closed, Augum saw the bolt smash into the Blade of Sorrows, his rotten face twisted with malice.

THE LABORATORIUM

Augum leaned against the doors, panting, feeling muted thuds from the other side. There was no time to relax though—Tridian and the others would find a way to get through, even if they had to play another one of Nefra's games to do it. Too bad the Blade of Sorrows survived Nefra's rat attack. Augum had no illusions that his First Offensive did any damage either.

He shone his palm light around. Before him was a long dusty table, on top of which sat scores of odd-shaped beakers and decanters. Shelves stood tall, crammed with books, scrolls, and exotic ingredients. Nearby, a large stone mortar and pestle sat on its own carved stand.

"Oh no, I forgot his spectacles—" Bridget said, tying up the last of Garryk's wounds. The boy was unconscious, face pale.

"We'll just have to manage," Augum said.

Leera dropped her rucksack and withdrew the Orb of Orion. "Damn spell *still* hasn't worn off ..."

"Do we have any provisions?" Augum asked.

"No food or water," Leera replied, "but I managed to nab our two books. Couldn't get Garryk's in time though."

"Guess we'll worry about that later then."

"I wonder why Nefra didn't stop us from coming in here," Bridget said.

Leera shrugged. "Who knows, though I bet it's more fun for her this way. Now she can pick us off twice as fast."

Augum looked into the darkness ahead. "Let's get to the other side of this room. We can leave our things there while we search for the recipe, that way if they get through, we'll just move to the other room."

"Good idea." Bridget snagged the first book she got her hands on off the table.

"What are you doing?" Leera asked.

"Making an alarm in case they get through." She leaned the book up against the crack of the doors and kneeled, laying open palms on the book. "Concutio del alarmo."

"All right, let's go," Augum said when she was done. "Horrick, follow us." He lifted Garryk, placing one of the boy's arms around his neck. Bridget quickly came to support the other side, and they hauled the unconscious boy off, necrophyte robe dragging. Leera, carrying the rucksacks, lit the way while Horrick shuffled along behind.

"Spooky in here," she said as they passed large stoppered jars with deformed creatures floating within. At least one of them looked like a human baby. Suddenly she let out a shriek. "One of those eyeballs moved!"

"It was just your imagination," Bridget said, huffing. "Place hasn't been used for fifteen-hundred years." Though Augum noticed she kept her gaze averted.

They passed a stack of barrels that had leaked a dark oozing liquid over the centuries.

"How are we going to find the recipe in this place?" Leera asked. "It's huge …"

VALOR

Augum awkwardly shone his light at the ceiling, but it was too high up. The walls were also too far. "I don't know, maybe with Unconceal?"

"This is *Occulus* we're talking about here." As she passed, Leera shone her light at a large array of flasks linked together. "I doubt he'd just hide it normally. If anything, it'd be protected by layers of arcanery."

Augum spied a long row of potions in the darkness, glittering like stars.

"Stop—" Bridget whispered, breathless. She nodded ahead. "What's that?"

Leera raised her palms. Two eyes reflected her light back from the darkness.

"Who are you?" Augum called out, but whatever it was did not move. "Let's just keep going, but slowly." Maybe it was a statue ...

They took one step at a time, until Leera's light revealed a beast of unknown origin. It had mangled limbs and cat eyes, but its head was like a misshapen bear's.

"I don't think it's alive," Augum said. "Let's keep going."

The thing did not move as they warily pushed past it. They snaked their way through a maze of strange obstacles—large cubes appearing to be made of flesh; curving walls with bone arms that stuck out; and rows and rows of wooden cabinets full of oddly-shaped teeth, bones, skulls, and what looked like rolled skin.

At last, they found another large pair of bronze doors depicting a figure rising from the ground. They gently lowered an unconscious Garryk to the floor.

"Is this really our only way out of this room?" Leera asked.

Augum nodded. "That's what the map showed. Horrick, is the recipe in here?"

"Mine villainous unworthy asks an unanswerable query."

"He's like Fentwick," Leera said. "Simple questions only."

Bridget raised her palm. "Shyneo," and a shining vine curled around her fingers and wrist. "Let's just hope that recipe is in here."

Leera placed the rucksacks near Garryk. "I hate to say it, but the only way to search this place quickly is to split up."

They exchanged tentative looks, perhaps each hoping the other would demand they go as a group. No one spoke up. Augum knew she was right—they simply had to take a calculated risk.

Bridget glanced down at Garryk lying motionless. "Will it be safe to leave him here?"

"Horrick, guard this boy," Augum said.

"As my unworthy fouling wishes."

"Shyneo." Augum's palm lit up with crackling lightning. "If anyone gets in trouble or if you find the recipe, call out." Wishing each other good luck, they went their separate ways.

Augum picked the near wall and began searching shelves, lecterns, cabinets and chests of drawers—all without success. He refrained from opening any sarcophagi, of which he found more than a few, some disturbingly small. He used Unconceal often, but nothing panned out. He'd often catch one of the girls' lights out of the corner of his eye, searching distantly like beacon fires. Judging by the dead silence, they weren't having any luck either.

After pushing aside a large barrel with Telekinesis, he spotted a pair of shining eyes again. This time, he approached without hesitation, finding a hulking man-like beast with a pointy horse head. Its arms and legs were massive, making the torso appear small by comparison. As he examined it closer, he spotted seams at the joints, sewn together rather crudely, though the hide was real. A thick bronze chain hung around its neck, a runic emblem on the pendant.

VALOR

His eyes took note of a fat bronze ring sitting on a table amongst a sheaf of vellum. It had the same emblem as the collar. On a hunch, he picked it up, took a few steps back from the beast, and slowly placed the ring on his left hand. The ring was so large he had to make a fist to prevent it from falling off.

There was a strange ethereal tug similar to casting Unconceal coming from the beast. His finger tingled, though he didn't know if that was from the cold bronze or from something else.

"Do something," he told the beast. "Lift that barrel," but it only stood there. Ring had to be broken, he thought. Or maybe it worked with certain commands. He glanced at the barrel. Or maybe ...

He imagined the beast picking the barrel up. The moment the thought concluded, the thing strode past him and picked the barrel up.

"Awesome!" He imagined it throwing the barrel at a nearby table. The beast did so, and the barrel splintered, coughing out a slew of animal bones.

"What's happening!" Bridget shrieked.

"Oh, it's fine—I just found a new pet!"

"What!"

"You'll see! Keep searching!"

He turned to the beast standing completely still before him. "I think I'll call you Osbert," the name he had given the first horse he learned to ride with Sir Westwood—and because Horsehead was a dumb name.

Augum kept looking, though his attention was somewhat divided between commanding the beast and keeping an eye out for the recipe. He was clumsy with it at first, upending tables and knocking over shelves, though he soon learned he actually had to imagine it stepping over or going around obstacles.

In another time and place, he pictured some wicked pranks he could play with it.

"I think I found it!" Leera waved her lit arm. "Over here!"

They quickly converged at her location.

Leera immediately pointed behind Augum. "What is that!"

"Osbert. He's our new pet." He held up his left hand. "I can command it with thoughts using this ring. Maybe he can help us somehow, especially with defense. Anyway, never mind him, what have you found?"

Leera light up an area behind her, revealing a great podium on top of which sat a highly ornate black oak desk. "Let's see what it is—" but she froze the moment she placed a foot on the steps, face pale, pupils dilating. Her mouth steadily opened and she began screaming, louder and louder.

Augum and Bridget yanked her back and she fell, shivering. "It was ... horrible. Horrible ..."

Augum helped Leera stand.

"It's been cursed with Fear." She gestured vaguely at her head. "Couldn't block the spell though. Too powerful." She glanced at the podium while holding herself, still shivering. "I saw myself ..." She looked to Augum, face as white as snow. "I *saw* myself burning alive on that step. It was ... it was so real ..."

He gave her a quick hug. "I'm just glad you're okay."

Bridget reached out a hand and arcanely tried to pull the desk, but it didn't move. "Telekinesis doesn't work."

Leera nodded at the horse beast. "What about that thing."

"Osbert, come here," but it didn't move. "Oh, right, it's not like Horrick." Augum imagined Osbert walking up the steps, then watched as the beast did exactly that, all the way up to the desk. He imagined it gingerly picking the desk up and slowly bringing it to them. Its muscles strained as it ripped the desk from the floor. Bolts tumbled as he paced back down, seemingly unaffected by the curse.

VALOR

"I think I want one of my own," Leera said as Osbert dumped it before them.

On top of the desk was a black iron tablet engraved in an unfamiliar language. The contours were smooth and sleek, with golden ivy adorning the borders—but it was the symbol at the top that captured their attention.

"That's the Helix!" Bridget said. "The symbol for Ley. This has to be it—this is the recipe!"

Augum reached for it, but Bridget grabbed his arm. "Don't—it could still be enchanted or cursed or something."

"I'll get Osbert to do it." He imagined Osbert picking up the tablet. The moment his unnatural hands touched it, a series of huge thin blades swung across the podium, some from the floor and some from the ceiling, built to miss the desk but slice anyone standing near it.

"Classic," Leera said dryly.

"Occulus would have cast Object Alarm on it," Bridget added.

Leera snorted. "Yeah, well, too bad he's dead."

Augum imagined that skeleton back at the Occi camp suddenly getting up from his throne. He worked up the courage and plucked the recipe from Osbert's grip, waiting to be struck down by something.

But nothing happened.

It felt heavy and ice cold. He glanced around. "Should we, you know ... destroy it now?"

They thought the matter over silently.

"Yes," Bridget said at last, taking the tablet from him. "We're going to destroy it anyway, right? Might as well do it now." She ran her fingers over the carving. "Seems kind of a shame though, it's so full of ... history."

"No, we're not giving it to the academy to study, Bridge," Leera said.

"Of course we aren't! I was only saying how important an artifact it is—"

"What if there are copies?" Augum asked. It was a simple question, but one that gave them pause.

"We can't worry about that," Bridget said. "Now how to destroy a piece of iron …"

"A forge," Leera replied. "It's the only way."

Augum glanced at the far wall. "There was a smithy on the map next to the Laboratorium, but the only way to get there is through the Legion."

"But then there's the challenge of firing it up," Leera said, "and a forge takes a long time to heat up."

"Unless it's arcane," Bridget said.

"Right, so there's that route …" Augum took a breath. "Or we can take our chances through the spawnery. I remember the map showing a back passage that returned to the sentinel room."

Bridget picked up the tablet. "Even with Osbert, it's too risky to fight the Legion, especially with Garryk injured. We have to go through the spawnery. Maybe it's dormant or something."

"Let's go then," Augum said.

"I think I'd have preferred a fight," Leera muttered as they made their way back to Garryk. The boy greeted them with glazed open eyes.

"You're awake!" Bridget said.

He swallowed weakly. "What … what happened …"

She explained everything while changing some of his bandages. Most of his wounds had healed, though not all, especially not the one on his neck.

"Thank you for … saving me …" Garryk said when she finished. His eyes wandered to the iron tablet. "What's that …?"

"We think it's the recipe." Augum held it near. "It's really important, but can you confirm it?"

Garryk was already out of breath. It was obvious it also hurt him to talk. "Need … spectacles …"

"I'm sorry but we left them behind," Bridget said.

VALOR

Augum held the tablet closer.

"Ancient Tiberran ... Yes, it is ... the recipe ..."

They exchanged relieved looks.

"We're going to go through the spawnery," Augum said, "and loop around to the smithy."

"Hurry then ... Lord Sparkstone ... is coming ..."

Suddenly Bridget's head whipped around to stare back into the darkness. Her voice was full of quiet urgency. "The alarm ... they're inside."

She and Augum lifted Garryk while Leera commanded Horrick to open the doors to the spawnery. They rumbled open, sending a hot blast of steam in their direction.

"Get in," Augum said, hearing shouts from the back of the room. He imagined Osbert following.

The sleek stone floor gave way to rock slabs, and then, ahead of them, squishy moss. The air here was strangely warm and moist.

"Close the doors, Horrick," Leera commanded in a whisper.

"As mine vile unworthy witch commands."

The rushing of warm air died down as the great bronze doors rumbled closed.

Leera pinched her nose. "Putrid. Stinks like a bog in here." The moment she stepped on the moss, there was a muted groan. She recoiled as the moss began to move. A hand shot out and gripped the ground, pulling itself up.

"Undead!" Bridget cried out, pulling Garryk back along with Augum. They lowered the boy and lit up their palms. The thing gurgled another moan, spitting up dirt. Its flesh was black and rotten and wet with debris from the earth. Bones were visible through its rags. Its ancient breastplate had the crest of a jousting knight.

"A walker," Augum said, mentally commanding Osbert to come forth.

Bridget backed away. "The crest ... he's Canterran."

"Scion ... war ..." Garryk gasped from the ground.

Osbert grabbed the walker by its bone arms just as it freed itself from the ground. The walker flailed, jaws clacking, but was not strong enough to escape Osbert's iron grip.

"How do we kill it?" Leera asked.

"Fire ..." Garryk replied. "Or strong ... arcanery ..."

Leera slammed her wrists together, palms open. "Annihilo!" A powerful jet of water slammed into the head, blasting it apart. The walker fell to the ground in a heap of bones. "That ... that worked!"

Augum ran to the walls and began examining them.

"What are you looking for?" Bridget asked.

"A torch rune." All along the walls, human rib cages covered what had to be torches. He quickly found what he was looking for—a depiction of a torch above a rune. "Here! Is this it?"

Bridget ran over. "Yes, but did we ever figure out the trigger word for torch? I can't remember."

Leera dropped her rucksack. "Let's check." Bridget ran to her side and the pair began rifling through Mrs. Stone's blue book on arcaneology.

Augum saw movement behind Osbert. "Another one's rising!" He imagined Osbert grabbing it and squeezing the walker's head. Osbert did as he was commanded, snatching the flailing thing by the head. There was a crunching sound and the walker fell to the ground in a heap. But there were echoes of distant noises now. Inhuman noises ...

"Horrick, defend us against the walkers!" Augum called as another walker rose where Leera had been only moments before.

"As mine vile unworthy guest commands." Horrick stepped between them and the walker, releasing his wooden practice blade. The moment the undead thing was free of the earth, it sprinted forward. Horrick met it with an expert blow to the shins. It fell on top of him and the pair fought.

VALOR

"I got it!" Bridget tore away to the rune and slammed her palm against it. "Firemente!" but nothing happened.

"Don't forget to envision it!" Leera said, hurriedly packing the book.

"Oh, right—Firemente!"

One by one, torches burst into life, quickly circling the room. As the darkness was beaten back, it was replaced by hundreds of forms, and every single one was moving. Some of these forms were gargantuan demons, so large they had to duck below the vaulted ceiling. Some had mangled wings, others malformed limbs. Every one of them looked like it had crawled up from hell.

Bridget went pale as death. "Gods help us ... We have to go back!"

Leera was steadily retreating. "They'll get the recipe though!"

Augum saw a sea of movement. Moss quivered and trembled as more things began to dig their way up from the ground. "I don't believe it ... it's an entire army!" They had no choice now. "We have to go back!" Behind him, he could hear muted thumping on the doors, with an echo of rattling laughter. Tridian and Robin had to be just on the other side.

"Lee, help me pick up Garryk!" Bridget called.

The undead throng began running their way, the walkers—the fastest among them—leading the charge.

Augum made the shoving gesture. "Baka!" and the walker that was pinning Horrick to the ground flew off him. He then slammed his palms together, aiming at the next closest walker. "Annihilo!" blasting a leg off with a shot of lightning. It rabidly continued crawling toward them though.

"Horrick, open the doors!" he shouted.

"As ye wish, unworthy and uncouth scoundrel."

"Just hurry!—"

Horrick shuffled along before making a motion at the doors. They rumbled open.

Augum heard a flurry of activity behind him, but his focus remained on the surging army. Suddenly a terrible rush ran up his spine with the realization that Horrick wouldn't get the doors closed in time once they were through.

"Augum, the recipe, they're com—!" but Leera's voice was suddenly muffled, as if someone had grabbed her mouth.

Augum did the only thing he could think of—he flung the iron tablet as far as he could into the horde, before bringing his hands together.

"Annihilo!" In the space of a moment, he focused the surge on the advancing walkers. He pushed his boundaries, tapping into every last reserve of energy he had. His heart thundered as the arcanery peaked—and broke through. He felt as if his insides were sucking inwards and being propelled through his palms—and he couldn't stop it. His entire being exploded electrically and uncontrollably—he glimpsed moss being flung along with the first wave of walkers, before his palms exploded, sending him flying back. He felt a sickening thud and all went black.

A HARD DECISION

"He's still out cold," Augum heard Temper say. Her foul breath had been enough to wake him. "Got to admit, that was some spell." When he heard her trundle off, he opened his eyes.

He lay on his side on a cold stone floor, hands tied behind his back, breath fogging. His head throbbed and his body ached. Torch fire rustled within ribbed cages nearby, illuminating a tall corner with two royal crimson settees. A marble bust on a pedestal stood in between, depicting a man with an iron stare. Bridget and Leera sat tied on one of the settees, mouths gagged with cloth, fur coats scorched.

Leera subtly elbowed Bridget and they glanced Augum's way.

"When'll the commander return with His Lordship you think?" Temper asked absently. She was behind him, and apparently picking at her nails.

"When he's good and ready," Raina said in clipped tones.

"Place gives me the creeps."

Raina made no reply.

Temper spat on the floor. "Do you think we'll at least get some reward?"

"You disgust me. If you were my daughter, I would have given you the throttling of your life for such a show of disrespect."

Temper sighed. "I only spat on the floor. Wow, it's not like it's the end of the world or anything. Don't be so serious."

There was a tense silence as Augum imagined Raina glaring at Temper. He strained his peripheral vision, trying to see around without moving. A muddy foot lay near. Was it Garryk's?

"This is boring. Why can't we just kill them?" Temper went on.

"You thick little brat. Would you prefer to be the one killed in one of the witch's games? We've lost enough soldiers. Now we have to wait until His Lordship arrives."

Temper leaned over. "He took a bunch of them, but did you see him almost explode himself doing it?"

Augum twitched from the memory of a powerful blue flash emanating from his palms, so powerful it had sent him flying back.

"He's awake," Raina said. "Drag him up."

Temper grabbed Augum's shoulders and roughly sat him up, cackling to herself.

He spotted Garryk and gasped—his eyes were closed and he was wrapped in new, blood-soaked bandages.

"Oh, don't like your own work?" Temper said with an evil smile. "You should be proud—even questioners wish they were that good at pain while keeping someone alive."

No no no no no no ... Mrs. Stone had warned him how dangerous wild arcanery could be, and now he'd done something so horrible it made him woozy. Temper shoved him back to the ground, but all he felt was an overwhelming nausea that churned his stomach. He had hurt poor Garryk, hurt him terribly.

VALOR

"We should end his misery," Raina said.

"Robin wants him alive for questioning. You better do what he says, because one day he'll be your commander. You know, he doesn't look right without his spectacles, does he? Kind of dumb."

Augum barely heard what they were saying—the blood shooting past his ears was deafening. What had he done? It was unforgivable ...

"Drag him back up," Raina said. "We have to question him too."

"This'll be fun." Temper yanked him up. He was limp in her arms, mouth hanging open, silently cursing himself a thousand times over. Bridget and Leera were moaning through their gags, no doubt furious with him.

Temper made an impatient sound with her teeth and let Augum fall back to the floor again. She strolled over to the girls, grabbing a handfuls of raven and cinnamon hair and sharply tugging.

"Shut. Up. Get it?" Temper gave one more yank before letting go. She marched back to Augum and dragged him to a sitting position.

Raina paced over and kneeled before him. "They said you threw the recipe into the horde. Is this true?"

He tried to focus on her, but all he saw was Garryk's blood-soaked bandages. That's what wild lightning does, that's why it's so dangerous. Now you know, fool. Now you know ...

Raina's hard jaw flexed. "Are you going to make me repeat myself?"

"Hit him!" Temper said. "You'll see it feels good."

Raina spoke through gritted teeth, still focused on Augum. "He is the lord's son. The lord is on his way here now. Think. Use that oafish carrot brain of yours."

"Yeah, but Robin said—"

"Enough!" She gave Temper a cold glance. "I will do the talking. You will keep an eye out for the witch. Is. That. Clear?"

Temper gave an annoyed grunt. "Keep sitting up." She maliciously pinched Augum's sides before standing, arms folded.

He barely felt the pain, nor did he care about her little amusements. He had done a great wrong, a wrong no one would ever be able to erase.

"Now, boy, did you or did you not throw the tablet into the horde?"

"You just repeated yourself," Temper mumbled, but Raina ignored her.

The soldier slowly grabbed Augum's coat and brought him near. He got a subtle whiff of scented berry oil and roasted meat. "Just because I do not think it wise to harm you, does not mean the same for your …" she glanced at the girls, "… friends."

"Yeah, that's right!" Temper kicked Leera, who surrendered a muffled gasp.

"Don't you touch her!" Augum struggled in Raina's iron grip.

"Then answer the question," Raina said in a deadly whisper.

"Yes, I threw it into the horde! And you'll never get it out."

"You are a fool."

Suddenly Augum remembered a beast with a horse's head. Was Osbert still back in the spawnery? And the ring—was it still on his finger? He couldn't tell because his hands were numb from the rope. There was only one way to find out—he envisioned Osbert walking from out of the darkness, grabbing Raina, and throwing her against the wall.

"What are you looking over there for, look at me when I'm talking to you!" Raina grabbed his jaw and yanked it back. She glared at him, features as chiseled as the hard bust

VALOR

in the corner. "Where's that crone of yours? Can we find her with the orb?"

No, he thought, but she can find you as soon as that Sphere of Protection spell wears off ...

"Maybe it *is* time your friends suffered for your silence—" but suddenly a great pair of hands clamped around Raina's neck and pulled. Augum witnessed the veins bulge on her forehead before she was sent flying against the wall, slamming into it with a dull thud and crashing to the ground, still as pond water.

"Baka! Baka! Baka!" Temper screeched, flailing her arms in a windmill pattern. Predictably, the spell had no effect, as she hadn't performed the correct gesture. Augum envisioned Osbert slamming an open palm into Temper's stupid face. A moment later, there was a tremendous smacking sound and she was sent sprawling with a yelp. Augum then envisioned Osbert picking her up with one hand and gagging her with the other. The task was clumsily done the moment the thought concluded.

Bridget and Leera were struggling while he sidled his way over to Raina's unconscious body. He turned himself around and grabbed her dagger, using it to cut through the rope. Once he was free, he did the same for Bridget and Leera.

"Aug, you didn't do it!" Leera was sputtering.

"She lied—" Bridget added quickly.

"What are you talking about?"

"Garryk—it was Robin that cast the First Offensive at him."

Augum didn't know how to feel. There was a sense of relief, but it didn't changed the fact that poor Garryk was suffering horribly and again on the brink of death.

"I wish we still had some Golden Vitae," Bridget said, kneeling by the boy's side.

"We need to get out of here," Leera said. "Aug? Concentrate."

"Right." He glanced at Raina's still form. "Where are Tridian, Robin and the other guard?"

Leera and Bridget began tying up Temper, who struggled in Osbert's powerful grip, a giant hand clamped over her mouth. One entire side of her face was beet red from the slap.

Meanwhile, Augum tied up Raina.

"Spiller's dead," Leera said. "He got locked in with the horde. And Tridian and Robin went back to the doors with Horrick. I think they want to try to get the recipe. They could be back any moment though." She nodded at Osbert's hands clamped around Temper's mouth. "Make him let go so we I can gag her."

Soon as Augum gave the thought commands, Temper gave Leera a head butt, only to break her own nose doing it.

Leera rubbed her head from Temper's clumsy attempt, smirking all the while. "Serves you right." She shoved a cloth in Temper's mouth and tied it around her head.

Augum spotted Leera's rucksack. "The orb—is it in there?"

"Yes, still enclosed though."

"We have to make a decision—we go for the recipe before my father gets here or make a run for it."

"We have one injured already," Bridget said. "Garryk needs help as soon as possible, and we don't know how long it'll be before the Orb of Orion is free of that spell, or even if Mrs. Stone can get us out of here. Though if your father gets that recipe …"

Augum glanced between Bridget and Leera. Dark circles ringed their eyes, their faces were gaunt, and they had to be at least as thirsty and hungry as he was. Yet Garryk fared much worse—his forehead was red and he was shivering, perhaps from fever, and the bandages were dripping blood. A decision *had* to be made …

He grabbed the other rucksack and handed it to Bridget. "You two take Garryk through the throne room and on to

Occulus' quarters. There might be an escape portal there. If not, hide and wait for Sphere of Protection to expire. I'll come as soon as I can, but if you run into trouble, don't wait for me. There's one closed door to go through, and you know what that means ..."

Leera stood. "No, we face them together. We stand a better chance that way."

"And leave Garryk here alone? What if my father comes? They won't harm me, but you two ..." He left it unsaid. "I can do this."

"He's right, Lee, we can't risk it," Bridget said.

Leera gave him an angry look. "Have to play hero, do you?" and stormed past to check on Raina's bonds.

Bridget gave him a sympathetic smile. "We'll do our best, Aug. How will you find us?"

"I'll cast Object Track on the orb like you did."

She helped him withdraw it from the rucksack and he went through the motions and imagery associated with the spell. "Vestigio itemo discovaro."

"Leave ... me ..." Garryk wheezed when Augum finished. "My ... family ..."

Bridget gently took his hand. "They'll kill you, or use you in one of Nefra's sacrifices. We're taking you along whether you like it or not." She turned back to Augum as Garryk made a disagreeing moan. "Aug ... be careful."

He held up his hand with the fat ring. "I have this. Should keep Tridian busy." Leaving him to face Robin ...

Leera stomped back and suddenly wrapped her arms around him. "You brave fool." She kissed his cheek quickly and let go, pacing to Garryk and gently lifting him up.

Bridget hugged him too. "Don't be afraid to run. We'll see you soon."

He watched them struggle with Garryk, wondering if he'd see them again.

THE HORDE AND THE PRETENDER

Augum prowled into the laboratorium, often checking over his shoulder to make sure Osbert wasn't too far behind. Keeping the creature quiet with nothing but thought was proving a challenge, so he kept him well back. His heavy winter coat was a burden, but if they were going to escape into the icy wilderness, it would be needed to keep him alive.

He soon spotted orange light on the far side of the room—it had to be Robin's palm. Had they opened the doors to the spawnery yet? As he crept closer, he began to make out their voices.

"I don't know how he did it, Commander," Robin was saying. "Maybe it was the stupid talking armor thing." His palm light fell upon Horrick, who stood near, silent as the grave.

Tridian paced. "We cannot afford to play another of her games—"

VALOR

"I can hear them on the other side. There's too many of them. Lord Sparkstone will be here any—"

"Do not doubt my new-found strength, Apprentice."

They were standing right in front of the doors—Augum saw his chance and took it.

"Horrick, open the doors to the spawnery!" he shouted.

"As mine baseborn inferior guest commands." Horrick made a gesture and the doors began to rumble open, spilling torchlight through the ever-widening crack. There was the sound of clacking and growling as arms struggled to get through.

"You take the boy, I'll get the recipe," Tridian said, as if expecting Augum's arrival all along.

"Yes, Commander." Robin grinned and strode in Augum's direction. "Show yourself, gutterborn!" He checked to make sure the horde hadn't made it past Tridian. The Commander's thin Dreadnought blade deftly zipped through the air, sending limbs and torsos flying. So far, none made it through.

"You'll pay for what you did to Mya," Augum called out from the darkness, unable to keep the bitterness from his voice.

"Ooo, I'm scared." Robin's left hand went into a pocket and he withdrew the Destiny Stone.

"Should have had the banyan beast smash your head in when we had the chance."

"You didn't because you're a weak fool. Now why don't you stop cowering and come out to play."

"Shyneo." Augum's palm lit up as he stepped out, keeping Osbert in the shadows. He wanted a face-to-face match. His fist clenched as his two lightning rings ruptured to life around his arm.

Robin scoffed at Augum's display, lighting up his three fiery rings. Suddenly he slammed his hands together. "Annihilo!" but Augum was ready, summoning his arcane shield. The fire blasted off, the force making Augum grunt.

Robin immediately leapt into another spell. "Itak oos iu azim!"

Augum remembered this spell and rolled away from the swooping specter, its dagger barely missing his neck. He shoved the air before him. "Baka!" but Robin summoned his own shield made of glowing embers, and leaned into the force of the spell, holding his ground.

"Vakari vikarei!" Robin shouted the moment the shield disappeared.

Augum cried out as his left leg began to burn in the same spot Robin had burned before, back at Hangman's Rock. He fell to the ground and quickly raised the hem of his woolen pant. The area had blackened. The loss of concentration had snuffed his Shine spell.

Robin made a sweeping gesture. "Closs pesti!" summoning a swarm of wasps that shot forward.

Augum scrambled to get away but slipped on his bad leg. The swarm descended on him like an angry cloud. He rolled and swatted madly, taking dozens of stings, before plowing into a shelf of ingredients. It fell over with a great crash, smashing bottles and jars around him. When the swarm cleared, he realized he hadn't been stung it all—it had been an illusion.

"Dreadus terrablus!" Robin called, but Augum immediately used Mind Armor to shield his mind from the terrifying effects of Fear, then used Telekinesis to send the knocked-over shelf flying at Robin, who had to duck as it flew past. The effort of it had pushed Augum's boundary—he'd never done anything like that before, especially in combo with Mind Armor.

Robin made to throw at the ground. "Grau!" There was the sound of an immense fireball, so real Augum couldn't help but roll aside. Robin used the dodge as an opportunity to crash another shelf on top of Augum with Telekinesis. This one was full of mortar and pestles—one struck Augum over the head. A blinding light erupted behind his eyes.

VALOR

So this was what a real warlock duel was like. Everything was happening so fast—no time to think.

"Voidus aurus!" Robin shouted, steadily marching towards Augum, hand held forward. But Augum, again thanks to Mrs. Stone's difficult training, blocked the Deafness spell with Mind Armor.

"Why isn't it working—!" Robin shouted, running forth and withdrawing a dagger. "I'll slice your throat like I sliced that wench's—"

Those words made Augum see red, but he forced himself to focus and made a quick yanking gesture. "Disablo!" The blade went skittering across the floor.

Robin put his hands together. "Annihilo!" and another blast of fire shot toward him. Augum rolled underneath a toppled shelf and it exploded in flame.

Robin winced as he clutched the side of his head. "Annihilo!" he said again, but this time nothing happened.

He had drained his arcane energies, Augum realized as he rolled from under the shelf. He made to shove at the air. "Baka!"

Robin made the shield gesture but summoned nothing, and instead was sent flying back, slamming into a shelf of vials with a crash. He picked himself up. "You damn gutter—" but was barreled over by a vicious charge from Augum.

The pair slammed into the same shelf, shattering more glass and shelving as they rolled together. Augum, who was used to wrestling with bullies since he was a boy, pinned Robin and rammed a fist into his face, breaking his nose. "That's for Mya—" then landed another punch, opening a large cut above Robin's right eye that began gushing blood. "And that's for Garryk—"

"Baka!" Robin said, but nothing happened. His face turned purple as Augum grabbed his neck and squeezed. "Commander ... help ..." Robin wheezed.

Somewhere behind them, the sounds of battle ceased. Suddenly Augum felt a tremendous kick and was sent flying off Robin, plowing into a pyramid of barrels. He tumbled through them, slamming into a table, breaking its legs and pinning him underneath. He made raspy noises, trying to inhale, but the wind had been knocked out of him.

The battle at the doors resumed quickly, Tridian shouting cries of victory with each swing of his sword.

"What the hell is that!" Robin wheezed.

Augum, who struggled to catch his breath, managed to shove aside the table in time to see the reflected torchlight on the ceiling crowded out by something gigantic.

"RUN!" Tridian yelled as the thing roared. The sound was so loud it shook the very floor. There was a great cracking and a swoosh—a giant block of stone smashed into the shelving nearby, rolling on and crushing everything in its path.

Augum felt a familiar creeping at the back of his mind and immediately slammed the door on it, just as Robin began screaming in sheer terror. The spell emanated from the giant beast and was strong, using up a lot of arcane stamina defending against it.

There was the sound of boots running. Augum pushed aside some of the debris in time to see Tridian making a hasty retreat, carrying a shrieking and bleeding Robin. He frantically made a shoving gesture at the Blade of Sorrows, but only managed to wheeze the Push incantation. Of course, nothing happened. He cursed, desperately wanting to get Robin, to stop him from getting away again. He wanted to keep smashing his fist into the idiot's face.

There was a monstrous grating noise behind him. He rolled to witness something huge with two horns duck underneath the giant door, barely squeezing through the frame. It was built like a giant bull with muscles as large and thick as castle columns. Around it flocked clacking walkers, shooting after Robin and Tridian. They flowed around Osbert as if he was a rock in a river.

Osbert. He had completely forgotten about Osbert!

Suddenly he realized that the horde hadn't yet spotted him behind all the debris, and he ducked. This was his chance, his *only* chance to get the recipe.

He had to let Robin go ... for now.

He quietly crawled on his hands and knees around shelves and desks as the giant demon bull sniffed at the air, blowing great blasts of steam through its nostrils. It flexed and began following the streams of walkers, each footfall sending tremors through the floor.

Augum scurried along the wall and hid behind a pedestal, on top of which sat a dusty vase. He checked his ankle and still found it to be black, but at least it didn't sting anymore. Luckily, Robin's necromantic spell casting was weak still, not to mention he didn't have the arcane stamina Augum had.

He gently massaged his temple. His head throbbed as if someone was pounding it with a giant hammer, but he forced himself to ignore the pain and concentrate on what was happening.

"Come forth, my darlings ..." Nefra's voice hissed in the darkness. "Sweet babes of the night ... The pretender this way comes ..." Her tongue rattled, the sound echoing off the walls.

Augum watched as streams of all kinds of monsters walked, slithered, limped and ran by. He dared not move a muscle, not even to breathe. All it'd take is one of them seeing him ...

At last the stream thinned to a trickle, until nothing walked by. He spotted Horrick standing by the other open door, watching him. Thankfully, the evil little rust bucket had not raised the alarm.

Augum envisioned Osbert walking up to the doors. Nothing disturbed the horse-headed beast as it stopped in the doorway.

He crept forward and peeked around the bronze frame, seeing an empty room, except for a fat lizard-like creature so wide it would hardly fit through the door. It was slowly slithering towards him on its belly. Its giant lizard eyes focused on him and it doubled its pace.

And there, between them, lay the iron tablet, shining in the torchlight.

He had to risk it ...

He imagined Osbert running at the lizard creature. The moment Osbert set off, Augum sprinted for the tablet. There was a squeal as the two beasts collided, except Augum had forgotten to have Osbert actually *do* something to it, and so the giant lizard simply knocked Osbert aside.

Augum got to the tablet first and snatched it up as the lizard opened its maw, shooting out a venom. It splashed on the moss, melting it with a hiss. He raced back, desperately trying not to trip on the various obstacles, as more venom landed near. The lizard trundled after him. Augum hoped Osbert was all right. He stopped at the doors to imagine his animated friend running from behind, jumping on top and squeezing the lizard's eyes—except when it actually happened, Osbert lost his footing on the slippery scales and fell off, still as a statue on the ground, awaiting the next command.

The lizard thumped along, its fat legs propelling it at a faster pace. Augum bolted, tablet under his arm, right past Horrick, who stood statue still. He sprinted for the door to the Hall of Ceremony and the tail end of Nefra's army. He imagined Osbert running to catch up. Behind him, he heard the sound of shelves, barrels, desks and tables crashing or crunching as the lizard slithered through them. Hurry, Osbert! He imagined the horse-headed beast sprinting now.

VALOR

Ahead, a walker turned and immediately shot toward Augum. He shoved the air. "Baka!" It was thrown back into a set of shelves, scattering parchment into the air like leaves. It soon recovered and charged again. Augum chose to conserve his arcane stamina and instead imagined Osbert tackling the thing—only to watch it happen a moment later. So his ugly horse-headed friend had survived being run over by a giant fat lizard after all ...

Augum ran past a few lumbering creatures. They swung clumsily and moaned, but he didn't stop, shooting through the doorway and running on to the throne room. The torches had all been lit now, revealing a great room decorated with tapestries and paintings. To the left, the undead army bottlenecked at the doors to the sentinel room, awaiting his father's arrival.

As he ran by the corner where he'd been kept prisoner, he noticed Temper and Raina were gone, and there was no sign of Robin or Tridian. The doors to the throne room were open as before, the stench thicker than ever. Soon as he ran through them, he halted, for before him, standing atop the pile of rotten bodies, stood Nefra, crimson robe flowing. Her legs bent in the wrong direction, and he saw that instead of feet she had hooves. Her hair was a great frizz of snakes, constantly moving and rattling and hissing. Her arms gracefully rose and fell. With each gesture, an ancient soldier rose and stumbled off the hill.

"You," said a surprised voice from his left. Augum turned to see Peyas standing near a bunch of bodies. A walker was already up and lumbering to the door. When the thing saw Augum, it clacked its jaws and rushed, but Peyas made a quick gesture and it veered away, walking on to the army. When some of Nefra's creatures tried the same, Peyas again intervened.

"What are you doing, Peyas ...?"

"Not this one, Nefra ..."

Augum looked over to the pile and Nefra was suddenly steps away, every snake on her head watching him. Her skin flicked between colors like reflections of torchlight on rough seas.

Bumps rose on his arms. "Where are my friends?"

Peyas glanced at the open door behind the throne but said nothing. Augum searched for the subtle pull of the Object Track spell, but couldn't sense it through his distress and exhaustion.

Nefra's tongue rattled. "I heard them speak of this one ... He is the pretender's son ..."

Peyas' eyes fixed on Augum like two gleaming bloodfruits. "This I did not know."

"We have something in common," Augum blurted. "You're Occulus' son, and I'm—"

"—nothing more than a pretender's bastard ..." Nefra finished in an angry hiss. "He has the tablet they want as well, Peyas ... The little thief shall witness his father boil ... He shall witness the resurrection of the true Lord of Death ... before joining his father in the sacred waters of the fire ..."

Nefra made a graceful gesture at the tablet.

"No—!" but despite Augum trying to hold on, she effortlessly yanked it from his grip and floated it over, her Telekinesis too strong. She placed it in a large leather pouch at her belt, securing the strap.

"Make him watch, Peyas ..."

"As you command, my queen ..." Peyas took Augum by the arm and guided him to stand aside while Nefra stepped back onto the pile of bodies, her movements strange with those goat hooves.

"Are my friends all right?" Augum asked Peyas as she resumed raising the dead.

"This I do not know, mortal one."

"Please, did they have to play one of her games to get into Occulus' quarters?"

"I believe they did."

"Did ... did one of them—"

"I do not know."

Augum's breathing was quick. "Is there an emergency escape portal in his quarters at least?"

Peyas was aloof, not making eye contact. "I have never been there."

Nefra seemed to expand as she cast a powerful spell on a rather large soldier. The man stood with bursts of fire and crackling light. Some of the rot on his body mended as he flexed.

"A revenant ..." Augum said.

Nefra increased her pace at raising dead bodies, sometimes even raising three or four at once, though those did not move as quickly as the ones raised singularly. She did this until all but a few remained. Then she turned her head of writhing snakes to glance at the door, voice slithering.

"He comes to the gate .... I go to let him in ... He will feel the power of the master's army ..."

Peyas took Augum by the arm. "Come."

Augum shrugged him off. "I can walk on my own."

Peyas gave him a cold look but let him walk between the two Occi. Nefra left a scent trail of putrid decay, and Augum had to avoid breathing through his nose.

He worried about the girls and Garryk. What kind of test had they undergone to get through the door to Occulus' chamber? Please let them be all right ...

He glanced through the doorway of the laboratorium as they passed, but it was too dark to see Osbert. He imagined the horse-headed creature standing behind the frame of the door. A lone walker soon exited the room, probably the one Osbert had kept pinned.

The undead army had pushed into the sentinel room, a great throng of stinking, clacking, writhing and moaning undead. They parted as Nefra walked between them, gesturing for Peyas to stay at the entrance of the room. She waved at the great bronze doors and they closed, trapping them inside.

Augum had to maneuver to see past the giant bull demon that sat like a dog in the middle of the room, its horns near the ceiling. He saw wraiths, walkers, revenants and other monsters. There was a space between the horde and the doors to the pit room, where Raptos had died to form a bridge for them, though the bridge was not connected to the platform right now.

Standing on the ledge where the bridge would have met the doors was the Blade of Sorrows, Raina, Robin and Temper, robes and hair whipping from the wind of the great cavern hole behind them. Robin's face was a mess after repeatedly meeting Augum's fist—one eye was puffy and black; he held his nose, from which blood flowed; and one side of his face was streaked with yet more blood from the cut above his eyebrow. Temper, too, held her nose.

Augum scanned the horde of monsters. "Why aren't they attacking?" he asked.

Peyas waved a lumbering creature aside and it pushed into its undead companions. "They have been commanded not to."

Nefra stopped near the center of the room, beside the giant demon, allowing herself to be surrounded by the horde. She raised a single arm. "I give you entry, Pretender."

A light briefly flared on the distant floating platform. Augum strained to see, but it was pitch-dark. The Blade of Sorrows and his group turned around to watch. There was a brief scream, probably from a sacrifice, and the stones of the bridge began to form.

Robin and Temper lit their palms. Their light soon touched upon a man dressed in highly ornate and sleek Dreadnought steel armor. It was the color of night, shining like the moon, with the burning sword emblem of the Legion upon the breast. A wispy black cape rolled from his great shoulders. At his side hung Burden's Edge, the family Dreadnought blade. Yet he wore no helm—his head was free to look upon the army before him, his eyes crackling electrically, the lightning sometimes spidering down to his strong chin.

"My new children," the Lord of the Legion, Death and Dreadnoughts said, voice magnified arcanely, booming off the walls. "Join me. There is no reason for us to quarrel."

"Imposter ..." Nefra's voice was silk, slithering through the horde before her. "Pretender ... submit yourself to the cauldron ... and raise the true master ..."

Lord Sparkstone's lips creased with a smile as his lightning eyes fell upon Augum. "I see you have my son."

"He will boil in the purifying waters along with his pretender father ..."

Sparkstone's arched brows rose. "You think it is I who is the pretender? But you are not even Occulus' true wife."

"You *dare* ..."

"Oh, but you know very well someone else had his heart. He never loved you." He raised a finger at her. "*You* are the pretender."

Nefra's tongue rattled angrily as the horde stirred, eager to pounce.

Sparkstone made a casual gesture and a globe popped out of a pouch, hovering near. Then more floated free, until four scions buzzed around him like attentive bees.

Augum almost swore aloud. His father had four scions now ...

Sparkstone watched the ancient orbs hover. "You have no idea how much I have learned; the true extent of my powers. You see, I *am* the true Lord of Death."

His lightning eyes returned to her. "Let us strike a bargain—I will give you a kingdom to reign. You can have Tiberra, if you like, for I know that was *his* kingdom once. You will be a queen, as you were meant to be, with a kingdom to rule as you see fit. In return, you will teach me the secrets of this castle. You will teach me everything Occulus knew, and more. I want it all."

What a horribly evil match that would be, Augum thought. She'd enslave or torture or play malicious games with an entire nation. It couldn't be allowed to happen, yet what he could do about it, he did not know …

Nefra stood silent as if actually entertaining the offer. It became deathly quiet, until she spat the words out like venom: "No, you will boil! Take him!"

The horde lumbered forward, groaning and screaming and clacking, the fastest of them, the walkers, once again in front. Robin and Temper scurried to hide behind the doors while Tridian stepped forward to assist in the battle. The Lord of the Legion merely raised a hand, staying him. He then pointed at various walkers. Some of them immediately attacked their brethren, while others continued to charge at Sparkstone. The ones that refused his command, he vaporized with thick ropes of lightning.

As soon as the first wave was destroyed, the second, composed of wraiths and small demons, charged. Nefra was pointing this way and that, casting spells, enchantments or curses. Sparkstone shrugged most off. The ones that actually hit his Dreadnought armor dissipated or did little damage. He watched her with a disdainful smile, toying with her, allowing certain strikes to hit him.

Soon Peyas began directing some of the larger beasts, including the great bull demon. The battle became thick and loud, with light flashing and explosions bursting. Meanwhile, Augum backed away to the door. Nefra was going to lose, this much he knew. He had to get out of there; he needed to open the doors, but how?

Then an idea came to him, but was it possible? He imagined Osbert, who he had left behind in the other room, running back to the entrance of the Spawnery, where Augum had last seen Horrick, and scooping the enchanted armor up in his arms. Then he imagined Osbert carrying

VALOR

Horrick back to where Augum was and setting him down just on the other side of the closed doors.

The battle raged on. His father had summoned an elemental to fight the bull demon, and the mighty but frantic brawl was making the ground shake. After obliterating two wraiths with forked lightning, the man reached to the ceiling and summoned a small lightning storm. The noise of thunder was deafening.

Augum hoped his plan had worked. "Horrick, open the doors! Horrick—!"

Peyas, who had been concentrating on the bull demon, looked his way just as the doors began to open.

Augum met his bloodshot eyes. "Please, let me go ..."

The bull demon suddenly roared and fell, crushing a slew of undead, but Peyas did not seem to care. "The battle is lost," and turned away from him.

Augum was about to run out when an idea occurred to him. He turned toward Nefra, watching her movements carefully, particularly the large leather pouch on her belt where the tablet was hidden.

He had to time it just right ...

He raised his arm and beckoned for the pouch to open with Telekinesis, trying to undo the strap. But at this distance, the spell required complexity and skill he did not possess yet.

The battle raged as Augum dropped his arm in frustration. But he couldn't give up, not yet. There was one other thing he could try, as foolishly dangerous as it was ...

He focused all his remaining arcane stamina and concentrated on the pouch, the way it moved, the way the strap bounced, how her body reacted to the ebb and flow of battle.

"Centeratoraye xao xen."

Centarro immediately sharpened his senses, brightening the lights and amplifying sounds. Augum ignored the chaos around him, a plan forming beautifully in his mind like a complex puzzle coming together.

The pounding in his head was a drum now, but he fought through it. He raised his arm and focused on the strap, focused all his concentration, even as things exploded nearby and bones flew at him; even as he was struck by fleshy debris; even as time quickly ran out.

The strap slowly undid itself like a leather snake. Soon the pouch was open and the tablet sprang free. Augum kept all his attention on that iron tablet as it carefully floated out of Nefra's pack, escaping her awareness. He ignored the blood trickling from his nose, the black walls of unconsciousness creeping into his vision. He weaved the tablet through scrambling walkers and bursts of lightning, until at last he was able to snatch it from the air.

He held on to that piece of cold iron like his life depended on it.

"Horrick, follow me!" he shouted, collapsing to his knees. He was about to lose awareness, but not before sending one last carefully imagined set of instructions to Osbert.

Find me. Pick me up. Carry me to the doors of the smithy. Do not let me go.

CUNNING

Augum slowly became aware of himself struggling in the grip of strong and unyielding arms. It dawned on him it was Osbert. He quickly envisioned the animated creature letting him go, and was suddenly dumped to the floor. There he lay a moment, trying to get his bearings. He felt his nose and saw blood on his fingers. It was hard concentrating through the dull haze, not to mention the pounding headache. Somewhere, not too far away, were the echoes of a battle.

Horrick stood quietly nearby. A large bronze door loomed ahead, decorated with a hammer and anvil.

The smithy ...

"Horrick, open the door to the smithy!"

"As mine disgustingly wretched unworthy commands." Horrick stepped before the great door and made a gesture. It rumbled open, releasing a stale mineral smell.

Augum scrambled to his feet, suddenly aware his hands held nothing.

Where was the tablet!

He glanced around, only to find it laying a few steps back. He must have dropped it in his Centarro-induced stupor. He grabbed it and raced through the door, commanding Horrick and Osbert to follow. Inside the pitch-dark room, he quickly found a torch rune on the wall.

"Firemente," he said, and watched as torches flared to life along the walls of a vast tall room, making visible an array of large forges, each matched with an anvil, a stone basin, bellows, and assorted other smith equipment. All of it was oversized and dusted with ancient soot.

He raced from one forge to the next, sliding on the dusty black marble floor, yet none of the runes he found made any sense. At least they were arcane forges. Now all he needed was a way to—

"Horrick! How do I fire one up—?"

"Only Dreadnoughts used thy smithy, wretched cur."

He could hide the tablet maybe. No, they'd easily discover it with an Unconceal spell!

A concussive boom echoed distantly. The battle quieted down a little after that, sounding as if it was coming to an end. He better figure something out fast. The First Offensive definitely wasn't strong enough to melt iron. He needed something more …

He spotted an exquisitely carved ebony cabinet. He raced to it and flung open the doors. Inside he found an array of chisels. He recognized the craftsmanship immediately—all were made from Dreadnought steel.

And suddenly the idea hit him. He threw the iron tablet to the ground with a clang.

"Osbert, come here!" Augum called, before realizing his mistake. He pictured the horse-headed creature doing his bidding instead. Osbert ran over, grabbed the largest chisel and a hammer, and began carving the intricate writing off the tablet.

It was working! Sliver by sliver, the words peeled off in crinkled strips like butter. Augum could barely contain his excitement. It had to be the stupidest way to destroy something so important, but who cared? He kept his imagination focused on Osbert, making sure none of the inscription survived.

Just as Osbert finished chiseling off the last strip of writing, Augum hit upon a horrible realization—his father could easily repair it! He still had to destroy the strips!

There was a distant mighty boom and then a grinding noise. There was no time. He quickly stuffed the precious shards into a pocket and ran, leaving the scraped-clean tablet behind.

"Horrick, follow me!" he shouted as he raced through the doors into the grand Hall of Ceremony, imagining Osbert keeping pace. Osbert had dropped the precious Dreadnought chisel though, as Augum forgot to imagine him holding on to it.

No time to go back—to his far left, the horde was retreating from the sentinel room, pursued by bursts of lightning and fire. Something large was squeezing through the doorway, but he did not stick around to find out what. He raced past the laboratorium and on to the throne room, where he tripped and scrambled over unraised ancient bodies, all while trying not to leave Horrick or Osbert behind—he might still need them.

Augum charged up the steps, past the mighty throne, and crashed through the open door just behind. It was dark on the other side.

"Shyneo," he said, gasping for breath. His blue light crackled to life, revealing a semi-circular grand guest hall with plush carved chairs, pedestal tables, and low mahogany shelving. A coat of untouched ancient dust clung to everything—untouched except for fresh footprints that led through one of a series of fine black oak doors.

The girls and Garryk had to have gone that way.

"Horrick, follow me!" he said, imagining Osbert doing the same.

Beyond the central door was a corridor of dusty paintings that reached all the way to the vaulted ceiling.

Every single one was a portrait of the same woman—a petite girl with porcelain Henawa skin and milky hair. Her face was plain but pretty, eyes full of sad love.

Occulus' beloved.

Augum tried to still his heart so he could feel the subtle pull of Object Track, but again failed—he simply wasn't practiced enough with the spell. He raced on, Osbert right behind, Horrick shuffling along in the rear.

At last, he barreled through an ornate oak door, into what looked like a grand bedroom furnished with a towering tester bed carved in the shape of a dragon. All the furniture was carved from the same black oak. There were dragon dressers, wardrobes, tables, chairs, and even shelves. The floor was covered with the finest Tiberran silk carpets, the walls with Tiberran tapestries depicting all manner of natural creature. At the foot of the bed hung another portrait of Occulus' beloved, this one the finest of them all. She wore an exquisitely embroidered robe, cheeks lightly brushed with crimson, an ivy coronet resting on snowy hair ornately done up.

There was no time to stare though; who knew how long until his father came looking for him.

Augum searched for a secret door. He looked everywhere, even in the wardrobe and privy, but found nothing. Yet they *had* to have come this way—there were even dusty footprints, which seemed to disappear right in the center of the room.

He forced himself to relax and tried focusing on the Object Track spell again. At last, he felt a very subtle tug pointing him onward and downward.

But downward? So there *was* a hidden passage here ...

He extinguished his lit palm and concentrated on finding something purposefully hidden. He splayed his fingers. "Un vun deo." In the darkness, the Unconceal spell tugged him to look underneath the dragon bed. There he found a page torn from a book, roughly written over with charcoal.

VALOR

Augum, we are all right. We hope you are too. We have gone down into a chamber below the bed. You must say the phrase written above it. Take this note with you or destroy it. Hope to see you very soon. Yours, Leera.

A wave of relief washed over him. They're all right! But written above what? The note? He looked around. "Horrick, how do I get down there?"

"I do not presume to understand thee ravings, mine twisted fiend of a guest."

"She must have meant the top of the bed," Augum muttered to himself, and searched. There was indeed a phrase there, but it was written in ancient Tiberran. Garryk must have read it—except they had forgotten to transcribe it for him!

He was doomed ...

"Leera, Bridget—can you hear me!" but there was only silence. He glanced back at the door, expecting his father to burst through any moment now.

He got up and paced like a madman until his eyes fell upon the ancient suit of armor with the empty skull helm. "Horrick, read this phrase aloud to me." He tapped at the top of the frame.

"As mine discourteous and unwelcome unworthy commands." Horrick shuffled over and looked up with his empty skull helm. "Andromus iu vectus, mio satus unudeus."

The bed creaked and came to life, folding almost mechanically, back and up. It took a portion of the floor with it, revealing a spiral stone stairway. Augum, absently playing with the pocket that held the tablet shavings, couldn't help but be impressed.

He took a step down and stopped, thinking he should set an alarm. He snatched a blue and white ancient vase from a dresser and placed it before the door. "Concutio del alarmo," affixing a bell sound to the object if it should be disturbed.

"Horrick, I want you to repeat that phrase you read on the bed frame as soon as we're gone, then guard that door there. Do not let anyone inside, and *don't* tell them where we've gone."

"As mine eternal unworthy foe commands."

Augum imagined Osbert following and began descending the spiral steps, palm shining in front. The walls were rough cut stone blocks, the stairs the same. The air was cool and musty and smelled of ancient earth. Above him, he heard the grind of the bed as it closed. Horrick would probably betray them, but hopefully they'd be long gone by then.

The steps spiraled down for some length, opening up into a rubble-strewn anteroom. This one was made of old gray stone, different from the rest of the castle. He walked through an ancient archway ahead and into a vast cavern. Towering black marble monoliths circled a raised platform, on top of which sat an ornate sarcophagus. But it wasn't the only sarcophagus—there was one at the foot of each monolith.

He quietly climbed the steps of the platform, stopping at the top, Osbert right behind. The lid of the sarcophagus was carved with the face of Occulus' beloved, a single rose below, and some ancient inscription he couldn't read.

As he stood there in the silence, he could hear a muted scratching noise.

"Bridge? Leera?" but no one responded. Soon a similar noise began from the other side of the room. His breath quickened as he suddenly realized where the noises were coming from—the sarcophagi!

The hairs on his neck stood on end. This is where Nefra had entombed Occulus' women ...

The noises quickened, soon joined by muffled howling and cries of old agony. How many centuries had those poor women been here? Their suffering was unspeakable.

VALOR

He played with the idea of setting them free, yet what if they attacked him in their madness? What if they weren't those women at all, but walkers?

"Bridget! Leera! Where are you!" but there was only silence. He ran about, searching the walls for engraved portal symbols. Had they already teleported out?

He spread his fingers and let his Shine extinguish. "Un vun deo," but couldn't concentrate in the darkness with that scratching and howling. He tried focusing on the Object Track spell he had cast on the Orb of Orion. He felt the pull, and after re-lighting his palm, discovered it pointed at a pool of water ahead, below an archway. As he neared, he saw it was a set of flooded stairs. Amidst a fresh puddle at the very top lay a rock.

Augum picked it up. It was wet but unmarked. Was it a signal left behind by the girls? How did they get through the water? It had to be near freezing ...

Suddenly a bell went off in his head and a thrill shot up his spine—Occulus' bedroom had been breached!

"Goodbye, Osbert, and thanks," he said, before imagining the odd horse-headed creature running up the steps and battling anyone that tried to pass him. The beast immediately set off to his unspoken command.

At the same moment, the water began to glow. A form took shape from its depths, swimming towards him. At first, he thought it was an undead fish, and took a step back, when out popped Leera's head. Her wet raven hair stuck to her freckled face in ribbons. Her palm was lit, but it also made the water glow all around her, as if it was made of light itself. She wore only her linen undergarments. His cheeks colored at the sight.

She was shivering and her teeth chattered. "Augum! I'm so glad it's you, and you're all right—"

He glanced over his shoulder. "We have to hurry, someone's—"

"Well come on already—!"

He jumped in. The water was frigid, sucking the air out of his lungs and immediately extinguishing his palm.

She gave his hand a squeeze. "Take a deep breath and follow me."

"Wait, I have to try something." He stretched out his hand and used Telekinesis to drag the lid off the closest sarcophagus. It was difficult to concentrate through the numbing cold.

"What are you doing—!"

"Saving them, or buying us time, we'll soon see."

He did the same to another three sarcophagi, before something began to slither out of the first one. It was a bony hand sleeved in a grimy crimson robe. A head soon appeared, draped in a sheer wispy veil, but the visage underneath was still visible—a sunken skull, plastered with the remains of skin. It hissed when it saw him.

Leera yanked on his sleeve. "Enough already, come on—"

They swam down, his thick coat and robes slowing him down. He just hoped he did not lose the tablet slivers. He struggled to catch up to her as she pressed on through a submerged tunnel, past a series of connecting hallways, before taking a break in a pocket of trapped air at the ceiling. He swam up beside her and emerged, panting. His teeth joined her in chattering.

"How did you survive this?" he asked, keeping an eye out behind them. He half expected to see one of the veiled women appearing from the darkness and snatching at their feet.

"You'll see. Now take an even bigger breath, this next one's a long swim."

They took a big gulp of air and continued on, turning a corner. The water glowed a small distance around them, but behind and in front was pitch-darkness. Augum wondered how she could possibly have found the right path through all these other corridors, let alone supporting a badly injured Garryk.

Suddenly he felt the oversized ring slip off his finger. He stopped to catch it but missed. It tumbled down into the darkness where he couldn't see it. Leera hadn't noticed and continued to swim ahead. There was simply no time to get it, he realized, even with Telekinesis—and so he followed her.

At last, they scrambled through a window and swam upward toward a fiery glow. Augum felt himself turning purple from lack of breath. When his head finally broke the surface, he coughed and gasped for breath.

Leera had already climbed out, dripping water.

"You made it! Both of you!" Bridget immediately rushed over and draped Leera with a coat, guiding her to a huge, blazing hearthfire that appeared to be woodless. Garryk lay before it, breathing weakly, face a tortured shadow of its former self.

"Leera's the hero here," Bridget began as she helped remove the coat from Augum's shivering shoulders. "Took forever for her to find the right route for us. She almost drowned countless times, and had to do two trips. I think she has the blood of a fish or something."

Leera smiled coyly. "Well I am studying the *water* discipline. And I finally found a use for this stupid Shine extension—"

"It's not stupid, it saved our lives!" Bridget said. "How else would we have seen anything underwater?"

"Anyway," Leera continued, "we saved the books by wrapping them tight in our coats. It wasn't fun, but at least it'll take a while for anyone else to figure out which tunnel we used."

Augum spied a strange rune above the hearth and figured that was how they turned it on. "What game did Nefra play with you at the door?"

"We had to fight a ghost," Bridget replied. "It took the First Offensive from both of us at the same time to defeat it."

"I'm so glad you made it," he said, teeth clacking.

Bridget gave him a hug. "I didn't know if … if we'd see you again."

"I didn't know either … My father came. He's here. There was a battle. Peyas was there. He and Nefra used Occulus' old army to fight him. When I escaped, the Occi were losing … but guess what?"

Leera smacked him on the shoulder. "Don't make us guess, just spit it out!"

He went over to his coat and dug out a handful of tablet shavings.

Leera scrunched her face. "What is that?"

"What remains of the iron tablet," and he explained how Osbert had carved it up.

"Maybe we can melt them in the fire—" Leera said.

Bridget shook her head. "No way, need something twice as hot at least."

"How do you know?"

"Brother was an apprentice blacksmith, remember?"

"What if we hid the pieces far apart?" Augum asked.

This time Leera shook her head. "Wouldn't work. Remember the map in Castle Arinthian? We walked around trying to repair it until the pieces were in range. No, the only way is to use something hot enough, like a kiln or something, and melt them down completely."

His eyes found the Orb of Orion, sitting on one of their soggy rucksacks, still enclosed in its shimmering green prison.

"Yeah, it's still trapped," Bridget said. "Not all spells expire when their caster dies. Hopefully it will fizzle out soon though, and Mrs. Stone can teleport us out."

"If she's tuned to the orb," he said.

"She's had plenty of time with it, I'm sure she's tuned by now." Yet her voice betrayed her doubt.

Augum took a look around the room. It was simply adorned, with an ancient stone trestle table and chairs. There was a stone chest in one corner. Even the door was made of gray stone.

"What is this place?"

"The Rivicans ..." Garryk's voice was weak. "Known for ... trying to transmute ... stuff into gold ... ancient alchemy."

"Shh, don't speak," Bridget said. "Rest up and get warm." She turned to Augum. "Some kind of ancient people built these chambers."

Augum strode to the door but was caught by Bridget's hand. "Please, Aug, get warm first. It's cold over there, you'll freeze."

He knew she was right—if they moved on while wet, especially out into the snowy mountains ...

He plopped down, resolving himself to rest and dry out by the fire, hoping something did not emerge from the depths of that black pool.

HOLE

We should go," Augum said when he felt his robe growing hot from the flames. "My father could emerge any moment." He had been staring at the black pool too long and it was starting to spook him.

"They'll harm my family," Garryk said. "Leave me ... here ... by the fire ..."

"We discussed this already, Garryk," Bridget said. "We're not leaving you. Besides, there's no guarantee they'd save you after finding you here, or if they'd even venture this way."

Garryk wheezed a resigned sigh and nodded.

Augum found a stone and placed it on the edge of the pool. He splayed his hands over it. "Concutio del alarmo." Then he helped Bridget with Garryk.

Leera gathered their rucksack and pushed on the stone door. "Shyneo."

They traversed passage after ancient passage, each sculpted from smooth stone, cracked by time. Leera's pale watery light lit the way, casting long shadows on the occasional stone bench or stone block chair. Crude torch

VALOR

sconces jutted from the walls. Rooms were barren and dusty. Their steps left visible footprints in the thick dust, something that could not be helped.

At last, they ended up in a great chamber with a wide shallow basin and copper spouts, as if a pool had once been here.

"Some sort of ancient bathhouse," Leera said.

"Need ... rest," Garryk wheezed. Augum and Bridget immediately set him down, lighting up their palms to give Leera a casting break.

"I've been ... thinking ..." he went on, eyes unfocused without his spectacles. "The armor thing ... it held your orb for a bit ..."

"You mean Horrick?" Augum said. "Horrick held the orb? When?"

"I think it was ... outside of the library. When we had returned ... I saw him place it ... back into one of your rucksacks."

"Are you saying Horrick enchanted it somehow?" Leera asked.

"Maybe ..."

Bridget quickly opened the rucksack and brought out the orb, shimmering in its greenish prison.

"It's not moving," Leera said. "The field ... it used to squirm slowly, but now it's not moving!"

Augum looked closer. Had the Sphere of Protection spell moved before? He honestly couldn't recall.

"Are you sure?" Bridget asked.

"Yes, because I took a good look at it once. I'm telling you, the field thingy used to move! Nefra must have heard us talking about the orb and Mrs. Stone and come up with some kind of plan."

"I don't know ..." Augum picked it up. It felt just as heavy as before, and looked identical, as far as he remembered it.

"What if Leera's right?" Bridget stepped away from the orb. "But what spells would she cast on it that would help her—" She stopped, locking eyes with Augum.

"—Object Track," they chorused together.

"It's the only spell that makes sense," Bridget said. "Then she could track us, and therefore the Legion—"

"Yeah but she was losing the battle anyway," Augum said.

"Then there's no harm taking it with us, is there?" Bridget said. "Even *if* Nefra cast Object Track, wouldn't she have more important things to worry about, like boiling the pretender alive—assuming she even survived the battle?"

They glanced at the orb between them. It suddenly appeared dangerous.

Leera picked it up. "I say we dump it."

"Not until we're sure," Bridget said. "We might be wrong, and it could be our only way out of here via Mrs. Stone."

The girls looked to Augum.

"I agree with Bridge. Keep it for now. If anything, we ditch it later."

Leera frowned but stuffed it back in the rucksack. Augum and Bridget picked up Garryk again and they continued.

They soon came upon a room with hundreds of pots filled with ancient earth. Some of the pots were on ledges. Others hung from the high ceiling on long chains, looming out from the darkness. In the center of the vast room were large stone basins holding the husks of long-dead trees.

"Reminds me of the forest room in Castle Arinthian," Augum said, being careful not to trip over scattered branches.

Bridget shifted Garryk's weight as he groaned with pain. "All the plants are different too."

VALOR

They passed through the room to another, this one filled with all kinds of piles of sand and rock and minerals, each a different color.

"Must be hundreds of them." Leera made her palm light a little brighter, but it was still not strong enough to find the walls.

"Rivicans …" Garryk wheezed. "Alchemists …"

They moved through this room on to a thin passageway of stone doors.

"We could easily never find a way out of here," Leera mumbled, inspecting each door as she passed.

Augum saw something glimmer on the ground. "What's that?"

Leera shone her light closer. "Looks like … is that gold dust—?" She pushed on the smooth stone door the gold dust led to. It swung open with a grinding noise.

"Empty," Bridget said, eyeing the tiny barren room, decorated with nothing more than stone block seats. "Let's keep going."

Leera held up a hand. "Wait. Something doesn't make sense here …" She followed the smattering of dust to a block. "Aug, can you take over?"

He nodded, gently lowering Garryk to the floor. "Shyneo." His palm crackled to life with lightning as hers extinguished.

Leera splayed out her palm. "Un vun deo," and was immediately drawn to one of the blocks, nestled against a wall. She pushed on it but it didn't budge. "Help me move this."

"We don't have time for this—" Bridget said.

Leera smirked. "There's always time for treasure hunting. Aug?"

"We'll just be a moment—" Augum said apologetically.

"Ugh."

Augum helped Leera push on the stone, but it ended up requiring all three of them to move it with Telekinesis. It ground across the floor, revealing worn steps.

"Oh, this is so neat—" Leera squealed, and disappeared down before anyone could stop her. "Get down here, you have to see this for yourselves!"

Augum scrambled after her, emerging in a small room filled with thousands of small vials, each on its own wooden stand. Some of them shone back the light, glittering brightly, while others were as black as coal. Some had liquid, others powder, others pebbles. There were books and scrolls and a table of beakers and a small furnace—

"Are you two all right—?" Bridget voice echoed from up top.

"Yes!" Augum called. "It's beautiful! Some sort of alchemy room. Bring Garryk down here and see for yourself!"

"We don't have time though—"

"It's worth it, Bridge!" Leera called, running to fetch them. "Trust me!"

"The books are all in some sort of old language," Augum said when they had rejoined him, taking one off the shelf. It was heavy and black and the pages were so old they practically turned to dust in his hands.

"Look at this!" Leera said, placing her hands on an exquisitely carved case. "Think it's safe to open?"

"Well you haven't died touching it—"

But Leera had already opened it. The old hinges squealed in protest. The contents immediately reflected their light.

"It's a book!" Leera said, reverently picking up the most beautiful tome Augum had ever seen. Its cover was made entirely of exquisitely ornate gold. The very center depicted a simple spiral.

"What do you think it is?" he asked, unable to take his eyes off the artifact.

She turned to him with the biggest smile he had ever seen. "It's gold! We're rich! Look! Even the pages are made from gold leaf! And it weighs more than stone—"

The pages were indeed made of fragile and thin gold, and written in the finest hand Augum had ever seen. It was graceful and loopy, and tinted with copper to stand out against the gold.

"I kind of meant what the book was about ..." he mumbled.

"Who cares! This could buy us a castle—"

"Leera Jones—" Bridget's stern voice began, "are you seriously handling some ancient artifact without checking to see if it's cursed or booby-trapped or—"

"And how are we supposed to do that?" Leera asked, drawing the book close to her chest. "Look at it!"

Augum helped lower Garryk to the floor while she inspected the room and the book.

"What language do you think it's in?" Leera asked, bringing it close to Garryk.

"Don't ... know ... very ... old."

"What about this one?" Augum asked, pulling off a random book and showing the spine to Garryk.

"Ancient ... Tiberran ..."

"So you can read it?"

Garryk only nodded.

"What are you doing?" Bridget said.

"I'm packing the book away," Leera replied, shoving it into her rucksack. "What does it look like?"

"What about this one?" Augum asked, shoving another book under Garryk's nose, genuinely curious about the books.

"It's about ... alchemical ... properties ... how to mix ... make—"

Bridget placed her hands on her hips and glared at Leera. "You're not seriously going to *steal* a valuable artifact from a historical site of ancient—" suddenly she stopped and turned to Augum. "That book, what did Garryk say it was again?"

Augum had already tossed it aside though. "I don't know, something about alchemy properties or whatever—"

Bridget hurriedly picked up and began carefully rifling through it, holding each page in front of Garryk, making him read out the contents while explaining her plan to him in hushed tones.

"What are you doing?" Augum asked when he got bored with the bookshelf.

"Shh! And this one, Garryk? What's it say?"

"Pyra Magnimunt."

"Will that work?"

"It might …"

"Then help me decipher the ingredients."

Now Leera had come over too. "Bridge, what are—"

"Shh! Listen carefully. Garryk?"

Garryk indicated for her to hold the book closer, and read out a short list of ingredients. He pointed at the page. "These ones … find them."

Bridget took the book and began trying to match the symbols beside each of the ingredients with the symbols on the stoppered vials.

"Now who's crazy—" Leera said.

"No, wait—" Augum dug in his pockets and withdrew the iron tablet shavings. "You want to destroy these, don't you?"

Bridget did not even look up from her frantic searching. "Exactly! Now help me—"

Augum and Leera joined in the search. Together, the trio found all the necessary ingredients. Then they worked with Garryk on how to exactly mix the stuff together and light it, as the recipe dictated.

"White fire," Bridget explained while holding a crude beaker full of their concoction. "It's called White Fire, and it's supposed to burn hot enough to melt steel, which should

VALOR

definitely burn iron." She carefully carried the beaker over to the stone furnace, and emptied its contents within. "Aug, the shavings—"

He searched his robes for every last one, getting pricked multiple times in the process, and dumped them onto the pile.

Then they stared at it.

"Now what?" Leera asked.

Bridget gave a nod at the pile. "Now, uh, we light it."

"We light it. Great. And with what? Legion's got all our supplies, *including* our lamp oil, our flint and—"

"All right all right, let me think!" Bridget began pacing.

Leera crossed her arms and glanced over at Augum. "She's pacing."

"But thinking," he added. Suddenly a loud bell sounded in his head.

Leera uncrossed her arms. "Aug? What is it?"

"The rock—" He did not need to explain.

"We have to get out of here," Bridget said. "We can destroy them elsewhere—"

"Wait ..." It was Garryk. "Help ... up."

Augum and Bridget quickly brought him to a stand. Garryk nodded at the vials. "Let me ... see them."

They carried him over, letting him inspect the shelves of vials. "This one."

"This black one here?" Leera asked, picking it up.

"Gentle. Yes. If you break it ... with enough force ... it will make ... a small flame."

"How do you know?"

Garryk winced, adjusted his arms around their necks. "When I was training ... as an arcaneologist ... there was an ... alchemy class."

"Of course," Bridget said. "We were supposed to take one too, but the Legion took the academy over before we even got a chance to—"

"Never mind all that," Leera said, running over to the furnace. "So I just have to smash it hard enough—"

"Use some parchment to get it going," Augum said.

"Good idea." She crumpled up an ancient leaf of parchment and stuffed the vial inside. Then she placed it on the ground, picked up a large nearby mortar, and smashed the vial. It instantly burst into a small fire, catching on to the parchment. Leera quickly picked it up by two corners and flung it into the furnace. There was a sizzling sound as the compound caught fire. The color of the flame transitioned from orange to red to blue to a hot white. They heard more sizzling and bubbling noises.

"It's working," Leera reported. "I see the iron melting!"

"There goes the only known recipe to make a portal to Ley," Bridget whispered.

Augum expelled a long breath. "Good, now let's get out of here—" and that they did, quickly closing the block over the entrance, the door to the room, and then hurrying along the passageway.

"No idea where I'm going," Leera said, lighting ancient corridors with her pale watery light.

Augum froze. "Do you feel that?"

They stood silent for a moment.

"I *do* feel something actually," Leera said. "Some sort of deep and constant rumble."

"What do you think it is?" Bridget asked, eyes wide.

Augum immediately pictured a giant bull demon plowing through the passageways. But that wouldn't be a constant rumble ...

"Sounds like ... wind." Leera shone her light ahead. "Let's find it. Might be an exit—"

The rumbling grew louder as they moved from chamber to chamber, until greeted by a pair of great stone doors. They were plain except for a single word inscribed across the face of them, with a thick circle underneath. The rumbling was accompanied by a steady roar, as if a windstorm were right on the other side of the doors.

"Can you read that, Garryk?" Augum asked.

"Closer please ..." Garryk studied the word a moment, squinting without his spectacles. "I think it says ... 'Agonex'."

"Does it mean anything?"

"I think it's a name ... though I don't know for what."

Leera highlighted something by the side of the doors with her lit palm. "There's a rune here. Shall I try to open the doors?"

Augum glanced behind him, still expecting something to crash through the hallway—either his father, or a large and demonic beast. "Definitely."

Leera placed her lit palm over the rune. "Entarro." The doors began to open inwards. A fierce wind immediately barreled into them, like an invader breaching a besieged castle. She peeked around the door, hair blowing wildly. "Steps!" she shouted over the roar. "They go down some kind of giant hole! I can't see far though—"

Bridget locked eyes with Augum, Garryk hanging limply between. "Do we really want to go deeper into the mountain?"

"It's a labyrinth back there," he replied. "Someone's coming after us. I say we go down. Like she said, maybe there's an exit. The wind has to come from *somewhere*."

They moved out into the roar, hugging the walls.

Bridget placed her lit palm over another rune. "Entarro," but nothing happened. "Do we know the runeword for closing doors?" she yelled above the din.

Leera shook her head. "No! Let's just keep going!"

Shoot, Augum thought. That wind will be easy to follow and a dead giveaway of their direction.

They began the descent, hugging the gently curving walls. The cavern was a giant round hole carved out of the rock of the mountain, similar to the one they had first seen upon gaining entry to Bahbell. The steps were thin blocks impaled into the wall, leaving spaces between. Augum had to take Garryk as three astride wouldn't fit. Wind hammered at them incessantly. It was filled with fat drops of water that slammed into their faces from below, like upside down rain.

Suddenly Augum's stomach jammed into his throat as a step gave way right underneath him and Garryk. He just managed to grab hold of the one in front with one arm and Garryk with the other. The pair dangled in the roaring wind like a couple of ripe apples ready to fall in an autumn storm.

"Aug—!" Leera dove and grabbed hold of his arm.

"Don't ... you'll make me fall," he said through gritted teeth. His body shook trying to hold on to the step and Garryk at the same time.

"Telekinesis!" Bridget yelled.

Leera quickly stood and extinguished her palm. "We'll have to do it together."

"Hold on, you two!" Bridget extinguished her palm, plunging them into roaring darkness.

Augum felt his grip on Garryk and the step slipping. He was weakening rapidly; if the girls didn't hurry, they were done for. But could they do it in the dark?

Garryk's voice was a whimper. "Please ... don't let go ..."

Augum couldn't even respond, fear choking him. He soon felt an arcane force pawing at him, but it was clumsy and ineffective. The more it tried to tug, the more he thought he'd fall, until he felt Garryk's weight lighten and his body scrape by him, leaving Augum to dangle in the dark. His muscles thoroughly exhausted, he didn't even have the strength to climb up.

The arcane force soon returned, but it was weaker. It lifted him a little, but suddenly failed. There was a frantic moment where he clawed at the step, but he knew it was no good. There was barely enough time to yelp.

VALOR

The girls' screaming was instantly lost in the rushing roar of his plummet.

THE FALL

"Centeratoraye xao xen!" It was the only spell Augum could think of. He immediately felt the effects course through his body, sharpening his mind, his senses. Any moment, he'd slam into another set of steps, yet he took one of those precious moments to study his predicament.

What exactly was happening?

He was falling.

It was pitch-dark.

There was rain, but it came from the wrong direction, which was slightly disorientating.

There was a great wind coming from below.

His coat and robe billowed, the coarseness of the fibers scratching at his skin. Would it be the last thing he felt? The question was strange and almost consumed his thinking. Suddenly he thought of birds, soaring through a hot summer breeze. But he didn't have wings—so what *did* he have?

He recalled an etching he had seen in one of Sir Westwood's books, of a ship in full seas, its square sails full. Under the influence of Centarro, the thoughts came together beautifully. He snatched the coat in such a way as to make it catch the wind, and immediately leaned right. There was a quick *thwoom* sound as he heard steps fly by—he had actually diverted his fall! Now the trick was to guide himself down somehow. He was aware of every movement, every nuance of his body and the way it hurtled through the darkness.

Then it occurred to him that he needed light.

"Shyneo!" His palm ripped to life. The vividness of seeing walls and stairs flying by at unimaginable speed almost made his heart stop. Yet the light was too feeble to see what came below through the upside-down rain.

He had to slow his fall somehow. He brought all his concentration to bear on one single task—holding on to the two corners of his coat in such a way as to make a sail, and billowing it above him.

The spell would soon expire. The side effects began to take hold—the drowsiness, the dull thinking, the confusion ... He roared as he held on to the coat, held it a certain way, a way that allowed for maximum resistance against the wind.

Thank the Unnameables it was a fat coat.

But it was slipping from his fingers ...

This was it. All he could hope for now was that he had slowed enough for the wind to compensate.

And then it happened just as his fingers let go—he crashed into something hard and cold. It yielded and took his breath away, freezing his very core. As the light extinguished from his palm, he gave his rapidly dimming mind a final command.

Swim.

* * *

Augum slowly came back to awareness in pitch-darkness. Everything before that moment seemed a hazy dream. At first, the dream was black, harrowing even—a long fall—but then tones of gray entered; some past life lived—a farm, beatings, a burning village, an old woman in a cave, friends, another burning village—until he dreamed in full color—a marvelous old castle, a distant world, a tower ... Eventually, he saw the face of a beautiful girl, a girl with porcelain skin, jet hair and almond eyes. He felt her shaking in his arms, dying.

Suddenly his body connected with his mind.

It was *he* that was shaking—shivering, in fact, and he was soaked through. Below him, he felt a rocky surface, and all around was noise, nothing but great, windy noise. His head throbbed as he sat up, trying to make sense of where he was.

It all crept back, one thought at a time, until he put everything back together. This was the giant hole in the mountain, and he was on the bottom. He had plunged into an underground pool, using his coat to slow the fall.

Centarro had saved him once again. Though he supposed he could just as easily have drowned.

He groped around for the coat but couldn't find it—probably lost in the water. He drew his robe tight and stood. His back was sore, along with every muscle in his body, but at least he hadn't broken any bones.

"Shyneo." His hand fluttered to life, the light pulsing along with the throbbing in his head. His arcanery was weak—that particular use of Centarro had pushed his boundaries.

He glanced around, but his light only reached two things—slippery rock below him, and water, only steps away. There was a trail of wetness to the water from where he had crawled.

It was raining. The drops were fat and tasted earthy. Suddenly he realized how thirsty he was and dropped to his knees, lapping at the water like a dog left out in the desert.

Thirst satisfied, he stood. Now he just needed to get out of the wind and dry himself. He stumbled about, eventually finding a crudely cut wall, and followed it, the wind steadily dying at his back. He sensed a great many passageways, the wind from each uniting to create a massive updraft. Dark oil sconces protruded from the walls, protected by pierced stone mesh. How they could ever be lit in this gale was beyond him.

One particular passageway stood out from the others. It was carved to appear like a great ribcage, as if one would enter the belly of some great beast. At the apex of the entrance was the same thick circle he had seen on the door. He stared into the black depth, feeling no wind come from it. The lack of wind meant it had to be a dead end.

He pushed on, muscles aching, stomach protesting its hunger, body vibrating from the cold. Bridget, Leera and Garryk had to be on their way down still. He should go back and find the spot where the steps met the cavern floor. Then again, they wouldn't come for some time—that had been a long fall. He might as well explore a little, maybe find some warmth. Besides, he needed shelter for a bit.

His light strengthened as he found more and more relief from the wind, until he entered another cavern, the steady roar distant and muted. His blue light found bulky shapes in the darkness. They were statues wearing matte black sleek armor. The helms were sharp and brutal, the weapons elaborate yet simple. There were axes, staves, maces, swords, but also plenty of other kinds he did not recognize. They, too, were matte black. Moss grew on some, while dust and dirt coated others.

Augum wondered if this was Occulus' army. He shone his light between the visor of a helm and immediately sprang back. The eyes dilated! And the face ... it was ancient flesh long dead! Are these warriors eternally alive as well? Was that part of the witch's bargain, that Occulus have an eternal army? Or were they just walkers? If so, why weren't they attacking?

He raised his lit palm, finding rows and rows of these warriors, and no doubt plenty more beyond his light. It appeared they all wore that same matte Dreadnought armor.

He thought of taking one of those blades, but decided against it lest the creature awaken.

He strode on to another chamber, finding more warriors, even a great wraith dressed in customized Dreadnought steel armor. There were other creatures he didn't recognize, ones with bull horns and great muscled physiques. He ran to another room, finding even more, and more and more—entire caverns of them.

Gasping, he leaned against a wall. An entire army, hidden in the depths of Bahbell. Occulus somehow teleported it in and out from the field of battle. He imagined them suddenly coming from nowhere, wreaking havoc on countless towns, Occulus in the rear. Then he imagined his father in Occulus' place, the flames of a burning village reflected in his cold eyes ...

No, the Lord of the Legion mustn't be allowed to possess an army outfitted so perfectly with Dreadnought steel.

Augum sprang to his feet, forgetting his shivering body. There had to be some kind of controlling artifact, just as the Orb of Orion had a controlling pearl, or just as Osbert had a controlling ring! He ran from room to room, finding thousands more soldiers, every single one armored from helm to boot.

At last, he came upon a different passageway, carved in the same plain stone as above. It led him to a vast room, in the middle of which loomed a great hollow rectangle made of stone, like a giant picture frame missing canvas. It was carved with ivy, demons, windswept trees and hairless forms.

Hairless forms ... could it be a portal to Ley?

Augum stepped near. But why the demon carvings? Were there demons in Ley he had not seen? Nonetheless, this had to be the portal Occulus had been working on with the recipe! Augum felt a tinge of pride—thanks to them, this portal would never be finished.

VALOR

He hurried on through another series of corridors and rooms until he found himself once again back in the central room with the pool. The wind curled around him as he searched for any sign of the others. They were nowhere to be found, but he did manage to find the spiral steps, which were as slippery as soap.

The wind had to come from somewhere, he thought, and that somewhere might be an exit. Then again, he recalled reading about mythically endless caves that stretched for leagues underground without ever surfacing. Perhaps that's what Bahbell really meant—it wasn't the entrance to hell, it was the entrance to eternity underground.

"Bridget! Leera!" but his voice was lost to the great updraft. Some of the fat drops made their way back down, pelting him like small stones. The wind sucked up the pool water into the giant vertical tunnel, causing the upside-down rain effect.

He began to shiver again and retreated, huddling in a nook. The wind had helped dry him, but the cold had long seeped into his bones. All he could do was bear it. He kept his palm lit in case Leera and Bridget saw it, yet visibility in the rain was a meager thirty paces or so.

They must surely think him dead, he realized. Oh, please don't let them fall!

Suddenly he thought he saw a torch reflection in one of the tunnels nearby. He extinguished his palm and listened. Just as he began to think he had imagined it, the flickering orange light returned. It seemed to be retreating. Was it his father? Had he found another way down?

Augum prowled forward, keeping close to the wall. The light turned a corner, but he could still see its dim reflection. He followed at a quick step, feet muffled by the noise of the tunnel. He could smell the burn of oil as he spied the tail end of a robe flicking around a corner. Checking to make sure there wasn't anyone behind him, he hurried after.

The deafening roar lessened, until he caught up in a quiet room that held some of Occulus' soldiers. A lone figure turned and the sound of a rattling tongue filled the air. Augum's skin rose as Nefra spoke.

"It is time to awaken them …"

"Awaken them …" echoed the Occi. They wore their crimson robes and held torches.

"The usurper underestimates us …"

"Underestimates …"

"I must object, Nefra—" It was Peyas—he was here too! But how did they escape his father?

"My patience is wearing thin with you, Peyas …"

"Wearing thin …"

"I understand that, my queen, but the usurper is too powerful. We do not have the forces to defeat him. Our fallen brethren must wait for the full moon to rise again. We only barely escaped the usurper, yet he is on his way as we speak."

"He stole the recipe, Peyas …"

"Recipe …" echoed the crowd.

"Perhaps he did. But now we have a greater worry—should the usurper gain control of the entire army—"

"We do not fear death, Peyas … We *are* death …"

"Death …" the crowd echoed.

"We should hide the Agonex, Nefra. Let him spend eons reading every book in the library trying to figure out how to control the army."

"I will not give up the castle … to a pretender …"

"Pretender …" the Occi murmured.

Nefra's tongue rattled menacingly. "He cannot defeat us … He has but one Dreadnought armored warrior … I have *tens of thousands* …"

"Tens of thousands …" came the echo.

"Tens of thousands you do not know how to use, Nefra. Free the orb. Let his nemesis face him—"

VALOR

"All his nemesis wants is the younglings ... I should have never listened to you, Peyas ... We should have kept them ... for her to fight on their behalf ..."

"Kept the younglings ..."

"I had Horrick make a false orb and cast a trace spell on it. We can find the younglings again if need be, but there are other matters more urgent—should the pretender get hold of the Agonex—"

So the Occi *do* have the real Orb of Orion, Augum thought, and apparently Horrick could cast spells. Now if only he could steal it back without them noticing and let Nefra's confining spell expire. Suddenly a devious plan came to him, but he needed to find Bridget and Leera first ...

"That is why we are here ..." Nefra said. "We will find the Agonex and use it ..."

"The Agonex ..." the Occi whispered.

"But how?" Peyas asked. "We have never seen it. By all accounts the Agonex is difficult to understand."

"It is written that we must follow the sign of the circle ..."

"Follow the sign ..."

Of course! Augum thought. The sign was on the door, and he had seen it above the ribcage passageway. But where was it again?

"Spread out and find the sign!" Nefra commanded.

The crowd parted ways as Augum snuck off in the direction he hoped was that particular passageway. He agreed with Peyas—his father was too strong for them, but if someone like Mrs. Stone had a Dreadnought-equipped army at her command ...

He ran blindly in the dark, not daring to light his palm. Instead, he used the wind, which he kept at his back, to return to the pool. Once there, he retraced his initial steps. At last, he found the ribcage entrance just as torchlight entered the pool cavern.

"Shyneo," he said after entering the passage. The tunnel was carved every bit of the way, sometimes narrowing and sometimes widening. Even the floor was carved to resemble stomach lining and tendons … or something.

He finally stepped over a great stone tongue and rows of teeth. When he looked back, he saw that it was the head of a dragon carved out of the mountain. Why a dragon, and here of all places? Had it once been real?

He strode on to a low platform, on top of which stood a statue of a man with powerful eyes and a stern jaw. The carving depicted him dressed in armor of ancient design, with a thick cloak around his shoulders. The man's hand was extended palm up, on which rested a bronze disk decorated with skulls and runes, the center empty.

The Agonex, Augum thought, reaching for it. Then he stopped. What if it was booby-trapped somehow? What if his hand withered upon touching it, or worse? Just to be safe, he stepped back, extinguished his palm, and used Telekinesis to float the Agonex off the man's hand. It clattered to the floor, the sound ringing down the passageway. It was tough using Telekinesis in the dark.

Suddenly there was a grinding sound.

"Shyneo." Augum's palm lit up, revealing the statue moving before him. One powerful hand reached for the sword at the hip.

"The master's son commands you to cease," said a voice from behind, and the statue froze.

Augum turned to find Peyas standing at the doorway, torch in hand. The ancient Henawa then stepped aside. "You must hurry. Take the Agonex to your father's nemesis. Defeat him."

Augum hesitated before picking up the Agonex from underneath the giant warrior, ready to jump aside any moment. But the figure stayed still. He ran past Peyas, only to stop in the dragon's mouth. "The orb. I need it back."

VALOR

"Do not bother with it. It is with one of the followers. Besides, Nefra's spell will not expire for some time—"

"But it's our only way out of here—"

Peyas' gaunt face darkened. "There may be another. It is said these passageways have an entrance somewhere, though it is far away. You might be able to find it if you follow the wind. It is dangerous and long, but you have a chance because you are a warlock and can provide your own light."

"Why are you helping me?"

Peyas' voice fell as he took a single step forward, his bloodshot eyes fixed firmly on Augum. "The pretender is not a pretender at all. He is the true rebirth of the Lord of Death, just as my father was. Nefra does not know it yet, but she will soon enough. Do you remember the story I told you about my father's pact with the witch?"

Augum nodded.

"And you recall I mentioned I studied in his library. Well there is a portal here in these caverns. It is far more ancient than one would think. The witch's pact had a second intention—not only is the portal able to reach Ley, but—"

"It can reach hell too," Augum murmured. "That's what they said Bahbell meant, that it was the gateway to hell ..."

"Imagine a man conquering Ley while unleashing the very fires of hell. It must not be allowed to happen. Although I am cursed, I do not want the world to suffer so. The portal is not finished, but it is now only a matter of time until the new Lord of Death completes it—"

"He won't finish it now."

Peyas stared at him. "It was you that retrieved the recipe. Did you—"

"—destroy it? Yes."

Peyas smiled, his gruesome teeth exposed. "Take the Agonex to his nemesis."

"But what about you? Will Nefra not—"

"Let that be my concern."

"Peyas … thank you." He turned his back on the ancient Henawa, the son of Occulus himself, and ran through the stone dragon.

RISKS

Augum ducked into a nearby passage as torchlight gathered near the entrance of the ribcage tunnel. The Agonex felt heavy and cold in his hands. Nefra will discover it missing any moment now. Then she'll use Horrick's trace spell to find Garryk and the girls. He simply had to find them first, even if it meant running up those stairs.

"Shyneo," he said as the throng of torches disappeared from sight. He dimmed his light just enough to see the ground. He ran to the windy pool only to glimpse the flicker of another torch on the other side, where the steps were. Then he saw yet another light, this one dim and green, descending those very steps—oh no, that had to be Bridget and the others, and they were heading right for an Occi!

He raced around the water's edge, watching as the two lights neared each other. The wind was too loud to shout a warning over.

Suddenly the torchbearer saw Bridget's light, turned, and ran, no doubt to warn Nefra. Augum happened to be standing right in the Occi's way. The face of the man was nothing but a rotten skull, with only the remains of one eye sitting putrid in the socket.

Augum dropped the Agonex and brought his wrists together, splaying his palms. "Annihilo!" He felt a great rush of arcanery surge through his body, depleting his reserves, and bolting through his hands right at the Occi's head.

The skull exploded; the body stumbled and fell. Within moments, it had turned to ash.

Leera, who had been helping Bridget carry an unconscious Garryk, ran forward. "Augum—!" She jumped on him, embracing him so tightly he couldn't breathe. "We thought you were dead ..."

He hugged her back. She held his head with tender hands, lips drawing closer. But Augum, who wasn't prepared for a kiss in that moment, hesitated and missed his chance. Her dark eyes registered disappointment as they let go of each other.

"I thought I had died too," he said lamely, "and it's good to see you, but listen, the orb is a fake—Horrick can track us with it!"

"I knew something was up with it!" She dropped her rucksack and hurriedly reached in. "We have to get rid of it."

"I'm so glad you're all right, Aug," Bridget said, face red from the exertion of helping Garryk down the steps. "But if we can, we should retrieve the real orb. It's a precious artifact, and probably our only real way to get to safety—at least once that protective spell expires and Mrs. Stone can teleport us through it."

"My thinking exactly," he said. "Anyway, I have a plan. One of the Occi has the real one. We find him and *switch* it somehow without him noticing. Then we make a run for it."

"Sounds crazy daring," Leera said, dropping on her knees and slurping from the pool, Bridget quickly joining her. Augum, meanwhile, picked up the Agonex and searched the Occi's clothing, careful to avoid the dusty remains of its body.

"What is that bronze thing anyway?" Leera asked once they had drunk their fill and replenished their only waterskin.

Augum stuffed the Agonex into the rucksack. "I'll explain later," and threw the creature's possessions into the pool, disappointed he hadn't found anything useful, not even an Occi horn. It had probably been lost in the fight above.

Bridget explained how frightfully dangerous the walk down the steps had been, how worried they were about him, and how Garryk passed out half way. She pointed at the water. "Aug, is that your coat floating there?"

"Yes, but we have no time to—"

"No, it's not that. Why don't we throw the fake orb into the water? Let them think we died from a fall. Then we're not being tracked and can steal the real orb back without them knowing where we are."

"Hmm, Peyas knows I'm alive, but I don't think he'll tell. Leera?"

"Might work." She retrieved the fake Orb of Orion. "So can I finally ditch it now?" He nodded and she threw it at his coat. It splashed into the water, lodging in the hood. She watched it drift away. "Looks like a ghost has drowned."

Augum spotted torchlight across the pool and dimmed his lit palm, gesturing for them to do the same. "We have to hide Garryk somewhere safe before going after the orb," he said in the cold and wet darkness. He lifted the unconscious boy and they hurried off into a nearby tunnel, all the while quietly explaining what had transpired since his fall.

"So wait, you can control Occulus' entire undead Dreadnought-equipped army with that bronze thing?" Leera asked.

"Looks like it, but I don't know how to use it."

"Maybe Mrs. Stone will know," Bridget said.

"Exactly. Though something tells me it's not as easy as controlling the Orb of Orion." He nodded at dark shapes ahead. "There's the Dreadnought army. At least a small part of it. They're in almost every room around here."

Leera inspected a particularly large brute with a sleek horned helm. "So ... are they statues or something?"

"I looked inside the visor of one. I think they're undead. I think it was part of the witch's pact she made with Occulus, maybe even the same arcanery that kept the Occi alive this long."

"Either that or they're from hell," Leera muttered.

The thought had occurred to Augum too, especially after seeing that giant bull-horned demon in the spawnery. "Let's keep going," he said, leading them deeper into the labyrinthine caverns than he had been. At last, they found semi-hidden steps descending to a small cave-like room.

"I'll stay here with Garryk," Bridget said. "You two go and get the orb back. Just ... be careful."

Leera withdrew the Agonex from the rucksack and kneeled over it.

"What are you doing?" Augum asked.

"Making sure we can find our way back." She splayed her hands above the disk. "Vestigio itemo discovaro."

Augum promptly did the same.

"Make sure it worked before you go too far," Bridget called after them like a mother hen. "And please, be careful—!"

"We will!" they chorused.

Augum and Leera hurried back, palms discreetly lit. The spell had indeed worked—he could feel a subtle arcane tug whenever he thought of the Agonex. It had replaced the tug he used to feel from the fake Orb of Orion. Object Track was turning out to be a very useful spell ...

Augum stopped Leera suddenly in the dark. "Look, if anything happens, go back and get them and try to get out of here without me, all right?"

VALOR

"Never—"

"You have to. The Agonex has to reach Nana. It *has* to. It could be the only way to defeat my father—"

"I'm *not* leaving here without you."

"Leera—" but suddenly she grabbed his robe and pulled him close, pressing her lips to his. It was a soft kiss, and Augum's first. He was so surprised he didn't know what to do.

She smiled warmly as she let go. "We never did get to kiss at the dance, and I didn't want to die without, you know …"

His tongue didn't work properly, but she seemed to understand, yanking on his cuff with a giggle. "Now stop your gawking and come on! We've got an orb to rescue."

Augum floated along the corridors. The tunnels didn't seem as dark as before and his aches had receded. He wasn't even hungry anymore. He only wished he hadn't just stood there like a fool, and actually kissed her back. He almost laughed at the idea of it—first kiss in the bowels of Bahbell …

Leera stopped to peer around a corner, extinguishing her palm. "They're searching for us." Torchlight flickered in distant tunnels, but all Augum could think about was her soft lips; her freckles, soot sprinkled on silky peach skin; and how the wind scratched at her raven hair. He ached to be away from all this danger, spending simple time together.

She snapped her fingers. "Hey, concentrate."

"Sorry."

"So what do we do now? How do we find which one has the orb without being seen?"

"Horrick."

"What? Why would—"

"No, look." He pointed at a squat figure standing near the rainy pool, barely visible in the darkness. "Horrick. Must have followed his trace spell to the fake orb floating in the pool."

"Well we can't use him, he'll just tell on us."

"I'm not so sure, I don't think that's how he works."

"What do you mean?"

"Remember Fentwick? He served the castle. Anyone could command him. I think it's the same with Horrick."

Leera scoffed. She looked pretty doing even that. "So we ask him to bring us the real orb," she said lamely.

He shrugged. "Sure, I guess."

"I was *kidding*."

"Well I wasn't. You have any better ideas?"

She thought about it a moment. "All right, but if Horrick tries anything, we push him into the water."

They checked for Occi before approaching Horrick from behind. Augum cleared his throat and Horrick spun about.

"Wouldst either of thou repugnant wretches care to duel?"

"No, uh, thanks, Horrick, but we need to ask a favor of you. Please bring us the real orb, right away."

" 'Orb', mine depraved clod?"

Leera shook her head, muttering, "How does he comes up with these things?"

"Yes, the Orb of Orion," Augum said. "You made a copy of it earlier. Bring it to us."

"As mine ungracious and boorish guest commands."

"Wait—" Leera said. "Be sure to tell the person that *Nefra* demanded it of you."

"As mine loathsome wench commands."

"Ugh, did you hear that?" Leera said as Horrick shuffled off. "*Wench*. What a little …"

"Nice touch," Augum said absently.

She gave him a furious look.

He swallowed. "Oh, no, I meant about the Nefra thing—"

She snorted and they took shelter around the corner.

"I'm still not convinced this'll work, you know," she said.

"Let's just be ready—we'll have to make a run for it soon as Horrick comes back."

VALOR

A robed figure exited a tunnel, trailed by another.

"There's Nefra," Leera said as the Occi woman began pointing firmly at Peyas' chest. "She looks livid."

"We can guess what she's saying." He could just make out her skin tones flashing rapidly. The memory of seeing Nefra kissing Masius as he writhed in her grip still haunted him. He hoped Peyas would get off easier than that ...

Just as he finished the thought, Nefra's hand shot to Peyas' throat. She squeezed, glaring at him, but he stood as passive as a deer. Just as she began bringing him closer, there was a low and powerful sound, almost like a great horn, that penetrated the rumble of the wind. Both Nefra and Peyas looked up only to immediately jump aside as something absolutely enormous smashed into the pool. The water exploded in a great wave, engulfing Augum and Leera before they could do anything, and washing them down a tunnel.

Augum's hand extinguished as the freezing water sapped his breath and stabbed at his brain. He rolled, slamming into a wall. The current dragged him across the ground, or ceiling—he couldn't tell.

Suddenly the area to his right lit up. It was Leera's underwater Shine extension! He swam towards the glow, kicking against the current, struggling not to take a breath. The flow moved fast, taking them to who knew where in the labyrinth of tunnels. Whatever had hit the water had to be gargantuan to displace this much of it.

The light up ahead seemed to flail. Then he saw it get sucked down into a whirlpool before it extinguished.

Panic gripped his heart like an iron fist. Ignoring the alarming fact that he desperately needed air, he kicked and scrambled until he too caught the whirlpool. He strained not to breathe as it sucked him down, finally jamming him through a hole in the floor, scraping his arms and legs in the process. He felt himself fall, splashing into another pool. At last, he was able to take a large breath upon surfacing.

"Leera!" he called, gasping as he tried to swim away from the waterfall. "LEERA—!" but his voice only echoed off cavern walls.

LETTING GO

Augum refused to lose her too. Not Leera, please not *her*. If it happened, he might as well let the dark waters take him.

Suddenly he saw a pale light flash briefly below. He immediately dove, kicking harder than his body would usually permit. His arms waved and clawed at the darkness before him, until latching onto a soft body. He pulled and rose through the black waters, finally breaking the surface.

"Leera!" but she did not respond. He held her with one arm while thrashing with the other, praying for ground, the darkness a relentless obstacle. "Please, Leera," he gargled, "not you too! Not you too—!"

He dragged her onto dry ground and immediately began beating on her chest and slapping her cheek. There was something he was supposed to do, something Sir Westwood had tried teaching him once, but he couldn't remember in his frantic state!

He had her robes in his fists and was shaking her now. "Leera! Please, wake up! LEERA—!" but she lay completely still. For a moment he just gaped stupidly, disbelieving what was happening. This wasn't real, he kept telling himself. It was a bad dream. He must have died in that water. This wasn't real ...

He gently gathered her close, feeling a tingling numbness that gathered around his shattered heart. "Please, not you too ..." He pressed his lips to hers and kissed her like he should have the first time, saying goodbye in his mind.

Suddenly she sputtered a cough and shuddered to life.

"Leera, I don't believe it—!"

She regurgitated water all over him again and again. He didn't care in the least, heart bursting with sheer joy. He rolled her onto her side and helped her through it, all the while thanking the Unnameables, the fates, and any and every force known to a commoner.

"It's a miracle," he mumbled when her spasms subsided. He embraced her tenderly.

She moaned and limply placed her arms around him, squeezing ever so gently. "Aug ..."

"I thought I lost you," he whispered, rocking her slightly. "I thought I lost you ..."

"I'm still here ..." Then she snorted a gurgling laugh. "You kissed me ... and I woke up ..."

He chuckled a laugh bordering on a cry. "I did, didn't I?" and they laughed together, allowing their spent bodies that moment of blissful amusement.

Then they held each other in silence, recuperating from the trauma of it all, until a distant horn sounded. Augum suddenly remembered where he had heard that sound—it had to be another giant bull-horned demon loosed from the spawnery ...

"Your father is up there," Leera said. "What do we do?"

Should they risk trying to get the orb? It seemed stupidly foolish now, especially after almost losing Leera. For once, he felt completely all right with the idea of not pushing his luck.

"We have the Agonex. We're alive. I say we get the hell out of here."

VALOR

Leera smiled. "I'm so glad you said that."

He wanted to mention getting out of these labyrinthine tunnels without food or the Orb of Orion would probably be next to impossible, but chose to stay silent and helped her stand instead.

"Shyneo," the pair chorused as the ground rumbled above. Their palms lit up a large and wet cavern. In the center, a thinning spout of water fell twenty feet into a dark pool.

"There." Augum ran to an area that seemed to have suffered a rockslide and began climbing. It was a hard slog because trickling water from above made it slippery and squishy.

"Careful with your light," Leera said, dimming hers.

Augum waited to do the same until they were free of the debris. He barely noticed he was shivering. It was the vibrancy and panic of the moment that made him not care, but he knew there would be a price to pay later, for him and for her.

He finally found a perch and hauled himself up before helping Leera. The sound of arcane battle rose above the din of the wind. The ground shook periodically, dropping a loose stone from the ceiling. Murky water moved past their ankles like a shallow stream.

"Come on." Augum felt for the arcane ether, the subtle pull that would take him and Leera back to Bridget and Garryk, but had a hard time concentrating. The spell was fickle, he knew, and required concentration and stillness, none of which was present in this moment.

"I can't feel it," he said. "You try."

Leera paused. A moment later, she grabbed his hand. "It's this way," and the pair ran together. Holding her hand made everything feel so simple and brought a thrilling elation to his heart. He curled his fingers around hers and allowed her to lead.

The ground rumbled and there was a distant piercing cry, followed by a tortured rattling that slowed to silence. Augum and Leera exchanged a look—Nefra had fallen. He wondered if Peyas was still back there somewhere, fighting a losing battle.

They pressed on, winding through the underground labyrinth, hands lit.

"Should be right up ahead here," Leera said.

The tunnels all looked the same to Augum. If it wasn't for Object Track ...

They turned the corner and descended the steps.

"You made it!" Bridget ran to give them each a hug.

Garryk sat against the wall. "Glad you made it back."

"Didn't get the orb though," Leera replied.

Bridget returned to dabbing a moist cloth to Garryk's forehead. "You didn't get the orb?"

"Don't worry, we'll figure something out," Leera replied, wringing out her robes.

"We're going to die down here," Garryk blurted.

"I *don't* want to hear talk like that," Bridget said.

"We should go," Augum said. "Peyas told me we can follow the wind to get out." But how to make it with Garryk?

"I'm not going," Garryk said. "You don't understand, they think I'm a traitor. You already know what they do to a traitor's family. You have to take me back." His voice turned desperate. "I'm too weak to make the journey and you know it. I'm exhausted and hungry. I'll tell them I tried to attack you and you ran off. I'll tell them ... *something*. Just please, I can't go with you, it'll ... it'll kill me ... it'll kill my family." He sniffed. "I want my spectacles. I can't see ..."

Bridget kneeled before the wretched boy and took his hands in her own, voice a whisper. "Garryk, they'll torture you—"

"—we'll all die if you try to drag me along. You don't know the kind of cave system this is. It's absolutely

VALOR

impossible for someone in my condition. Besides, they probably *won't* kill me. I know it because I can serve them with my book smarts. I can be of use ... I can ..."

The trio exchanged a knowing look.

An idea occurred to Augum. "If we did leave him to be found, why can't he just tell them what he knows?"

"Aug—" Leera tried to say.

"No, think about it. So what if they discover the recipe is destroyed, or that they find out we have the Agonex? What difference does it make? Garryk will live at least. He can say he spied on us the whole way, fully intending to report what we've been doing."

Leera pointed at Garryk. "But he knows where we've been staying—"

"No he doesn't," Bridget said slowly, turning to Garryk, still holding his hand. "Do you?"

Garryk shook his head. "I don't. You've never mentioned it. And don't say it now."

Bridget sighed. "It's a big risk. They might ... they might kill you anyway."

"I'll take the risk. Look at me, I'd die on the trek. Allow me to be found. I'll ... I'll minimize the damage."

Bridget closed her eyes but eventually gave a single nod.

Garryk released a relieved breath. "I promise I'll say as little as I can." He squeezed Bridget's hand. "It's really what I want. I will not let my family suffer. You have to understand."

"I do," Bridget whispered, standing and letting go. "I really do."

"Thank you for saving my life." He glanced at each of them with eyes that were unable to focus without spectacles. "Thank you all for fighting for the kingdom."

THE BOTTOM

They had left Garryk in a meeting of corridors nearby, a spot they determined yielded the highest chance of him being found. They could hear the last rumbling of battle as they bid him good luck, with hopes of seeing each other again in good spirits, in a time without war.

Sometime later, the trio stopped before three tunnels, palms lit.

"So which one?" Leera asked.

Augum stood before each of the gaping maws. "Wind is strongest from this one."

They resumed the trek. The tunnel began a steady descent.

Augum noticed how waterlogged the rucksack was on Leera's shoulder. "Let me take a turn."

"Thanks but no. I'm a saddler's daughter."

Quiet hours passed in the dark tunnels. Trying to ignore his shivering bones, Augum occupied his mind with thoughts about what had transpired.

"Don't think there was a copy of that recipe, do you?" he asked.

"Let's hope not," Bridget said, navigating around an ancient boulder.

Leera hopped over the same boulder. "And if there was?"

Augum flashed her a smirk. "Then we'd just have to destroy that one too."

Leera snorted. "I'd rather be torn apart by a walker than come back."

"No you wouldn't."

"You're right, I wouldn't."

"At least I got to see Temper get slapped by a horse thing. And you got to re-arrange Robin's stupid face."

"Please, you two," Bridget said, extinguishing her palm and stopping to rest. "Enough is enough. We're in great danger here. Let's stay focused."

Leera crinkled her nose. "I suppose you're right." She stared off into the darkness ahead, voice strangely grim. "The Fates might not be done with us yet. Maybe none of us are getting out of here alive. We're hungry and lost in some ancient cave system." She turned to Augum. He noticed the rings under her eyes, the scratches on her freckled face, the tangles in her muddy hair. She took his hand and gave it a squeeze. "I'm just glad that I'm not here alone, that I'm here with you and Bridget. If I'm to go …"

For a moment, he thought she was going to kiss him again. He was about to take the initiative and lean in when she let go, giving Bridget a nervous glance.

But Bridget only flashed an exasperated smile. "You two …"

"What?" Leera said.

"Nothing."

They journeyed on for another few hours through tunnel after winding tunnel, pacing through caverns and crawling under low-hanging ceilings. Augum and Leera's clothes slowly dried. Surprisingly, the further and lower they went, the warmer it became. At the same time, the cave seemed to devolve, becoming a hodgepodge of sharp rock and tight squeezes.

At last, they stopped by an underground stream. Augum refilled the waterskin, trying to ignore the cavernous empty feeling in his stomach and the throbbing ache in his bones. He noticed something soft growing on the walls. "There's moss here. Think it's edible?" At this point, he'd start eating rock.

Leera finished laying her moist coat on the ground and shrugged. "I don't know …"

He tore the moss off and took a nibble.

"How is it?" she asked absently.

"Has an … earthy taste to it, like unwashed artichoke."

"Well I'll start eating my coat if I don't have *something*." She snatched it from him, taking a larger bite, made a face, and handed it back. "Ugh, worse than turnip."

Bridget tried some and immediately spit it out. "We should get some sleep." She got comfortable and extinguished her palm.

"The Fates know how long it's been since we last had some," Leera chimed in.

"Since when did you start swearing by the Fates?" he asked in the darkness.

"Since you survived that fall. Since you brought me back to life with a kiss just like in those stories, like some handsome knight with his fair maiden—"

"—before you vomited all over me."

They laughed despite the crassness of his comment.

"Go to sleep, Augum Stone," she said at last.

"You two are adorable," Bridget said with a barely audible sigh.

He extinguished and tried to get comfortable. "Bridge?"

"Hmm?"

"You all right?"

"I'm just worried about Garryk."

VALOR

"He'll be fine," Leera said in sleep tones. "Tough little wart."

"Please don't call him that."

"Just a joke, Bridge, just a joke …"

Augum's lids quickly grew heavy as the exhaustion of the entire ordeal dragged him into a deep and dreamless sleep.

He startled awake what must have been many hours later, stomach aching with emptiness. It was dark and quiet except for the trickle of the underground stream and the gentlest breeze.

He sat up. "Shyneo." His hand flared to life. The light was weaker than usual, and it slowly throbbed to the rhythm of his heart, as it did every time his energies were low. Leera slept beside him, face nuzzled up against his robe. He gently moved a lock of muddy hair from her forehead and rested it by her ear. He watched her snooze quietly, wondering if they'd find a way out of there.

Bridget slept nearby, curled up into a ball. He watched her steady breathing, listening to the darkness.

It was a miracle they had made it this far. He lay there for a while longer before gently waking the girls, telling them they should get going.

"I'm going to gather more moss," he said as they came to. "Might be the only thing we have to eat down here, and it's better than nothing."

There were three kinds of mosses—orange, green and black. The green he had tried and disliked, the black tasted bitter, while the orange tasted mildly sweet. He recalled Sir Westwood saying to use that as a measure of edibility, and chose the orange one, gathering an armful.

"Better than the one that tasted like turnip," Leera said after taking a bite. "Still tastes like moss though."

"It's either that or we start eating our boots like sailors stranded on ice." He had read harrowing tales in one of Sir Westwood's books, of square-sailed ships going for months without food, and the sailors resorting to eating leather, rope and wood chips. There was even a story involving cannibalism.

"Bet the boots would taste better," Leera said, finishing the moss. "You might as well hand me another."

They ate their fill and moved on.

* * *

Uncountable days passed as they descended further and further, feeding on nothing but orange moss and stream water, slowly weakening. They followed the gentlest of breezes, hoping it would lead them to safety. They conserved energy by talking little, refusing to practice arcanery, and sleeping tightly together like puppies. Eventually, deep underground, the caves grew so warm the trio took turns carrying Bridget and Leera's coats, along with their one and only rucksack containing their worldly goods.

They passed through gaping echoing caverns; squeezed through tight spaces that provoked anxiety in each of them; swam across mirror ponds; skirted bottomless pits; and descended cliffs that callused their hands. The cliffs were hardest on Bridget, who possessed a crippling fear of heights. Cliffs aside, she already had the toughest time adjusting to the constant quiet, the impossibly dense darkness, the primordial nature of the cave. She would often stop, refuse to voice aloud what was the matter, and simply shake with fear. Sometimes these strange fits would last for hours. Augum and Leera would sit patiently by, encouraging her to take her time and drink lots of water, but her fears had a strong grip. "I don't belong down here," she would mumble, holding herself. "This isn't right. We're descending to hell …"

No matter what Augum and Leera told her, it did no good. She would panic and return to that state every few hours. Then she would calm down and they could continue. The very prospect of negotiating a cliff would turn into an hour-long argument, not that it was easy anyway without rope. Descending into sheer darkness and not knowing if there was a drop-off just below was a harrowing thing, even for Augum and Leera. But that wasn't the only danger—Bridget's flailing sent rocks falling. One had almost knocked Augum out. He and Leera used Shield often after that. Then there was the time Bridget slipped. Augum and Leera were ready for such an eventuality though and caught her with Telekinesis, as they had once before at Evergray Tower, though it cost them greatly in arcane energy and over all endurance, something they could barely afford with such little nourishment.

At long last, at some unknown remote depth, they came upon a different kind of structure—a vast room of nothing but faceted crystals. It gave off every color of the rainbow with their light and stole their voices. The place was hot and damp, making them sweat profusely.

"This is the most beautiful thing I have ever seen," Leera whispered.

"I don't like it," Bridget said, trying not to touch anything. "It's too hot. *Dangerously* hot. We have to get out of here."

Leera sighed. "We *are* getting out of here, Bridge. The wind says we have to go through it though. Don't worry so much."

"Don't worry? *Don't worry?* We're as thin as sticks; we haven't had a proper meal in ... in who knows how many days now; we don't have a way of getting back to Mrs. Stone; the moss is getting harder and harder to find down here; Garryk could be getting tortured as we speak—I *knew* we shouldn't have left him behind! And we're lost in some ancient super cave that probably leads straight to hell. And you're saying ... you're saying *not to worry?*" She was panting at the end. Even raising her voice seemed to exhaust her.

Leera just stood there with a sorrowful expression.

"You're being a touch harsh, Bridge," Augum said. She might have been right on some points, but he didn't want them wasting precious energy arguing.

Bridget plopped to the ground, extinguished her palm, and closed her eyes. "I'm sick of eating moss, I'm sick of being in the dark all the time, and I'm sick of ... I'm sick of this endless cave."

Augum wanted to give her a hug but was too tired. "We all are, Bridge. We all are ..." Heights and confined spaces didn't suit her, especially for prolonged periods. He hoped they found a way out sooner than later. Then they'd have to tackle the problem of winter without mitts and lacking one coat. And where would they go? What would they do for food? He'd have to hunt, he supposed, though even thinking about constructing traps made him feel even more tired.

Leera broke a few crystals off and stuffed them in the rucksack.

"You shouldn't do that," Bridget said.

"Why in Sithesia not? They look valuable."

"Because ... it *feels* wrong. Like we're stealing from a sacred place or something."

"Sometimes a cave is just a cave." Leera closed up the rucksack, flashed Bridget a rebellious look, and began navigating the crystalline structures.

Augum extended his hand to Bridget. "Come on," he said quietly, silently agreeing with Leera—who knows what use those crystals might come to.

She sighed in aggravation but took his hand.

The crystal cavern was short, a gem in the abyssal depths of a black ocean. After passing through, they turned to get a last glimpse of its sparkling magnificence. They stood for some time, none of them wanting to venture on into the darkness after seeing something so graceful, so sacred ...

They walked and climbed in silence for the better part of the day, or night—no one was sure when exactly it was, or how many days had passed, or how many countless leagues they had traversed. It buoyed Augum's spirits that at least they began a steady ascent. Maybe they'd reach the surface before starving. Only to freeze to death, he thought, snorting at the idea of it. To have come all this way ...

As more time passed and the moss became scarcer, their bodies withered to emaciation. Their appearance turned haggard and hollow. Movements slowed to a crawl and voices softened to whispers. Breathing became rattled, interspersed with coughing.

The cold once again sharpened and Augum found himself longing for a coat. They took turns with the two they did have, though it always left someone to shiver more than the others.

Nonetheless, step by dreary step, they battled the wind, keeping only one of their palms lit at a time, until even that one light was as weak as a dying candle, ready to be snuffed out by the incessant wind.

Another day passed and they weakened further still. It was a day Augum thought a miracle in their condition. They had survived this long, but he knew death was nearing. Obstacles like small boulders that would have required little effort to overcome now expended time and energy they did not possess. The wind bit deeply, the cold shrinking their hunched forms to shuffling stumps.

The ascent dragged on and on. The darkness began to fool with their minds. Sometimes one of them would turn around, thinking they had heard something, or seen food where there was only rock, or light where there was only gloom.

It was Bridget that fell first. "I'm ... done," she mumbled between gasps. "Leave me ..."

Augum, who had been dragging the rucksack for the last while and refusing to give it up, was happy to let it slip from his fingers. He fell to the ground beside her. "Let's ... rest ..."

Leera collapsed on her other side, extinguishing her palm and their only source of light. "Not ... going ... without ... you ... Bridge ..."

"This ... is ... it ..." Bridget wheezed. "I'm ... done. Really ..."

Augum took her cold, bony hand in his own. Her skin was dry to the touch. He gave it a gentle squeeze. "If ... you ... stay ... we ... all ... stay ..." and he meant it. There was no way he would be able to go on without her. "You ... must ... be ... strong ..." The effort of speaking was sapping his reserves, not that he had any really.

"Sleep ..." Leera gasped. "For ... a while ..."

Augum was afraid to sleep. He feared death taking them. He listened to the girls' short breaths, hoping to keep hearing them, tortured by the fact that he was as powerless as a kitten. His mind feebly grasped at ideas. What could they eat? How could they get out? Damn it, what could they eat!

Food consumed his thoughts like sickness, until he swore he was eating roasted chicken, only to suddenly discover it was the edge of the rucksack. The thought would have been amusing at some other time, some other place. But down here in the dark labyrinthine depths, probably their final resting place, it was coldly sobering.

He pushed the rucksack away and turned to the wind, only to see a faint light in the distance. His mind was dying along with his body. It was flailing with hope, though there was none down here.

He turned away from the fake light. No, this was how he was going to die—right here with his friends. He lay still, continuing to listen to the girls' breathing, wondering which breath would be their last. The count had to be small, perhaps in the hundreds of breaths now ...

He turned back towards the light. It was still there, pale as the moon.

Pale as the moon.

VALOR

Could it really be? He reached deep inside himself for strength, scraping the bottom of the pot, and found just enough to move. "Shyneo," but his palm would not light.

"Leera ... look ..."

She stirred with a groan.

"Do ... you ... see ... it ...?"

She moaned. "Yes ..."

Hope surged like a spring fountain. "Let's ... go ... look. Bridge ... come on ..."

Bridget made a feeble noise.

Leera shook her. "Come ... on ... Bridge. There's ... light ..."

"Leave ... me ..."

"No ..." Augum laced his arms around her and tried picking her up, but he was too weak. "Leera ... help ..."

The two of them managed to do it together. They began the long shuffle to the light, Bridget flopping between them like a sack of apples, Augum dragging the rucksack by the strap. He could feel her ribs and held her tenderly, wishing he could do more for all of them.

It took forever to get to the light, and the wind only increased, its cold biting through their meager garments, their malnourished and stretched skins. They stumbled often, too weak to light their palms. This was it, Augum realized, the final push ...

They climbed and climbed, at last coming upon a great cavern, or more like a sheer vertical hole. Somewhere far, far above, was the moon, its pale light reflecting off the massive earthy walls.

When they saw the enormity of it, it became clear how impossible a climb this would have been in the best of circumstance, let alone in the shape they were in. They collapsed together, without words or hope.

"Sinkhole ..." Leera gasped. "It's ... the ... damn ... sinkhole ... We're ... finished ..."

ONE AFTER ANOTHER

Time stopped then and there at the bottom of that great sinkhole. It was the same one they had passed on the way to Bahbell, Augum was sure of it. Had they really traversed such a great distance underground? The thought seemed ludicrous and impossible. Yet what did it matter? They were going to die here at the bottom, and that was that.

He amused himself with thoughts of the future. One day, someone will come across their bodies and find some peculiar objects. Crystals, books, the Agonex. An entire army at their command, if they figure out what the artifact was …

The trio curled up tightly together, preserving the last of their warmth. The wind and the cold raked at them with demon fingers, hurrying them along in their final moments. They held on to each other as deep friends, determined to leave this life together.

And then, at some late and grave hour, with Leera and Bridget's heads buried on his chest, Augum heard a peculiar metal shuffling. It was so unexpected and so out of place that he thought for sure it was his mind finally breaking, until a form appeared before him, perhaps with a few extra dents and scratches.

Horrick carried an orb, an orb Augum remembered to be the Orb of Orion—and it *did not shimmer in its protective cocoon.* The thought sent a surge through his body, so much that he actually sat up, startling the girls.

"I don't believe it," he said without gasping. "I don't believe it …!"

"Thy orb, as mine repugnant detractor commanded." Horrick shuffled forth and gave Augum the orb while the girls sat slack-jawed.

"I don't believe it," Augum kept saying. "How did you … how did you find us? How did you get through the cave, through *all that?*"

The skull helm tilted slightly. "Mine lord?"

Of course he didn't understand the question, how could he? But it hardly mattered, for Nana was going to save them now!

"Nana …" Augum gasped desperately, bringing the orb to his ear. "Nana …!" but unbelievably, there was no response. He exchanged a perplexed look with the girls.

Suddenly there was another noise from the direction Horrick had come. Augum looked past to see two figures emerge from the shadows, carrying torches, one in armor that reflected the light, the other garbed in black Legion plate. Soon as he spotted that grisly face and those pale eyes, Augum dropped the orb and squeezed Bridget and Leera close.

"How pleasant it is to see you all again," the Blade of Sorrows said in his deep voice. "What a trek that was." The revenant commander turned to Raina. "And to think they doubted our trusty companion was up to something. Now feast your eyes on this sorry sight."

Raina reached into their rucksack and withdrew the Agonex. Augum could no more stop her than he could curl his fingers into a fist. Her hard features creased with a mirthless smile. "There it is. Our lordship will be most pleased."

"Most pleased indeed," Tridian said. "You know, you put us through an awful lot of trouble, boy, an awful lot. My apprentice has lost his good looks, I daresay, and he is most angry. You, unfortunately, are to live, for His Lordship has demanded your return. But you can guess what that means for your friends—"

Augum's grip on Bridget and Leera tightened. "Don't you dare touch them!" He didn't know where the strength to shout had come from. "If you want to kill them, kill me too, you damn cowardly dogs. Kill me too!" And if they didn't do it, him shouting and depleting the very last of his strength certainly should do the job.

"You have grown bold," Tridian said. "Too bold, in my opinion. I would put you to the question if the first caress would not end you." He nodded at Raina. "Finish the little witches."

"No!" Augum screamed. "NO—!"

The girls barely resisted, not that their wasted muscles were any match for Raina, who looked like she had been well provisioned for the journey that had so sapped their strength. She tore Leera from Augum's feeble clutches first, drawing her dagger. Yet as she did so, Augum heard the most beautiful sound in all of Sithesia, one he dreamed of hearing for days and days in the darkness—the sound of an implosive crunch.

There before the Orb of Orion stood Anna Atticus Stone, head held high, silken white robe shimmering in the moonlight.

The Blade of Sorrows took a stumbling step backward. "You …"

"Me," Mrs. Stone said simply.

Raina's jaw clenched. "Don't you do anything or I'll cut her open—" She pressed the knife against Leera's throat.

Augum couldn't breathe—for a moment, he saw Mya standing there in Robin's arms.

Mrs. Stone's brow rose ever slightly. "You will *not*," and without any apparent gesture, Raina's arms began to fold up and away, so far, in fact, that that there were loud snapping sounds. She screamed and fell to her knees, arms dangling limply.

Leera, meanwhile, crawled back to Augum. He placed an arm around her shaking body and drew her close.

Mrs. Stone turned to the Blade of Sorrows. Perhaps the revenant knew it was futile to try anything against the only living warlock to have achieved mastery, for he stood frozen in place like a winter waterfall.

Mrs. Stone stared at him coldly, as if daring him to make a move.

"I yield," Tridian said at last. "And we both know you cannot kill a soul who has surrendered. It is against your principles."

Mrs. Stone raised her arm slowly. "For that to apply, revenant, you would have to have a soul."

Tridian's eyes widened as Mrs. Stone's arm ruptured with a crackling blue sleeve. A bolt of thick lightning leaped from it, uniting with the Blade of Sorrows. The man lifted off his feet, convulsing, crying out. He began to burn alive while screaming, finally imploding into the armor with a pop. The hulk of metal and guts fell to the ground, smoking.

"Gods …" Raina gasped, shaking, kicking the ground to crawl away, arms limp and useless.

Mrs. Stone ignored her and crouched before Augum, who held the girls tight in his embrace, afraid to let their frail bodies go. Her hand lit with a soft white light. She pressed it to each of their foreheads. A soothing sensation, like taking a warm bath, consumed Augum's body. It eased the many pains, the hollowness in his stomach, and gave him a measure of peace he thought he'd never feel again.

Mrs. Stone smiled sadly. "I have listened through the Orb of Orion, as powerless as a newborn babe. But I heard nearly everything of import. Your struggle is over now. You are victorious in your quest. The recipe is destroyed. Lividius will not reach the plane of Ley."

Augum didn't have the strength or the words to reply. He only held on to Bridget and Leera, glad they were all right, glad that it was over.

"Please return to Lividius Stone," Mrs. Stone said to Horrick, "to the one they call the Lord of the Legion. Tell him the hole in his heart is growing larger. Tell him that one day it will consume him. And that day comes ever nearer."

"As mine mighty antagonist commands." The small suit of arcane armor shuffled back the way it had come.

Leera managed to give Augum a look. Was that a compliment from Horrick?

Mrs. Stone strode over to Raina and took the Agonex from her limp hand. She was still trying to feebly crawl away.

"You can't just leave me here!" Raina struggled to get up without the use of her arms. "Save me, you cold-hearted hag!"

"You were about to murder the girls, were you not?"

"I was commanded to!"

"Some commands should never be followed." She studied the Legion woman a moment with no pity. "You can find your own way back."

Raina looked at Mrs. Stone with horrified eyes, hard lips quivering, knowing what that meant.

Mrs. Stone picked up the rucksack, put the Agonex and the Orb of Orion inside, and turned to the trio. "I hope you are ready to leave."

Augum took a last skyward look, at the towering sinkhole directly above, at the pale moon and its soft but cold glow. He squeezed the girls close. "We are, Nana. We really are ..."

ANNOCRONOMUS TEMPUSARI

Mrs. Stone teleported the trio directly into the Okeke home in the dead of night, waking Mr. Okeke and Jengo. Both expressed great shock at seeing the trio in such a state of health. A fire was quickly built up in the hearth and water boiled. Mr. Goss, who was staying in the Miner's Mule Inn with his son, was promptly fetched. He nearly fainted upon laying eyes on them. Floorboards creaked as the household scampered to see to the trio. Mrs. Stone patiently administered more arcane healing.

For his part, Augum was just happy to be near a fire, knowing Bridget and Leera were safe beside him. He glanced up at Mrs. Stone, whose brows were furrowed in concentration as she gently washed Bridget's muddy face with a cloth.

"Is ... is Haylee—?"

"She is well, my dear child," Mrs. Stone said without shifting her gaze. "You will see her tomorrow. Now I urge you to conserve your strength. You have been through a most harrowing ordeal and need plenty of rest."

"How frightful they look," Mr. Goss whispered to Mr. Okeke, unable to take his eyes off the trio. "Like the undead raised."

Jengo, looking taller than ever, brought over a bowl of steaming leek soup. His ebony face was creased with worry as he placed the bowl between Augum and Leera.

"I was certain you would all meet your end in that hellish place," he whispered.

Mrs. Stone sharply cleared her throat and Jengo stiffened. "B-b-but I'm very glad to have been wrong of course, very glad." He spooned some soup and brought it to Leera's mouth, then another to Augum's. It was the most delicious thing Augum had ever tasted, and something he had been dreaming about for who knew how long.

"More," Leera wheezed.

"Not too quickly now," Mrs. Stone said.

"Haylee ..." Augum mouthed before eagerly accepting another spoonful.

Jengo's eyes lit up. "Sensational news—she was carried into town on Chaska's back!" His eyes zipped between the trio. "The two are quite the, uh, item now. Oh, and she moved in with my betrothed, Priya!"

Augum glanced at Leera and could tell she would have snorted with laughter if she had the energy. Haylee living with Ms. Singh ... indeed!

The trio exchanged relieved and amused looks. It was good to be back. Good to worry about the little things again. Good to hear about ordinary things. Good to not have to fight rabidly for one's life.

"Mercy, child, you must not excite them," Mrs. Stone said, now on to washing Bridget's hair with the help of a basin of warm water.

"Yes, Mrs. Stone. Sorry, Mrs. Stone." Jengo lowered his voice but plowed right on. "Mrs. Stone teleported her to see

VALOR

an arcane healer not long after she arrived, but they couldn't heal her broken leg completely. Apparently it was much worse than when I broke my arm and stuff. Anyway, now she walks around with a limp. And the two of them told me all about your adventure—wolven, harpies, and those ... those cannibals! I must hear every word! Oh, I can't *wait* to hear about the castle too. Every. Word—"

"Son, enough." Mr. Okeke brought a pot of tea over. "You may speak with them tomorrow."

"Yes, Father." Then his voice dropped to the barest of whispers as he spoke in rapid tones. "And just you wait until you meet our mentor. The vilest and ugliest—"

"I said, *enough*, Jengo! Fetch more cloth and replace the water basin. Now, if you please."

"Yes, Father." Jengo gave Augum a look that promised more news tomorrow, but did as he was told.

"About the quest ..." Mr. Goss began. "Were they ... was the recipe ..."

"It was destroyed," Mrs. Stone replied, delicately wringing Bridget's hair. "They are victorious. A great evil has been prevented."

"Most marvelous news indeed!"

Mr. Okeke and Mr. Goss congratulated each other with handshakes and hugs while Jengo pumped his fist in the background.

But the look on Mrs. Stone's face was as troubled as ever. "I am afraid I cannot stay. I risk Milham more with every visit. I shall return briefly in a tenday, when they have sufficiently rested. Please keep me informed of their wellness through the orb."

"They managed to save that too?" Jengo caught himself and quickly bowed his head. "Yes, Mrs. Stone."

Mrs. Stone worriedly glanced over Augum, Bridget and Leera one more time before standing. At her age, constantly being on the run was obviously taking its toll. There were more creases on her face and her posture was more stooped than Augum remembered it.

"I shall return," and she teleported off with a THWOMP.

* * *

The trio slowly recuperated over the next tenday. They regularly received visits from Jengo's betrothed, Priya; as well as Leland of course, who was as spritely as ever; and some notable others, such as Hanad Haroun and his daughter, Malaika, whom Augum had danced with; and even Panjita Singh, who did nothing but complain about the trio's ridiculously dangerous quest. They were also visited by Haylee and Chaska, who seemed more distracted by each other than anything else. Haylee indeed did walk with a limp, but as long as Chaska was near, had not a care in the world. The two were an odd couple, but Augum was happy to see Haylee in a warm place in life.

The trio also heard all about the cruelty of the new mentor brought in by Mrs. Stone, but had yet to meet him as he was currently away on an errand.

Jengo pried the adventure of the castle out of them, every juicy detail, expressing not only incredulity but also a gratitude that he had not come along, for if he had, he would have certainly met a most untimely end.

As they rested up, their faces took on color and rounded out again. Leera's insatiable appetite for sweets even abated somewhat. They slowly began studying and training. Much to their surprise, they discovered—talking to Mrs. Stone via the orb— that the crystals Leera had taken from that deep underground cavern were rare "reflecting prisms". Mrs. Stone promised to teach the trio a difficult 6th degree off-the-books spell that paired with the crystals, a combination that, once mastered, would allow them to reflect a spell back upon its caster once daily, for they were *Sun-tuned*. It was something that made them squeal in delight. However, the crystals had to be carved into a mirror shape first by a special arcaneologist, something that would take time. She also expressed great interest in the golden tome and the Agonex, but said she would wait until her next visit to study them better.

News soon reached them in the form of the Blackhaven Herald. Bahbell had been declared a "historical treasure now under the guidance of His Esteemed Lordship." Robin Scarson was trumpeted as a boy hero for trying to stop "a most villainous and heinously treasonous trio of criminals." There was a portrait etching of him and Temper, noses notably crooked, faces resentful.

To their great relief, there was a brief mention of Garryk, thanking him for being "cooperative with the cause". There was no mention of Peyas or Nefra or any of the other goings on, except a new addition to *The Great Quest*—and that was the search for the Agonex, raising the trio's infamy level to new heights and thus placing the village of Milham in even greater danger.

At long last, Mrs. Stone returned for a brief visit one evening to give some critical personal arcane tutelage. The Agonex she decided to take with her for further study, but when she got around to opening the ancient golden tome, she gave an audible gasp.

"What is it, Nana?" Augum asked, nursing an arcanely-induced headache with mint tea.

"Merciful spirits, it is real …"

Those words instantly made everyone crowd around the tome.

Mrs. Stone turned the golden pages delicately. "This is Annocronomus Tempusari, otherwise known as Cron, an ancient off-the-books Rivican spell arcaneologists deemed to be myth. It long predates the Founding. There are legendary stories of its use in duels. But it is mostly known for the price it exacts on the caster."

"What does it do, Mrs. Stone?" Bridget whispered.

"If the stories are true—and mind you, we are talking about more than three thousand years ago—then this spell allows the caster to travel back a short length of time, making it particularly lethal in battle."

"And the price, Mrs. Stone?" Leera asked.

"Each casting ages the warlock ..."

"By how much, Nana?"

"That I do not know, but there are stories ... one of note tells of a man repeatedly casting the spell for the purpose of gambling, only to shock his wife and children upon returning home."

Solemn looks were exchanged around the table.

"Perhaps it is not a surprise the spell had been banned at the Founding." Mrs. Stone suddenly froze mid page turn. "I understand now ..."

Leera swallowed. "Mrs. Stone?"

"I had not understood the Seers' meaning before, but now ... now we have found the path." Her eyes were glassy and distant, voice the barest of whispers. "I daresay I struggled with the problem ... "

Jengo had to steady himself against a chair. "What ... what problem, Mrs. Stone?"

Mrs. Stone let the golden page slip from her fingers. "The problem of youth." Her gaze washed over the trio before settling on the fire. "How could ones so young and inexperienced face an impossible challenge such as this ... but now it comes together in simple beauty. Of course ... A destiny entwined by a single strike of lightning ... and thus three would fight and learn as one ... at the sacrifice of their youth ... perhaps more ... and when the fires burn from east to west ... and the blind lead the dead ... then, and only then, may the battle begin."

"We don't understand," Bridget said, voice wavering slightly. "Sacrifice of their youth ... what does that mean? We don't understand—"

Mrs. Stone continued as if in a trance. "The history of it. The enormity of the challenge. A battle repeated through countless eons. Sometimes lost. Sometimes won. Always different, for the lessons have not been learned. Lessons lost to time ... Every sacrifice ... all to reach this point ... and go further."

Augum's breathing intensified. "Nana, what are you saying?"

Mrs. Stone's countenance hardened. "This will change everything."

"What ... why—?"

She slowly turned her blue-eyed gaze on him. "Because the three of you must attempt to learn this complex spell, Great-grandson ... for it may be your only hope against the Lord of Death."

FOR FANS OF *THE ARINTHIAN LINE*

Sign up to my mailing list and get the next unreleased book in the series for only 99 cents. You'll have a window of 24 hours to purchase it for this special discounted rate, only available to mailing list subscribers. After that initial 24 hours, it'll go back to regular price, so make sure to open that email as soon as you see it (and be sure severbronny@gmail.com is white-listed in your email settings).

Go to severbronny.com/contact and subscribe using the link on the page.

BE A HERALD—SPREAD THE WORD

Honest reviews are critical in today's highly competitive market. I'd be grateful if you would consider leaving one on Amazon.com and/or Goodreads.com for Arcane, Riven, and/or Valor.

Word of mouth also helps. It makes a huge impact when you share a link to Arcane's Amazon page on social media like Facebook, Twitter, etc.

Thank you so much, it really means a lot to me :)

ADVANCE REVIEW TEAM

Want to take things to the next level? Read my books before anyone else does for free? Receive secret special rewards? Apply to join my Advance Review Team at:

severbronny.com/team

CONNECT

I love hearing from readers. Email me anytime at severbronny@gmail.com — I respond to everyone :)

Website: severbronny.com

Twitter: @SeverBronny

Goodreads: goodreads.com/severbronny

My other passion: **Tribal Machine** www.tribalmachine.com

ACKNOWLEDGMENTS

The Arinthian Line has been in the making for years, and I couldn't have done it without the loving support of my amazing wife and editor, Tansy.

Thank you to my family, friends, my ART team, and my loyal readers for supporting my work.

Want to get hints about book 4? You guessed it—you'll have to sign up to my mailing list above ;)

Thank you for reading, and I can't wait to reveal what happens next!

All my best to you and those you love,

Sever Bronny

ABOUT THE AUTHOR

Sever Bronny is a musician and author living in Victoria, British Columbia, Canada. He has released three albums with his industrial-rock music project Tribal Machine, including the full-length concept album *The Orwellian Night*. One of his songs can be heard in the feature-length film *The Gene Generation*. His love of fantasy began with Dragonlance and continues on with Harry Potter. Connect with him at severbronny.com.